BLOOD AND BURNING

A hundred yards from the stockade, small fires had been laid in the darkness, but not ignited. Now torchmen trotted out and lit them. By their flickering light, Frazier saw warriors dip long, nocked arrows into them, tipping each with flame, then wait for a signal that must quickly come.

On the walkway, Frazier spoke to his bugler. A patter of notes sounded, and hundreds of defender arrows took flight from the palisade. Flaming arrows answered, arcing over the walls. Stricken livestock bawled and bleated, human voices screamed with pain, arrows struck roofs and walls, and commands were shouted. Frazier had foreseen this too, and the people had drilled it. Ladders leaned against every building, and boys scrambled up. Bucket lines formed quickly from cisterns to ladders. Voices called "Here! Here!"

Fire arrows kept coming, and now, out of the night, tribal horsemen charged by the hundreds, shouting war cries, swinging lariats. The defenders too were yelling. Within seconds, warriors were scrambling up the walls. Sabers cut lariats, arms, shoulders, heads. Hatchets chopped, knives struck. The walkways were quickly slick with blood; men slipped in it, or stumbled on the fallen. Bodies fell or were thrown from the walkways, some out over the merlons, others inward, into the bailie.

And increasingly there were warriors who jumped from the walkways into the bailie, to expand the violence.

THE HELVERTI INVASION

JOHN DALMAS

THE HELVERTI INVASION

Copyright © 2003 by John Dalmas

A Baen Books Original

Baen Publishing Enterprises
P.O. Box 1403
Riverdale, NY 10471
www.baen.com

ISBN: 0-7434-7169-5

Cover art by Bob Eggleton
Interior map by Randy Asplund

First printing, November 2003

Distributed by Simon & Schuster
1230 Avenue of the Americas
New York, NY 10020

Typeset by Bell Road Press, Sherwood, OR
Produced by Windhaven Press, Auburn, NH
Printed in the United States of America

This book is dedicated to

Ruth Beebe Hill and her Dakotah collaborator Chunksa Yuha, for her novel *Hanta Yo*, a historically rooted epic of the Grizzly band of the Dakotah, 1794–1835

to

David Matheson, a Schee-chu-umsh traditional, raised on the Coeur d'Alene reservation in a traditional family, for his novel of the pre-contact Schee-chu-umsh

and to

Tony Hillerman, a white-eyes like myself, for his numerous novels of the contemporary Navajo that have provided my wife and me with much pleasure and many insights

ACKNOWLEDGMENTS

My thanks to the following writers for critiquing this at one or another stage of development: Jim Glass, Patty Briggs, Mary Jane Engh, Kathie Healy, and Bob Lovely. And to the Spokane Word Weavers for listening to, reading and critiquing a number of chapters.

CONTENTS

Part One—Roots

Part Two—Scouting the Ground

Part Three—Shell Games

Part Four—War

Part Five—Aftershocks

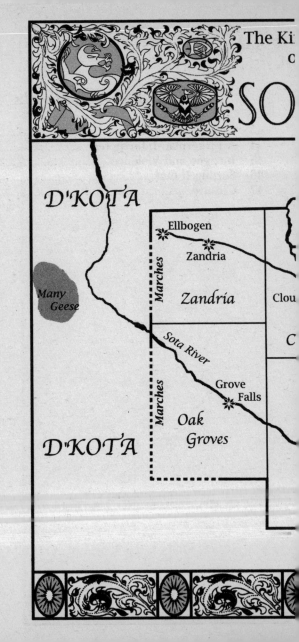

The Ki
c

SO

D'KOTA

Ellbogen

Zandria

Marches

Zandria

Clou

Many
Geese

Sota River

C

Grove
Falls

Marches

Oak
Groves

D'KOTA

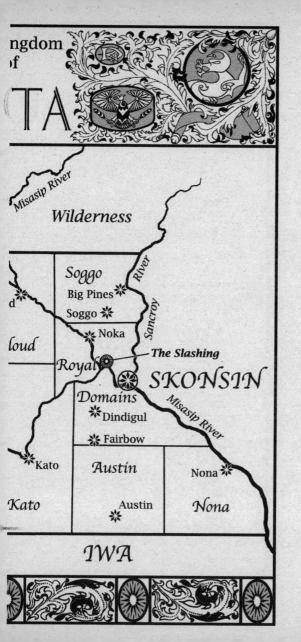

Part One

ROOTS

ROOTS
Vision Quest

Trail-worn and half-starved, Mazeppa slipped through the undergrowth. His face, body, limbs, recently shaved head, all bore what was left of medicine paint. Its symbols were to help on his vision quest—a very unusual vision quest—and only incidentally served as camouflage.

He was pursued by the shrieks of a blue jay in a giant silver maple. "Man! Man! Man!" it shrieked. "Man! Man! Man!" Mazeppa ignored the racket, and settled onto his belly beside a growth of red osier on the riverbank. After a bit, when he failed to move again, the jay's clamor became erratic, confused, as if the bird had forgotten what it was shouting about. Finally the youth heard its departing wing beats. Somewhere on the terrace behind and above him, a nest of baby robins renewed their querulous cries for food. A parent began sharp, demanding chirps. A little later there was the sound of wings again—one mate returning to the nest, the other departing.

For a time, the only sound besides the peeping nestlings was the barely perceptible murmur of the

Misasip: the soft drag of its current along the bank, the faint play of interweaving eddies and subcurrents. The youth's empty belly no longer distracted him as it had the first days, and at a subliminal level each sound registered. He heard it all, understood it all, ignored it all. Had there been a hint of anything worrisome, it would have caught his attention. Meanwhile he simply watched the great river.

Upstream on the far side, another sizeable river joined its waters to the Misasip. At the juncture was an area of many structures, a walled town, and rising within it on the high bank, a higher enclosure of stone, with towers. Mazeppa knew of the great town, and of the towered enclosure called *Palace*. When he was a little boy, a wandering storyteller had stopped among the people and told of it.

Briefly Mazeppa examined it. Then, on the Misasip itself, a great raft came into view, riding the current, a broad tent near its center. Men lay or moved languidly about. On the stern a man stood holding a long pole that trailed in the water, a very long paddle, Mazeppa realized, for steering. As the raft passed, some hundred yards out, a long canoe overtook it from behind, driven by twenty paddlers, their strokes slow and synchronized. As it overtook the raft, men shouted back and forth. Briefly the raft's steersman sculled as if to keep ahead, but after a few powerful strokes he stopped, his cheerful call belying the fist he shook.

Shortly both craft disappeared downstream. Soon another great canoe appeared, this one from the south, moving slowly upstream, its paddlers digging more quickly, but still synchronized. It too had a tent near the middle. It seemed to Mazeppa a great chief must lie in its shade, perhaps napping. He watched it approach and pass. After a bit, it landed below the enclosure's high stone walls, and men disembarked.

Leaving Mazeppa alone by the hypnotically murmuring river, sunlight dazzling on its water. After an indeterminate time of near-trance, a voice spoke to him, not in his ears but in his mind. He'd expected a voice, but this one? It was, he realized, the voice of Jesus. "Mazeppa," it told him, "someday you will rule all this, you and your people. All of it: the great river and the land along it. Including the great town, and Palace, and all they contain. It is what you were born for."

Then Mazeppa slept. When he awoke, the sun was behind him, low, missing the water entirely, glowing gold on the treetops along the distant bank. Where he lay, dusk was settling. Quietly he crept backward, away from the shore, quietly got to his feet, and quietly returned to his tethered pony, which had spent the day browsing the undergrowth within its reach.

Despite days of fasting, Mazeppa vaulted onto its back, ready to return home, no longer a boy, a man now, his vision quest completed. He'd ride west as he'd ridden east, following or paralleling the great trail the Sotans had beaten in the earth with their comings and goings.

And mostly he would ride by night, for in this land he was the enemy. Ride watchfully, listening, his nostrils reading the air, and not just for danger. Because now his fast was over, and it was time to kill and eat. There would be something: a porcupine feeding audibly in a treetop, the smell of its careless evacuations rank in the still night air; or a beaver taking advantage of the darkness, dragging a branch to a streambank. Then he would dismount, string his bow, nock an arrow and wait, letting his eyes find the target if they could. Wait till dawn if need be. And after he had killed, thanked his prey and eaten, he would lie up in a thicket well away from the Sotan trail, and sleep, to dream whatever after-dreams might follow Jesus's message. Lie up till sunset. The moon would be halfway up the eastern sky then, mostly full, and he could travel swiftly.

From Galactics 202
Studies in Cosmology

Parallel universes are not generated randomly or regularly. They result when a sophont chooses, knowingly or not, between alternative actions of *sufficiently effective differences*.

Like a stone thrown into a pond, the results of choice propagate outward in what can be likened to a ripple effect. But unless the matric location is suitably unstable and the initiating decision suits the circumstances, the difference will not maintain itself against the tendency toward the conservation of established universes. The separation does not perpetuate, and only one of the two alternatives continues.

But if the changes are potent enough, "parallel" universes result, or "divergent" universes, if you prefer. (We deal in metaphor here.) Neither universe has any *material* trace of the other. However, the causal complex persists for a considerable period as shadow events. Thus adepts, by focusing on the divergence zone, can discern and penetrate the event cloud. And with sufficient knowledge of pre-event conditions, can give those perceptions context, and to a degree, identity. In fact, it is by recording the deep-questioning of adepts that the following reconstruction has been assembled.

In year 1983 of the Terran Common Era, in what we can call the stem universe, a sequence of political events and posturing led to an American naval task force holding exercises in the vicinity of Korea. Within weeks, the government of the Soviet Union replied with a large-scale demonstration of naval power within five hundred miles of the Hawaiian Islands.

Given the experience of 1941, the American Pacific Fleet was sent out to confront it: a response sufficiently threatening, it was misread as an impending attack. Ordered by Soviet Pacific Fleet Command, the Soviet force commander ordered a single tactical nuclear missile launched to destroy the American flagship. However, the order was incorrectly transmitted, and *all* his missile ships fired.

The Soviet admiral, appalled by the error, immediately notified Moscow. At the same time, an American satellite monitoring the confrontation reported this multi-missile launch, and the U.S. responded immediately with a launch not only against the Soviet task force, but against naval shore targets in the Soviet Far East.

The Soviet chief executive, Yuri V. Andropov, had acted almost as quickly. Assuming the Americans would launch a wider-ranging nuclear response than they actually did, he ordered an ICBM attack on numerous strategic American targets. This massive launch was reported promptly, and the Americans raised the ante "while they still could."

The critical mistransmission of the Soviet admiral's firing order resulted from a choice made by the admiral's signalman—to covertly drink ethanol on watch. It was the kind of choice made innumerable times at every moment in every universe, but this one occurred at a time and place of extreme pregnancy. The result was a space-time bifurcation, and two resultant universes. In one, the drink was taken, in the other it wasn't.

In each, choices made during the next few minutes created a veritable spray of incipient new universes. This seems to be characteristic in the violent decline of sapient life forms. In the universe of interest here, which we will call Universe Terra One, hundreds of fusion warheads exploded in the atmosphere and on the surface. The possibility of such a war had been foreseen. Scientists had predicted not only extensive shock wave and radiation damage, but extensive urban, forest and grass fires; a resulting major increase in albedo that would take years to decline to pre-war normal; the effective destruction of planetary technical infrastructures, including food production and transportation; enormous direct and indirect human fatalities; and the collapse of law and order.

Their predictions, however, were not met. Instead, an unforeseen effect resulted which still is not understood: a major imbalance in the local sector of the underlying creativity matrix. Which was promptly adjusted by the effective *erasure* of the still localized universe of the cataclysm, that is, its morphing into one in which Terra differed from its precursor in some but by no means all respects. In it, many effects of then-recent Terran history disappeared, remaining only as more or less vague memories *in the surviving, ethnically redistributed sophonts*. Sophonts confused not only by the new and unexplainable world they found themselves in, but by vague images of horrors in the spray of *stillborn* universes, horrors that never quite happened.

This is the only known case of a reality matrix rebalancing itself in that manner. Its study gave rise to whole new areas of research, and in time to the cosmology that today we take for granted.

From the HOLY BIBLE
The Book of Renewal, Chapter 1

1 The second millennium had passed since the birth of the Redeemer, and the Lord GOD looked at what man had wrought upon the Earth. 2 HE saw the waters and the air fouled, greed rewarded and virtue scorned. 3 Liars were empowered, their voices entering every home, and their pictures which moved with the semblance of life. 4 And the cities of man were beset with murderers and thieves, tempters and corrupters. 5 Great armies there were, and fleets of warships that

fared upon the sea and beneath it, and there were other fleets that flew swiftly in the air. 6 Still other fleets flew above the air, and these were the most terrible, for they had in them such power that a single one of them could destroy a great city and all its people, and poison whole regions of the Earth.

7 And even as HE watched, GOD saw the armies of man move and clash upon the Earth; the fleets on and under the seas destroyed each other; and the fleets that flew in the air wrought havoc upon all they flew over.

8 Then those other fleets took flight which flew above the air. 9 And when they came to earth, the walls of the cities fell as less than rubble; fire and great winds reaped the people like mighty scythes; the sun was masked with blood and the moon hid its face; days became like nights; myriad were the dead, and loud the cries and lamentations. 10 And the Earth in its sorrow was cold beneath the pall of Death, so that the corn did not grow; hay rotted in the windrows and potatoes in the ground.

11 And the armies of man were without rule, sacking and killing, and the children of man were without bread. 12 Pestilence and famine spread across the face of the Earth, even pestilence that was sent not by GOD but by the hand of man, so that few remained of man's multitudes. 13 And bands of the wicked wandered the waste place the Earth had become, murdering with knife and gun, bow and club, stealing bread from the widow and blankets from her children, making slaves of them, and violating them.

14 And many men raised their faces to GOD, crying aloud for mercy, but only a few there were who fell upon their knees, calling out to GOD that they repented, and saying that all which had befallen them was just.

15 And among the Host of Heaven were those who spoke to GOD saying that man was too iniquitous, that the time had come for the final judgment and

that the Earth should be cleared of man and all his works.

16 GOD listened to the hosts, but also HE listened to the supplications of those men who were righteous. 17 And in His infinite mercy and His infinite justice, GOD stopped for a space the passing of night and day on Earth. 18 HE made the suffering and dying and life itself to pause and wait, while HE renewed the Earth, recreating it. 19 And on the renewed Earth HE left few works of man; simple tools whereby man could have shelter and bread by the sweat of his brow.

20 For GOD did not return man to the paradise of Eden and the innocence of the beginning. 21 Instead HE took the remnants of the nations of man and divided them into small portions separate from one another in distant places, mingling them, and caused them to forget their pride and their shame, and much else. 22 And charged the Church to teach man to love GOD and his fellow men.

---

from "Catechism for Cadets"
Commentary on Force and the Order,
Based on Certain Axioms of Saint Higuchi

As Saint Higuchi put it, "the Tao ensouled a suitable primate species here on Earth to evolve out of barbarism in the direction of the angels." But "given the nature and range of human variation, it is often necessary to apply force." Which, acting with the authority of the Church, is the function of our Order. The trick is to choose actions that offer high long-term benefit-to-harm ratios for humankind.

With the corollary that we *wield no more force than necessary, drawing no more notice than need be,* while being "as honest and truthful as the circumstances permit." Because "to deceive and defeat in a good cause can be pleasurable and *addictive.*"

That is an explicit part of the rationale behind our vows of temperance in all things—including temperance in righteousness, and in temperance itself.

For "what is called 'righteousness,'" he wrote, "is too often *self*-righteousness, which poisons decisions while providing a spurious sense of superiority." Furthermore, humans can seldom comprehend true righteousness, only suppositional righteousness, which the Saint, in his 11th Axiom, calls "a snare and a pitfall. Suppositional righteousness," he went on, "was a serious contributor to Armageddon, and no doubt to most of the earlier debacles in human history."

So said the Saint, whom Senior Operations Director Eskonsami Tahmm has called a truly enlightened being by standards anywhere in the Commonwealth of Homid Worlds. Higuchi-sama's 11th Axiom caused the Cultural Oversight Bureau to adopt and support the Order, and the External Security Secretariat to approve the establishment of the Sangre de Cristo Academy. . . .

In theory this is a straightforward partnership, and the best we're likely to have on Terra until we've grown a lot, spiritually and philosophically, which means for quite a while. Meanwhile we in the Order do the best we can, which, based on performance, is rather good. Perfection is *unavailable* to human beings (Axiom 5), or to any ensouled life form in the physical universes. Except of course in the most basic sense, in which perfection is unavoidable.

Certainly our principal weakness seems unavoidable, given the free-will character that accompanies sapience in the known and implied universes. For sapience (again according to the Saint) carries with it goals and principles which differ among individuals, and cultures, and societies. And looking beyond humankind, among life forms. Goals and principles which inspire and empower conflicts as minor as what to serve for supper, and as major as whether to destroy a world.

Love and compassion are our saving graces, but (again according to Tahmm) they are not known to manifest sufficiently, in the physical universes, to eliminate conflict. Nor are love and compassion enforceable. Let me repeat that: *Nor are they enforceable.* Control is often necessary, but it is at best a mechanism for coping, not for healing. Spiritual evolution—with the consequent enlightenment—is the mechanism for healing.

—Kabibi Christian
Instructor

The Vicinity of Sol 9
GPV 1219-28-99206

The ship had begun as an express package carrier in the Borgith Sector. After forty-seven years it was put up for sale, and through an intermediary was bought by a Fohannid chaos cult that called itself "the Helverti."

The Helverti had the vessel modified as a yacht, and renamed it what best translates as *Satan's Delight*, or *The Delight of Chaos*. For in Fohannid mythology, the Evil Principle is personified as the Lord of Chaos.

Now, nearly four long hyperspace years from their home world, her skipper watched the shuttle emerge from the *Delight's* shuttle lock. For a few seconds the shuttle's navcomp read and analyzed the gravitic plexus, then she disappeared into warp space with seven cult members.

With that, the *Delight's* skipper activated his gravdrive and took his ship down to the dead, frozen surface of what, in a different universe, was known as Charon. There, he and his crew—all but one—would take to their stasis lockers. At the end of every shipsweek, the crewman on duty would waken his or her replacement to stand watch, to monitor the automated systems checks, as required by the owners and by prudence.

In not too many years, with a bit of luck, the owners would lift shuttle and beam a signal to the ship, which would read it and waken the entire crew. If there was no signal, eventually the ship would waken them without one, and they'd be free to leave. For the Commonwealth's Cultural Oversight Bureau would have monitors on Sol 3, and no one could guarantee a successful mission. In fact, risk was an important part of the charm that had drawn the Helverti so many parsecs from r'Fohann.

Another part of the charm was the indigenes. From all the Helverti could learn—and they'd studied everything available and seemingly pertinent—the indigenes themselves presented risks. Opportunities and risks.

A Message from God

Helverti Chief had scratched politely on the tipi flap. Mazeppa Tall Man's junior wife, Trains Horses, had unfastened the flap and let him in. Mazeppa gestured Helverti Chief to sit beside him, on a buffalo robe near the fire. Trains Horses quickly refastened the flap, for autumn was well advanced, and the day raw and windy. And cloudy, and the fire had burned down to little more than embers. Much of what light there was in the tipi entered through the smoke hole overhead.

When both men were seated, Mazeppa's senior wife added small pieces of dry aspen to the fire.

Mazeppa was an imposing man, his wide shoulders muscular, arms long and sinewy, hands large. His hair was sun-bleached, pale as straw on top, his large mustache red-gold, and his eyes chestnut brown. From a rack he took a pipe, not his long-stemmed ceremonial pipe, but of redstone nonetheless, inviting serious talk.

Filling its carved bowl with tobacco, he tamped it, and using a wooden-handled trade spoon, lifted an ember from the fire. Holding it to the bowl, he inhaled, a series of short kiss-like inhalations. The resulting smoke was fragrant, even amidst the pungence of burnt buffalo dung.

He held the pipe upward, offering it first to God, then to Helverti Chief, who called himself Jorval. As always, Jorval took a single mouthful of smoke and released it without inhaling. He'd learned earlier that his lungs and throat did not tolerate such concentrated fumes; they'd nearly strangled him.

For a long minute the chief smoked thoughtfully, seeming to ignore his guest, who had thoughts of his own. Before leaving r'Fohann, Jorval had viewed all the publicly available cubes that long ago survey scouts had covertly recorded among the buffalo peoples. Solitary scouts, Fohanni like himself because of their resemblance to humans. Faces depilated, they'd posed as holy wanderers, staying a few days or perhaps weeks at a camp, their physical oddities adding to their acceptance as holy.

The first Xiox survey team had arrived in post-Armageddon Year 14, discovered the totally unexpected Shuffling, and created rough and ready policies and procedures for anthropological studies. Since then, new, better-prepared expeditions had been sent, first at thirty-year intervals. Recorded on cube, the raw data, with commentaries and analyses, was voluminous.

Jorval had begun by reading the written summaries, then formed a basic project concept centered on the buffalo peoples of what once had been called North America. Next, using illicit language cubes, he'd invested two weeks on "forced learning" and drilling the Merkan language. Afterward he reviewed the publicly available survey cubes on the buffalo people. Their oral traditions were not particularly rich, and less perceptive than those of the tribes who'd dwelt there before Armageddon. The indigenous tribal survivors, more at home, and less traumatized and confused, had been leaders in the recovery. This, along with the nature of the environment, had inevitably caused the emerging new tribes to assume certain features. But the "inshuffled" elements had been much more numerous, and arrived with their own cultural inclinations. Thus, while the cultural similarities between the traditional Dakotah and post-Armageddon Dkota were conspicuous, the differences were significant.

Based on maps, Jorval had chosen the Dkota to work with; they'd seemed the most suitably located. During the weeks since his first visit, he'd enlarged and refined his knowledge, while carefully nurturing Mazeppa's trust and friendship.

He had not, however, foreseen the tipi's smoky reek. It had bothered him from the beginning, even though the tipi had not been buttoned shut on his previous visits. And immunological wizardry, so important in interplanetary commerce, didn't cover every allergy, every idio-sensitivity. So he minimized his exposure by minimizing the time spent inside.

With a sharpened and feathered stick, Mazeppa dug the dottle from his pipe and looked again at his guest. "The time of ponds freezing will soon be upon us," he said, "and soon after that, winter. Then some of our bands will move into soddies until the time of mud. Which will be a long time from now."

"I have never experienced a Dkota winter," Jorval replied. "Perhaps you will advise me."

"You will need warm clothes."

"We brought some with us. All we will need."

Mazeppa wondered what those warm clothes would look like. Not, he supposed, like his own. Nothing about the sky people was like the Dkota, except their basic human appearance, and even that was peculiar. "What do you eat in winter?" he asked.

"We have brought food with us, food we are used to, but to ensure we have enough, I hope to trade with your people for meat."

Mazeppa nodded gravely. "We have smoked much buffalo, and soon, when it is colder, we will kill more, freezing it."

Again they sat briefly without talking. It was polite to talk about lesser topics before discussing what was on one's mind. Mazeppa knew too little about the sky people for easy small talk, but after a minute or two he spoke again.

"Before, when you visited, you came in a smaller sky canoe. Today you came in a large one. Why is that?"

"With your agreement, this time I would like to stay for several days. The larger sky boat will be more comfortable, and has room for more of us to stay in. So I have brought my nephew, Ench, son of my sister. Also Lorness and Harmu, whom you have already met. And others. But we are a shy people. Those of us who do not need to be among your people will keep largely to themselves. That is why we landed a little distance away."

Mazeppa nodded thoughtfully. "Did Helverti Chief come to my lodge to speak about something in particular?"

"I did. It has been waiting to be said since I came here the first time, but it was too important to speak of so soon. Now the time has come. That is, if Mazeppa Tall Man feels ready to talk about something greatly important."

Again the stolid nod. "I am interested in hearing what the Helverti chief, my friend Jorval, has to tell me."

Even now Jorval was not quick to speak, as if considering how best to start. When he began, it was with a story already part of Dkota lore, recorded early by survey scouts. In fact, it had been recorded among the other buffalo tribes as well.

"The story began a long time before Armageddon and the Shuffling," Jorval said. "Buffalo people dwelt on these same grasslands, living as you live. And then as now, dirt-eaters lived in the country east of the grassland. Over time, the dirt-eaters became more and more numerous, and decided they wanted the grassland for themselves. So they chose to behave against the way of the Great Spirit. They invented new and more deadly weapons that enabled them to kill many at once, from a distance. Then, because the dirt-eaters were not brave, they attacked the buffalo instead of the people of the buffalo, killing them in great numbers and leaving them to rot, until none were left. When the buffalo were gone, the buffalo people grew weak with hunger, and the dirt-eaters attacked them in force. They killed most of the buffalo people, and the rest they turned into two-legged dogs who had to do what the dirt-eaters told them to do."

He shrugged with both shoulders and hands, in the manner of the Dkota. "Afterward the dirt-eaters fought each other, until they destroyed the world."

Mazeppa had heard all this before. His people had told it through the generations. But he didn't say "yes yes" as if to hurry Helverti Chief. He simply, stolidly listened.

Jorval continued: "Then the Great Spirit remade the world, and the people who were left, He scattered. He renewed the buffalo people, along with the buffalo, the wolf, the yellow bear and all the rest. And the dirt-eaters. And He told all those who walked on their hind legs that if they destroyed the world again, they would receive no further chance. They would dwell forever in the place of fire.

"These things you know without my telling them."

Only now did Mazeppa nod, still waiting. Helverti Chief's gaze remained on the small flames dancing on the shrunken branchwood. Mazeppa wondered what he saw there besides the fire. "But there is more to the story. You Dkota have not heard it all. Along the Misasip, the dirt-eaters have once more begun to look at the grassland. In their greed, they have begun to think again that they would like to have it for themselves. Some of their chiefs have begun to talk about destroying the buffalo, and once more turning the buffalo people into dogs. So the Great Spirit has sent us, the Helverti, to warn you: you must not let them do this evil. You must attack them first, defeat them in war, burn their villages and towns, kill their cattle. And let them know the buffalo people are not theirs to rule."

A chill ran through Mazeppa. It had been one thing to hear Helverti Chief repeat what his own people already knew. That had been only a story. But this? This was prophecy!

Jorval got to his feet. "That is why I have come to Mazeppa Tall Man. The Great Spirit has chosen the Dkota to carry out His wishes, and He has chosen Mazeppa Tall Man to lead the Dkota.

"Now I will return to the large sky canoe, and give you time to contemplate my words. I have not come to command you, only to tell you that the Great Spirit has appointed the Dkota and Mazeppa Tall Man to carry out his wishes. To do it or not is up to you. But if you decide not to, He will not turn elsewhere. He will let the dirt-eaters do as they please, and when they have destroyed the world again, He will not put it back. Instead, all the beings who walk on their hind legs will dwell in the sea of fire forever. Except for His servants, the Helverti."

Trains Horses had heard all of it. She unfastened the door for Helverti Chief, whom she thought of as Sky Chief, and refastened it when he'd left. She and Mazeppa's senior wife did not look openly at their husband, but sat on their robes, their bone needles, teeth, and sinew threads busy. Neither entirely trusted

Sky Chief, and wondered if his words could possibly be true.

Mazeppa, however, did not wonder. Remembering his vision quest, and what Jesus had whispered to him, he believed with certainty. For years he'd been preparing for this day without ever wondering why Jesus had told him what he had. He'd even succeeded in allying the Ulster people with the Dkota. And contemplated doing more, but had delayed, for it seemed to him his people would not yet agree to it.

Now he knew what to do. Not do it now, for winter would soon arrive, but after the snow had melted and the willow buds were opening.

Memorandum of Transmittal
dated GPV 1211-27-931130

Furg,

You should already have seen the official report on the Helverti incursion. Now I'm sending a detailed, *verikal*-assisted debrief of the mission leader, filled in with sections of *verikal* debriefs of others involved. No one was coerced to talk.

I have filled minor gaps with my—ahem!—own judicious conjectures.

Precautions were taken to safeguard technical security, an interesting exercise in misdirection.

It's been quite a project. Enjoy!

Tahmm

Part Two

SCOUTING THE GROUND

Chapter 1
The Moleen Brother House

(Luis Raoul DenUyl)

"About five minutes now."

The pilot's words woke me, and I raised my seat-back. It had been nearly night when I'd fallen asleep, right after we'd lifted from Momiji Tani-gawa, most of an hour earlier. I'd been dreaming that Lemmi and I were drilling Dakotah verbs and idioms, a kind of dream that happens after deep-learning a language.

Seen through the cabin windows, forest stretched black beneath us, interrupted by farm settlements, their fields and pastures side-lit by a crescent moon. Across the aisle, Lemmi was looking out his window. Tahmm and the pilot sat up front, identifiable by their white hair. Fur. Carlos and Peng had taken seats toward the back.

Five minutes.

I remembered the map. Tahmm had routed us via Mizzoo, to drop off another new master at the Momiji Tani-gawa brother house, so it would be Ilanoy we were flying over. Northern Ilanoy, where Jamila had come from. Lemmi was probably looking out at the

23

Misasip, and at Iwa on its west bank. It would be high spring down there. Back in the Sangre de Cristo, that noon, the snow had still been deep, in the spruce forest and above timberline. But at Momiji Tani-gawa they'd already put up the first cutting of hay. I hadn't actually seen it—it had been deep dusk—but there was no mistaking the smell.

Below us the clearings slowed, nearly stopped, and I felt us dropping. I could make out a large building a short way off, dark with shadow, and growing. The brother house. We were settling toward a field, or more likely a pasture, with a lane on one side bordered by hedge-apple trees. Closer by, real trees were reaching upward, their tops climbing past us, exciting my stomach. This was the beginning of a new life.

We slowed, stopped. The windows were still on one-way transparent, but when the cabin lit up, it was faintly. We didn't want light shining out the door when it opened. Tahmm stood up. "Time to unload," he said, then walked down the aisle, passing me. Grinning, Lemmi got to his feet and I followed him aft. We four new graduates—Lemmi and I, and Carlos and Peng—picked up our baggage and carried it down the ramp.

The scout floated inches above the ground. We were in the shadow of the woods. It was chilly enough, the mosquitoes were lying low; I didn't even hear tree-toads. It smelled like high spring—new foliage, the damp mull of last year's fallen leaves and, faintly, cow manure. Toward the middle of the pasture, cows and calves stood watching.

A man on horseback approached, leading a string of saddle and pack horses. He'd been waiting in the hedge shadow, by the lane. He didn't call to us, and when he arrived spoke quietly. "I'm Brother Krikor, the majordomo here. If you'll load your gear, Fedor and Freddy are waiting."

After lashing our baggage on the pack saddles, we

mounted, and rode toward the lane with its fifteen-foot hedge. The chance of any local having seen the scout was as good as zero. As we approached the hedge's narrow gap, I looked back. The scout was already gone. Standard security procedure. He'd probably go up ten or twelve miles, park on a gravitic vector, and catch up on his sleep and reading, then pick Tahmm up after dark tomorrow.

I remembered another country lane, in a beaver meadow in Adirondack, when the first scout I'd ever seen, barring the lizard scout, had loaded Lemmi and Jamila and me in the dark, and changed all our lives. But that was then. This night didn't feel anything like that.

The Moleen brother house was bigger than the one I'd done my brother training at, back in Mizzoo. Brother Krikor opened the heavy oak door and led us through a vestibule to a sitting room. "Your guests, Master Fedor," he announced, then left. He was in the know about floaters, but probably not about magisterial mission ops. A pair of lamps gave off light and the smell of fragrant oil. Two of the waiting men wore master's sashes; I could guess their names. The third, well-fed and graying, wore a bishop's habit.

It was Tahmm who introduced us; he was senior to us all. "Fedor, Freddy, Bishop Foley, I'd like you to meet my new magisterial missioners: Master Luis Raoul DenUyl and Master Lemmi Tsinnajinni." He gestured. "And teaching masters Carlos del Passo and Ho Peng, who will establish a brother house and school near Hasty, and provide ops support for Luis and Lemmi." He turned his attention to us four new graduates. "You know something of Fedor and Freddy," he said.

We knew one thing certainly: it was they who'd broken with tradition and trained Jamila as the first female brother. Their Moleen brother house was the most prominent in the Archdiocese of the Central Misasip Valley, with three resident masters training novices and brothers. The Order was expanding everywhere, since the "need-to-know limitations" had run out, and the chaos cults had learned about Terra.

"And this is Bishop William Foley," Tahmm was saying. Normally a bishop wouldn't have known about Lemmi and me, and surely not about Tahmm, so this was no ordinary bishop. "Besides being bishop of the Moleen Diocese," Tahmm went on, "Bishop Foley is in charge of the Ecclesiastical Network from Sanlooee north to the wilderness. He knows a lot about the Kingdoms of Sota, Skonsin, Iwa and North Ilanoy, and what goes on there."

The Ecclesiastical Network, the "EN," is the Church's basic hierarchical layer: the parishes and their priests. All centered on their dioceses and bishops, in the next layer up. The bishops in turn are centered on the archdioceses and their archbishops, which in turn are centered on the Holy See in Norlins, with its ecclesiastical bureaucracy centered on the Holy Father. The general structure had existed long before Armageddon, though with differences, but only after Archbishop Kuczinski had been raised to cardinal had it become the Ecclesiastical Network—big E, big N— Norlins' intelligence network. Call it quality control. We'd learned that in Church 101.

As a junior parish priest, Kuczinski had been one of the first clerics selected to the Academy. Earlier, only Higuchean brothers had been selected. After returning from the Academy, he'd had been elevated rapidly to bishop, Archbishop of Chocapoako, and then to Norlins as assistant to Cardinal Bau, in the Sacred Congregation for the Defense of the Church. As Bau's chief of staff, Kuczinski had his finger on the ecclesiastical pulse of North Merika.

I glanced at Lemmi, catching his eye. Foley was another Academy grad; had to be.

It was Fedor who spoke next. "Bill," he said to Foley, "tell our guests what you've learned about the Helverti."

The bishop spoke seated. "To start with," he said, "they're Fohanni. Tahmm's world-kin."

Tahmm smiled ruefully. Foley continued: "They're from a different culture than the Kelgorath sado-hedonists you dealt with in the People's Democratic Republic. They're here illegally, and they're in illegal contact with—" he paused, grinning "—with the indigenous sophonts. The likes of you and me. Beyond that, not even *Uncle Arvind* knows anything about them." *Uncle Arvind* is the nickname for the artificial intelligence at the Academy. "The little we know is from informants.

"Consider their name: *Helverti*. That's what they call themselves. You all recognize *helvert* as a Xiox adjective meaning 'excellent.' Attach the suffix and you get the derivative noun *Helverti*. But Arvind doesn't list it as a proper noun, which means it's either secret, or has very limited use.

"Still, to me, when first I heard it, the name Helverti didn't imply anything negative. I'm proficient but not fluent in Xiox. And not surprisingly, when you think about it, each Xiox-speaking world has its own usages, rooted in the specific life form and planetary culture, and influenced by the indigenous language, even when effectively extinct. Often this results in a distinctive dialect of Xiox. And Tahmm assures me that on r'Fohann, where the indigenous language is tonal, the word *helverti*, given a certain tonality, means 'scoundrel.' In the literal sense.

"We don't know how the Helverti pronounce it, but Tahmm is confident they selected it for its double meaning. Which suggests an attitude: they take pride in their criminality.

"Our informants are two traveling ironmongers who trade with the buffalo tribes, dealing in pots and pans, arrowheads and axes, glass beads, silver and copper for making wire and ornaments . . . that sort of thing.

"The buffalo people travel a lot, following the buffalo, which often takes them across tribal boundaries. And the tribes tend to be territorial, so sometimes they clash. To some, a territorial boundary is a temptation and a challenge, rather than an exclusion. Mostly their clashes aren't very bloody—skirmishes and an occasional punitive raid—but they can be more. And more, the Dkota occasionally prey on farm settlements in the marches, the border zone with the Kingdom of Sota. But until the last ten years or so, their raids were infrequent and on a small scale. Then the Dkota elected a new war chief, Mazeppa Tall Man, a leader of exceptional charisma, especially for young warriors. Sometime during the next few years he became principal chief. Principal chiefs are generally older men, less interested in fighting, but Mazeppa is neither old nor peaceful. Under his leadership, the Dkota raided deeper than ever into Sota, with more warriors than ever, and more killing and burning.

"Three years ago, Mazeppa made a peace treaty with the King of Sota, actually signed his name to it, and smoked the peace pipe. Then promptly turned his attention to his neighbors on the west, another buffalo tribe calling itself the Ulsters. Beat them soundly in what for the tribes was a large-scale battle. Afterward he praised the Ulster warriors for their bravery and skill."

"Wait a minute," I said, "Signed his name? We were told the Dkota are illiterate."

"Mostly they are, Luis. But Mazeppa's senior wife is said to be Sotan, a nun taken captive on a raid. The story is, she taught him, whether simply to sign his name or to actually write, my informant didn't know."

"So he defeated the Ulsters," Lemmi said, "and softened the blow with praises. Then what?"

"He arranged a lot of marriages between the tribes, took Ulster boys into Dkota tipis and sent Dkota boys to Ulster tipis, to live with foster families. All with big ceremonies, while proclaiming the two tribes to be part of a new and larger one."

I wondered what the exchanged boys thought of that. Novices at a brother school can be as young as thirteen, and generally like it fine, but they're there because they want to be.

"We know of no buffalo tribe ever doing such a thing before," Foley went on, "and the elders of the other northern tribes—the Yellow Bears and Wolves—are said to have agreed to stand together if the enlarged Dkota tribe harasses them. The assumption among Mazeppa's own people seems to be that he'd annexed the Ulsters to build Dkota strength. Might he have signed the treaty with the Sotans to lull them into carelessness? It seems well to operate on that assumption."

"What do the Sotans think of all this?" I asked.

The bishop grunted. "It depends on what Sotan you're talking about. I'm not sure the Sotans even know the Ulsters and Dkota have joined ranks, though they may have heard of the battle. But they differ bitterly on trusting Mazeppa. King Eldred, along with Archbishop Clonarty of the Upper Misasip Archdiocese, believe absolutely in Mazeppa's honesty. Or claim to. They insist he'd had a religious epiphany, and that the treaty grew out of it. But most of the nobles consider Mazeppa a liar, and the king a gullible fool."

"Hmm. Any prospect of an uprising against the king?"

"There's a Williamite parish a few miles northwest of Hasty," he answered. "Pastor Linkon there has numerous contacts, in Hasty and elsewhere in Sota. He follows its government and politics closely. I have other sources there, but Linkon's the man I rely on most. When you get there, look him up."

❦❦❦ ❦❦❦ ❦❦❦

That led to an hour of discussion that left things hanging. Afterward I spent forty minutes meditating before going to bed, and seven hours sorting things out in dreams. At least that's what seemed to be going on.

Chapter 2
Assignments and Catechism

(Luis)

A tolling bell wakened me at 0530—me and everyone else in the Moleen brother house. It gave us time
to dress, go out to the latrine, come back in and wash,
and brush our hair. At 0600, everyone went to chapel
for morning prayer, something not part of the Academy day. The Cultural Oversight Bureau, the COB,
isn't part of the Church, for all their importance to
each other, and now we were in the world of the
Order again.

Meditation, on the other hand is part of life at both
the Academy and the brother house. At 0640 we all
went to one of the two zendos to meditate. There was
a zendo for masters and brothers and one for novices and for any brother needing coaching. Freddy was
the exception; he'd meditated before the bell woke
the rest of us, so he could guide the novices in their
meditations later. Supervising meditation is an art
form.

At 0740 we went to breakfast, and at 0815, we four
new masters met again with Tahmm and Fedor. Freddy

was tied up with novices all morning. With the assistance of selected brothers, he worked with novices not only on meditation and the Catechism of St. Higuchi—but on martial arts. (The Catechism of St. Higuchi is a lot different from the Catechisms of the Council of Ponshtou, both the Complete and the Simples. It's not that they contradict each other; they simply cover different ground. And the Catechism of St. Higuchi is said to be nowhere written down. You memorize the whole thing, word for word, then gradually over the years, peel your way through new layers of meaning and application.) It was primarily Freddy who turned novices into Higuchians, spiritually and martially.

By contrast, Fedor's job was to supervise the entire operation—brother house, school, farm. He also lectured on, and supervised study in history, and in tactics in the broad sense. Higuchian tactics. And planned and debriefed brother missions, which were the great majority of missions. Tahmm had paired them. He's been known to keep a graduate around an extra year, getting further training while waiting for the graduation of an underclassman who'd be a really good match with him.

Tahmm and Lemmi and I, and Carlos and Peng, were in the briefing room a few minutes ahead of time. Fedor came in on the minute, and not alone. Our two assistants—"brothers" assigned to the Moleen brother house—came in with him. Lemmi and I recognized one of them: Paddy Glynn. Jamila and I had saved Paddy's life, back in Allegheny, and taken him under our wings. Supposedly I recruited him, but in a sense he'd recruited himself, as a big, remarkably brawny sixteen-year-old. And because of the emergency, he'd been exposed to things as an unprepared boy that even brothers weren't supposed to know about.

He'd handled all of it well.

The other was a black girl, or young woman. Brown,

actually. Fedor introduced her as Kabibi Christian. Apparently he and Freddy had been encouraged to train more female brothers. She was taller than most women, but not as tall as Jamila had been, and she didn't have Jamila's charisma. On a good day, Lemmi and I combined wouldn't match Jamila's charisma. But Kabibi was no one to brush off. Like me, she had a warrior's aura with a good tinge of scholar, and strong self confidence. During the introductions, her glance took us in without self-consciousness. Though I didn't know it, she was still short of her eighteenth birthday, but she'd been on two brother missions.

When the introductions were over, Brother Krikor ushered the brothers out. Apparently Tahmm didn't want them exposed to some part of the briefing.

It was Tahmm who briefed us, of course. Lemmi and I, and Carlos and Peng, had been briefed back at the Academy, and this was pretty much a summary, but it tied in things Foley had told us. And hadn't told us; I had no doubt he and Tahmm had sat together into the wee hours, discussing things.

He began by repeating something we already knew—something obvious: "If the buffalo people massacre large numbers of Sotans, it will result in generations of hatred and violence between the kingdoms and the tribes. Which is what I believe the Helverti have in mind. So what you need to do is prevent a war between the Dkota and the Sotans. If you can't prevent it, keep it as minor as possible.

"Meanwhile, we need Sota militarily strong, to help prevent massacres. But His Majesty, Eldred Youngblood, and his confessor, Archbishop Clonarty, are confirmed 'mollies,' convinced that the way to peace is to mollify anyone who threatens you. And that all violence—all war at any rate—is evil. Meanwhile, Eldred has already weakened his kingdom's ability to defend itself.

"On the other hand, he's demonstrated willingness

to use force brutally against rebellion, so if the Dkota attack, he may fight. But how effectively, given his weakened defenses?"

We already knew the basic problems, and our assignments. Lemmi was to learn what the Dkota planned, and what their military potential was, along with what he could find out about the Helverti. I was to learn the political and military dynamics in Sota, and what their potentials were, good and bad. Explore how pacific the king and his archbishop really were, and what the nobility was able and willing to do about it. We were cross-trained and cross-briefed, to help us interact and provide backup when needed, and whatever we learned, we'd share by radio.

This final briefing had been a last opportunity for questions. Now Tahmm dismissed us to see to our supplies and equipment for the long ride north to Hasty town.

We had everything ready before evening prayers. We'd leave in the morning. Supper followed vespers, and after supper, Tahmm called Lemmi and me to talk with him.

"I'm going to ask you some questions," he said. "Call it a catechism. Some of it will seem obvious, but bear with me.

"Luis, we were aware a year ago that an illicit shuttle was approaching Terra. Why didn't we jump it right away?"

"You wouldn't dare shoot on sight. It could have been from some ship in trouble. And if you'd simply challenged it, it could have generated warpspace and been out of this dimension before anything could be done about it.

"Once the intruder lands, *then* you might send the marines, but if they jumped it within sight of some locals, you'd be in serious trouble with Dzixoss. Because it's not all right for us indigines, present company excepted, to know we're being monitored. And that some material 'higher power' is hanging around. Even a beneficent higher power."

Tahmm raised an eyebrow at that. Not in surprise— I know his eyebrows—but to draw a response. An elaboration.

"To think that *God* is looking out for you is one thing," I went on, "because when nothing appears to happen, you shrug it off. God being unseen, and operating at a different level, his actions are indirect and hard to pin down. But a marine fighter swooping in, shooting up or scooping up whatever's threatening you? That kind of higher power is something else, especially for people who never imagined such things exist."

"Combat aircraft are mentioned in your Bible," Tahmm countered. "In 'The Book of Renewal.' "

"Even to strict constructionists, the Biblical universe isn't real in the same way the world around them is."

"All right. Are there situations in which the COB *might* intervene openly—visibly and conspicuously— in the Helverti's little game?"

"It would have to be *very* carefully. With the understanding that it automatically triggers two things: It will almost certainly enter the local—" I paused, groping; the word I wanted you don't run into every day. My experience with it had been in Psych-Soc 201. "The local folklore," I said. "The *mythos*! That's the word.

"And you'd have to be able to justify it, because it automatically triggers a COB board of inquiry. We indigenes are supposed to be responsible for ourselves. You people are here to train and guide some of us, help us get started. Not to intercede visibly."

"Good," Tahmm said. His grin was easy, impressing me because the ESS's Terran Command station, parked thirty thousand miles out, had sent Tahmm's report to Dzixoss, describing the mission against the Kelgorath chaos cult. And Tahmm's effort to camouflage the COB's role—to minimize the effect on the locals. The message pod could be arriving at Dzixoss even as we spoke; unmanned pods travel more rapidly in hyperspace than manned ships can. I could imagine a great scurrying of bureaucrats in the huge External Security Building we'd "visited" via holo cube, in *Introduction to the COB*. Scurrying, and shouts of "sacrilege!" Not really; I exaggerate.

Tahmm didn't seem to worry. For one thing it would be a long time before a replacement could arrive, or be assigned from local staff, and he'd commented once that he could have whatever decision they made. They had their problems to deal with, he had his. And if he could go back and change what he'd done, he'd leave it as it was.

I also remembered something Professor Sorvok had said: that the Bureau had never before dealt with anything like the Terran situation. That it was a learning experience, and the Bureau's manual for Terra was a work in progress.

Meanwhile Tahmm had turned to Lemmi. "Doesn't that seem a little silly," he asked, "being so careful with the Helverti? With a little skillful stalking, or an ambush, the marines could send a covert hit team, wipe them out or snatch them, and be done with it. I could even have you do it."

Lemmi shook his head. "A major key to the dynamics of spiritual growth is freedom of choice. Including the choice to do seriously destructive things. Sometimes the potential damage of an impending destructive action is too great to accept, so we prevent it, by force if necessary. By killing if necessary. But even coercion creates negative energy and mucks up the reality matrix: it's harmful to everyone."

Lemmi paused just long enough that Tahmm started to speak—did it on purpose I think—then cut him off. Lemmi's more of a gamesman than I am. I'm pretty sure he knew what Tahmm was going to bring up.

"To forcibly block choice generates futility," he went on, "and deep and protracted—or repeated—futility can generate destructive compulsions. So in the case of chaos cults, the Bureau tries covertly to let the game play out with minimum destruction. Using indigenes like us." He shrugged. "One of those indigenes—" he gestured at me "—who'd been stripped naked for purposes of torture, tricked the lizards out of their shoes. Got hold of a steel bar and went on a rampage in their engine room, shutting down power and shields. Allowing a troop of samurai to storm aboard with swords and bows, and it was more than futility the lizards felt. More than dismay. But it wasn't the same as being blocked by some overpowering Commonwealth military force. More like a force of nature."

I was impressed. That was no paraphrase of some Academy lecture. But Lemmi had it right. That's how it had been.

Tahmm nodded. He'd enjoyed it. But he wasn't done with Lemmi yet. "A lot of Dkota have seen the Helverti spacecraft. How might you explain it—or the Helverti—to a tribesman?"

"That they're probably survivors from before Armageddon, living on the other side of the world. I'll be posing as a healer, and to the buffalo people that means having a direct line to God." He grinned. "It's simpler and less intrusive than your old scout and bullhorn technique in the dark of night over Eisenbach."

Tahmm got to his feet. "Good enough, both of you. You're ready." He turned to me. "One more thing. I've been waiting in case you spotted it yourself, but you should know before you set out." He paused, making me reach mentally for what followed. "Kabibi Christian," he went on, "is Jamila's baby sister. Brought up in a different family; that's why the different surname."

Chapter 3
Change of Plans

The invasion plan proceeded without haste. The winter camp of the Beaver and Buffalo Bands was a large open-ended hoop of tipis near Mink Creek, less than an hour's ride from the soddies of the Tobacco and Corn Bands. It was the largest single concentration of the Dkota people. Jorval had visited the hoop only about once a month, to spare his lungs, and on the principle that familiarity breeds contempt. Furthermore, by nature he was a student, and by habit (outside his chaos compulsion) a dabbler. Once-a-month meetings with Mazeppa left him time to explore. He visited and recorded numerous sites on Terra, from the polar regions to the tropics. He experienced the monsoon deluges of the Ivory Coast, the thick heavy snowfalls of the Pacific coastal mountains, the idyllic beaches of Pacific islands (fishing from time to time), and from within the shuttle, the fierce ground blizzards of the Greenland and Antarctic ice caps.

On the prairie, the winter had been severe. But with the arrival of spring, the bands had dispersed, and the Helverti spent more time with the Dkota.

It was an agreeable season. The mosquitoes were still only wigglers, and despite showers, a late snow and occasional thunderstorms, the lengthening days were mostly sunny. Larks trilled, and red-winged blackbirds chattered and sang amongst the cattails.

The shuttle or scout might sit all morning near the hoop, even all day, with none of the Helverti showing themselves. Then it might leave without explanation, and be gone for days. All of which, as intended, maintained a useful degree of otherness. Twice Jorval created sonic booms immediately before landing, for the Dkota considered thunder an important attribute of God.

And sometimes Jorval emerged from the shuttle, or the scout, always before midmorning, his burly form (the locals had unknowingly resurrected the name White Bear, from the survey days) striding to Mazeppa's tipi, where he would announce himself in the standard courteous manner by scratching on the flap. If the chief was in, they would talk by the fire, or better yet, leave the tipi to walk alone together. Jorval had been impressed by Mazeppa. Although less powerfully built than Jorval, the Dkota was strong and athletic. Sinewy, even for a Dkota. Having far less body hair than a Fohannu, he was a living chart of the human skeletal muscles. And he stood half a head taller. But what impressed Jorval most was Mazeppa's charisma—he was an innate leader and at the same time invariably courteous.

On one gorgeous spring morning, Jorval sent Ench, his fifteen-year-old nephew, to Mazeppa's tipi with an invitation to the scout craft. Not for a ride—he'd given him one the autumn before, and it wouldn't do to let flying become ordinary—but a courtesy lunch, including the Fohannid equivalent of hot chocolate. None of it was familiar to Mazeppa. He ate it in trust, and found it interesting.

While the two chiefs ate, they made the small talk

that was part of Dkota manners. They spoke of the weather; of the great flocks of migrating geese and swans whose formations crossed the sky day and night in this season, their honking cries audible far below; of the broad rafts of ducks that gabbled and muttered on the lakes at night, lakes whose thick roofs of ice had recently melted.

Jorval found Dkota lives and folkways interesting, and covertly recorded their conversations. "I'm surprised not more of your people are out hunting them," he commented, gesturing at a formation of geese settling toward a nearby lake.

"Of birds we kill only what we want to eat at one time. And the meat of birds is not so nourishing as buffalo. It is the meat of hoofed creatures—especially true meat, the buffalo—that makes the people strong, enduring. Also we would have to kill many ducks or geese or swans or cranes, and skin and clean them, to make as much meat as one buffalo. And we can kill numerous buffalo in a day, when we find them."

Jorval nodded. "Ah! I understand."

For a minute they sat unspeaking, sipping. Then Helverti Chief asked a question of greater interest. "How went your council with the Ulster-Dkota?"

Mazeppa grunted. "They did not disagree with any of my plans, but they are still uncomfortable about my decisions. They believe I am too much influenced by the Helverti, who are not buffalo people."

He chuckled. "So I have given Chief Gallagher a very important role in the planning." He paused, a smile playing around his lips. "And I have left them little time to grumble. We will destroy the Sotans soon after the horseflies come out."

Uncertainty tightened Jorval's chest. *Destroy? After the horseflies come out?* "When will that be?"

"By then the young geese will wear feathers." Seeing that neither reference had meant anything to Jorval, Mazeppa tried something the sky people would surely know about. "The moon will wax and wane two times by then."

Now it seemed that Jorval understood. "You will destroy the Sotans this summer?"

"Yes."

"That wasn't what we decided last fall."

"Things have changed since last fall. After the Sotans have been defeated, the grass has cured, the bracken is dead and brown, we will set fire to the land. We will burn it every year it's dry enough, and when the new grass greens in the ashes, buffalo will go there. Then Sota will truly be fit to live in, all the way to the Misasip."

This shook Jorval. Last fall they'd *agreed*! On a raid in force, when the Sotan grain had matured, and the stems and leaves had dried. The Dkota would raid widely into Sota, burn the grain fields, storage sheds, barns, villages, then return to their hunting grounds, driving the Sotan's spotted buffalo westward with them. Leaving the Sotans to face a winter of hunger, their grain crop burnt up, and with little breeding stock from which to rebuild their herds.

The following spring, the Sotans would emerge from the long winter weakened, disheartened by hunger, and by the sickness and deaths that would come with it. Much less able to repulse the Dkota. They would plant what potatoes they'd saved for planting, and what grain they'd saved for seed. Then the Dkota would return— in high spring they'd return—and the Sotans would lack the strength and energy to fight strongly. Those who weren't killed would flee.

Mazeppa had defined the strategy, it was he who had the necessary knowledge. It would almost ensure victory, and save Dkota lives. Yet he'd changed his mind! Drastically! Jorval felt the urge to argue, to accuse the chief of breaking his word! The impulse shocked him. It would undo, perhaps beyond repair, all that Jorval had accomplished. For the first time the extraterrestrial understood how fully he was committed to this people and its chief. It was go with Mazeppa—or go back to r'Fohann unfulfilled. And that he would not do. He'd invested too much of himself in this.

The soul of the project was its potential: refugees fleeing Sota, carrying their tale of tribal savagery, of fire and murder and rape, eastward to the Sea of Mishgun, southward along the Misasip, and up the valley of the Ohio. Meanwhile, he in the shuttle and Lorness in the scout would visit tribes throughout the plains, spreading word of the dirt-eaters' plan to exterminate the buffalo, and of the great Dkota victory, inspiring alliances and war plans. Plans doomed to fail, in the long run, because the tribesmen were too few and disunited.

At the same time, the eastern kings would begin to build armies, and create their own alliances and plans, perhaps first to defend the frontier, but sooner or later to eradicate the tribes. Plans also doomed to fail, because of the mobility and self-sufficiency of the buffalo peoples. It would be chaos—a beautiful mess— creating cruelties, hatreds, appetites for vengeance that would persist for centuries.

So instead of outrage, Jorval chose the way of reason, reviewing for Mazeppa the scenario they'd agreed on the previous autumn. Mazeppa listened patiently against the backdrop of his own wants and considerations. And his secret, which he was not ready to share, because it could still fall through. Success was probable, or so it seemed to Mazeppa, but if it didn't work out, *then* he could revert to last autumn's agreement.

Not until Jorval had finished did Mazeppa speak again, directing his gaze past his listener, to avoid seeming confrontational, though he looked at Jorval from time to time. "Helverti Chief has been a good guest," he said calmly, "and you have given me much to think about. Much of value. But the People of the Buffalo have their own ways. The Great Spirit whispers in the minds of men, and he has whispered differently to me than to you.

"Also, the Ulster haven't gotten used to us, or to our dominion over them. And only three of their four bands have joined with us. The Swift Current people are unlike the others; they have taken refuge in their stronghold, the Black Mountains, which are covered with forest. A broken land with many draws and canyons. It is easy for them to defend themselves there.

"And because of them, the Ulster-Dkota must wonder now and then if they surrendered too easily to us. But if I lead them to a great victory—if together we drive the dirt-eaters from Sota—and if then I praise them, and they share equally in the spoils, they will be pleased, and the union will be strong."

Now he looked openly at Jorval. "The sooner all this happens, the better. Then we will parley with the Swift Current people—and if need be hinder them from coming out of their hills to hunt buffalo. Which will make their women thin, and their infants . . ."

Ench had been standing behind his guardian and to his left. Now he stepped forward, interrupting and confronting Mazeppa. "Why don't you just do what my uncle tells you?" he said. "What you plan is foolish. Lots more of your warriors will get killed, and it will be your fault. The Sotans will fight you from their forts, and when enough of your men have been killed . . ."

"ENCH!" Jorval cut off the youth's outburst more in shock than in anger, but the Fohannid words that followed snapped like gunshots: "FOR GOD'S SAKE SHUT YOUR MOUTH!"

For a long moment the scout craft was absolutely still, no one moving, no one speaking. Then Mazeppa got to his feet and folded sinewy arms across his chest.

"I will follow the way of the buffalo people," he said to Jorval. "You are free to stay, for you have been courteous. And he—" he gestured at Ench "—he may also stay, because you are his uncle. But your people did not raise him very well."

Then he turned and left the sky canoe.

Jorval stared, watching Mazeppa leave. Then he turned, and his voice hissed. "Do you realize what you just did? The good will of that human is vital to our project, and I've spent much of a year cultivating him. To the Dkota, simply interrupting is offensive, and to call him foolish? To his face? Didn't you see the knife he wore? You're lucky he didn't cut your throat! You made an arrogant fool of yourself, and by extension you made a fool of me."

He paused, his eyes impaling the boy. "I wish I'd given you back to your mother, left you on r'Fohann with her." Now his words became measured, crisply enunciated. "In the future you will keep your ignorant mouth shut! Or I will have Widhros take you back to the *Delight* and put you in stasis till we get home."

Ench had turned so pale, for a moment Jorval thought the boy might have a seizure of some sort, and it brought him up short. *You have,* he told himself, *let your temper run away with you.* Reaching, he laid a hand on a thin young shoulder. Thin but stiff. "Ench," he said, trying now for temperance, "these people may be primitives, but they're observant, intelligent, and experienced. Mazeppa knows far more about this world, its conditions, and how to live here, than we ever will. And more about the psychology of the buffalo people: what they can be gotten to do and what they can't."

It struck him then that he himself had taken far too much for granted. Mazeppa probably *did* know best. *Listen and watch,* he told himself. *You'll learn something, and between what you know and what Mazeppa knows, things will turn out well enough.*

Meanwhile Ench still stood frozen-faced. *His mother's acid tongue had scalded the boy's spirit from early on,* he told himself, *and now you have made it worse.* "Ench," he said, "I'm sorry I lashed out at you. It was inexcusable. You need a change. Go outside. Walk around and observe the indigenes. Find one your age, talk with him courteously, question him, learn what he's like. Visit his family if he invites you. When you get back, I'll be interested in hearing what you've learned about them."

Ench didn't meet his eyes, simply left, looking whipped.

It occurred to Jorval that he knew very little about young people. What had *he* been like at that age? Cocky; probably hard-wired that way. He'd told Ench more than once to be bolder; might even have used the term "self-assertive." This morning the boy had decided to try it out, apparently, and self-destructed.

Jorval shook his head and looked toward the cockpit. Its door had been open since before Mazeppa had entered. "I suppose you heard all that, Lorness."

"Every word." Lorness, his pilot, confidant and chief enforcer got up from his seat and stepped into the cabin.

"How does anyone handle a pup like that?" Jorval asked.

Lorness's lips quirked. "He's still a boy, Jorval. His mother resented him, and for the most part you haven't done much better. And today you flogged him in front of company, so to speak. Do that a time or two more, and he won't be worth worm shit. But that was good advice you gave him at the end—if he's not too far gone to make use of it."

Inwardly Jorval cringed. Too far gone! Terrible words! He hoped they weren't true. He couldn't imagine ever *liking* his nephew, but the boy was family, and he'd accepted responsibility for him.

⋖⋗ ⋖⋗ ⋖⋗

From his sentry post outside the door, weapons technician Harmu Griss had heard some of it too— all of it, beginning with Jorval's explosion. Now the boy stood slump-shouldered at the foot of the ramp.

"Hey, Buddy," Griss said quietly, "need a friend?" Ench didn't look at him, but he didn't leave, either.

"I kind of know how you feel. My old man used to jump all over me sometimes. Then I'd go talk to my older cousin. If you need an older cousin, look me up when I'm not on watch.

"As for what Jorval said about talking to some local, someone about your age . . . that was good advice. Let me see if I can do him one better. When you find one, *ask him to teach you how to be a Dkota*. He might like that. And I don't know about you, but I think I'd like being a Dkota. Riding around on those big animals they've got looks like good stuff."

Ench walked away without answering or glancing back, his gaze still on the ground, but Griss was pretty sure his words had registered. Whether anything would come of them, though . . .

Chapter 4
Hasty

(Luis)

It was nice to renew my acquaintance with the Misasip after so many years. This far north it wasn't as big, and the water was clearer, but it *was* the Misasip. Riding north to Sota, we crossed it three times on ferries. Fedor had sent a brother along to guide us, and there were stretches where travel was better on the west side while others were better on the east.

We were a goodly company—four masters, seven brothers including Kabibi, and three teamsters driving freight wagons with things for the new brother house. All of us were carrying sabers and bows; highwaymen weren't likely to bother us. According to Brother Sandip, highwaymen weren't often reported in the region anyway, and I could see why. Several times along the way we met highway patrols: six men, or eight, with sabers, bows, helmets—and hauberks, which had to be sweaty on late spring days.

Mostly the road was bordered by forest. On river terraces, forest was almost invariable, often with big old silver maples, and ancient sycamores three men

49

together couldn't reach around. Must have been there since Armageddon. On the uplands, besides woods, there were fields, farmsteads, and patches of meadow or prairie, rich in flowers where they weren't grazed. The upland woods were mostly oaks, but often with shagbark, walnut, pignut and what have you. All in all it made for pleasant traveling.

It was three hundred miles from Moleen to Hasty, and we took eleven days to cover it. With the freight wagons, we never once broke into a trot. We spent the nights at rectories and inns, sleeping beneath the sky only once. All in all it was like a pleasure trip—except that each evening we four masters would get together away from the others, each of us with his radio to his ear, and check with Fedor in Moleen, for any news he might have for us. We didn't call Tahmm. He'd told me before we left the Academy, and repeated before we left Moleen, that I was chief of mission. Its management was my responsibility. If I wanted help, I could ask for it, and he might or might not provide it, but he wouldn't be advising or bypassing me. All he wanted was reports on what was happening, and a successful conclusion.

Which was how I wanted it, too.

We four masters knew one another well. We'd lived together and been classmates for more than five years. But the brothers were new to us, excepting Paddy, who Lemmi and I had known really well during the so-called Lizard War. By the time it was over, he was functioning more or less as a brother, without a day of training, learning on the job in the wildest operation the Order had ever taken on.

He'd grown a lot—not so much physically as mentally—in the five years since Lemmi and I had said goodbye to him in the Peoples Democratic Republic. He'd done a novitiate at Aarschot, graduated as an actual brother and been transferred to Moleen, where he'd come off a mission only days before we got there.

We got to know Kabibi pretty well, too. Jamila's baby sister! They were a lot different, partly because Kabibi was younger and less experienced than Jamila had been. But her basic personality was different, too. Though Kabibi was decisive, she didn't have Jamila's charisma. (Who did?) This wasn't her first mission, either; that one had been in Shy Free-Town, over east on the Sea of Mishgun. The first evening out we tested her saber drill. She was good, very very good, but not overwhelming like Jamila had been. Her aura showed her warrior essence tinged with scholar, like mine, though probably with a different focus.

At the inns and rectories where we stayed, we struck up conversations with innkeepers, travelers, and clergy, asking questions, getting a sense of the region and its people. There's usually a lot of conversation in inns, but rectories usually had a better ratio of fact to rumor. Of course, rumor is useful too; it gives a sense of people, attitudes, and situations.

The only rectory where we weren't well received was Carlian. The Carlian Order disapproves of Higuchians. The pastor there didn't even meet with us. His majordomo put us up in the stable, in the hayloft, saying their guest rooms were full. We saw no sign of other guests or their horses, but I thanked the man.

After all, he had confirmed, indirectly, what we'd been told about the Archbishop of Sota.

We deliberately bypassed Hasty, Sota's capital. Passed it on the other side of the Misasip, riding some three miles beyond Hasty Crossing to West Crossing, where tradition said Hasty had been before Armageddon. From West Crossing we rode a ferry to North Landing, four miles upriver of the capital, near the farm the Order had bought. When we got off the ferry, the clock on my belt com read 1820. We went straight to the farm, where the newly built brother house stood. Milo Bambino, the middle-aged caretaker, had already milked his cow. He helped us move our things in while his wife prepared a simple supper— bean soup with spicy sausage, rye bread, butter—and buttered sassafras tea. Delicious! At 2130 we bathed in the wash house, using buckets, at 2200 held a brief prayer service in the tiny chapel, and at 2215 went to the zendo for meditation. Ordinarily masters meditate in their cells at night, but to Carlos and Peng, this night was special. It was their first night as masters of their own Brother House.

By midnight, the last of us was in bed.

Chapter 5
Meeting an Ally

(Luis)

Bishop Foley at Moleen was a Williamite. Saint Higuchi had begun as a Williamite, and the Williamite Order had been instrumental in founding the Order of Saint Higuchi. Bishop Foley's number one listening post in the north was the Williamite church at Sugar Grove, just four miles north of what would soon be known as Brother House Junction. Along with his pastoral duties, Linkon had been the Holy See's agent in purchasing the farm, getting the brother house built on it, and hiring Milo Bambino to take care of it till Carlos and Peng arrived.

So on our first day there, while Carlos and Peng rode east into Hasty for their obligatory check-in with Archbishop Clonarty, Lemmi and I rode north to meet Pastor Linkon. I could see why the parish was named Sugar Grove. The woods along the road ran heavily to sugar trees, which for me were as pleasant to the eyes as their sugar to my tongue.

At first glance, the two-storied rectory appeared to be built of logs, but actually they were cants, sawn about ten inches on a side. And fitted so snugly, no wind could penetrate even if it hadn't been plastered inside. The outside was painted red, with nicely carved trim painted white. Very attractive.

The pastor recognized us at once by our Higuchian uniforms: gray breeches, black shirt with light blue clerical collar, gray cavalry cape, and flat-brimmed gray hat with low skull-cap crown. And saber of course. We introduced ourselves as missioners, Master Luis and Master Lemmi. He excused himself and left us standing for a moment. We heard him instructing an assistant pastor to take care of his visitations for the day. "If anyone asks where I am," he added, "I have visitors from Norlins. If they ask who, tell them bureaucrats. That'll be close enough."

He returned to us with a wink. "Father Sando is rather retiring for a priest," he said. "I'm trying to cure him of that." Pastor Linkon was a tallish man, lean and blond, with a complexion that didn't well tolerate the sun. His face was pink, his forehead white, his eyes blue as flax blossoms. His aura was blue too, mostly, with silver rays, areas of red and pink, with a golden tiara. He led us down a corridor, calling, in a voice not naturally big, but trained to reach the rearmost pews. "Norma! Sassafras for three please, in my study!" In the study he closed the door without latching it. For Norma, I suppose; it would open at a touch. He seated us at a table, then sat across from us, backward on his chair, leaning on crossed forearms, "When did you arrive?" he asked.

I told him, adding that Carlos and Peng intended to visit him the next day. "Today they're in Hasty, making themselves known to Archbishop Clonarty, and to the king if they get an audience."

"Ah. His reverence will be thrilled," Linkon said wryly. "He's been forewarned about them, I suppose, but does he know about you?"

"He'll find out today. Carlos was to mention us."

He nodded. "Obviously I know why Carlos and Peng are here, but not you. I suppose you're on mission, and you seem to be the spokesman, so presumably you're in charge."

"Actually we're on separate but connected missions. Lemmi will be mostly in Dkota."

The pastor's eyebrows rose. "Ah. And you've come to me with questions."

"That's right."

"Let me ask one first. What are your missions?"

We told him, interrupted once when his cheerful wife entered with a tray—three cups with saucers, a cream pitcher, honey bowl with spoon, and a steaming ceramic pot of sassafras. He introduced us, but she sensed we were deep in some issue, and didn't linger.

When I was done, Lemmi spoke, Linkon intent, saving his questions. Afterward he sat thoughtfully for a moment, stroking his chin whiskers. "I know nothing of Dkota intentions, only their past raids, and the general opinion that they'll raid again when it suits them. As for Eldred—he's a molli only toward outsiders. And it may be he'd reverse that, if provoked enough. Regarding internal issues, he can be bloody. Ruthless."

I nodded. "We've heard somewhat about the uprisings in Austin and Nona, and his reprisals. Presumably the archbishop approved. We've been told that Eldred consults him on anything important."

"Consults, yes, but not, I think, for ecclesiastic approval. Clonarty is his friend; they're like brothers. Closer, because the archbishop is Eldred's confessor."

"What kind of man, and leader, is Eldred? Aside from his ruthlessness toward rebellion."

"He delegates authority well, and his ministers are mostly relatives. His wife's relatives actually; the Youngbloods are a seriously infertile lineage. By contrast, the Maki and Lahti clans, his late wife's lineage, are quite fertile, with close ties to the Youngbloods."

"How infertile are the Youngbloods?"

"In Eldred's case, he has twin daughters and no son."

"Any prospect of problems in the succession?"

"It's been talked about. Eldred is only thirty-nine, and I've never heard of him being ill, but he's the only child of an only child. No brother waiting in the wings, nor male first cousin." Linkon shook his head. "What he does have is more than enough in-laws, some of whom might well covet the throne. But in that case the dukes might—*might* not approve."

"What are the daughters like?"

"They're seventeen, I believe. Maybe eighteen by now. In Sota, with no male heir, the crown could devolve on one of them. Mary, it would seem; she's said to be the eldest by half an hour or so. But she'd need an influential champion to help her through the hazards and stumbling blocks on the way to the throne. And to back her when she gets there, *if* she gets there.

"She's been courted, but nothing came of it. Eldred, always the indulgent father, didn't press her. The best bet for a royal husband might be a son of one of our own dukes—" Linkon paused, chuckling "—except that the only two dukes on good terms with Eldred are also kin to his wife. Norlins wouldn't stand for that.

"If the dukes could agree on whom, one of them might succeed Eldred. A year ago I would have said Edward Maltby was the best candidate. He's duke of Kato, and a widower. But last autumn he had a serious hunting accident. His horse stumbled at a full gallop, and ended up atop his rider instead of under him. Now Edward's a cripple—has trouble even breathing.

Linkon shook his head ruefully. "There'll be someone, of course, but it might take a bloodbath to sort things out."

It seemed to me he'd left someone out, probably for good reason. "What of the other twin?" I asked.

"Ah, Elvi. She and Mary look much alike, but

they're quite different, in expression, manner and soul. Those who know Mary say she's not only sweet-tempered but intelligent. While Elvi's said to be suspicious, ill-tempered, and holds grudges forever. And less than bright. If she were to try for the throne, I can envision the dukes joining to prevent it."

Our talk switched from Elvi to Eldred. According to Linkon, the king could easily live another twenty years or more. Then we talked about the kingdom in general, including its defenses, about which the pastor was not well informed. And its dukes, about whom he knew quite a lot, second-handedly. His parish being in the Royal Domain, there wasn't a local duke to know.

Even his knowledge of the king was less than I'd hoped. The two had never formally met. Considering the Carlian hostility and Williamite friendship toward our order, Linkon had never asked for an audience with him. I wasn't at all sure Eldred would see us, though the Order had had the favor of every Pope since it was founded. At any rate, if Eldred refused us, that was important to know.

Lemmi mined the pastor's knowledge of the Dkota. There was more of it than we'd expected. He'd learned much of it from a Williamite brother who'd gone to Many Geese to study the Dkota, and ended up spending four years there as a slave.

Finally we talked about Archbishop Michael Clonarty. Pastor Linkon knew less about him, too, than I'd expected. Clonarty was not someone who'd share confidences with a Williamite.

We left after lunch knowing a lot more than when we'd arrived. Hopefully enough to stay out of trouble the next day.

Chapter 6
Rulers Secular and Ecclesiastic

(Luis)

That evening, Carlos and Peng described their day. They'd visited the archbishop first, that being a duty call, and Clonarty's aura and demeanor had made clear his disapproval. But he'd contained it till Carlos mentioned Lemmi and me. Then anger flashed. "Missioners? Why aren't they here with you?"

Carlos and Peng both grinned at us. "I told him you planned to visit him tomorrow," Carlos said, "that you have no servants, and had things to take care of today. The archbishop's round face has a narrow, full-lipped mouth; he does a very good job of looking petulant. He asked the nature of your mission, and I followed your suggestions: told him it was my impression that Master Lemmi was going to investigate the state of the faith among the Dkota, and that I knew nothing at all of yours. That jarred him. *Worried* him. 'Surely,' he said, 'he told you something!' 'Not a word,' I told him back."

I went to bed looking forward to the next day.

The next morning, Lemmi and I rode into Hasty. The archbishop's mansion was easy to recognize. I expected we'd have to wait in line to see him, but there was only one person ahead of us, and our wait was brief.

Clonarty was standing as we walked in, and after his secretary introduced us, motioned us to cushioned, straight-back chairs. Then he sat down at his desk.

Things started out well enough. "I've never met Higuchian missioners before," he said. "What brings you to Sota?"

We'd agreed that Lemmi would speak first, implying seniority for the Dkota operation. "Your reverence, in two or three days I'll be leaving to visit the Dkota. To learn the state of their Faith, and report it to the Holy See."

"Hmh! I could tell you that without traveling to wherever the Dkota might just now be found. I was closely involved with their principal chief, Mazeppa, in the treaty negotiations three years ago. Mazeppa is a splendid Christian."

Lemmi bowed in his seat. "I'll include your observation in my report, your reverence. But I am to live among them for a time; I'm well trained for it. And—" he paused "—I am trained to perceive their state of mind. Their true feelings, you understand."

He said it with complete, matter-of-fact certainty.

Judging from Clonarty's aura, Lemmi's words had jerked the archbishop. *Trained to perceive their true feelings? What did he mean by that?* He dodged the question by turning to me. "And you, Master Luis, what will you be doing?"

"I shall be visiting the Kingdom of Sota, from Twa to the northern wilderness."

That alarmed him. "To what purpose?"

"To determine the state of the Faith here in Sota. It is well known that you disapprove of our Order, but Cardinal Bau trusts me to report honestly, and I will not fail him."

Clonarty reddened, and Lemmi moved in with a

non sequitur. "We are not a warlike order, your grace, regardless of what you may have heard." He paused, his hands half raised as if in earnest supplication. "Some call us 'the soldiers of the Pope,' but in fact we're more nearly his policemen, defending Church and people against the lawless and seducers—those who would coerce or mislead the faithful."

We both stood quietly then, while Clonarty, with an effort, recovered. Again it was to me he spoke. "You will find Sota strong in the Faith, for our King is the greatest champion the Church or our people could have. Both His Majesty and Mazeppa Tall Man have signed an agreement—on the Bible!—that neither nation shall molest the other. An agreement that has enabled the king to reduce the force at arms of every duke and baron in the kingdom. And further, has allowed him to reduce the taxes levied against the yeomanry." He paused, his gaze shifting from myself to Lemmi and back again. "Sota is blessed to have such a wise and benevolent king."

"Mazeppa reads and writes?" Lemmi asked.

"He signs his name, at least. His tribesman and confessor, Pastor Morosov, both reads and writes."

"Thank you, your reverence; that is welcome information, and casts a favorable light on the Dkota."

Lemmi's response changed Clonarty's aura at once—expanded and even brightened it. He still distrusted us, but his indignation faded, and after another minute or two, he dismissed us with a blessing. As we left, it seemed to me the archbishop was a true believer, in the Church and in the Carlian principle of mollification.

❦❦❦   ❦❦❦   ❦❦❦

Hasty Town was a fortress, in the sense of a walled town, and the royal palace, a complex of buildings, was a fortress within that fortress. And within it, an innermost fortress, stood the keep, its thick round walls built to resist pounding from cannon. For to produce its layered roundness, each of its great, cemented stone blocks was a keystone, a truncated granite wedge nearly impossible to drive inward.

The palace's main gate was a sort of tunnel through the ten-foot-thick stone wall, its squad of large, well-armed guards looking anything but molli-like.

The sergeant of the gate passed us through, in the custody of a corporal who took us to the royal residence and turned us over to a sergeant at its front entrance. There a sergeant sent a page hurrying off. A few minutes later an usher led us up a curving staircase and along a corridor to a waiting room. There we were met by a balding blond man at a desk. "May I help you, brothers?" he asked.

I introduced Lemmi and myself, and showed him our mission authorization from the Sacred Congregation for the Defense of the Church. He glanced at it, eyebrows arched, then asked us to be seated. Two other people were ahead of us; probably merchants. A guardsman with polished bronze helmet and breastplate stood by the door to the audience chamber. A minute later the door was opened from the other side, and a bailiff ushered out a short brown man who seemed pleased with himself. The balding man got up and went into the audience chamber with the bailiff.

A minute later they reappeared. "Masters," said the balding man, "the bailiff will take you to His Majesty now."

We'd been jumped ahead. The audience chamber was not large. The king, a rather large man, sat on a throne on a raised dais. A guard stood on each side of him, half a step to the rear. The bailiff stopped at a knee-high railing before the throne. "Your Majesty," he said, "these are the Higuchians," then he stood aside and gestured us to the railing. To one side, beneath a window, an angular elderly man sat at a writing table, a graphite pen in one hand, a sort of ledger open in front of him.

The king peered at us, his aura suggesting guardedness and curiosity, but not hostility. "Which of you is the spokesman?" he asked.

"Your Majesty," I said, "I will speak for us except as you specify otherwise, since I in particular will be spending time in your kingdom. I am Master Luis Raoul DenUyl. My partner is Master Lemmi Tsinnajinni. We have been directed to make ourselves known to you. Master Lemmi will spend the summer with the Dkota, but en route will travel through your kingdom, and may spend time in the marches."

Reddish eyebrows climbed the king's forehead. "With the Dkota? Are you aware we have an agreement with them? Each side respects the territory of the other. We have raised monuments along the border, to avoid misunderstandings."

"We're aware of that, in a general way. Perhaps Master Lemmi can be given a copy of the agreement, or be allowed to make his own copy."

The king turned to the elderly scribe. "Lord Brookins," he said, "please see that Master Lemmi is given a copy." He looked at Lemmi then. "Master Lemmi, what is your purpose in visiting the Dkota?"

"Your Majesty, I shall report on the state of the Faith among them, to Cardinal Markovic."

I wondered if the king would reply the way the archbishop had, but in fact he simply nodded, then surprised us both. "Are you a citizen of my kingdom, sir? You appear to be *Dinneh*."

It might have complicated things if the king thought of him as a subject, though churchmen are independent of secular rulers. But Lemmi handled it cleanly. "I am Dinneh, Your Majesty. Blood of Christ Dinneh."

This time the eyebrows curled inward and downward. "Blood of Christ Dinneh?"

"From the Blood of Christ Mountains, a very long journey west and south of here, Your Majesty."

That part was true enough, but before that? He'd grown up just two or three days ride from Hasty.

"Hmm! I never heard of the Blood of Christ Mountains. A beautiful name. Perhaps you can tell me about them sometime." For a moment he sat looking inward at some thought. "It is rumored that a sky boat survived both Armageddon and the Shuffling, and has visited the chief of the Dkota. Have you heard of that?"

Lemmi steepled his fingers, seeming to regard them. "Your Majesty, it is both easy and wise to doubt reports so far outside common experience. But on the other hand, there are realities outside of common experience. It's well to remember that, in his time, many doubted the Savior himself. And of course there is *The Book of Renewal*. Notably its first Chapter."

"Exactly! Exactly! But where on Earth could such a craft have come from, do you think? If it is real."

"That, Your Majesty, I will try to learn—if indeed I find evidence of its reality."

Eldred wasn't done with the subject. "The people who ride in it are said to be of powerful physique, and exceedingly hairy—one might say furry. And that the hair is white." He looked quizzically at Lemmi. "What do you say to that?"

"In that case, Your Majesty, one might expect an origin in some cold place, where having one's own fur would be useful. And white fur could help one hide in the snow."

The king laughed, his aura matching the mood swing. "Indeed! I would never have thought of that." He paused, his eyes curiously intent on Lemmi now. "That is very clever!" He turned to me. "And you, Master . . . Luis is it? What will you be doing while Master Lemmi visits the Dkota?"

"In one respect, Your Majesty, my mission is relatively

mundane: I will be right here in Sota. But in another respect my mission resembles Master Lemmi's: I am to report to Cardinal Markovic on the state of the Faith in Sota."

This time the eyebrows arched higher than before. "Sota? Really! Does His Reverence suspect anything amiss?"

"Your Majesty, it would be remarkable if nothing seemed amiss. The Holy See hears rumors of this, reports of that, from everywhere. And after enough of these sends one of their own to examine the facts. Here so far from Norlins, such visits are further apart." I flashed him a conspiratorial grin. "In Shy Free Town they come far more often."

He nodded with his whole body now, rocking on his throne, a bizarre sight. His next question took me by surprise again. "What is your opinion of fighting?"

That was his first allusion to our being Higuchians. "Your Majesty," I said, "God has assigned the Church one primary task: we are to teach humankind to love God and our fellow humans. Love is the very essence of God and Christ, and of the Holy Spirit that resides in every man but is too often ignored or suppressed. Fighting, on the other hand, is a manifestation of fear, and fear is the antithesis of love. Thus, the Church and our Order regard fighting as unchristian."

His gaze was intent now, fixed on me. As if he too saw auras, and was examining mine. "Yet your Order is referred to as the Soldiers of the Pope," he said.

"When we might better be called the Pope's police. His Holiness has need of police, just as kings do."

That blunted his intensity. Now I changed the subject. "As for the rumored sky boat people—if they are real, they may prove benign, even beneficent. I look forward to hearing what Master Lemmi may learn, but meanwhile I won't hold my breath."

I stopped there. Eldred's attention was inward again, and for a long moment no one spoke. Then he broke free of his thoughts. "Well, I am glad we've had this talk," he said. "Perhaps we'll have another." He looked toward the bailiff. "Thomas, conduct my guests to the antechamber, and see who Pekka has next for us."

We'd left Hasty before either of us said much. It was an attractive town—prosperous, and rather noisy with the creaking and grating of cart and wagon wheels, the clopping of shod hooves on cobblestones, shouts and oaths of teamsters and pedestrians, citizens calling out of windows, shrieking children at play in the alleys, the occasional barking dog. . . . And of course it smelled: the sharp pungency of horse urine overwhelming the smell of their manure, and over all, the tang of woodsmoke from kitchen fires. Once I smelled boiling cabbage. I could distinguish no clear smell of human wastes; obviously they had a law in Hasty controlling where chamber pots could be emptied, and enforced it. You could rather reliably rate the quality of a town by whether or not it enforced such a law. Probably they also required dumping one's wood ashes into privies, as a form of liming them.

After leaving through the town gate and passing the dumping ground, we rode through an attractive countryside more farmland than woods. "What did you think of the archbishop?" Lemmi asked.

"He's sincere in his beliefs, both in the Church and in the Carlian Order. His sincerity is his strength."

Lemmi cocked an eyebrow. "And the king?"

"How did he know you were Dinneh?"

"I suppose because I look Dinneh. Did you notice the guard on his right? He's almost certainly Dinneh. But I was asking what you think of the king himself."

"My impression, is that the king is insane. His aura brought to mind Tharkol's lecture on episodic psychotics. May he never decide I'm his enemy."

As I said it, it seemed to me he would so decide, almost certainly. If not soon, surely before this was over.

Lemmi laughed. "I'm glad my mission is among the Dkota," he said.

Before this was over, I'd remind him of those words.

Chapter 7
Stephen Nez

(Luis)

Now, with a good sense of the archbishop and the king, I needed to make contacts elsewhere in Sota. So two days later I rode to Sugar Grove again, to ask Pastor Linkon more questions. By that time Lemmi had already left.

I was lucky again; Linkon was at home. He asked what Lemmi and I thought of the archbishop and the king. I summarized without telling him we thought Eldred was insane. Someone who doesn't read auras misses a lot of clues, and he might think we'd based our conclusion on prejudice.

From what Linkon had said before, I'd pretty much concluded that Edward Maltby, Duke of Kato, should be my next serious contact—if his health wasn't too precarious. Linkon turned out to be more helpful than I'd expected: he wrote me a letter of introduction to Bishop Joseph of Kato, a good friend of his from their youth together in seminary—and the duke's confessor. Joseph's opinion on the duke's health should be worthwhile, too, and he could advise me on who else in Kato might be helpful.

I spent the rest of the day exploring the country around the brother house, learning my way around. After supper I talked awhile with two of Carlos and Peng's new novices, ages fourteen and fifteen, local farmboys who'd learned their way around hunting.

We were interrupted by the duty lad, who announced that a royal guardsman was there to see Lemmi, and would I talk to him?

Who in Sota, and a guardsman at that, would be looking for Lemmi? Who even knew he was there, outside the brother house, the Sugar Grove rectory, and Clonarty's and Eldred's offices?

I went down to the parlor, and recognized the throne guard Lemmi'd thought was Dinneh. *What,* I wondered, *is this about?* He was eighteen or twenty years old, I guessed, and tall. Not really filled out yet, but strong and tough. Physically. His aura was something else.

"I'm Master Luis," I said. "Who am I speaking with?"

"My name is Stephen Nez," he answered, not meeting my eyes. "I'm a royal guardsman. I was with His Majesty when you and Master Tsinnajinni talked with him. That's how I knew your names, and how to find you."

He looked worse than uncomfortable; judging from his aura, he might run out of the house at any minute. Whatever was troubling him, Nez hadn't been sent by Eldred to spy. To relax him, I offered my hand. He shook it in what Lemmi called "Dinneh fashion"— a soft grip, though his hand was well callused. "Master Lemmi's on a trip, I told him. "How can I help you?"

"I don't think you can," he said apologetically. "You're not Dinneh."

"Let's go outside and talk, where no one can overhear us."

It was still twilight, rich in night singers—tree frogs, crickets—and somewhere in the hedgerow a hermit thrush trilling "sweetly enough to break your heart," as my mother used to say. "All right," I said, "tell me your problem."

That worked better than "how can I help you?" He'd come to confess a sin, he said, one he was afraid to confess to the chaplain at the palace. If he did, it would get him in bad trouble, so he'd hoped Lemmi would hear his confession.

"I can hear confessions," I said, and led him back inside to a confessional off the chapel. Higuchians confess differently than other orders; they confess face to face with a master, or with a brother if no master is available. And if the confessor is a master, he provides more than an ear. Keying on the aura, he helps the penitent find the root of the problem, or nearly enough to handle the grief or guilt.

A few nights earlier, Stephen told me, he'd taken part in a murder. Under orders from a Guard captain, he and a corporal had taken a captive from a dungeon cell to a room used for executions. There, while Stephen held the captive, the corporal had stabbed the man through an eye socket, the dagger going deep inside, mangling the brain. Then they'd wrapped the corpse in a tarp and loaded it into a small horse cart, a sort of cage on wheels, used to transport pigs or sheep or poultry to market. After changing into civilian clothes, they'd hauled the body out of town and buried it, then returned to the guard barracks and a sleepless cot.

One thing that got my attention was the way his aura behaved as he told his story: it shrank, darkened and muddied worse than it was to start with. No recovery at all.

"So," I said, "what part of that was the worst?"

He started to tremble, and sparks flew out of his aura like grinding an ax on a dry grindstone. *He'd handled the corpse,* he told me, *and all Dinneh knew that meant.* Then he got hold of himself and thanked me for hearing his confession; said it had helped a lot. "If you'll give me my penance now, father, I'll carry it out, and square myself with God."

There were two things wrong with that. One, he was still caved in. And two, he was blameless in this. If he'd refused to carry out an order like that one, he'd have been buried beside the other victim. "Something's preventing absolution," I told him. "Tell me what it is."

His brown face paled to something like mud. "I can never be clean," he said, "till I am freed of that one's *chindi*."

It turned out that when someone dies and the soul goes to Purgatory, his people believe that more than a corpse is left behind. Associated with it are all the evil acts and thoughts, all the fears, hatreds and griefs of the dead person's life. Its *chindi*. And if someone handles the corpse, the chindi sticks to him. That even to say the dead person's name is dangerous.

Fortunately, all this is easily corrected by a religious ceremony called a "sing." It's routine for people who have to handle the dead. But as far as Stephen knew, he couldn't get a sing except in the township he was from—the only Dinneh community he knew of—because it not only required a skilled shaman who knew the ceremony, it took the participation of the community. And he couldn't ask for leave to go home, because he'd have to convince the sergeant major, who didn't know about the murder. A certain captain had ordered it, and no one else was to learn of it. And in any case the chaplain would have to approve, and Archbishop Clonarty had declared sings to be pagan, and mortal sins. If a guardsman asked for one, he'd be locked in the dungeon.

"Stephen," I told him, "I have the solution. No one, not even guard commanders—not even kings!—can prohibit someone from joining a religious order. That's Church law. And if you join the Order of Saint

Higuchi, I guarantee you can go home for a sing.
Afterward you can resign from the Order if you want
to, without penalty as long as you haven't completed
your novitiate and been accepted as a brother. Master
Carlos is the chief of the brother house and school,
so if you want to do it, and Carlos agrees, your problem is solved. It's up to you."

He brightened a little, and so did his aura, tentatively,
but he needed to get used to the idea, so he asked some
questions and I answered them. He brightened a little
more and said he'd do it, so we talked to Carlos. Briefly
it seemed we might have a problem after all, because
Stephen *liked* Eldred. It seemed the king had been
friendly to him—a king friendly to a Dinneh from the
northern frontier! So Stephen wanted to go in to Hasty
and tell the king he was leaving to join the Order. "It's
the honest thing to do," he said.

Which was true, but I was pretty sure that if he did,
neither I nor anyone else outside the palace would ever
see him again. "Stephen," I said, "if you do that, the
king will surely ask you why. And you'll tell him the
truth, and who knows what will happen then. You could
be put in the dungeon for helping murder someone.
You could be! And while you're in there, still infected
with the dead man's *chindi*, that captain you were
worried about might have you murdered too."

Luckily that was real to Stephen.

From there I went to the washroom, filled a bucket
and bathed, then went to my cell and meditated for
half an hour or so. After that I went to the brothers'
quarters. Paddy and Kabibi had been supervising novices in their studies and training, while waiting for me
to assign them mission duties. It gave Carlos and Peng
more time to visit parishes round about, recruiting for
the Order. But the evening study period was over, and
Paddy was in the quarters he shared with the other

male brothers, meditating in preparation for sleep. I walked in quietly and laid a hand on his shoulder. His eyes focused, and he looked up at me.

"Paddy," I whispered, "we need to talk. I have an assignment for you."

He got up grinning, and followed me without a word. In my cell, I gave him the chair, sat down on the cot, and told him about Stephen Nez. There would, I went on, be a vacancy in the royal guard, and I wanted him to apply for a job there. The next morning. I'd give him money for room and board in town while he waited.

"Tell them you're from Allegheny," I said. That part of the world is known for wars and fighting men. "From Galway Town—" that much would be true "—and that you served three years as a guardsman for the Count of Connemara." That's where the lying began. "If they ask why you left, tell them you got a wanderlust, came down the Ohio as a crewman on a freight raft, then took a job guarding a party of merchants headed for . . . for Kato. That you have kinfolk there, or used to. But when you got to Hasty, you knew *this* was the town for you."

He was grinning again.

"I know that's laying it on pretty thick, but they'll like it, even if they're skeptical. Recruiters are used to bullshit, and if they like your sword forms, they'll not likely worry about the rest. Be good enough to get the job, but not so good they'll start wondering. Fit in."

He laughed. "It sounds interesting," he said in his Connemara brogue. "Will it be all right to get promoted?"

I looked at that for a moment. "It's fine with me," I said. "I trust your judgement."

When he left, I changed into my night shirt for bed. I had several busy days ahead of me before starting for Kato to meet its duke. But where I might go *from* Kato, I had no idea. And if things soured, or even if they didn't, I needed to know my way around the Royal Domain—the king's personal duchy, so to speak. Especially within a half-day's ride of Hasty. And Hasty's back alleys, and what the country and townsfolk thought of their king, and the state of the kingdom. Maybe even find some people who seriously disliked him.

Before I lay down though, I realized something I needed to do before I slept. I'd been ignoring Kabibi, maybe because she was Jamila's baby sister, and now I'd given Paddy an assignment without having anything for her. So I dressed again, went to her cell, and rapped on the door. "Who is it?" she asked.

"Luis. I need to talk to you."

"Just a moment."

Not just a minute. Just a moment. I'd noticed before, she used language more carefully than most do.

She stepped into the hall wearing her loose meditation blouse and trousers. I told her what Paddy would be doing, and that I hadn't forgotten her. That when something came up, I'd get back to her. Saying it, it seemed like a lame sort of comment, but she set me at ease.

"Luis," she told me, "I know you will. Meanwhile I enjoy helping Peng with the novices. He's as good as Freddy at martial arts." She put a hand on my sleeve then, and smiled a little sadly. "Am I as good at martial arts as Jamila was?" she asked.

Her question wrung my heart. "I'm not sure any of us is," I answered. "Tahmm I suppose. But you're very good. *Very* good."

"Some day," she said, "when we both have time, I want you to tell me all you can about her." She teared up then, a little, but her calm quiet voice didn't change. "She was such a good big sister. But I was only a tiny little girl when mom and dad were murdered, and I never saw Jamila again."

"I *will* tell you," I said. "That's a promise."

"And I want to hear how she died. Fedor and

Freddy didn't seem to know, except that the Kelgorath cult killed her."

Lord spare me that, I thought. "I'll tell you all I know about it," I said. And I would, God help me. "But this isn't the time."

As I walked back to my own cell, I wondered how much she knew about Jamila and me. Not everything; no way she could. But she surmised there'd been something between us. Comradeship if nothing more.

Chapter 8
Arrival at Many Geese

Lemmi set out with two mounts, and a single pack horse lightly burdened, neither pushing them hard nor loitering. Stopping at deep dusk, he stripped and cross-hobbled them to graze, and rolled out his bedroll to sleep beneath the sky, the shrill tiny hum of mosquitoes in his ears. Chilled and stiff, he awoke at dawn, caught and saddled the animals, removed their hobbles, and set off without striking a fire. Mostly he ate in the saddle—jerked beef, dense and tough, popular with herdsmen and hunters. Each day, as long as there were farms, he stopped at one to purchase a dark, pungent loaf of rye bread, and before he'd left the brother house, Milo Bambino had given him a cheese and a bag of dried and shriveled apples for variety.

Between the jerky and the hard bread, Lemmi's jaws ached from chewing.

Much of the time he trotted his horses, but at times eased them to a walk, to rest them and allow them snatches of grass as they went. Every hour or so he changed mounts. Occasionally he dismounted and led them, as much for himself as for the animals.

All in all, he made excellent time.

On the first day, the road had passed mainly through forest. By the fifth, the land was mostly prairie, with groves of bur oak and occasionally of aspen. Scattered bands of cattle or sheep grazed there, tended by horsemen and dogs. Late on the fifth day he passed a rock cairn, marking the agreed-upon border with the tribal lands of the Dkota. Beyond that were neither wheel ruts nor cattle; the road had become a trail. The bluestem and Indian grass that crowded it was sometimes shoulder deep to the horses.

Two days later he entered the loosely defined region known as Many Geese: prairie, with groves of scrubby aspen. And countless lakes, mostly small and often bordered by marsh. At one point the trail climbed a slope through aspen scrub. At the top, the aspen ended. Some eighty yards ahead, four young boys on ponies trotted unnoticing toward him, in lively conversation. Lemmi stopped, and raised a hand above his head.

"Hello!" he called. The boys too stopped; this was clearly a stranger. Three of them, heavily tanned, wore only moccasins and breech clouts. The fourth and largest wore doe-skin leggings, a light doe-skin shirt with sleeves, and a broad-brimmed hat of woven grass. His face was red and peeling. A mile beyond them lay a large encampment, many tipis in a hoop, and it seemed to Lemmi this was the place he'd come to find.

He walked his mount up to the boys, speaking as he rode, in Dakotan to see how they'd react. As he'd half expected, they were uncomprehending and confused. Presumably at least part of their confusion was because of his Ilanoyan broadcloth.

It was the larger boy who answered. Respectfully. "None of us understands Dkota," the boy said in Merkan, carefully and rather loudly, as if unsure whether Lemmi understood.

"Ah, then I will speak Merkan. I have come seeking Mazeppa Tall Man." With his head, Lemmi gestured toward the encampment. "Will you take me to his tipi?"

They did, without hesitating, but no one was at home. Nearby some adolescents were wrestling, slick with sweat. Lemmi called to them, and reluctantly they paused. "I am looking for Mazeppa Tall Man," he said in Merkan. "I have come a long way to find him; all the way from Hasty."

The largest youth's eyes narrowed. "Hasty." He sneered the name. "That is in Sota, and you—are a dirt-eater." He paused, and Lemmi waited, giving him time. "You have an ugly saddle," the youth added. "Does no one like you well enough to make you a better one?"

Lemmi answered in Dakotan now, his voice mild. "I am a healer, who wanders from place to place. I do not stay anywhere long enough to have a sweetheart who will make a fine saddle for me."

The lad flushed, embarrassed. He recognized Dkotan, though he himself knew only a few words and idioms. He looked hopefully at one of his friends, who then translated Lemmi's words for the others. When he'd finished, the interpreter turned to Lemmi and spoke careful Dkotan. "I apologize if I understood that wrong. You speak the language differently than my family does."[1] With his chin he gestured at his embarrassed friend. "Because you wear dirt-eater clothes, Big Peer did not realize you are Dkota. Let me take you to Pastor Morosov. He speaks better Dkotan than I do, and he may also know where Mazeppa Tall Man has gone."

---

[1] The Dakotan which Lemmi had deep-learned was based on extensive recordings made 70–85 years before Armageddon, by the COB's first Terran survey, a remote/covert survey. At that time, Dakotan was still the Dakotah vernacular.

The youth led Lemmi to the tipi of Pastor Morosov, then respectfully departed, leaving the two men alone except for the pastor's wife and infant daughter. Lemmi nodded to the pastor. He'd have to ad-lib Dkota ways; hopefully they weren't too different from those of his own people. "I am a healer," he said in Dakotan. "My people live in the Sancroy River country in northern Sota. We have been apart from all other Dakotah since the Shuffling."

They spoke at some length, Lemmi in Dakotan, Morosov in Dkotan, the exchange halting, lapsing into Merkan when necessary. Lemmi discerned a pattern of vowel changes, mainly in unstressed syllables, which accounted for some of their difficulties, and Morosov was a patient if quick-minded man.

The pastor didn't tell Lemmi much more than Lemmi told him, but he spoke more truthfully than Lemmi dared to.

"And you are a healer," Morosov said. "So am I, though I am not so good as some." He looked intently at his guest now, not avoiding eye contact. "How good are you?"

"Try me."

The pastor nodded. "Very well. There is a boy in our camp whom I have been unable to help. He sees a great yellow bear where there is no yellow bear, and is frozen by fear of it. He first saw it a year ago. Now he sees it more and more often, and believes it will soon kill him. Do you think you can heal someone like that?"

"Let me wear leg coverings of yours," Lemmi said, "so the boy will not be alarmed by my appearance. Then we will go to him."

The boy—his name was Alexei—was reluctant. Previously Morosov had tried two different approaches—the first a simple exorcism, the second a purging that included fasting, sweating, and a powerful purgative that had made the boy violently ill. Neither had helped, and Alexei had lost faith, wanted no more of it.

Lemmi's approach was entirely different. He asked Alexei questions, personal but easily answered, till the boy's aura was notably cleaner. This led to questions about yellow-bear stories he'd heard, and the earliest dream he could recall about yellow bears. Finally he hypnotized the boy, and kneeling beside him, laid a hand on his shoulder, saying nothing, simply intending that the boy revisit the earliest yellow-bear dream he could remember.

After a long minute, Alexei began to tremble. Soon he stilled, then after a minute began to shake again. That too quieted, and repeated. Now a tension built in the tipi, as if a great bear was about to charge inside. Alexei began to thrash around on his robes, arms striving, and he cried aloud in a language none of them had heard before. After a minute of that, he lay back limp and pale.

Lemmi's calm eyes took in the boy's aura, shrunken but clean. No one spoke, not even the mother. After another minute, Lemmi returned his hand to the boy's shoulder. "Alexei," he said, "what did you just learn?"

The boy spoke in what seemed to be the same language he'd cried out in, but now his voice was his own, calm and relaxed. Morosov opened his mouth as if to speak, perhaps ask a question, but he thought better of it.

"Very good, Alexei," Lemmi said. "Tonight you will dream about a bear one more time, a different kind of bear dream, and wake up laughing. And that will be the end of it. Now I will count backward from ten to zero. When we reach zero, you will wake up." He paused. "Ten . . . nine . . . eight . . ."

At zero, Alexei sat up. "Mama," he said, "I'm hungry."

Lemmi grinned at the woman. "Feed him," he

told her. "Bear meat, if you have it and he wants some."

Alexei thought bear meat sounded good, but his mother didn't know of any in the camp. There was fresh antelope in the tipi though, and wild strawberries picked that morning for the baby, so he had some of those.

Before they left, Lemmi was gifted with a recently sewn wolf-skin parka.

Walking back to his tipi, Morosov looked thoughtful. Lemmi kept silent, waiting till the pastor spoke. "What did the boy tell you when you asked what he'd learned?" Morosov said at last.

"I don't know; I couldn't understand it. But it's not important that *I* know what he learned. What's important is that *he* knew. That he looked at it and realized what it was." He turned to the pastor. "Meanwhile the yellow-bear nightmares will not come back, and he will no longer imagine a bear waiting in ambush for him."

At Morosov's tipi, Lemmi changed back into his own clothes. Then they went together to the tipi of Mazeppa Tall Man. This time the chief was at home. The pastor introduced the stranger as a healer from Sota. "He seems to have healed the child Alexei Ivanov," he added. "Certainly he did more for him than I had. Much more, I believe."

Lemmi and Mazeppa were already examining each other, even while courteously avoiding eye contact. Through his Higuchian training, Lemmi had become comfortable with eye contact, though mostly avoiding it with anyone he felt it might offend. Mazeppa, an undiluted Dkota, tended to treat it as discourteous, though when it served his need to dominate, he used it without thinking.

Just now he felt a gut need to establish dominance over this stranger, but avoided eye contact anyway. He could not have said why. At six-foot-three, he was taller than Lemmi by three fingers. Lemmi was tall himself, by the standards of the time, slender and sinewy. Mazeppa was also lean, but larger framed and more muscular, outweighing his visitor by thirty pounds.

For all his alertness and athletic bearing, Mazeppa gave an impression of rigidity, of spirit, not of body. Lemmi was supple in all respects, and showed it now: he grinned. Nor did he stop with grinning. "I heard about you in Sota," he told Mazeppa, "from a man who feared and distrusted you. To him you are a dangerous giant."

The comment astonished Morosov; he'd had limited experience with men who were not Dkota or Ulster. Even after preliminary small talk, to say something like that on first acquaintance would have been presumptuous, and as the very first thing said, outrageous.

But Mazeppa didn't raise an eyebrow, for now, suddenly, he felt kinship with this foreigner. "He said that, did he?" And now he did make eye contact, not in challenge, but in curiosity. "Where are you from?"

"I grew up in the township of Big Pines, in the Duchy of Soggo. In the very northeastern part of Sota, the upper Sancroy country. But I left Big Pines to wander. Among my people, sons are raised as warriors, so I have served as an armsman, as well as a healer."

"You speak of your people. What are they called?"

Lemmi answered creatively. "My father's clan is Dinneh, my mother's is Dakotah." Said it without thinking; his warrior muse was strong, and he was always open to it.

"Dkota?" Mazeppa said. "We are Dkota. And far west of here are a people calling themselves Dinneh. The Swift Current people of the Ulster, dark like yourself. They are not friends to the Dkota."

Morosov spoke again. "Lemmi speaks Dkotan," he said. "We have spoken it together."

Now the chief's reddish eyebrows did raise slightly.

"Our beautiful ancient tongue," he said. "I wish I'd learned it. Do you then think of yourself more as Dkota than as Dinneh?"

"I speak Dakotan, but I also speak Dinneh. In the Great Shuffling, God put the two peoples next to each other in Big Pines." Lemmi chuckled. "On the Sancroy, we have often intermarried. With our mother's family, we speak their tongue. With our father's we speak theirs."

He changed the subject then, with a smoothness that did not escape Mazeppa. "So I grew up as both, but some of us like to wander, see new places, so I left Big Pines. I have been told the Dkota also wander; that in the great grassland, the buffalo wander and the Dkota hunt them."

"Both are true," Mazeppa said, then returned to the subject. "You are young for a healer."

"That is so."

"Who taught you?"

"My first teacher is named Dorje, in the Kingdom of Ilanoy. The second is called Kellam, and claims to be from a very distant place."

Taking in the rangy, sinewy body, Mazeppa turned the subject again. "Are you a good wrestler?"

"For sport I wrestle. For more serious fighting, I strike with hands and feet."

"No knife? No spear?"

"Only for killing, which is not good in the eyes of God. But if necessary, I can also kill with hands and feet." He paused. "If you have in camp a man who is a bully, I am willing to show how such fighting is done."

Mazeppa turned to Pastor Morosov. "Do you know if 'Always Angry' is around?"

"He may be, but I haven't seen him lately."

"Let's go to his lodge." The chief turned to Lemmi. "Always Angry's wife put his moccasins out of her tipi, for striking her. Now he lives in a bachelor lodge."

The three men left the chief's tipi, walking. "Always Angry is not *always* angry," Mazeppa said, "but often. And when he is, he looks to attack someone. He is like you: he strikes with hands and feet. But he is larger than you. If you would rather not fight him, this is a good time to change your mind."

Lemmi grinned again, nonchalantly. "I will fight him. If he beats me, he beats me."

Recognizing a true warrior, Mazeppa nodded approval.

The bachelor tipi where Always Angry lived was two furlongs distant, and at the moment held four young men. Always Angry was the largest, not so tall as Mazeppa, but more thickly muscled. The young men got to their feet when Mazeppa arrived. "I have come to see Joshua," the chief said, courteously using Always Angry's baptismal name.

"I have just returned from hunting," the young warrior answered respectfully. "I brought four fat geese with me. I would like you to have two of them."

"Thank you," Mazeppa said. "That is good of you. I will give one of them to the widow, Martha Lost-Her-Knife."

Always Angry nodded. To share such a gift was according to custom, and part of the tribal fabric. Just now, though, he felt distracted by the stranger.

"I have brought a visitor with me," Mazeppa said. "He is Lemmi the Healer, a Dkota of the Sancroy band. They dwell in the forests north of Sota."

Always Angry looked Lemmi up and down, disapproving the strange clothing but saying nothing. Mazeppa continued. "He says he is more than a healer; that he is also a fighting man. One who has learned to fight without weapons, using hands and feet. I asked him what that was like. He said if there was a man in camp who also fought with hands and feet, he would be willing to show me how he does it. I thought at once of you."

Always Angry nodded, scowling. "I will fight this man," he said. "We will see if he is any good."

The lodge quickly emptied. The pastor and bachelors formed a loose line to one side. The bachelors might have made bets, but they weren't eager to antagonize Mazeppa Tall Man, of whose preference they weren't yet sure.

Lemmi was already pulling off his boots, which he put beside Pastor Morosov. Then he stripped off his shirt and folded it over his boots. His breeches he left on. Always Angry simply watched, waiting. When Lemmi was ready, Mazeppa stepped between the two. "I do not know the ritual or rules for such a contest," the chief told them, "but I will tell you some things you must not do." Then he looked at the bystanders. "Those who are watching must stay out of the way and not interfere." Now he gave his full attention to Lemmi and Always Angry. "There must be no taunting, and I want neither of you to die in this fight. When I have seen enough, I will tell you to stop. You must then stop at once." He backed out of the way. "Now—begin!"

For a moment, neither contestant moved. Then Always Angry rushed Lemmi, who at the last instant stepped aside, leaning away from a roundhouse right and executing a spin kick that sent Always Angry stumbling forward without quite falling. The Dinneh did not take advantage. The Dkota regained his balance and turned, aware now that he was in trouble. He shuffled forward warily, cocked fists moving up and down, his left shoulder and left fist intuitively forward, his right prepared to follow with power. Lemmi stood almost casually, right foot forward, hands open and about waist high, knees flexed. Unsure what to do next, Always Angry threw a lunging left, prepared to follow with a right hook, but somehow the left was slipped aside, and a rock-like hand struck him in the sternum hard enough to shock him. He dropped to hands and knees, then rolled onto his back. Though the fight was only seconds old, Mazeppa had seen enough.

"Stop!" he ordered.

The bystanders—bachelors and pastor—stared without a sure sense of what had happened. It hadn't seemed like much, but there was Always Angry on his back, ashy pale, struggling to draw breath. For a long moment it seemed to him his heart had stopped; now it hammered rapidly. He didn't know what had happened either.

Lemmi knew: his warrior muse had taken over with precision. He might now have helped Always Angry to his feet, but that could be taken as an insult, so instead he turned to Mazeppa.

"Let no one speak ill of Joshua," Lemmi said. "He was never taught, nor does he need to be. He is strong and quick and brave, and if we had wrestled instead, things might have gone differently. I was taught because I would travel alone, sometimes among those who prey upon strangers, and I might not always have weapons at hand."

He went to his clothes then and put on his shirt, while Always Angry got unsteadily to his feet. Next Lemmi pulled on his boots, left foot, then right, seeming not to fear a surprise attack. The other bachelors went into their tipi. Always Angry didn't follow them. He simply walked off in the direction of the horse herd.

As they neared Morosov's tipi, Mazeppa said he wished to speak privately with their visitor, so the pastor left them. Mazeppa and Lemmi continued to the chief's tipi and went inside. It was beginning to rain, large uncertain drops. The two sat against backrests on the men's side. The chief's two wives had begun to prepare the evening meal. The senior wife, Consuela, was still young and quite beautiful. The younger wife, Trains Horses, was perhaps eighteen or nineteen, and not so lovely, but tall and athletic. Mazeppa hoped to have strong sons by Trains Horses, but so far she, like Consuela, had not conceived. Still, he was fond of her. Also, and this was especially important, she was a bond between the Dkota and the Ulster, for she was Chief Gallagher's eldest daughter.

For a few minutes the two men sat without speaking. The sky had a ceiling of dark clouds now, and the light was poor. Rain pattered dully on the tipi's buffalo skin shell. Mazeppa gazed thoughtfully toward the fire, then spoke to his guest.

"After you defeated Always Angry, you spoke well of him. Why?"

"I owed it to him. He is a person, a proud man who has demons to fight. Yet I used him, demonstrating my skills at his expense. It was not something to boast of. Perhaps one day I can heal his spirit as I healed the spirit of Alexei Ivanov."

The chief turned his eyes to Lemmi, who could see the firelight reflected in them. "I did much the same thing to the Ulster chiefs after we defeated them in battle. I praised honestly their bravery and their fighting qualities, and they became our friends. I do not think Always Angry will become your friend, but I do not think he will be your enemy, either."

Again they sat briefly silent, and again it was Mazeppa who broke the silence. "You said you speak Dinneh. You also said you like to wander, see new places. I would like you to go somewhere you have not been before—to the Black Mountains, six or eight days' ride to the west. Go and speak with the Swift Current Dinneh. Few of them know much Merkan. Do you think you can understand them?"

"It seems probable. I am willing to try."

"Good. They are a difficult people. Let me tell you what my problem is with them . . ."

Chapter 9
Kato

(Luis)

I reached Kato Town in mid-morning. Sota's second city, it covered about as much acreage as Hasty, though Hasty, crowded inside the town walls, had many more people. The cathedral tower rose near Kato's center, but the bishop's manse and offices were at the edge of town, on the bishop's farm. I tied my horses in front of the manse and knocked on the door.

Half a minute later it was opened by a man about my age, his face and aura wary. My Higuchian uniform? After introducing myself, I showed him the letter of introduction from Pastor Linkon. He examined it, then seated me on an upholstered settee in the vestibule, and left.

He was back in a minute. "His reverence will see you," he told me, and led me down a hall to the bishop's office. The bishop got up and shook hands warmly. "Sit down! Sit down!" he said. "I'm glad to see a Higuchian presence in our kingdom! How is Pastor Linkon?"

Happy, hearty, and busy, I told him. Then we talked

about the new brother house. He said he might have some prospects as novices; he'd speak with them. I didn't bring up the archbishop or king. His aura, and his pleasure at "a Higuchian presence" told me enough.

"Was that your steward who let me in?" I asked.

He laughed. "He's a new usher, who takes his duties too seriously. We're working on him. Edgar's letter says you're a missioner. How may I help you?"

I told him that to start with, I'd like to lodge at the manse while I was in Kato, and put up my two horses in his stable. And that I was there to meet the duke, to question him about the state of the kingdom and its defense. That's as explicit as I got. He would, he said, have a room arranged for me; and stalls, feed, and grooming for my animals. "Mrs. MacNeff serves supper at six o'clock, but if need be you will find bread, cheese, and beer in the kitchen, and buttermilk in the ice house.

"As for meeting with Edward, the man to see is Captain Keith Frazier, commander of the duke's force at arms. Since Edward's accident, Keith acts as his deputy. A good Christian, highly ethical, and capable in every respect. I suspect he can answer any questions with full authority."

Taking out a sheet of paper, he dipped his pen, wrote a brief letter of introduction to the captain, blotted, folded and sealed it, then marked it with his signet and handed it to me. He wasn't smiling now. "I wish you success in your mission, Master Luis. As for King Eldred Youngblood—in most respects I have found him a decent ruler . . . though more brutal toward his enemies than God would wish. Between you and me, I lack confidence in his treaty with Chief Mazeppa."

"Thank you for confiding in me," I told him. "I'll respect that confidence." I held up his letter. "And thank you for this. I'm sure Captain Frazier will speak more freely to me with an introduction from his confessor."

⊲∋-∈⊳ ⊲∋-∈⊳ ⊲∋-∈⊳

The ducal palace was a large, handsome, two-story structure, built of massive timbers—logs slabbed off into snuggly fitting, twelve-inch cants, planed smooth, carefully fitted, and painted sky blue. I'd never before seen a timber building so large, and it was no doubt less cold in winter than the king's stone palace.

A guard stood at the main entrance. After glancing at the bishop's sealed letter, he rang for a page, who led me to the "guardhouse," a one-story wing appended to a rear corner of the palace. Captain Frazier had a cozy office where the guardhouse joined the palace proper, with a door into the adjacent room where he lived. Between the two rooms, the lower two feet or so of wall was brick—eight courses of them—no doubt forming flues from the brick stove in mid-wall, warming both rooms in winter. Brother houses use similar arrangements.

The captain recognized the Higuchian uniform, and rose to greet me. He was middle aged, of medium height and weight, but gave a larger impression. And still strong—dangerous in a fight. I handed him Bishop Joseph's letter, which he opened and read. "*Master* Luis," he said. "I'm familiar with Higuchian brothers, but not with masters. What is the distinction?"

"Most masters," I told him, "operate the brother schools, and supervise the brothers' work. Others, like myself, carry out missions for the Sacred Congregation for the Defense of the Church. Candidate masters are selected from the corps of brothers, and spend more than five years preparing."

"Five years! What did you learn to master in those five years?"

I'd never heard that question before. "More than

anything else," I said, "each of us learns to master himself. And his talents."

Frazier nodded, gesturing me to a chair, then seated himself, crossing his arms. "So, Master Luis, why have you sought *me* out?"

"I've heard the duke is in seriously poor health. It is my hope, and Norlins', that you will tell me more about that. Afterward I'd like to meet him."

His eyes appraised me. "Surely there's more beneath your question than that."

"Excuse me. There is indeed. I'm afraid I take it for granted. The Sacred Congregation, and of course the Order, are concerned for the safety of Sota, and do not trust the Dkota to abide by the treaty, though we hope we are wrong about that. Nor do we trust Sota's ability to defend herself against them, should they attack."

"What is it you want to know from me?"

"First, just how serious is your duke's injury? My information is that until his accident, he was the man most able to influence and perhaps lead the other dukes—should the king need to be replaced."

Frazier's gaze sharpened. "You speak frankly, Master Luis, and dangerously, should it come to some ears. But you're right about what our duke might have done, had he not been injured. He *was* injured though, most grievously. A man of lesser will would have died. During the first days, he coughed blood a good deal, sometimes strangling on it, and suffered greatly. Even now he breathes only shallowly, exhales and speaks weakly, and sleeps with the aid of whiskey. Also he eats little. It is my belief that when his horse fell on him, it crushed his ribcage, and damaged inner organs. I dread what might happen if he is afflicted with a lung infection.

"Prior to his accident, he was vigorous and strong. He drilled and contested with sword, spear and bow, ate with gusto, hunted a great deal, and seldom drank anything stronger than beer. Even beer he took mainly with meals."

"Does he still function as duke?"

The captain answered glumly. "He functions largely through me, I'm afraid. Each morning we breakfast together and talk. I tell him my plans for the day: what orders I intend to give staff; what baron, or merchants, or other petitioners I expect to see, and about what, and the advice or orders I expect to give them. Edward comments, advises, and as need be gives orders. But he tires quickly. And if something comes up that cannot wait, I deal with it out of hand.

"At first we assumed he'd recover, bit by bit, to something like he'd been before, but his condition has not improved for months."

"Is he married?"

"He was, and therein lies his first wound: his wife died of a tumor, of the lungs, ten years past. A terrible affliction for her, and for him a grim time. He has not remarried, and now is unlikely to."

"I've heard he has a son. What manner of man is he?"

Frazier gazed thoughtfully at me. "His name is Donald. I take it you've heard something of him."

"Only that he's not the man his father was."

For a long moment Frazier sat silent, then began slowly. "He is a fine young man, but has . . . limitations. Your interest, I suppose, is in the sort of duke he might be, when Edward steps down. Or dies. I believe he will rule adequately, but he will not replace his father as a leader of Sota's dukes. I doubt he'd accept the role, nor would they invite him."

His eyes met mine. "I suggest you ask his father about him. If you then have further questions for me, I will answer them as best I can.

"Now, is there another subject you would question me on?"

"I'm sure there will be," I told him, and got to my feet. "But later."

"Ah," he said, and stood. "Then I have something to ask of you. I know the Higuchians as a martial order, and in the Anti-Pope's War, in Shy Free-Town, I've seen them fight. Rarely have I seen such skill with sword or spear, or such fearlessness. But you have been named a Master, and I would like to see you fight. Edward will ask how good you are; he's a born warrior." He leaned forward. "I have an armsman who's a superb swordsman. As good, I believe, as the Higuchians I observed during the War. At the moment he's on duty, just down the hall; he's sergeant of the guard today."

"Let's go see him," I said.

The young armsman's name was Hamus, and we contested outside with ash practice swords. Several guardsman watched. I started out holding back. It's policy to let people know we are very very good—it's essential to our reputation—but not *how* good. We call the difference our safety margin. Besides, humiliating people creates grudges, even enemies. Young Hamus, though, didn't allow me to take it easy. I had to take the fight to him. When after several minutes Frazier cried "Hold!", the corporal and I both stood slick with sweat, breathing hard and grinning at each other.

Hamus looked at his captain. "Sir," he said, "I have never seen such swordplay before. I will remember this each time I oil my bruises."

"Hamus," I told him, "I enjoyed the match. But with real swords, I'd much rather fight beside you than against you. Captain Frazier tried to tell me how good you are, but I had to see to believe."

The two of us sluiced off at the horse trough, then donned our tunics again. Hamus returned to duty, and Frazier and I entered the palace by a rear door.

"Master Luis," he said quietly, "I've been a soldier

for twenty-six years, and I've never seen anyone who could match you with the sword." He looked at me shrewdly. "And without, I believe, extending yourself."

"From you," I answered, "that is high praise. But the credit belongs to the Order. Beginning with the brother schools, which train us skillfully and hard. Thus the Academy has an excellent pool of candidates, it is extremely selective, and its system . . . is unique."

Inside the palace proper, the corridors were bare of rugs but floored with red oak; quite handsome. The duke's bedroom was on the second floor. Frazier rapped quietly. After a moment the door was opened by a woman of perhaps thirty years, the duke's nurse. She smiled at Frazier, who greeted her as Sara. "I knew your knock, captain," she said. "His lordship's on the balcony, perhaps dozing, but feel free to wake him. He'll want to see you."

He was awake, lying on a couch beneath an awning. He turned his face to us as we stepped out. It jarred me. If the rest of him was as badly wasted, he might not scale a hundred pounds.

"Milord," said Frazier, "I have a visitor I believe you'll want to talk with. He has questions."

Despite how wasted he appeared, Edward Maltby's gaze was firm and evaluative. His spirit aura was that of a man born to action, to dominate—and who'd come to terms with what had happened to him. His shrunken body aura, on the other hand, was predominately a dark murky violet, with a black irregular hole over his chest. For some seconds he did not speak. When he did, it was to Frazier, his voice breathy, weak but firm. "Introduce us, Keith, and we'll see."

Frazier's introduction was thorough, and included my trial at arms with Hamus.

"Thank you," the duke answered, this time without a lag. "Stay with us. You'll have, more to say, than I do." His breathing was so shallow, the words came a few at a time between breaths.

Frazier and I both were on the duke's right. Now I saw the utility of that: his lordship changed focus from one to the other of us simply by moving his eyes, his head still. "So, Master Luis, I am ready, for your questions."

I told him what I was there for, giving him more detail than I'd given Frazier. Ending with "tell me, your lordship: do you walk?"

"Daily. Today I walked, from my bed, to this balcony. But, at a cost. I spent, the next, twenty minutes, recovering, my breath, and the hour, after that, exhausted. I do it, that I may not lose, what little strength, remains to me."

He paused then, eyes closed, as if having spoken those short sentences required a rest.

"Master Luis," Frazier put in, "it would be well to preface questions with the reasoning behind them. His lordship will be saved the drain of providing more answer than you need, or of mistaking your need and answering the wrong question."

Some of the questions I'd intended to ask, I decided to postpone. I'd wait till I heard more from Lemmi, and perhaps till I'd spoken with other dukes. Clearly leadership couldn't be expected from Edward Maltby. Knowledge yes, perhaps direction, even wisdom, but not visible leadership.

Meanwhile I gave the duke and his deputy the situation as the Order saw it, as a matter of policy not mentioning the Helverti. And so far, at any rate, we saw the Helverti not as an active force, but as instigators and advisors. Troublemakers.

It was Frazier who responded, with a question. "In some respects you know more about the Dkota than we do. How did you learn it?"

"There are traders," I told him, "who travel among the tribes selling pots, knives, glass beads. . . . Some report to us."

"Ah." Frazier gnawed a lip in thought. "You voiced

concern that if the Dkota attack, Sota will not be able
to defend itself. But they have never attempted a
sustained attack—a campaign of conquest. They've
scourged the marches from Zandria to Oak Groves,
burned ranches, hamlets, even stockades. They've even
raided into the western reaches of our duchy here,
though they've never reached Kato Town. They do it
more for adventure and brags than for loot.

"We've recovered strongly each time, though
scarred a bit, and some argue another raid might be
worth the cost." He paused for emphasis, then spoke
crisply. "Because if they raid again, it will break the
treaty, an act we believe even Eldred can't ignore.
Then surely the kingdom will arm, mobilize, and
punish. For when Eldred feels betrayed, he *does*
respond, brutally."

Ah brutality, I thought. *It tends to be habit forming; begets further brutalities*. "Meanwhile," I said, "his
treaty has given you a period without raids."

"There have always been periods without raids,"
Frazier replied. "All of them longer than this one. And
Eldred's reductions have hurt our ability to defend
ourselves, and rally."

"Reductions?"

"In the ducal and baronial forces at arms."

He elaborated. Previously each duke kept forty-six
armsmen, well-trained, well-armed, and always at
hand. Now they were allowed only thirty-five. Each
baron had kept eighteen; now the number was fourteen. Cumulatively the reduction was serious.

"And the king's force?"

"We have heard, and believe, that the king's force
at arms has not been reduced. But it's quartered at
Hasty, and of no use in defending against raiders.
Unless the raiders reach the Royal Domain at least."

"I suppose you have militia."

"We used to. Eldred disbanded them after the
uprisings at Nona and Austin. They dare not drill even

in secret, for he has informants everywhere. When the dukes complained, the royal answer was that militias aren't needed: that the treaty with Mazeppa has erased the threat."

"Are the ex-militiamen still armed?"

"Their weapons are their own. Together the militias might have been potent, but they've never combined, even within a duchy. They'll retain some potential for a few years, though dwindling, because the king is not so rapt in his molli doctrine that he'd try to confiscate their arms. For many years, all men between ages fourteen and forty were required to drill weekly through their eighteenth summer, biweekly through their twenty-second, and monthly after that. They had to own a fighting spear, sword, or battle ax; a longbow and at least thirty arrows; and a bullhide hauberk and steel cap. And to pass an annual archery test for range, accuracy, and rate of fire.

"But they had their shortcomings against raiders. For one thing, they were infantry. Most were farmers, of course, with a horse or horses. But except in the marches, few farmers are truly skilled horsemen, and their horses, most of them, are better suited to the plow than the saddle. And the law and the Church forbade training militia as cavalry; mounted militia could too easily dabble in brigandage.

"While for the most part, the raiders ride like the wind, arriving without warning, before the militia can gather. Thus the militia fight in small groups, perhaps after sending boys galloping eastward, hopefully to spread the alarm. And when at length the raiders find villages defended by platoons and companies, they flow back to buffalo country, with loot, captive girls, and stories to tell around winter fires.

"So the first line of defense is the baronial stockades, defended by armsmen and any militia at hand. There, as many people as possible take shelter. Any who can't get to a stockade, which is commonly most

of them, flee to the woods and hide, or get out of
the raiders' path, or die, or get carried away. Mostly
the raiders don't take the trouble to search them out.
They simply grab what catches their eye, then race
on till they meet an effective defense."

As he'd spoken, Frazier's aura had darkened. He
paused now, lips thin, eyes . . . thoughtful.

"The crown has never provided protection," he
continued. "As far as that's concerned, most of the
kingdom has never seen a raider. We haven't here at
Kato Town; they've never gotten this far. Until some
hundred years ago, raids were unknown, and only in
the past twenty years have there been raids by forces
larger than twenty or thirty. Except the first one of
all, some hundred years ago, said to have been by a
hundred or more. But the last two raids were the
largest, with two, possibly three hundred."

"What if they arrive a thousand strong?"

"It's hard to imagine them sending that many. In
summer the Dkota live as scattered bands. And raids
are by volunteers: youths looking for excitement and
reputation, older men looking for status. I doubt
Mazeppa could marshal half a thousand, let alone
direct or control them."

I nodded, examining my palms as if looking for
answers there. Actually I was thinking that someone
had done well, evaluating and pulling together what
was known and supposed. And wondering whether
that someone was Frazier. Meanwhile the silence set
up both captain and duke for what I had next to say,
based partly on Lemmi's reports.

"It would seem like it," I answered. "But . . . have
you heard of the fighting between the Dkota and the
Ulster?"

"We know they raid each other. Small raids, fed
mainly by youthful energy."

"About two years ago they fought a battle with
hundreds on each side; a battle deliberately planned

and led by Mazeppa Tall Man. The Dkota won, and
when it was over, Mazeppa lavished praise on the
Ulster chiefs and warriors, for their bravery and skill.
Then, after they'd smoked the peace pipe together,
many prominent men or their sons married a daughter
or grand-daughter or sister of some prominent man
of the other tribe. And swore that the enemy of one
would be the enemy of the other.

"It may be that the treaty with Eldred was simply a screen, and that when Mazeppa is ready, he'll
strike with far more warriors than before." I shrugged.
"Or not. Who knows?"

Frazier and I talked about that for a few minutes,
with Edward adding occasionally. I'd worried them,
though not as much as I'd expected. They didn't know
about the Helverti, and I couldn't tell them. But I'd
planted the seed.

Meanwhile Edward was used up. "Milord," Frazier
said, "I think it's best we leave you to your rest."

"Yes, your lordship," I put in. "And before I leave,
I'd like to ease your discomfort."

His eyes questioned.

"Masters are also trained as healers," I told him,
"and while my skill is less than some, I believe you
will find it worthwhile."

I didn't wait for his reply, simply began running
my open hands over his aura, feeling the major energy
loci, and the flows. The aural hole over the chest felt
hot, and the flows around it tangled. Gently I stroked
what I'd been taught to call his "energy field,"
emphasizing the upper torso, but including long
strokes reaching to the crown locus, the feet, and the
hands, letting my own energy interact with his. After
a few minutes I straightened. By that time the aural
tear showed softened margins and a tinge of color,
and felt different. It wouldn't hold like that, but bit
by bit . . .

"That's enough for now," I said. "If you'd like, I'll come this evening and do it again."

Edward opened his eyes. "You will be, more than welcome," he murmured. "I've never before, credited claims, of healing hands, but I may, have to change, my mind."

I returned with Frazier to his office, where his orderly brewed sassafras tea for us. Frazier had his with honey, the most popular way, but I sipped mine straight. It was mild, pleasant, and hot.

"What can you tell me about the king's force at arms?" I asked.

"Hmm." Frazier took another sip. "To begin with, his is stronger than those of all the dukes combined, if combining was even possible. The last I heard, there were five companies trained both as cavalry and mounted infantry, one of them especially for defense of the palace and town. Companies of one hundred men each, plus officers and senior sergeants, each man with a longbow, saber, and fighting spear, all well-drilled and confident. And two companies of musketeers, with *rifled* muskets, deadly at ranges much greater than smooth-bores. They number the same as other companies, and are trained mainly for defense of the palace. But all *are* able horsemen, well drilled with the saber, and with the long dagger they attach to their rifles in lieu of spears."

Frazier's recital had turned his face grim. He took a long breath, then continued.

"In addition there are cannon, forbidden to the nobles. Four of them firing six-pound projectiles, and eight or a dozen firing three-pound projectiles. Clusters like steel grapes, actually, that separate when fired. Horrible weapons.

"The kingsmen would make a strong shock force against the Dkota, while the militia, if they could be gathered under a single command . . . but *that* would truly be a challenge."

"What kind of commander does Eldred's army have?"

"His name is Jaako Jarvi, one of the late queen's many cousins. In our soldier-of-fortune days, Jaako and I served together against the forces of the Anti-Pope. Jaako is well-known as a fighting man, and an excellent trainer and disciplinarian, well-liked by his troops for his fairness. But as a commander unimaginative, at least when we served together. Unfortunately, like the Lahti Clan in general, he is entirely loyal to the House of Youngblood."

"A bit ago, it sounded as if you know a lot about the Dkota," I said. "How did you learn it?"

"Ah! That I owe largely to Gavan Feeny, a peasant lad from Killibegs, in the west of the duchy. As a child, Gavan was captured by Dkota raiders, and so far as I know, he is one of only two captive boys ever to come back." Frazier's face soured. "It seems they come to prefer a life of hunting to one of farm work. When stolen, he was not yet twelve. His mother was killed defending him, and he in turn defended her. His bravery could have cost him his life, but instead it brought him admiration, and he was adopted by the chief of the party that captured him.

"He soon came to like being a boy among the Dkota. And not only was his mother dead; his birth father had died the year before, of lung fever. What brought him back to us was his twin sister. When Dkota raiders were reported, everyone who could, in the barony, flocked to the Flussdorf stockade. But the weather had been very dry, and the Dkota pushed a loaded haycart against the palisade and set it afire. Then shot arrows at anyone who tried to put it out.

"Meanwhile, inside the stockade, Gavan had lowered his sister into a well used to water livestock. During the drought, it had gone nearly dry. He'd always wondered if she'd survived, so when he was seventeen, he came back to find out. And she had.

She'd married and was with child, so he stayed. Meanwhile I learned about him and went to question him; it seemed a good opportunity. I stayed a week. Then his sister died delivering a girlchild, and Gavan disappeared, no doubt returning to the Dkota. He'd told his Dkota foster father where he was going, and why, and the man gave his blessing. Something I found . . . encouraging, I suppose."

Frazier shook his head. "Gavan explained much to me, but he did not, could not explain how such a good man as his foster father could lead a raiding party against people who'd done him no wrong.

"We'd thought that raid was bad. The next one was worse: the raiders were more numerous and more destructive. They took time to hunt people down and murder them, so of course word spread ahead of them. Despite greater numbers, they didn't penetrate as far before the militias blunted them and sent them home.

"Then, two years ago last fall, Mazeppa led an embassy to Oak Groves, asking to speak with the king. In *November*! A good month for the early blizzard, a strange season to ride so far. He said Christ had come to him in a dream, telling him he must become a man of peace, must have a treaty by Christmas. It was just what Eldred wanted to hear—Eldred, the archbishop, and the rest of the mollies—so he and Clonarty came to meet him.

"There were more than just Carlians who believed the chief, but there were more still who distrusted Mazeppa. The Dkota had sent raiders twice in four years! Still, Mazeppa asked nothing of us except a peace treaty, and the right to hunt buffalo in the marches, so there was little more than grumbling against it.

"And men do change, so I'm hopeful it will hold, and that Mazeppa intends us no harm. Hopeful but not expectant. To me, the man *felt* deceitful. Meanwhile our greatest complaint—and it's serious—is Eldred's abolition of the militias. That wasn't part of the treaty. If it had been, there'd have been a strong public outcry against it. But Eldred's proclaiming it independently, a year after the treaty, didn't or shouldn't have surprised anyone. It goes with the Carlian philosophy."

"And none of the dukes resisted?"

"Two. Takeza of Nona, and Jozef of Austin, whose duchies border each other. They sent a joint message to the other dukes, urging them to rise against Eldred and his treaty, and suggesting Edward as their leader. It was the wrong time. Two days after sending off their couriers, they got word of Edward's accident. Probably the other dukes had the message of the accident before they had the one from Austin. At any rate, away from the Marches, public misgivings about the treaty had eased; they'd never been very hot. And with the reduction of the ducal and baronial forces at arms, Eldred had ordered a proportionate reduction of local taxes, so a lot of people consider the treaty a blessing.

"Meanwhile Jozef's steward was a spy. He sent a message of his own to Eldred, with a copy of Jozef and Takeza's call for rebellion. So Eldred sent a strong military force to Nona, under Jarvi's command. When it finished there, it went on to Austin. Stories of the bloodbath at Nona had preceded them, so at Austin there was no resistance.

"With Jarvi, Eldred had sent two reliable supporters as the new dukes, along with hand-picked aides for them. Jarvi installed them. Takeza's drawn and spread-eagled body decorated the main gate of his fortress for weeks. The last I heard, his head still looked down from a spear in front of the palace." Frazier shook the image off, and exhaled through pursed lips. "I guess you could say Jozef was the lucky one, though I doubt he thinks so. He got away barely in time, and fled south to Iwa, leaving his family behind. I'm sure he never imagined what would happen to them."

"Which was?"

"They were executed; publicly beheaded. All of them, including his cousins; even a foster cousin."

I stared. "Do you know that as a fact?"

"The word is 'publicly.' Publicly executed. Many believe the new dukes ordered the butchery, and I could believe that of François. As a baron he'd been known as a brutal man. But Alfred? I don't believe it. He might have voiced the order, but it came from the king."

That was essentially the end of our conversation that day. I'd sleep on what I'd heard, and ask further questions later.

I rode around Kato Town till supper, which I ate at the River Inn, listening to other people's conversations but speaking only with the tap man, who was also the owner. He asked about my uniform, and I explained I belonged to a religious order—my collar had told him that much—without naming which one. I was from Norlins, I said, which formally was true: my assignment to this mission had been confirmed by the Holy See.

After supper I returned to the palace, where I gave Edward another healing session, longer than the first. When I finished, he told me he felt better than at any time since his accident.

Back at Bishop Joseph's manse, the bishop and I talked for a bit over wine. I didn't tell him what I'd learned, only that I'd had an audience with Frazier and one with the duke. Then I retired to my room and meditated till my com chirped. It was Lemmi reporting to Tahmm, Carlos and myself. The next morning he'd begin his trip to the Black Mountains, as Mazeppa's emissary to the Swift Current Dinneh— or Swift Current Ulster, take your choice.

Appropriate. Who else was suited to the job?

When he'd finished, I told them what I'd learned. Major food for thought.

Chapter 10
Realizations

(Luis)

The next morning I was at the bishop's kitchen early, though not as early as the Widow MacNeff. She'd just taken the barley porridge off the fire to cool. Now she ladled a bowl full for me, hot enough to scald Satan's gullet. I cooled it with thick cream from the ice house. A bowl of maple sugar waited on the table, and salt pork perfumed the air, sizzling on a sheet of iron over the coals. She turned the slices as I watched, and after a minute reached with tongs, getting me two of the most crisp. On a sideboard was a rye loaf, several slices already cut, and a bowl of butter, probably yesterday's churning. Given the dry weather, it was no longer spring yellow, but as tasty as if it were. I washed it all down with a mug of milk still warm from the cow.

I'd been told the day before that no morning hour was too early for the duke, whose pain invariably increased through the night as the whiskey wore off. He was usually awake by the first light of dawn. A guardsman met me at the palace's main entrance, and rang for the usher, but it was a quick-footed page boy who came. The usher, the boy told me, was at breakfast. He trotted off to tell Widow Sanders I was there to see the duke. Two minutes later he was back. The duke was still asleep; she'd send for me when he was awake and ready to see me. I suspected our healing session had something to do with his sleeping later.

I told the boy I was going to the guardhouse to see Captain Frazier, and that I'd come back later. I found Frazier having breakfast with the day's guard detail. He introduced me as "Master Luis of the Order of Saint Higuchi," which earned me looks ranging from respectful interest to wary awe.

All in all, the morning had begun nicely. I tried to refuse a second breakfast, but ended up with a large slab of warm fresh wheat bread spread with butter and honey, and a mug of sassafras, then sat listening to the small talk of armsmen, constrained in the presence of their captain and a churchman, while Frazier finished a modest breakfast and had a second cup of sassafras.

When he was done, he left the guard detail to the duty sergeant, and the two of us started for Edward's sickroom. Frazier had been surprised to hear that Edward had slept late. Judging by his aura, it worried Frazier; was the change for the worse? Widow Sanders met us at the duke's door. He was hunched over his table with a cup of duck soup, a soft-boiled duck egg, small slice of buttered bread, tiny cup of raisins, and new baby carrots barely cooked. And sassafras. Frazier and I had another cup "to keep him company."

The duke looked more alive than on the day before. His voice even sounded a little stronger. "If you didn't have such urgent matters, to take you away," he told me, "I'd suggest you stay, a week or two."

"I'll be here at least till tomorrow," I said. "Why don't I give you a session later today, and another in the evening?"

"It will be, appreciated, Master Luis."

When he'd finished eating, he hobbled slowly and carefully onto the balcony, leaning on a cane. The morning was cool, and Frazier bundled him in blankets before helping him lie down. Then I gave him a ten-minute session. By the time I'd finished, he was actually smiling. "God bless you, Luis," he said.

"And God bless you, Edward Maltby," I answered. I turned to Frazier then. "Captain," I began . . .

"Please, Master Luis, my name is Keith."

"Fine, Keith. And mine is Luis."

"Indeed. I'm afraid I interrupted you."

"I wondered if there is any resource Sota might have for her defense that I am unaware of."

"Ah. I lay awake almost till cock's crow this morning, thinking of what you said yesterday. And it seems to me your evaluation of the threat to Sota is correct. As for resources, there may in fact be one you're not aware of. Not exactly a resource, perhaps, but . . . Many of our youths, in their teens, show an adventurous streak. I'm sure that's true elsewhere as well, but here in Sota, with the Misasip on the east and the wilderness on the north, it's more easily indulged, and become a tradition. 'The faring time,' it's called.

"Generally by seventeen or so, a boy has learned good basic military skills in the militia. Some then go off hunting employment as an armsman, mostly outside their own duchy. Perhaps hiring out as oarsmen on a freight raft, seeking service at arms in lands as far as Loozyana, Ohio, even Allegheny or Susky Hannah. They may never find such service, but the journeying itself is an adventure. In any event, after a time, most return home, take a wife, and a farm or a trade, and of course reenter the militia. In fact, most of our militia officers and some of the sergeancy have served as armsmen somewhere, and bring to the militia their skills and experience.

"And perhaps as often, at sixteen or seventeen, lads will turn north to the wilderness, sometimes alone, but usually two or three together. They've trapped and hunted from childhood, if for little more than skunks around the hen house, coons around the corn patches. They've become good bowmen, and skilled with snares and deadfalls. And traps and setlines for fish. They've grown up with the ax, of course, cutting fence rails, mountains of firewood . . . till finally, some autumn, they trek off north on foot, to spend a winter in the wilderness, sheltering in some rude hut they've built, or found abandoned. There to hunt furs, and meat for their bellies. Sometimes over-hungry, and often freezing, but too proud to come home till spring. At April's end, when the snow has disappeared, most do come home, wiser and with a better-founded self-confidence. Others stay with it for a full year or more."

He paused, a finger tapping meaningfully on the arm of his chair. "And whether armsman or wanderer or fur hunter, when they come back, they have a new stature, a changed bearing. They add a certainty and sense of boldness to their militias, even among those who never left.

"In fact, my impression from the Anti-Pope's war is that our militias here in Sota are better than others. But they are strictly local. What they lack is an overall command to direct them. A command that all respect. All: the militias, the various forces at arms, the barons and dukes. Except at Nona and Austin, which seem irretrievable while Eldred sits the throne."

His eyes challenged. "The overall command I speak of is yourself, sir, or your Order. The scores of Sotans who served in and survived the Anti-Pope's War as armsmen, brought home stories of the Higuchian brothers: of their fighting qualities, and of their loyalty to one another and the Pope.

"Whether and how you make use of that reputation, I leave to you. The little I have observed of you, convinces me you're as well suited to the task as anyone could be. Nor do I doubt my duke will lend his authority and my help to your efforts."

I'd almost forgotten we sat beside the duke's couch. A soft chuckling reminded me. "You see now, Master Luis," Edward murmured, "why I so trust, my friend's wisdom, and judgement."

I did see. After discussing for a bit the training and qualities of Sotan forces at arms, I gave Edward another healing session. Then Keith and I left him relaxed, and as comfortable as his broken body allowed.

Late in the session I'd sensed something stirring in Edward, a result of two interlocking human energy fields communicating. Some understanding waiting to be seen and grasped. But I'd let be, preferring he reach it with neither Keith nor Widow Sanders on hand. Their presence might constrain what he would otherwise say.

As we walked down the corridor, I told Keith I wanted to speak with him about the duke's son, Donald. Where we'd not be overheard. The little I'd been told of him had been phrased enigmatically, and I wanted to know more before I met with him. So the two of us went to the stable, saddled our mounts and rode off. Alone except for a swirl of horseflies, which not liking the darkness in the stable, had hung around outside waiting.

Frazier took me not through town, but across a pasture into green and quiet forest, rich in basswood and ash. Donald Maltby, he told me, was nineteen years old, a youth with many strengths: honor, intelligence, self-discipline, outstanding physical strength and martial skills . . . "But unfortunately," he added, "the duke is a father who rarely praised his son, believing it would spoil him. Instead he stressed and criticized the boy's every error—even small ones, even in his successes—to improve him, he thought. Until the young man had little faith in himself. Now Donald lacks confidence in both his judgement and his actions—and has little love for his father. He fears and shuns responsibility, and is awkward in his relationships. Yet I have no doubt it's a sense of responsibility—to the duchy!—that has kept him from leaving.

"And in this case the tragedy is compounded, for in Donald Maltby I sense great potential. Potential stifled. And his father knows it now. The lad was seventeen when Edward gave him into my hands, asking that I 'make a man of him, fit to rule the duchy.' At least the duchy.

"It was too long delayed. Donald is no longer the sullen hangdog he'd become; by praise and affection I accomplished that much. But still he has a deeply ingrained view of himself as lacking, and it cripples his will. Nor do I know how to take him further. He probably *will* rule the duchy when the time comes, but I suspect the barons will take advantage of him, and I fear that in response, he may become heavy-handed."

We rode silently then, till we topped a terrain break. Below us through the greenery of floodplain trees, we glimpsed the Sota River. For a minute we stopped, the horses' heads tossing, tails switching, hooves stamping; I was sorry for them, and glad to be human, for horseflies are cruel.

"I hope I haven't discouraged you from talking with Donald," Frazier said. "Know that beneath that resentful, too often sullen surface lie stifled virtues. And I sense unusual power in you. Perhaps you can strengthen his troubled soul as you seem to be strengthening his father's broken body."

"My friend," I told him, "you have inspired me to try."

⬦—⬦ ⬦—⬦ ⬦—⬦

Riding back to the palace, it occurred to me that this had already been a major day in my life, and it was still morning. Five-plus years at the Academy had changed me a lot; I'd known while it was happening. But there, everyone was select, the trainees among us being educated and trained by other, more advanced selects. It was by them I measured myself. But these two days at Kato, especially today, had shown me the kind of impact I could have on people in the world at large. Even on people like Edward and Keith. Especially on people like Edward and Keith.

<&><&> <&><&> <&><&>

I looked forward to meeting Donald Maltby, but meanwhile . . . Keith and I parted at the stable, and I walked to the palace's rear entrance alone. He had duties to take care of, and I hoped to draw Edward out on private, personal matters.

The guardsman at Edward's door knocked—properly it was his job, not mine—and Widow Sanders opened. Yes, Edward was sleeping. And yes I could come in, but to please not waken him. Such healthy sleep, she said—and almost without whiskey!—was a blessing too good to be interrupted.

Edward had left the balcony for his bed, and muted daylight filtered through the curtains. His body aura was far from expansive, but it was lighter and cleaner than it had been. The aural "tear" was smaller, its blackness "cleaner," its energies less "trapped" and "snarled."

I had no idea why I said what I said next, but I said it very softly. "You know, Miz Sanders, I can see the man he was. A handsome man, wouldn't you say?"

"Yes Master Luis, very handsome." She answered as quietly as I'd asked.

"How long ago was it his wife died?"

"Nine years, sir."

"Did you know her well?"

"I was—I am a nurse, sir, and well regarded. I was brought to the palace during her illness, to attend her."

"I'm sure you're a good nurse, Sara." I paused before going on. "I understand she suffered greatly in her illness."

Tears had gathered. Now one spilled from each eye, running quickly down her cheeks. "Toward the end she did, sir. Her physician treated her with laudanum, to ease it, and his lordship would sit by her for hours, holding her hand. He had a surgeon sent up from Sanlooee, but the man didn't cut her. There was no use in it, he said."

My mind had gotten a picture, of the surgeon I had no doubt—a dark and lanky man, with short kinky hair like Kabibi's. And I got a sense of his words. "I know," I told Sara Sanders. "I can hear him." I changed my voice, trying for his, deeper and fuller than mine. "In cases like this, cutting does no good. She'll go to God soon. Meanwhile keep giving her the laudanum."

I watched Edward as I said it. He seemed not to have heard at any level; his sleep remained calm. Then I looked at his nurse. She'd been stunned by what I'd said, and for a moment afraid of me. I put a hand on her arm. "I'm going to give his lordship a healing session now. Longer than the earlier ones. This time I want to break through his condition, if I can. Turn it around. Meanwhile . . . which room is yours?"

Still afraid, she whispered her answer. "I sleep in the small bed there"—she gestured at a nearby cot—"where I can hear if he needs me. His voice is so weak. But my room is across the corridor, the second door to the left."

"Good. Go there now, and pray for his lordship and myself. I'll rap when we're done, and you can come back."

She got up and left without answering, closing the door softly behind her. I spoke quietly to Edward, without attempting to waken him. "Edward," I said, "I'm going to give you a session now. If you wish, you may continue sleeping. If . . ."

His eyes opened, first vague, then focusing, shifting to me. "I believe I'm awake," he said, in little more than a whisper. "Yes. Awake."

"Fine. Now close your eyes." I began to stroke his body aura as I had before. "Pictures or thoughts may come to you," I told him. "Whenever you wish—if you wish—tell me one of them. We're alone, and I will listen."

Neither of us spoke for perhaps ten minutes. I continued to stroke, not knowing what to expect, except that something was going to happen. Finally Edward spoke again, his voice stronger than before: "Clarissa's tumor, was in her chest. It was suffocating her."

"Thank you, Edward."

His spirit aura was darkening. I continued to stroke. His breath became more labored, his head rolling back and forth on his pillow. He began to moan. "Oh Clarissa, Clarissa, if only I could take, your pain, onto myself, free you of it."

My skin crawled. It was beginning. Edward's breathing smoothed. His head lay still again, and after a moment he chuckled faintly. I continued to stroke. His spirit aura had lightened; his body aura expanded notably. Within four or five minutes, though, they'd darkened again, and this time his moaning was different.

"I'm *sorry* Clarissa, blessed saint, I'm *sorry*. Clarissa! Where are you? I beg you, to forgive me."

This time my skin rucked like a plucked goose, from head to foot, and my short hairs bristled. For now someone else was there, and I knew who. It seemed to me she was talking to Edward, though I got none of it beyond a sense of transcendent love, utterly pure, and a beautiful golden glow. Edward began to weep, then to sob, the sobs seeming to tear him apart. I wouldn't have thought his damaged lungs could create such paroxysms, and wondered if I was killing instead of healing him. But still I stroked, and in the essence of Clarissa, I sensed the difference between human pity and angelic compassion.

The episode was brief. The sobs died. Edward raised himself on an elbow . . . and laughed! The phenomenon was common in Xioxian therapy. It was joy at the passing of old guilt and grief; old suffering replaced by understanding. I'd experienced it myself, often, in the clean-up we got at the Academy, and I'd been told to expect it on occasion as a healer.

But I hadn't been told of anyone like Clarissa taking part.

I'd been weeping too, I realized, and wiped my face and tear-blurred eyes on a sleeve. Edward and I looked at each other, and this time we both laughed.

"Do you know what happened?" he said. All in one flow, on one breath. Again we laughed together. From outside the door, the guard called—quietly but audibly. "Are you all right, your lordship?"

I went over and opened to him. "Come in, man," I said. He hesitated, then stepped inside. And stopped, staring. I turned. Edward was on his feet now, in his nightgown, as thin and pale as he'd been the day before, but standing almost upright. Grinning.

"Tren," he said to the guardsman, "I have been visited, by an angel. An actual angel, and she has—healed my soul. Thanks to the good work, of Master Luis."

He raised a constraining finger. "Now stay a minute. I'll want your help, in dressing." He turned to me. "Master Luis, please call Sara. Tell her I want, trousers, and a loose-fitting shirt." He laughed again,

running his hands down his scrawny torso. "Ha!
They're all loose-fitting now. It's time for me, to
totter up and down, the hall a bit. Maybe a few,
stairsteps. I've been too long, in this sickbed."

I went down the hall to Sara Sanders' door and did
what I'd been told, then left to find Keith. Thinking
what a burden of guilt could do, for Edward had
unknowingly embraced his injury as an opportunity
for self-punishment. I knew as surely as if I'd been
there, that in the last days of Clarissa Maltby's life,
her husband and her nurse had become lovers, probably an unintended outgrowth of comforting each
other. And after his wife's death, Edward, filled with
remorse, had sent Sara back to wherever she'd come
from, well-paid and highly recommended.

Eight years later, with Edward broken and seemingly dying, it was probably Keith who'd sent for her
to nurse his crippled duke.

And the light of Clarissa's compassion had let Edward
forgive himself, had freed him to recover.

Chapter 11
Father and Son

(Luis)

The chief usher stopped at Donald Maltby's door and knocked for me. It's doubtful Donald even knew I existed, and at any rate I had no standing to introduce myself. Seconds later the door opened, and Donald looked out at us—the usher in livery, I in my habit. My *uniform*, as we call it. I doubt he recognized it as Higuchian, but the collar marked me as a churchman.

It was the usher he spoke to, as protocol would have it, paying no attention to me. "What is it, Jacques?" he asked.

"Your lordship, I've brought a gentlemen to see you: Master Luis, of the Order of Saint Higuchi. A healer who's been working with your father. Captain Frazier commends him to you."

Donald examined me thoroughly now, enough that some would have resented it.

"Thank you, Jacques," he said quietly. "You may go now." Jacques left, and Donald spoke to me. "Your name again, sir?"

"I am Master Luis."

"Please come in, Master Luis."

I did, closing the door behind me. I'm taller than most, but Donald is taller than I, more strongly built, and had more presence than I'd expected. His aura marked him as essentially a scholar, hardwired to learn, not contest. But scholars can fight and command if called upon, and he was also hardwired to dominate. As was his father; it had probably contributed to their poor relationship. And his father had the advantages of seniority and rank. And of essence: he was *born* to command, as Donald was born to study.

Another thing influenced his potential: he had a deep desire to be important. Usefully important. A common enough desire, at least in the Order, but in his case suppressed, probably for fear he'd make a fool of himself.

"Sit down," he said, gesturing toward a straight-backed, upholstered chair. I sat, and he sat down facing me some six feet away. Distant enough to support his aloofness. A means of defense, of holding people off and hiding his insecurity. But not so far our fields couldn't interact.

"What does a Higuchian want of me?" he asked.

"Your help, Lord Donald."

My answer unsettled him, though he hid it well. "My help? Do you ask as a Higuchian, or as a private person?"

I answered pleasantly. It wouldn't take much to close him off, but even a briefly felt essence contact could be helpful. "I'm afraid there's not much I do as a private person," I answered. "Norlins has sent me to Sota to learn its defensive posture toward the Dkotas, and to improve it if I find it inadequate. The king's is nonexistent. Now I'm visiting the dukes. Starting here in Kato."

"Then you're a military man."

I had his interest now: a cautious interest. "I'm

Higuchian," I said, "military by training and experience, but not agressive unless forced to it. My favorite weapon is knowledge."

Knowledge. He nodded, still wary behind his facade.

"Your father is said to have been the most influential of Sota's dukes, but he is not able now to play a role. While you, though inexperienced, are generally recognized as his successor." I could sense him backing away. "Captain Frazier," I went on, "has assured me you have the intelligence, character, and presence to present yourself to the other nobles as a man worth listening to. That you're well educated in government, politics, and military thought, but lack experience. He suggested I approach you, and offer to be your mentor."

His aloofness had weakened, but the offer scared as much as interested him. He feared I'd find him worthless. "You've told me what Keith thinks of me," he said. "What do you think?"

Was that a whiff of boldness? "You have strong potential. Keith tells me you've been well and thoroughly taught, but your education was flawed by over-correction and lack of validation. Not uncommon for men whose instructor was their father; fathers can be over-critical of sons." I grinned now, a friendly—a comradely grin, but with a warrior's edge. "I'd feel privileged to be your mentor. You might find the experience enjoyable; certainly different. In age, we're not far apart, you and I, not like a father and son. An older cousin perhaps. And as Jacques said, I'm a trained healer. My specialty . . . is the human soul."

He was staring now, the last of his facade gone, but the wariness still strong: was I a charlatan? At some level, though, he knew I'd been truthful, and that my intentions were honest.

"What do *you* think of Captain Frazier?" I asked.

"Keith is a noble man," he said, "honest, wise, and good-hearted. And very competent."

"Then let me suggest you ask his opinion of my offer. And do you know Corporal Hamus?"

"Hamus? He's sparred with me. He says I'm very good; that in the guard, only Keith excels me with the sword. And himself. He didn't say that, but I know it from experience."

Somewhere inside Donald, the boy was still alive. "Good," I said. "Ask him what he thinks of *me* as a swordsman."

I got to my feet. "I plan to leave the morning after tomorrow. If you decide to come with me, you'll need to be ready when I am. Let me know. I'm staying at the bishop's manse, but I expect to return here later today, and again tomorrow, to speak further with Keith, and give healing sessions to your father. That's all I have to say for now. The choice is yours."

I stepped toward him, invading the protective space he liked, and thrust out a hand. He hesitated briefly, then he met it, and we shook.

I left the palace feeling optimistic. It seemed to me the young lordling might play a larger part than I'd thought.

It didn't take long for Donald to act. He went first to Hamus, who verified it was Frazier who'd asked him to test me. As for my swordsmanship, Hamus insisted I'd won easily.

Frazier had been away from the guardhouse at the time, so Donald returned to see him after supper, and found him in his quarters with his boots off. They'd talked about me and what I'd said, and Donald decided on the spot to accept my offer.

"You'll have to tell your father," Keith said, "since you're to be his proxy."

Donald hadn't confronted that. "Well . . ." he replied, "will you come with me? In case he has questions I can't answer?"

So Keith pulled his boots back on, and they'd gone

to Edward's door. There the guard told them Edward's healer, "the Higuchi," was with him, and that he'd been instructed not to interrupt. Even Widow Sanders had been dismissed to her room.

Donald looked to Keith, and the captain said they'd wait. Minutes later I opened the door, and there they were.

"Hello, Luis!" Keith said, "Donald and I have come to talk with his lordship. And since you're here, and it's you we've come to talk about, you might want to stay."

Donald was visibly surprised to see his father on his feet, standing almost straight, and not holding on to anything. Both father and son were ill at ease, Donald especially. Their conversation was brief. Edward's only instruction was to follow my instructions. He even managed to sound casual; comfortable with Donald serving as his proxy. He extended his hand. Donald met it uncertainly. "Good luck, son," Edward said. "You go with my love."

Then he embraced the young man.

Donald was like stone, and when Edward stepped away, answered stiffly. "With your leave, your lordship, I must go to my room and prepare."

Edward recoiled almost visibly, and Keith winced. "Come then, Donald," he said. "Your father and Master Luis have last-minute words."

We watched as they left. When they were gone, Edward turned to me, deeply hurt. "He has no love for me at all."

The words touched me, burning in my chest as if the pain were mine. "My lord," I answered, "let me tell you what he'll do as soon as he reaches the privacy of his room. And he will do it precisely because of the embrace you gave him. He will weep, hard and bitter tears. For lost years, lost opportunities of affection. But perhaps he will change, these next weeks. There are strong grounds for hope. Meanwhile it seems to me we'll see him able to rule, when the time comes, and perhaps more than just the duchy. At least you'll see him happier than he's been since childhood.

"And when he gets back to Kato, I believe he'll return that embrace you gave him. Look forward to it, sir. Then the two of you can start over."

I gripped his skinny arm. *The man's both frail and tough,* I thought. "Meanwhile," I told him, "we must bring you back to strength. You have work yet to do. If you'll send the guard for Widow Sanders, I'll teach *her* to heal with the hands."

Chapter 12
Father and Daughters

Morning sunlight slanted through the broad, south-facing window, back-lighting three persons eating breakfast. Eldred Youngblood speared another chop and cut it into large, but for him bite-size chunks. Wide of frame and wide of mouth, he weighed considerably more than his seventeen-year-old daughters combined.

Elvi tucked a small fragment of poached duck egg into her mouth and chewed daintily. Though she'd made herself daddy's girl, it was her late mother from whom she'd learned table manners. Her father wolfed down duck eggs in two bites.

"I've been examining the tax accounts of the duchies," she said, "and do not like what I've found."

His Majesty turned his eyes to her. She'd long tried to be manly. When she'd been younger, she'd wanted to be a man-at-arms, so he'd had a helmet and hauberk made for her, a small saber forged, child-sized spear and bow crafted, and arranged for her instruction in military horsemanship and weapons. For a while she'd trained diligently, but in time had outgrown both her armor and her interest, and taken up government instead. "Mary doesn't want to rule," she'd told him, "and someone will have to when you've grown old and die."

Eldred's eyebrows had raised. "I'm not yet forty, you know. You may have a long wait."

She'd neither blushed nor laughed. "That's all right, father," she'd replied. "While I wait, I'll be your deputy, and help you do your work."

Actually he'd found it endearing.

She'd been fifteen then. So he'd let her sit with him at his work table in the afternoon, reading reports, and drafting what her response would be if she were king. At first he'd critiqued them, but after a bit stopped, for it was time-consuming, and she seldom understood what he was getting at.

She seemed bright enough, in her way, but her invariable assumption was that if something appeared wrong, evil was at work, or at least criminality. As occasionally it was, but usually not. He'd never been able to coach her through that, so he'd stopped trying. Actually he sometimes reacted much as she did, without recognizing it.

He'd assumed she'd tire of the deputy game, but she was still at it. He had boxes of documents she'd written: analyses, "orders," policy proposals . . . always thanking her, telling her she was learning. And in fact she'd learned the *system* well, but generally her evaluations were at least skewed. Soon he'd learned to ignore her written reports, but when she brought something up orally, certainly with someone else present, he felt compelled to reply.

"Don't like what you found? Tell me about that."

"You have ordered the dukes to reduce the number of their armsmen, and they say they have. Yet their defense expenditures are as high as before. They're withholding something from you! There is cheating going on!"

"My dear, there is always cheating going on. It's why I send inspectors out. Meanwhile, the armsmen they let go must eat, so they receive severance payments, depending on their length of service, and whether they have wives and children. And these payments are charged to Defense, because that's where the obligations were incurred."

"But that's not right! If they are no longer armsmen, then their time is free. Let them work for their living, like honest men!"

"They do work, my dear. Each has either been given a grant of land for a farm, or is authorized to partake in some trade. But they must build a dwelling, and outbuildings, and clear and break the soil if they are to farm it. Or learn their new trade if they are to practice it. And meanwhile they must eat. Would you have the dukes reward loyal service with hunger and need?"

"They drink their money up!"

"Some do I'm sure, what money they receive. But much of their severence pay is in suitable land, tools, livestock . . . or the payment of a training fee, for they come to their new trade late in life."

None of it really registered on Elvi; her eyes were bright with exasperation. "It's not right!" she insisted. "They were already paid for their services!"

He reached a chubby paw and patted her much smaller hand. "My dear, I suggest you take it up with Archbishop Clonarty. Our Lord Jesus explained long ago the responsibilities of wealth. Besides, loyalty works both ways, and it was I who cost those men their positions. Soon their period of eligibility will run out, and then you will see an improvement in the royal income."

He looked again at his plate; he'd been forgetting to eat! "But enough of that! I can't sit here all morning. I must finish my breakfast and get to my audiences. People will be waiting for my attention:

tradesmen, artisans, farmers . . . They depend on me. It's the burden of being king!"

Elvi bit back a retort. "Yes father," she said pouting.

He returned his attention to his food then, but his daughters finished ahead of him, and with his leave, wandered out to the palace gardens.

"I don't trust the dukes," Elvi said, "not even the ones father installed last fall. Nor the barons. Those so-called 'discharged' armsmen are still serving. They haven't even heard of the reduction. Nothing's changed except on paper."

"Father's inspectors would know," Mary said reasonably. "They arrive in their own times, unannounced, can inspect the armsmen's lodgings, watch them at drill . . . they can even visit the new domiciles of the men discharged, if they want to."

Elvi sniffed. "I trust the inspectors no more than I trust the nobles."

Mary nodded. Elvi was chronically suspicious—an unhappy way to be—and to argue with her was useless. Though Mary sometimes pointed out that counter arguments at least existed, without making an issue of them. *She's my twin, after all, and has no other friend. Father is patient, but too often condescending. She needs someone to speak freely to, without feeling depreciated.*

❖❖ ❖❖ ❖❖

Eldred often lunched in his office with some important person, the minister of the royal treasury perhaps, or a baron or merchant, or one of his spies come to report. Rather often it was the archbishop. On this day it was a cousin, Captain Carnes, commander of the palace guard.

Lunch was the king's lighter meal, a gesture toward controlling his weight. He raised a small spoonful of strawberry custard to his full lips, mouthed it with appreciation, then swallowed. "Tell me, Wesley, whatever became of my Dinneh throne guard? His name was Stephen. He seemed a nice young man, a backwoods peasant through and through of course, but with an innate sense of manners. He stood at my right shoulder. Then one day he wasn't there, and I haven't seen him since. I trust he didn't get into trouble. Or was it homesickness?"

"I wondered the same thing, Your Majesty, when he didn't show up at muster one morning. Not even his squadmates knew where he was. But he has relatives in Hasty, an uncle and his family, whatever 'uncle' means to those people, so I had the man brought in, and questioned him. It seems Stephen was afflicted by religiosity: he'd joined the Higuchians."

Eldred jerked as if slapped, and thoughts came helter-skelter. *The Higuchians were preying on his guardsmen! Had the Dinneh been their spy? Who did I give an audience to while he attended me? Clonarty among others. What might the spy have overheard? The Higuchians' farm had been bought months ago. They must have had an agent here to see that their building was properly built, and Stephen had been his spy. He must have been!*

He'd been victimized!

Chapter 13
The Swift Current Dinneh

Lemmi Tsinnajinni had spotted the four riders when they were more than a mile away, cresting a grassy hill against the backdrop of the Black Mountains a few miles beyond. They were coming for him, he thought, and kept riding.

He'd encountered his first Swift Current Dinneh the day before, a solitary youth scouting for buffalo. They'd talked, and Lemmi discovered their dialects were more alike than he'd expected. Then the youth had turned and galloped back toward the mountains already visible in the west, to tell Chief Nagani Yazzie he'd discovered a Dinneh from a tribe many days to the east. A stranger with a message for him—from Mazeppa Tall Man of the Dkota.

Lemmi had been right about the four riders, and they rode together into the mountains. There the land was rugged and rocky, the streams small, the forest largely of pine, and the trail much used. After a bit, they came to an encampment, its tipis much like those at Many Geese. Nagani Yazzie was sitting crosslegged by a small outdoor fire. As Lemmi and his escort approached, Yazzie unfolded his old legs, and stood.

"Here is the man you sent us for," said the escort's leader.

Yazzie greeted him with reserve. "I am told you are Dinneh," he said, "from a tribe many days ride toward the sun."

"That's right. I am of the Sancroy Dinneh."

Yazzie's wolf-like face looked past him, jaw set. After a moment he gestured. "Sit," he said, and lowered himself back onto the ground. Lemmi sat to his right, out of the smoke.

"What is the land like where you come from?" Yazzie asked.

So, Lemmi thought, in at least one respect beyond language, the Dinneh here are like the Dinneh at home; like the Dkota, for that matter. They don't get right to the point. "It is a land called Soggo," he answered, "in the north of the Kingdom of Sota. It is mostly flat, with many lakes and streams, and mostly covered with trees, many with broad leaves like the cottonwood, but also pines, some of which grow very large." With his hands, Lemmi gestured a diameter. "But when the trees are cut down, the land is fertile."

"Are the Dinneh numerous there?"

"In Sota, no single people is numerous. But counting all the peoples together, they are *very* numerous."

Nagani Yazzie looked into the fire, digesting what he'd been told. After a minute he went on. "I am told you have a message for me from Mazeppa Tall Man. What kind of Dinneh does the bidding of a Dkota?"

"The Sancroy Dinneh have no grudge with the Dkota. And Mazeppa wishes to be the friend of the Swift Current Dinneh."

Nagani Yazzie contemplated the small, burned-down fire before speaking again. "Mazeppa Tall Man consorts with witches who ride through the sky in a canoe.

He may have become a witch himself. I will have nothing to do with such a person. If he wants these sacred mountains, he will have to take them from us."

So he knows about the Helverti. "It isn't these mountains he wants. He told me they belong to the Swift Current people, and should remain so. He wants to take the land of the Sotans, east of the Great Grass. And he wants you to help him. It will be a large war, with many honors to be gained, and when the Sotans have been broken, the buffalo people will no longer need to fear the dirt-eaters."

Nagani Yazzie pursed his lips scornfully. "Cochran, who is called 'Kills Buffalo With His Knife,' told me all that. He is chief of the Ulster, and now calls himself brother to Mazeppa. I told him I already do not fear the dirt-eaters, and do not trust Mazeppa. He was to tell his new brother that. Mazeppa was a fool to send you, after I did not believe Cochran, with whom I have been friends a long time. Our peoples joined together in our fathers' time, to defend each other against the Wolves, who used to war on us. After that, the wolf warriors did not trouble us, but now our alliance is over."

"Mazeppa thought you might listen to another Dinneh, someone who speaks your tongue."

Nagani Yazzie shrugged. "Why does Mazeppa want land east of the Great Grass? It would be hard to hunt buffalo there, if there are any."

"In many ways, Sota is a good land," Lemmi answered. "The Sotans never lack for wood. They have more water than they know what to do with. They have many women famous for their beauty, and many gardens in which they grow food. And many spotted buffalo, tame and easy to kill."

Nagani Yazzie grunted scornfully, and gestured about them. "The Swift Current people have all the wood they want. They have all the water they want. Their women are better than Sotan women. Also, the

Swift Current People do not have to garden. They
have all the buffalo they can eat. Not the poor spotted
buffalo of which I have heard, but buffalo with thick
warm fur, and fat humps."

Lemmi nodded. He'd foreseen the answer. "I will
tell Mazeppa that. Is there anything I can tell him
for you that he will be *glad* to hear?"

"Tell him we do not fear the dirt-eaters. And we
do not fear his witches. Only Dinneh witches can
harm the Dinneh. Tell him his sky witches will bring
harm to his people. Witches are poisonous; when a
witch befriends you, you are doomed. Unless he kills
them, they will destroy him. Tell him that."

Lemmi nodded, a single nod. "I will tell him all
those things."

"Good. Would you like something to eat?"

They ate buffalo hump, and talked about their tribal
beliefs. The Swift Current Dinneh knew about Jesus,
but they did not worship him as the Dkota and Ulster
did. To the Swift Current Dinneh, the pope was at
most a vague rumor, and they'd never heard of
Norlins. Compared with them, the Sancroy Dinneh
were strict Catholics.

Nagani Yazzie invited Lemmi to stay with him in
his lodge that night, and Lemmi agreed. While they
finished eating, a man of perhaps thirty years trotted up. Nagani Yazzie invited him to join them, and
cutting off a large slice of meat, gave it to his tribesman, whose name was Tsosi Begay. Briefly they talked
about the weather, the upcoming hunt, and Lemmi's
errand. It seemed the entire village knew he'd been
sent by Mazeppa.

"As Nagani Yazzie knows," Tsosi said, "Mazeppa Tall
Man and I grew up together."

"That is true," Yazzie replied. "Enlighten this
Dinneh from far away."

At age nine, Tsosi Begay had been captured by a
party of Dkota. For six years he'd lived with the

Coyote Clan of the Beaver Lodge Dkota, but eventually ran away and returned to his people, partly for shame at the coyote being the totem of his adoptive clan, but also because he missed the holy mountains.

At first the Dkota boys had made fun of Tsosi because he knew no Merkan, and because he was so dark. That was how he'd learned to fight so well. And as he learned Merkan, and Dkota ways and beliefs, life became much easier.

But even when he'd been new there, Tsosi was not the one most picked on. Mazeppa, who was a year younger, had been the butt of many jokes. Something was wrong with his body. Often he stumbled. He couldn't run very fast, couldn't fight very well, and was a poor shot with the bow. His calling name was "Clumsy." More than once, in riding contests, he'd fallen from his horse.

But Mazeppa never quit, never gave up. While still a child, he began spending hours alone with his bow, shooting at anything that hopped or ran or slithered or flew, until his fingers were raw. When nothing else offered itself, he shot at gopher mounds. He never became the best shot, or the best rider, but he did become proficient. And he had an older brother, a very good wrestler, who could also walk on his hands, do handsprings, and kick a ball hung higher from a crossbar than any other youth his age. It hung higher than he could reach. So Mazeppa asked his brother to teach him to do those things. He almost killed himself learning to kick a ball hung no higher than his head.

After greeting the rising sun, Mazeppa, as he grew older, often left camp running alone, instead of with friends. If you watched, you would see his child form disappear into the distance, not returning till much later. Once another boy, who was thought the best runner of boys their age, followed Mazeppa's tracks, to see if he lay down somewhere under a bush to rest.

Mazeppa came back far ahead of him. The other boy, when he returned, told that Mazeppa had turned into a coyote, and ran around him in circles, a story much repeated.

After that, Mazeppa was looked at differently. Before he reached his fourteenth winter, he was not only the best distance runner among boys his age, but the best sprinter. And the best fighter; no other boy his age wanted to fight him anymore. He allowed no one else to prevail at any time; he'd lost all sense of proper balance, of harmony. His calling name became "He Who Must Win."

Having told his story, Tsosi Begay made his parting courtesies and left.

The next morning, Nagani Yazzie gave Lemmi his final message. "Tell Mazeppa Tall Man I will not ask my people to go far away and die because he needs help to get what he wants. What Mazeppa Tall Man wants is his business, not ours."

Then Lemmi left the Black Mountains, escorted by two warriors. It was a pleasant ride, the three of them exchanging stories and asking questions. The Swift Current men were intrigued, and at times amused by what Lemmi told them of the settlement of Dinnehville, in the Township of Big Pines. The strangeness seemed even stranger, knowing that generations of Dinneh had been born, spent their lives and died in that place. Finally they separated from him a few miles beyond the foothills, and returned home. They'd have liked to hear more, but a herd of buffalo had been located, and Nagani Yazzie's people were preparing to go on a hunt.

That evening when he camped, Lemmi radioed his contacts, summarizing for them what he'd learned. "The old chief is sending Mazeppa an earful," he finished. "Food for thought."

"Fine," said Tahmm, "as long as Mazeppa doesn't punish the messenger for delivering the message."

"I don't think he will, but if he tries, the messenger may challenge him."

Chapter 14
Taking Care of Business

(Luis)

Donald's room had a balcony, and on the day before we left Kato Town, we sat on it and talked. On side by side chairs angled so we could easily look at one another. And equally important, close enough that our energy fields interacted directly. By feel, I talked them into something like harmony while giving him my impression of the duchy, which is attractive and clearly fertile. And from there, about growing up in Aarschot, and amusing things that happened. All prompting reminiscences from him. As a child he seemed to have been reasonably happy. Certainly there were happy events to revisit, and our being in phase reenergized them.

Once he got underway, he talked more than I did—until I began telling stories about the Aarschot brother house; he ate them up. When I left to give his father another healing session, Donald was looking forward to our trip.

We left at dawn, with almost no one yet on the road. We wore used work clothes I'd bought the day before from the Diocese "poor bin." Two young bucks out for adventure and jobs, wearing wide-brimmed, hand-woven oat straw hats. The air was humid, and by mid-morning more than warm. Between the sweat and the road dust, our faces and clothes were soon dirty.

We didn't have a packhorse. Being heavier than me, Donald rode what had been my pack horse—it had been broken to riding—and I rode my saddle horse. Donald was now Gerald Redgrave, his choice, and he called me "Gus," finding the name amusing.

Just leaving the palace and Kato Town had a liberating effect on him. He was away from the surroundings of his past, with no real compulsion to return. As an expression of independence, he felt free to fart openly, and now and then we exchanged blasts, grimaces and laughs.

Mostly we kept to an easy quick-step trot, occasionally dismounting to walk a mile or so, leading and resting the horses. Donald was so cheerful, his father and Keith would have been astonished. I'd drilled mood guidance at the Academy, but had never used it in any serious way, prior to Kato's ducal palace. I knew I could do it, but I hadn't fully realized the effects it could have.

Mostly the road followed the Sota River through nearly continuous riverine forest, angling occasionally onto the uplands—prairie, fields and woods. Pretty country. We slept in haysheds. The weather had been dry, but in June, Keith had said, thunderstorms could roll through by day or night. And while we had the time and money to sleep and eat at inns along the way, Donald might be recognized, and *that* we couldn't afford. He'd traveled to Hasty with his father when he was fifteen, so his face was known, certainly to innkeepers, some of whom were no doubt part of a royal informer network, paid for useful information.

The word would get out anyway, of course. Eldred probably had at least one spy in every ducal court including Kato's. Within the next week he might hear of Donald's leaving with me. At least he'd learn that Donald was no longer at the palace, and maybe put two and two together.

Meanwhile we ate jerky from Keith Frazier's travel stock, while from farmers along the way I bought bread and cheese and prunes. And farm-brewed beer, which I carried in a large bottle, in a basket padded with grass. Occasionally we snacked on wild onions in bottomland woods; our breath and sweat reeked of them.

My mother wouldn't have approved of us at all.

I liked to think the horseflies didn't like it either. The deerflies didn't mind though, hitting without warning, with a special liking for our temples. But we were soon used to that. Meanwhile we talked a lot. I learned about his reading—he'd read and reread most of the palace books—and about his mother, whom he dearly loved. He'd have been much happier if she'd lived. He in turn learned more about my years as a novice and brother at Aarschot, back in Mizzoo, and found it as interesting as I intended.

He was curious about how I'd helped his father so much. So I told him, in simple, meaningful terms: various painful events in his father's life tied in with the accident, and I'd guided him through them—helped him unravel them for himself. It was a skill taught to all brothers being trained as Masters.

And of course I told him what I had in mind for him, as my assistant and his father's unofficial envoy, keeping it casual.

Meanwhile his young beard had gone unshaven since before he'd been embraced by his father, and perhaps a day or two before that. Fortunately it was showing up darker than his blond scalp, and dark would disguise him more quickly. As the days passed, he'd be increasingly hard to recognize, certainly by people not expecting to see him.

Finally we reached the little town of West Crossing, on the Misasip. There a ferry crossed to North Landing at the end of the Sugar Grove Road. Up the hill from North Landing, and half mile east, was the brother house.

Carlos and Peng were prepared for us; I'd radioed them each evening, when I'd leave our hayshed of the night to relieve myself by a nearby shrub. As planned, Donald was to stay awhile at the brother house, as an older than usual novice. With his scholarly interests, he'd find it enjoyable. Meanwhile I'd be getting local business handled.

It was Carlos who showed him around, introducing him to the facilities, novices, brothers and staff. As Gerald Redgrave, of course. Meanwhile I talked briefly with Peng. I needed Donald as confident and able as Peng could get him, and in our class at the Academy, Peng had been the best in cleaning people up. My prep work on Donald had gone well, but Peng was more talented and better trained, and he'd have him longer.

❖❖❖   ❖❖❖   ❖❖❖

I didn't know what Eldred might have learned the past few days, or might learn tomorrow, but a courier from the palace had arrived at the brother house just the day before, with a message from His Majesty: "I wish to see Master Luis as soon as he returns." It was as close to a command as a king could issue to a churchman acting for the Sacred Congregation, especially one whose mission introduction had been signed by Cardinal Termini.

It seemed prudent to humor Eldred, and at any rate my warrior muse wasn't ringing alarm bells, so the morning after my return, I rode to the palace, where I was escorted promptly to Eldred's audience chamber.

Paddy Gwynn stood at his right shoulder, half a step back. I didn't give Paddy a second look; not even a first. My attention was on the king. Eldred looked at me for perhaps thirty seconds without speaking, something which no doubt shook most who were exposed to it, wondering what he knew. I spent it examining his aura. Given his power mode and need to dominate, I'd focus on limiting the damage.

Finally he spoke. "Well, Master Luis, I suppose you've been traveling."

"I have indeed, Your Majesty. I'm just back from Kato Town, where I met the duke. And Captain Frazier, who is acting as his deputy until his lordship is able to carry the full burden of his responsibilities again."

"And when might that be?"

"Physically the duke is frail." I paused to cross myself. "But mentally he is strong and sharp, and each day reviews the matters of government with Captain Frazier, advising and giving orders."

"Hmh." Eldred's gaze was intent. Something was bubbling to the surface, and I wondered if he was going to ask next about Donald. He surprised me. "It has come to my attention," he said, "that you have stolen one of my throne guards. What have you to say for yourselves, you and Master Lemmi?"

"Stolen?"

His anger flashed. "Do not trifle with me, churchman! You enticed Stephen Nez into your Order."

The railing kept us far enough apart to limit the direct interaction of our energy fields, but I made do. "Enticed? Your Majesty has been misinformed."

"I speak of the young Dinneh who stood to my right when you first visited me. I have it on good authority."

This wasn't anything Carlos or Peng knew about;

they'd have told me. Or Stephen; I'd seen him the evening before, and his aura had reflected no hint of anything withheld. He'd told me he'd be leaving for Dinnehville the following Monday, to arrange for the sing.

"May I be privy to those reports?" I asked. "I do not imply that anyone is lying, though someone may be. But often what first appear to be lies are honest errors."

Eldred gnawed on that a moment. He wasn't used to being cross-examined. "I had missed the young man's presence," he said, "and asked the commander of my palace guard what had become of him. He'd wondered the same thing, and had asked Stephen's squadmates. They hadn't known, but they told him that Stephen had an uncle in Hasty. So I ordered Captain Uuka, my chief of Intelligence, to locate the uncle, and bring him to me for questioning.

"It seems Stephen had met with two Higuchians— a Master Lemmi and a Master Luis—and that he was going to the brother house. The uncle had never heard of Higuchians, and Stephen explained they were Churchmen."

I frowned as if considering. "Ah. Perhaps he'd told his uncle he'd 'seen' us, not 'met with' us. Lemmi mentioned, after our audience with you, that he thought one of your throne guards looked Dinneh. Clearly the young man you're concerned about."

Eldred was frowning again, his wide mouth pursed.

"As for our names," I went on, "he was there when we were introduced to you. If I remember rightly, Lemmi told you *he* was Dinneh—Blood of Christ Dinneh. Your Stephen would have noticed and remembered."

"Or," Eldred countered, "he may have said exactly what his uncle reported: that he'd met with you."

I nodded. "True. Tell me, were the gate guards informed of his—departure?"

"They would have been, yes."

"Would they have stopped him if he'd returned to Hasty to visit his uncle?"

Eldred looked thoughtful now. "If they'd recognized him." I could almost hear the rest of it in his mind: *and Stephen is tall, and there are few Dinneh in Hasty. He'd be hard to miss.*

"If he'd gone to the brother house to meet us, then come back to Hasty to tell his uncle, he'd probably have been noticed when he returned. Perhaps the gate guards could tell you. And if he didn't return, he couldn't have told his uncle. At least it would seem so. It would have had to be before he went to the brother house."

"Yes. Well. That may be."

Eldred was uncomfortable with it, juggling my suggestions and implications, trying to see how they fitted. I gave him a few seconds, then broke the silence myself. Best to remain in charge if I could.

"Meanwhile, Your Majesty, I've come bringing a matter of my own. It seemed unimportant when we first heard of it—Lemmi and I, that is. It's well known that the Dkota use iron pots, steel knives and hatchets, and they had to come from somewhere, so Lemmi looked into that. And learned of an itinerant iron monger, one of several who trade with the Dkota."

Now I shifted focus on him again, this time from steel, and possibly weapons, to religion. "Lemmi asked whether he knew anything of the Dkota faith, and the man told him that while they recognize Jesus as God's son, they're seriously pagan in most respects. For one thing, they claim that their great chief, Mazeppa, meets with witches who fly through the sky in a canoe. That supports the rumor you'd heard. One might wonder what such 'witches' have been doing there. If in fact they are real."

The thought distracted him, and I talked my way out of the audience chamber, leaving him with it.

Hopefully it would blunt his certainty about Mazeppa. Meanwhile his mind was off Stephen.

◁▷◅ ◁▷◅ ◁▷◅

Masters are also trained in disguise—a skill sometimes useful on missions—so after supper, Carlos blackened my hair, then widened my narrow face by gluing on mutton chops. Considering how bushy and curly they were, I suppose they were the shearings of some curly-headed novice's introductory haircut.

Then I rode off to Hasty again, with a message and package for guardsman Paddy Glynn. At the guardhouse I found the duty corporal perched on a tall stool behind a counter. In my version of Paddy's brogue, I said I was Paddy's cousin, that his grandfather had died, and the package was from him. If the corporal had chosen to snoop, he'd have found "granddads dager," which "the oud man wanted ye to hav as a kepsak," and that the family looked forward to seeing him soon. But without so much as a look, the corporal stuck it into a wall cabinet with several rows of cubbyholes.

The real message was hidden in the apparent message. Deciphered, it read: "Bow & Saber Tuesday evening. One-Eye." The key was simple to use and easy to remember—a key every brother learns when he graduates, and learns again whenever it's changed, which is seldom. It might not hold long against someone who suspected, but to a guard or page or usher, the message would look harmless.

◁▷◅ ◁▷◅ ◁▷◅

The next evening I walked into town. And into the Bow & Saber, wearing an eye patch. My hair was re-blackened, but my mutton chops were gone, replaced by soft lambskin pads in my mouth, behind my side teeth, filling out my cheeks. My left jaw had an ugly three-inch scar.

The Bow & Saber was one of several taverns in Hasty that catered to armsmen, guardsmen, and veterans. I arrived early. There were only eight men there besides myself, and only three in uniform. Paddy was nowhere in sight. I ordered a pint, then sat down at a small table with my back to the wall. From there I could see everyone in the room.

It was a decent brew, and I took my time with it. When Paddy came in, I had half of it left. He looked around, his gaze crossing mine in passing, to show he'd recognized me. Then he went to the bar. A minute later, a mug in his hand, he was chatting with the tapman, setting things up so he could leave early. Then he turned, leaning back against the bar as if watching the door. After a couple minutes I killed my mug, set it on the table, and without a glance at Paddy, left the tavern.

With the summer solstice near, it was still early dusk. On the other side of the street was a printer's shop, and I crossed, to stand at the window and watch the printer work. His quick hands took a printed sheet of paper from the press, hung it on a rack for the ink to dry, then emplaced another to be printed. He did about three pages a minute. Cranking the press down and back up took most of the time. It seemed to me a lever would be a lot faster.

At the Academy they print as many pages as they want as swiftly as they want.

My warrior muse told me Paddy was crossing the street behind me, but I waited till the last minute to turn. A good strategy if someone's stalking you; that way you take *him* by surprise.

"Hello, Paddy," I said.

He grinned. "Hello, One-Eye. Where'll we go?"

"Somewhere we can talk privately. You know Hasty better than I do."

We went to a small park in the shadow of the town wall, to a bench beneath a basswood tree. We could sit side by side and talk, while seeing anyone approaching. Dusk was thickening. Even one of the palace guard wouldn't likely recognize Paddy at twenty yards, and anyway a park wasn't where they'd be in the evening.

Paddy's "new job," he told me, wasn't too bad. Most palace guards were selected from among the armsmen, for size and bearing, but after a morning of tests, and maybe discussion, Paddy'd been assigned directly.

After a few days he'd been sent for an interview with the king. His throne guards had to impress nobles, merchants, and foreign emissaries. The interview lasted most of an hour; Eldred seemed to enjoy Paddy's fictitious adventures as a freight raftsman.

Throne guard was what I'd intended for him—he'd hear the king talk about all kinds of things—but just being a guardsman would have gotten interesting rumors and information.

The food was decent, he told me, and the duties easy. In fact, from Paddy's viewpoint, the guardsmen had too much free time. Instead of squatting in the zendo developing *fudochi*, they drank or threw darts in the taverns, or went upstairs with the girls. And when their pay was spent, instead of studying the thirteen strategies and eleven approaches, or practicing the fourteen postures and thirty moves, most of them played cards or shot dice for chits, while sparring orally. The gambling and prostitutes in particular caused quarrels and grudges. And there were cliques.

The guardsmen trained with weapons two hours a day, but few really worked at it. "The veterans," he went on, "are pretty good at their weapons drills, which aren't that difficult, but they think they're better than they are. When sparring, oi have to be careful not to make them look bad, or they'd have it in for me. Oi've already made one enemy." He chuckled. "He's bigger than me, but not much. Oi don't think he'd have tried me, but his clique expected it of him. And he's the kind that, if you beat him, he's apt to lay for you with a cosh or the like, unless he's *really* afraid of you. Oi mean *really* afraid. So oi worked him over good, really knocked him around—lots of bruises and cuts—leaving no doubt at all in his mind. At the end he had to gather his wits a couple of minutes before he could get to his feet. Him being a bully, most of the others enjoyed the watching, and his clique has pretty much left him."

He eyed me then. "Don't worry about me, Luis. Bhatti and Soong made sure we pay attention to our warrior muse." He chuckled, no doubt remembering the traps and ambushes they'd set to catch the novices, and sometimes a brother, unaware. Coming out of the messroom perhaps, or the latrine. "Talk about empowering!" Paddy finished. "I can smell a trap or ambush."

I knew his *ki* was strong, probably stronger than mine at that stage of the game. Letting my attention be distracted had been an occasional problem, before I went to the Academy. Partly because of having a strong secondary muse for what Tahmm called "scholar with a nature focus," that had blocked my warrior muse now and then. Most people have a pretty strong secondary muse, but judging from his aura, Paddy's warrior muse stood by itself; he's a warrior through and through. A good-hearted warrior. There was, of course, a false muse—an expression of false personality, whose essence is fear. The false muse can be very active—and seductive!—in producing and selling counterfeit messages. But Paddy's false personality was remarkably muted.

So far, nothing he'd heard seemed relevant to the mission, but he'd only stood a few throne watches, and probably some of the more sensitive matters were discussed without guards present. But I could hardly ask for a better spy. Of course, if he learned anything urgent, getting it to Carlos or Peng in time might be a problem.

So I decided to ask Tahmm to bend regulations and give me a radio for Paddy. If anyone asked, he could use the usual cover—"religious amulet." Tahmm would probably turn me down, but it seemed worth a try.

Stephen Nez, of course, had been a throne guard for weeks, and I'd hoped for important information out of him. But questioning had needed to be relaxed and casual. For two reasons: he still really liked Eldred, and he was new to the Order. But more important, when Carlos had asked what sorts of things were discussed in royal audiences, it turned out that Stephen hadn't paid much attention. He'd gone to the job ignorant, with limited perspective to help relate things.

Six years earlier, that had been true of Paddy, too. Then he'd ended up in the middle of the "lizard war."

Like Stephen, Paddy found Eldred likable. "Though he's a bit sly, and they say his temper can be really bad. But the problems oi've seen brought before him, he's handled justly. They've not dealt with matters of defense of course, or the dukes, or the Dkota. Mostly with property and business disputes, taxes, and complaints about officials."

Almost the last thing we talked about, before he went to the guard quarters for curfew, was the royal family. Since the queen's death, some years earlier, it consisted of Eldred and his daughters. It was the daughters who interested me. Paddy's description matched Linkon's: they looked alike, and they were pretty. And more interesting, sometimes a throne guard would be assigned to them, though Paddy had only glimpsed them in passing.

"You'd have little trouble telling them apart," he said. "Mary looks pleasant, Elvi looks sour. They say Mary likes to go boating, sometimes with Elvi, but usually with what they call a 'handmaiden'—a sort of hired friend. With a throne guard to row. They ride around on the river, the two young ladies talking with each other."

Finally I went to the night gate, where the guards let me out of town, and I walked back to the brother farm. It was time to give Kabibi something interesting to do. Inside the palace. It might come to nothing of course. There are no guarantees. Good old *fudochi*! The muse speaks, and you act without fretting. The Saint and our Academy instructors tell us this is a free-will universe, as far as people are concerned—Humans, Fohanni, or what have you—and things take their own course. Even our muses can't see the future with certainty. But they read the probabilities and vectors. They do that.

Chapter 15
The Spy

(Luis)

I needed a general cover identity to use in Hasty. It didn't need to be deep, or mean anything. All it needed to do was deflect attention. Mislead. And an accent can mislead. The Shuffling dumped a bunch of Flemish and Spanish at what would become known as Aarschot, and they intermarried till their old languages disappeared—before my time—leaving mainly a few cuss words. But the nearby settlement of Nedreby had been all Swedes, and kept the tongue. Three of my fellow novices at Aarschot had been from there, and I learned to mimic them.

While I'd been away at Kato, Carlos got to know Father Sando, Pastor Linkon's assistant, who it turned out is a Swede from Ilanoy. So I rode to Sugar Grove and talked with him. He said my put-on accent was good enough to fool non-Swedes at least. "Just don't lay it on too thickly," he warned. "It might draw attention instead of deflecting it."

I'd be out of luck if someone spoke Swedish to me, of course, but so far as Sando had ever heard, there was only one settlement in Sota where people spoke the language, so it wasn't much of a risk. "Tell people you're from Grassmark," he said. "It's in the barony of La Cienega, in the Duchy of Oak Groves. Not many people in Hasty even recognize a Swedish accent. They'll just know you have an accent." In the Royal Domain, he went on, there are a lot of Swedish names—the Youngblood, or Ljungblad clan was Swedish originally—but they married so much outside the community, their descendants speak only Merkan.

So I decided to borrow the name of my old Nedreby friend, Arne Asplund. Sando said it was as good as any.

The next morning I wore a floppy, hand-woven grass hat. I'd shaved for my meeting with Eldred, so my "beard" was only stubble, hardly noticeable. But workman's clothes completed the disguise well enough.

I rented a rowboat with an awning, and anchored it maybe seventy yards from the royal dock, in the Sancroy a little above the Misasip. I was willing to give this project two days—no more—though from what Paddy had said, two weeks might not be enough. I really needed to get about other business, but I also wanted Kabibi to have more information. At least that's how I explained it to myself.

Tahmm told us in lecture once that some people claim you can enforce your will on the physical universe—when conditions are right, and you're acting on the advice of your muse. But according to Tahmm, that's backward. How it really works, he says, is your muse knows the moment to moment odds for certain possible events, which is the closest we can come to knowing the future in a free-will universe. It can tell you when the time is ripe: when your chance is best. Nudge you, whisper to you to do such and such. That's what muses do.

And you can feel that nudge, if you're paying attention, and you choose to. It's up to you. And if your mind isn't too fixed on something else, or wallowing around in counter-intentions or fears or resentments or anger or poor poor thing or what-have-you—you may act on that nudge, that impulse. And the outcome may make it *seem* like the universe obeyed you.

Anyway there I was on a beautiful June morning, sitting under the little awning in my rented boat, holding a fishing pole but not watching the bobber. I hadn't even baited my hook; didn't want the distraction of a fish. It was the royal dock that held my attention. After ten or fifteen minutes, two young women and a man walked out on the dock. The women sat down on a cushioned bench, while the man, an armed guardsman, stood at a sort of parade rest forty or fifty feet from them. To give them privacy no doubt. Presumably they were waiting for a boat to pick them up.

I took the spyglass from my shoulder bag and looked them over. It looked like an ordinary pocket spyglass, foot long, but the optics had been designed by a technician at the Academy. The awning put me in the shadow, and the frame, and my floppy hat, broke up the silhouette; so at that distance the risk of being noticed was minor. The guardsman looked no more than twelve or fifteen feet away, and held a crossbow cranked and ready. But he was paying no attention to a fisherman seventy yards off.

It was obvious at once which twin was which. Switching on my belt com, I set it to "record," and began examining Mary and her aura, speaking quietly, telling what I saw. After two minutes or so I focused on Elvi and repeated the procedure. Their auras were as different as their facial expressions.

When I'd finished describing Elvi's aura, I turned back to Mary. She was looking at something, and pointing downstream toward the Misasip. I promptly capped my spy glass and put it back in my bag. Sure enough, the royal pleasure boat was approaching, with two servants or guards at the oars. They passed not more than thirty yards from me.

For whatever reason, I pulled my hook from the water, attached a ten-inch sucker from my bait bucket, and tossed it back in. The pleasure boat loaded the girls and their guard and pulled away from the dock, upstream against the current of the Sancroy. In my direction. Suddenly something hit my bait hard, and I horsed on the pole. A twenty-five-inch pike arced through the morning sunlight to land flopping in my boat.

And what do you know! Mary pointed at me, laughing in delight, clapping her hands! It gave me a chill; a good kind. I wasn't sure what our muses were up to, but something. I stayed there for a couple more minutes, then pulled the anchor up and headed back to the rental dock.

From her spontaneous response to the flying pike, and from an instant of essence contact so light and natural you could wonder if it had actually happened, I'd learned important things about Mary Youngblood. Especially—and this took me by surprise—I'd learned it was time for her to leave the palace. To change from Daddy's girl to Mary's girl. And now I knew what Kabibi's mission was.

I just didn't know why.

Chapter 16
New Status for Lemmi

When Lemmi Tsinnajinni arrived back at Many Geese, he stopped his horses outside the chief's tipi. He'd report to Mazeppa before taking his gear inside. The weather had turned hot and humid, the prairie breeze slept, and the flies were making the most of it. The sides of Mazeppa's tipi were rolled waist high for ventilation. They could see saw each other through the open door, and Mazeppa beckoned Lemmi in.

"It is good to see Mazeppa Tall Man again," Lemmi said. "I have been to the Black Mountains, as you instructed."

Mazeppa gestured at another back rest, and Lemmi sat down against it. "What have you to tell me about it?" the chief asked.

"The redgrass land I passed through is beautiful, and so are the mountains and forest. I can see why the Swift Current people live there."

"Indeed," Mazeppa replied. By the standards of the buffalo peoples, he was edgy, impatient. "Did you talk with Nagani Yazzie?"

"We spoke at length."

Mazeppa grunted. "What was said?"

"He asked why you sent me. I told him you wanted an alliance with the Swift Current people. He answered that Mazeppa Tall Man consorts with witches who ride through the sky in a canoe, and that he would have nothing to do with such a person." Lemmi shrugged. "I had no answer to that.

"He then said you want the Sacred Mountains, and that the Swift Current Dinneh are not giving them to anyone. I told him it wasn't the mountains you want, but the Kingdom of Sota, east of the Great Grass.

"He asked why you trouble yourself with the Swift Current people, if you want to war eastward? I answered as you instructed: that you would like his help. That the Sotans have many men; that it will be a great fight, and when it is over, those who fight beside Mazeppa will share in the wealth of the Sotans. And the buffalo people will no longer need to fear the dirt-eaters."

Lemmi's face and voice were calm, showing no trace of apology for the answers he'd brought. "Nagani Yazzie asked what this Sotan wealth consists of. I told him the Sotans have much wood; that the Sotan forest goes on and on for days. That the Sotans have much sweet water; rivers so wide, you cannot hear a man shout on the other side. That Sotan women are famous for their beauty, and that Sotans have great gardens in which they grow food of many kinds."

Mazeppa's lips thinned. He hadn't foreseen that question, and while Lemmi's answer didn't appeal to him, he couldn't think of a better one. He had not spoken of what Jesus had said to him. His own people would have difficulty accepting that. And among them, ruling was not an important concept.

"What did he say to that?" the chief asked.

"That the Swift Current people have all the wood they want and all the water they want. That their women are better than Sotan women, and they have

all the buffalo they can eat. And that his people do
not fear the dirt-eaters. That it is Mazeppa, not the
dirt-eaters, who wants to rule everyone. Also that he
does not fear your witches; only Dinneh witches can
threaten the Swift Current people. That the friendship of witches is poison; that unless you kill the
witches or drive them away, they will destroy you, and
afterward your *chindi* will poison your people for a
very long time.

"He said he will not ask his warriors to die far away,
that if you want to take the Sotan land, that is your
business, not his. That the dirt-eaters will not thank
you for bringing blood and fire to their villages. If
they had no ill intentions before, they will when you
do what you speak of."

Mazeppa's scowl hid vague discomfort. "Gallagher
told me Nagani Yazzie is senile and difficult," he said.
"Well. I will deal with him in good time. Meanwhile
things have changed. I no longer need his alliance."

Even watching the chief's aura, Lemmi couldn't
guess what went on in his mind. Finally Mazeppa
spoke again, slowly and quietly. "Do Dinneh warriors
adopt sons into their lodges?"

"Occasionally."

"So do we here." He fell briefly silent, then continued. "My loins have produced no sons, no children
at all, though I have two wives." He paused again.
"You are a warrior who has traveled far. Who knows
the Sotans. Who shows respect. Who in victory is kind
to the vanquished, and who does not fear to tell me
what he thinks. And who speaks the ancient and
beautiful Dkota tongue, which we must begin to teach
our children."

Lemmi knew what came next. "I would like to
make you my son," Mazeppa said. "My warrior son,
who will be a hero in the fighting to come. I can see
it in you. And you will have many sons, and they will
have many sons. Mazeppa and the sons of Mazeppa

will be known forever, throughout the world. What do you say to that?"

"I would be honored to be the son of Mazeppa Tall Man." Lemmi's mahogany face had turned sober. Mazeppa Tall Man *was* honoring him. The offer was rooted in self-interest, but it could have been made to any number of others instead of himself. And he would accept that honor to betray it. For a good cause, but a betrayal nonetheless.

"Good," Mazeppa said. "Then you must prepare. You have been tainted by the words and company of Nagani Yazzie. So go now to the tipi of Pastor Morosov. Tell him you must be cleansed of the poison of Yazzie's words before the next new moon. The Dkota will hold important ceremonies then, and when they are completed, you will become my son. Meanwhile you are to live in the lodge of the penitents. Now go."

Lemmi left, thinking about the moon. That morning he'd wakened to gray dawn, with the brighter stars and Jupiter still sharp in the western sky. But in the east, the bitten moon was well up, and the new moon a few days off.

⋘⋙ ⋘⋙ ⋘⋙

Still leading his pack horse, Lemmi rode to the pastor's tipi and told him what Mazeppa wanted. The chief had already explored the subject with the pastor, who now took Lemmi to the penitents' lodge nearby. "Move your things in," he said. "Some things are already here: waterbag, baskets and rocks for cooking, baskets for gathering buffalo chips ... You returned at a good time. Those who have lost harmony with the Great Spirit and the People will begin their cleansing tomorrow. But this evening you will eat in my tipi."

Judging from his aura, the pastor had some other matter on his mind, something he wasn't talking about. *Something to do with me,* Lemmi guessed, *and perhaps with Mazeppa Tall Man.*

It turned out the evening meal would be his last for three days. Three days of not quite fasting; three hungry days.

Each morning the penitents would be wakened by a deacon with an eagle bone whistle. After sharing pipe smoke with the rising sun, and washing in the creek, they would run the short distance to Coot Lake, then all the way around it. It was fairly large, more than a mile across and some two miles long. There were thirteen penitents besides Lemmi, all naked, all there for spiritual cleansing. While running, they were followed at a little distance by a swarm of children and youths wearing breechclouts, who treated the run like a festival. Afterward, slick with sweat, the penitents bathed in the lake, some distance from the others, and unlike them, not sporting in the water.

After returning to the village, the penitents sat together in a prayer lodge with the pastor and five deacons. There they prayed together, Pastor Morosov leading, the others following, to the beat of a lap drum played by an old man. The prayer was in Dkotan; Pastor Morosov had coached them, and told them what the words meant.

Afterward they partook of the Sacrament, each eating a single morsel of God's Great Gift, buffalo hump, handed them by the pastor; followed by God's Sweet Gift, a dollop of honey on a fragment of sacramental corn tortilla; and finally a sort of bitter tea, served in a hollowed-out gourd; all while a singer prayed, accompanied by drum.

Following that, they danced more or less in place while the singer sang a prayer of love: first to Sun and Moon; then to Land and Water; to the four-leggeds large and small; the winged people; the many-leggeds; the standing people, both trees and grass. To the Virgin and her Son; and finally to the Great Spirit, God who dwells in all things. After that they left the prayer lodge, each to go about his day aware that he was not to eat for three more, except for the Sacrament.

Lemmi didn't know what the other penitents did. The rest of his day was spent being instructed by a deacon, in Dkota lore. He found it interesting—enlightening on Dkota attitudes and folkways.

That evening they gathered in the penitents' lodge to be led in prayers by Pastor Morosov, and again drink tea, this time a soporific. Soon they lay down on their sleeping robes, to dream until dawn.

Most of the second day was much like the first, though some of the prayers were different. Lemmi was surprised that his legs weren't sore from yesterday's run and dancing.

Evening, though, was entirely different. The penitents gathered outdoors in deep twilight, bellies complaining. The mosquitoes were out in force, their stings annoying but momentary, for their prey had developed resistance to the itching and swelling. With the penitents were singers and drummers, trained in the ceremony. Morosov had explained to Lemmi what the penitents would do here. A large crowd of onlookers waited, chatting among themselves. They would, Lemmi thought, be familiar with the ceremony, its purposes and meanings.

The penitents stood six to eight feet apart in a circle, surrounding a tipi-shaped pyre of split bur oak. The pastor stood beside it. A single large drum began to beat softly, rhythmically. The crowd stilled at once. Then the drum stopped, and Morosov began to pray in Dkotan, pausing after every phrase to repeat it in Merkan. The prayer was not long. It asked the Great Spirit to be active within each of them, not only the penitents but the onlookers, bringing them all into harmony with His Wisdom, and thereby with each other, the Earth, the Waters, the Air, and everything living on and in them.

When he'd finished, the Great Drum began a heart-like beat: *thump-thump! Thump-thump!* A deacon entered the circle to hand the pastor a tightly woven basket, with the handle of a small metal dipper showing. Morosov took it, and presented each penitent with a dipperful of whatever was in the basket. The penitent drank it down without a pause. *Thump-thump!* spoke the drum, *thump-thump!* Lemmi was the last to be offered the tea. It seemed to him every eye in the crowd was on him—every eye that could find him. The brew was warm, verging on hot, and again bitter, but not the same as the tea of that morning.

Again the drum stopped, and Morosov prayed in Merkan to the Great Spirit, asking forgiveness for any imperfections in himself, the ceremony, the penitents and the onlookers, and to help them reach harmony. When he'd finished, another deacon entered, to hand the pastor a torch. He thrust it into the pyre, which Lemmi realized had been primed with fat, probably buffalo fat. It flared into flame, and Morosov left the circle.

Several drums began a strong synchronized beat, and the penitents began to dance, right, then left on the circumference, treading firmly without stamping. The onlookers began to sing. Lemmi quickly found himself at one with the other dancers and the crowd. *Partly it's the tea,* he thought. *Partly.*

The drumming speeded, and so did the dancers, sweating copiously from the exertion and the burning pyre. They gleamed in the firelight. At intervals signalled by changes in the drum beat, their back and forth circling paused, and they danced in place, jumping high. At certain points, deacons entered the circle to lay more wood on the fire, reverently despite the intense heat. Lemmi's last conscious thought was, there was meaning in this, and validity.

Despite two days of fasting, the dancers continued

for nearly two hours—longer than seemed possible. Several had slowed to a shuffle, while one by one, others ceased jumping but continued to dance. A few of the younger, immersed deeply in group consciousness and the tea, continued to jump, visiting their limits. Lemmi was one of them, his awareness of time and specifics vague. Finally the dancers began to collapse on the moccasin-packed earth. When several lay gasping, Morosov shouted a single loud cry. The drums crescendoed, crashed, stopped. The chanting crowd stopped with them. They'd been more than mere onlookers; they'd been co-celebrants.

⊰⊱⊰⊱ ⊰⊱⊰⊱ ⊰⊱⊰⊱

Again Lemmi awoke to an eagle-bone whistle, knowing exactly what day it was. The new moon would rise in another half hour or so, rise unseen, with the sun or very nearly. Meanwhile, gray dawn shone through the open door-flap of the penitents' lodge. Lemmi recalled being given more tea after the dance, and drinking deeply. Of being bathed with water and trade soap, rinsed off, then wiped dry by hands. Of drinking again, and later, vaguely, going to the latrine.

For one final morning, the penitents ran the path around Coot Lake, bathed, and took the Sacrament together. It seemed to Lemmi he should be immobilized by soreness, but he scarcely hurt at all; a little in the calves.

Afterward, followed by the entire village, or all who could travel, the penitents walked to a hill known as the Hill of Saint Gustav. A three-hour walk, more for the older people, who'd started early. There they found Dkota from camps so far away, they'd traveled several days to get there, bringing their own penitents, and had set up camp a little distance off.

Saint Gustav had been the holy man who'd "discovered" what the hill was: *the site where First Man and First Woman had met Jesus—Jesus riding on Pony,*

*accompanied by Buffalo, Elk, Bear, Wolf, Mouse, Eagle,
Raven, Goose, Snake and Spider; Cottonwood, Pine,
Cattail, Bitterroot and Camas, representing all living
things. Now all were there again, their spirits in the
costumed members of their totem lodges, reenacting the
Great Pow-wow in which, under Jesus's guidance, First
Man and First Woman were taught to live in harmony
with all the others, including each other.*

The implication was that this had happened long
long before Armageddon. But the pre-Armageddon
recordings—print or audio—had no such myth, not
for the Dakotah or any other buffalo people. It was
from the post-Shuffling surveys that Lemmi knew the
story. In the enactment, Coyote had been there too,
and tried to play tricks on Jesus, but nothing worked
for him. The crowd laughed with delight at his clumsy
failures. Still, First Man had been distracted by
Coyote's shenanigans, and had not learned all he was
intended to know.

Lemmi had hypno-learned the basic story before
leaving the Academy, but it was far more meaningful in the enactment. When it was over, those from
the nearer villages started home. There was no feast;
on this day *all* the Dkota fasted till sundown.

At Mazeppa's village, late that afternoon, two sweat
lodges were prepared to complete the cleansing of
the penitents. Meanwhile each confessed himself privately to the pastor or a deacon, before time to
sweat. Lemmi's confession, of course, was less than
frank. After sundown, each drank copiously of still
another tea, then relieved and washed himself. When
it was nearly dark, the naked penitents crawled on
hands and knees into the sweat lodge, followed by
Pastor Morosov and a deacon. The physical experience was not new to Lemmi; the Sancroy Dinneh
used the sweat lodge as well, though the ceremony
was different.

When they were all inside and the entrance closed, the only light was from the bed of red-glowing rocks near the middle. The heat was intense, but at first not oppressive. Pastor Morosov threw pinches of tobacco and sweet grass onto the rocks, their fragrance flavoring the air.

Only after the pastor's opening prayer did the deacon cast a dipper of hot water exploding onto the rocks. The result was instant humidity. Then one by one the penitents prayed—for harmony with the land, the waters, the air, all living things in and on them, and with Jesus and the Great Spirit. Each in his own way, his own words, from the viewpoint of his own experience. After every prayer, another dipper of water was splashed onto the rocks. The penitents were slick with sweat, trickling down their naked bodies till the ground they sat on was mud.

Again, as someone new to the Dkota, Lemmi was the last to pray. He did not fake it; but he *was* selective.

Once, using pitchforks obtained from traders, acolytes added new rocks, glowing from a fire outside, and the heat and humidity became almost intolerable. More tobacco and sweetgrass were thrown on the rocks. Then, in the darkness, the pastor handed out fragrant bundles of soft cedar twigs, gotten from Sotans by trade. With these they switched themselves till their bodies tingled. Then a deacon opened the door, and one by one they crept out into the night. Acolytes met them with more tea, all they could drink. Other acolytes added still more glowing rocks atop those from before. Then the penitents and their two leaders crawled back inside.

This stay was shorter. They scrubbed themselves and each other with trade soap and large wads of sphagnum moss, to emerge clean and glowing. This time the acolytes held baskets of lake water. The penitents were so overheated, having baskets of cool water poured on them was no shock at all.

⋘⋙ ⋘⋙ ⋘⋙

In the penitent's lodge, a feast had been spread: God's Great Gift and God's Sweet Gift, along with camas cakes, corn cakes, and other delectables.

Then they all went home, Lemmi to Mazeppa's tipi. He was too spent to seek the privacy needed for a report to Luis and the others. They'd have to wait another day.

The next day, Mazeppa sent Lemmi to Pastor Morosov again, this time to be instructed in the things a man of another tribe should know before marrying into the Dkota. Things he hadn't already been taught. For Mazeppa had chosen a wife for him, and had asked the pastor to be his new son's *hunka* uncle. Morosov led the young man out of the village to the top of a knoll.

It was there they talked, the pastor doing most of it. Lemmi was free to ask questions throughout the two lessons, but one question he saved till the last. He wanted it to be on Morosov's mind when they parted.

"Pastor," he said, "there is one matter that troubles me. The Dkota, your people and now mine, put great emphasis on harmony. On balance. Yet the principal chief of the Dkota now rules the Ulster as well. If my mission to the Swift Current Dinneh had been successful, he would have commanded them, too. And he wishes to rule Sota. Now he wants me to father many sons, so that Mazeppa and the sons of Mazeppa will be known forever, throughout the world. Where is the balance in this?"

Morosov's face was thoughtful, and for a while he simply gazed at the horizon. "Mazeppa Tall Man was born to rule," he said at last. "And he does it well. People tend naturally to do what he asks, especially the young men. If the elders object—if I object—the young men will follow him, not us. Also, his wisdom as a ruler is great, especially for one so young—thirty-one winters."

"But why rule so much?" Lemmi asked. "Many warriors of the Dkota and Ulster will die in the war, and many Sotans. Why is he not content just to rule the Dkota?"

The pastor's aura was considerably troubled now, and his lag was even longer than before. "Do your people know the story of how things were before Armageddon?"

"I will know when you've told me what story that is."

"Before Armageddon—a long time before—the buffalo people lived as we do, hunting the buffalo. And east of the Great Grass, the dirt-eaters lived as they do today. But they were numerous, and increasing, and decided they wanted the land of the buffalo people."

Lemmi nodded. That was history. Morosov wasn't looking at him, though, and didn't see him nod.

"So the dirt-eaters made many agreements and promises. If the buffalo people would agree to let dirt-eaters live on part of the Great Grass, other parts would remain theirs forever. But the dirt-eaters did not keep their promises. They took the land they'd said the buffalo peoples could keep, and when the buffalo people tried to drive them out"—Morosov's expression was desolate—"when they tried to drive them out, the dirt-eaters killed all the buffalo and left them rotting. With no more buffalo, the buffalo people became weak, and were required to do all that the dirt-eaters ordered. Finally the dirt-eaters fought each other, and when most were dead, God in his mercy renewed the world, and the buffalo, and the other living kinds, in their proper numbers and places. And the people who were left he shuffled together, and those whom he put on the buffalo land, and their sons and daughters, became the new buffalo people."

Lemmi saw where this was leading, but asked anyway. "What has this to do with attacking Sota?"

"The dirt-eaters are talking again about conquering the buffalo people, and making the land their own."

It was Lemmi's turn to lag. Then—"How does Mazeppa know this? If it is true, why didn't I hear of it in Sota? In Iwa and Ilanoy? Surely they'd know of it there."

Lemmi's questions startled Morosov. They hadn't occurred to *him*. He thought then of the sky people; he himself had never heard of the dirt-eaters' plan till after the first visit of the sky canoe. But it couldn't have been Sky Chief. Mazeppa had talked about attacking Sota almost as soon as he'd defeated the Ulster, before Sky Chief arrived.

"I do not know, Lemmi. Perhaps only a few chiefs know, in those places. Chiefs in those lands do what they wish, and do not discuss it until they are ready."

Lemmi looked thoughtful. "What do the Dkota think about this?"

"Many elders spoke against making war on the Ulsters, even after the Ulsters raided the Standing Rock Dkota. They said we should just raid the camp the raiders came from. That's the way such things are done. But Mazeppa said we needed to teach the entire tribe a lesson they would not forget, and most of the young men thought it was a good idea.

"Later, when Mazeppa began to talk about attacking Sota, more of us disagreed. But he answered that if we do not attack them—defeat them so badly they will never want to fight us again, and drive them far away from the Great Grass—if we do not do that, they will come in all their numbers, and possess the land of the buffalo. Just as they did before Armageddon.

"And the young men agreed with Mazeppa, and many who are no longer young. *I* agree with him! The old are not expected to fight, and anyone is welcome to stay home. But almost all the young will go. It is to defend the buffalo, a great purpose, a great honor. No one argued. And when the young men ride against the Sotans, there will be men of fifty winters who ride with them."

Lemmi nodded. "I understand, Pastor," he said. It was time to cover his rear now. "I will be there too."

They parted then, Pastor Morosov walking back to camp. Lemmi, on the other hand, stayed on the knoll, to meditate and pray, he said.

After watching the pastor leave, he took his belt com and thumbed it on. It seemed to him he had the missing piece now, and what the Helverti's role was in this.

Chapter 17
Job Interview

Kabibi was a rather tall and striking young woman—very attractive—and at 19 years, not much older then Mary. And though she'd never been schooled in the manners of royalty or nobility, in her childhood community, poise and dignity were valued, along with basic courtesy. In the Order, those had been matured and polished, made more cosmopolitan, less culture-specific. And her voice and accent were aesthetic.

She applied at the palace for employment as a scribe. Luis's hope was, she'd be assigned to the Princess Mary. When Kabibi asked "Why Mary?" he'd said he didn't know yet. His warrior muse seemed to be waiting for further developments.

That was real to her.

She'd come to the Order literate, and in it her reading had been considerably expanded. Her spellings fitted cultivated practice, she wrote legibly, neatly yet rapidly, and where desired, calligraphically. If hired, she was most likely to work for His Majesty's secretary, who employed scribes for making multiple copies of reports and correspondence. Elvi also used a scribe for copying her adminstrative reports, would-be regulations etc., but she preferred servants less good-looking than the face that peered back from her mirror.

Making copies was a duty of Mary's handmaiden, as well, because Mary carried on a considerable correspondence. And though Luis hadn't known it, her present handmaiden was about to marry and move to Noka, a good day's ride northwest.[2] The availability of the position had not yet been made public, so Kabibi was the first candidate examined.

It was the king's secretary, Lord Brookins, who screened her for the opening. Impressed, he commented briefly on being handmaiden to a princess. "Her highness," he finished, "has a pleasant personality, but she must and does require full and proper respect for her position. And it is she, guided by precedent, who decides how her servants shall conduct themselves. On the other hand, I have never known her to be unreasonable in dealing with anyone, and I believe you would find her a good mistress." He smiled benignly. "I do suggest, however, that you appear . . . less strong. Less in charge.

"If she approves you for the position, we will set a date for you to move to the palace and commence your duties. You must be prepared." He paused. "Meanwhile be aware that others are sure to apply, and the princess may choose someone else. If this happens, do not take it as criticism. You have demonstrated skill with both language and pen; you are attractive and intelligent, and so far as I have observed, you comport yourself nicely. But Mary is looking for someone to be a close friend and companion as well as a servant, so the applicant's personality must fit well with hers. You understand I'm sure."

---

[2] Do not confuse *Noka,* 40 miles northwest of Hasty, with *Nona,* 120 miles southeast of Hasty.

"Of course," Kabibi said. *We'll see,* she thought. *If not Mary, then perhaps Lord Brookins. He seems very nice, and the secretary to a king is bound to have privileged information.*

But she'd bet he was no gossip. And at any rate, the job Luis wanted her to have was with Princess Mary.

When Kabibi had left, Brookins penned a summary of the interview and signed it approved, then sent it to Mary. Who perused it, examined Kabibi's writing samples, then ordered her own appointment with the candidate. She sent a courier to Kabibi, who had taken a room with an elderly couple from Soggo to hide her association with the Order.

The next day Kabibi arrived at the palace and was taken to the princess's apartment.

Part Three

SHELL GAMES

Chapter 18
The King's Tame Dukes

(Luis)

It was, I decided, time to visit Nona and Austin, to gain a sense of how loyal the king's recently installed dukes were to him. Nona first, because its Duke was supposedly the more formidable.

Meanwhile, on my mental back burner, one aspect of Lemmi's report troubled me: Mazeppa had said he wasn't interested in a Swift Current alliance any longer. If true, why wasn't he?

As for things at Hasty—if anything came to Carlos's attention, he could com me. And if Paddy or Kabibi needed to let me know anything, they could get in touch with Carlos through Brother Ranjit, who today would be setting up a one-man courier business in Hasty, as cover.

I left the Brother House at the first gray of dawn, dressed as a working man but otherwise undisguised, carrying my habit in my bedroll. The sun wasn't up yet when I boarded the North Landing ferry. Me and a taverner with a wagon, team, and eight barrels of beer.

I kept a sour face to avoid conversation, and traveled with neither packhorse nor remount, the better to be ignored. With any luck, I figured to make it to Nona on the third day, if I slept under the sky, or the inns were spaced right.

They weren't and I didn't. By late afternoon, thunderheads were building, so I quit early, at a village called Rito Nogales, with a three-bed inn and a livery stable. The food was hotter than anything I'd ever eaten, with tiny green peppers that looked like a skinny bean, hot enough to scald your swallow pipe. The weather being threatening, all three beds were full, which was fine by me. After making sure my horse was properly tended, I slept in the hayloft over the stable. It didn't rain though.

It was the fourth day before I reached Nona Town. The ducal palace was a stone fortress built on a bluff above the river, to defend against attackers from downstream, not from buffalo tribesmen. In fact, Nona was as far from Many Geese as you could get and still be in Sota.

I stopped at a decent-looking inn at the edge of town, used the wash house and my razor, unrolled and straightened my uniform hat, changed into my habit, and left to visit the duke. Leaving my saber in my bedroll, and my bedroll in the lock-room. A Churchman carrying a saber almost had to be Higuchian, and I preferred that not be known.

The bodies I'd heard about, that supposedly had been drawn, quartered, and spiked to the town gate, weren't there anymore, if they ever had been. I passed the guards unquestioned. My collar marked me as Church, but they seemed not to recognize the order.

I didn't do as well at the palace, where I introduced myself to the door guards as Master Luis from the Holy See, and didn't specify my Order. I told them I needed to speak with Duke Francois Cheong. The

guards had me wait on a small bench, while they sent
an usher to his lordship.

I waited about an hour, which didn't surprise me.
What did surprise me was my growing unease. The
king had probably sent a letter to the dukes, warning
them about me. Finally I told the sergeant that if
his lordship didn't see me soon, I'd notify Norlins
that the Duke of Nona had refused to receive a rep-
resentative of the Holy See. So he rang for an usher
again.

I began to think that wouldn't work either, but after
about twenty minutes I was taken inside.

The duke's bearing, scowl and aura bespoke worse
than harshness, arrogance, and toward me, hostility.
The man was psychotic, and his bodyguards butch-
ers. It seemed to me I'd made a mistake leaving my
saber in my bedroll; he knew what I was and who I
was. So I switched on my com, on send. If anything
happened to me, Tahmm would know when and
where; Uncle Arvind records everything that comes
in. Everything.

Meanwhile I was polite enough to make you puke,
and every question I asked, he deflected scornfully,
giving neither reason nor alibi. Which was fine. I'd
gotten important information: Duke Francois Cheong
was an enemy and insane. I felt lucky to get out of
there alive.

At the inn I changed back into civvies, saddled my
mount, and left without taking time to eat, afraid the
duke might change his mind and send a party after me.
Saber at my side, I pushed my horse till I reached the
small market town of Sanggau, still well inside the
duchy. It was getting dark. I ate at the Sanggau inn,
then rode west out of town and slept in the woods.

The day had given me more than information about
Duke François. It had shown me something about me,
the hero of Eisenbach, survivor of Kelgorath captivity.
Today I'd been more scared than I'd thought possible.

Not of death, but of *evil*. The word had a new reality for me.

Before I lay down to sleep, I called Tahmm and Carlos, and Freddy in Moleen. And Lemmi, who announced his coming marriage, arranged by his new father. According to Mazeppa, the girl was tall, strong, and good-looking, of a lineage with large families.

I gave them my read on Duke Francois. "The man scared me, literally," I said. "The king must have sent word to expect a snoopy Higuchian, so I suppose Duke Alfred's expecting me, too."

One thing's certain, I added to myself: *At Austin I'll have my saber on my belt, instead of in my bedroll.*

The sun was well up when I awoke; both my horse and myself had benefited from the extra rest. And yesterday didn't seem as bad now. Scared I had been, but I'd functioned well, made the right decisions. And now I realized something about Francois Cheong that I'd overlooked the day before: someone that crazy is likely to make serious mistakes.

And more: I'd been in real danger of being killed, but my muse had steered me through it despite my fear.

I took it easy on my horse all that day, and bought another at a Williamite Church I came to, appropriately enough at a village called Saint William. With a remount I couldn't pass for a poor traveler, but I had a lot to do, and needed to get on with it. Meanwhile I enjoyed a wash, supper with the priest, a featherbed, and bacon and eggs for breakfast. And rode away on the new horse, the other trailing on a lead.

The next morning I could see Austin Town ahead, and stopped at a farm a mile before I got there. Paid for a meal, then went to the horse trough, where I stripped to the waist, washed, brushed my hair, and dressed in my habit again. Then I took lunch with the farmer and his family, and rode on into town.

A palisade had been built around the town, which

at the time had been a village. Now more of the town was outside the wall than in, but the ducal palace was in the old, walled part.

Unlike my reception in Nona, in Austin I waited only a few minutes, and Duke Alfred apologized even for that. But his aura didn't match his words. I took a different approach with him than with Francois: I identified myself as Higuchian, and told him I was inspecting the duchies in Sota for their preparedness, in case the kingdom was attacked. He informed me that Sota had the protection of God. I answered that God expected earthly authorities to do their part.

Then I asked to inspect the ducal force at arms.

"Master Luis," he said, apologetically again, "two of my three squads are away just now with Captain Bevins, on a routine round of the baronies. Because of last year's lawlessness, you know. The other squad is here on security duty."

His aura said "liar! liar!" but I didn't insist, nor say I'd be happy to inspect his men on duty. There was nothing to gain by cornering him. And though he might not be psychotic, he was dangerous.

"I can, however," Alfred told me, "introduce you to their sergeant major." Said it as if that would help. He turned to his page. "Tell Sergeant Major Banda we have a visitor who would like to meet him: Master Luis, of the Order of Saint Higuchi."

Neither his aura nor his face showed any hint of treachery.

The page hurried out, and Alfred had beer brought while we waited. Excellent beer. Chilled. No doubt in winter they cut ice on the river, and stored it in sawdust or such like, in an ice house, the beer with it. Meanwhile he faked cordiality, and I faked belief. He'd prefer to send me away intact and content, but ill-informed. I was agreeable to the first two, and as for ill-informed—if nothing else, I had a character read on him.

The sergeant was slow in arriving, and it wasn't something the duke had set up; his annoyance was genuine. "What's keeping him?" he asked. The page said some of the guard had the flux, and the sergeant had said he'd "be right along," so probably he had it. I hoped it wasn't something in the beer.

When the sergeant major arrived, he proved to be a burly, muscular-looking man of ordinary height. His aura marked him as an inborn warrior inclined to recklessness. His gaze was direct, and I expected his grip to be strong. Actually he kept it moderate—but there was something in his palm: a piece of paper folded small. If this meant what it might, the sergeant had more guts than a slaughterhouse. I moved my hand to my pocket, swapped the paper for a handkerchief, and blew my nose mightily.

"Excuse me, gentlemen," I said. "It's the season— something in the air. When it tickles, it's either clear my passages or have a sneezing fit."

I asked the sergeant a few questions, and he answered them. Yes, he liked his job. Yes, the troops were good, and their training stringent. Morale was high. No, they had no militia; it had been disbanded. No, he didn't think that weakened the duchy; the militia had never been very effective.

His aura told me he lied like a horse thief; they'd been forewarned. So I turned my attention back to Alfred. Did he think the Dkota would abide by the peace treaty? He was sure they would. If they didn't, how would he deal with possible raids? There'd be none. If they did attack, and the marches asked for help, would he send any? It could never happen, to contemplate it was to invite it. What did he think of the reduction; could he keep the peace with only three squads? It was not a problem.

He obviously wasn't going to tell me anything on purpose, and I really wanted to look at that piece of paper. So I offered him my hand. "It was good of your lordship to indulge me," I said. "I appreciate your time—and that of the sergeant major. Meanwhile Sota has numerous dukes, and my orders require that I visit all of them, so I'm afraid I must leave. Get this trip over, and back to Norlins."

Then I wished them a pleasant summer, and left. Eager for privacy, to see what I had in my pocket.

Back in the saddle and out of Old Town, I unfolded the paper. It was about three by three inches, with the name Wolf and Badger written on it, and a time: 7 OC—of the clock. The sergeant hadn't had a flux; he'd needed privacy to write his message. So I rode back to the farm, changed into my road clothes, and snoozed in the hayshed till supper. After eating, I rode back into town.

I figured The Wolf and Badger would be a tavern. Actually it was an inn on the Fairbow Road north of town. Not the sort of place guardsmen would likely choose for drinking. Obviously Banda's warrior muse was healthy, and he paid heed to it. I was right. I figured he'd be inside wearing civvies, to deflect attention. He looked up questioningly as I walked over to him, as if wondering who I was.

"Excuse me, friend," I said, "haven't we met somewhere down the line?"

He frowned, then brightened. "Yeah, I believe we have. Up north of Long Portage, back in our trapping days. We had a, um, discussion over the rights to a beaver flowage."

"That's it," I said. "We settled it by throwing axes at a tree, and you won. And I found a better flowage the next day."

He laughed. "That's an advantage to getting *way* back in the bush. The farther back you go, the more good stuff you find."

I grinned at him, and we took his pitcher of ale to a back corner. "That was a helluva risk you took today," I said.

He smirked. "I knew you wouldn't give me away. You're Higuchian. We'd been warned two, three weeks ago to expect you; you've got somebody worried in Hasty."

This guy not only had guts. He was even smarter than I'd realized. "So," I said, "what do you know that I need to hear about?"

"First, this duke is like the king. In fact they're cousins. He's half good guy, half butcher, and the good-guy half, being real, lowers your guard. Then the butcher guts you.

"He's not as smart as Eldred though. Eldred hired one of his wife's cousins to command his force-at-arms, but the cousin is Jaako Jarvi, a genuine fighting man who knows what he's doing. Alfred, when he took over the duchy, brought a boyhood friend, Adam Bevins, to command his guard. *Captain* Bevins, who doesn't know his ass from a cupboard mouse. When Jarvi put down the uprising here, all of Majesky's old force-at-arms— those who surrendered—were executed anyway. Eldred's orders. And Bevins replaced them with guys he'd had recruited for him in Hasty. Some of them, you tell them to stomp someone to death, they'll draw straws for the privilege. You can always find guys like that, but you can't always control them."

"Then how," I asked, "did you get on here?"

He laughed quietly. "Why ain't I surprised you asked?" He took a draw on his ale. "I was on the guard here before the uprising. Master sergeant, like now. But I crossed horns with Captain Ho over some dumb shit, and talked when I should have listened. Ho was mostly a good man, but there was only one way to do things, his way, and he wanted no discussion.

"So this time he told me, 'Sergeant, you bring that up one more time and I'm going to send your ass back to the farm.'

"So I told him that's it, I quit. And went off south

to Iwa, where I've got a brother-in-law with a dray
service on the docks in Riverton. Hard work but
honest pay, and very little bullshit. A few months later
I heard about the rebellion, and how Jarvi put it down.
Brutal. But it was worse at Nona. On Eldred's orders,
so I've heard. The story is, Jarvi had to get puking
drunk to carry them out.

"So when spring arrived, I came back. One of the
first things I saw was Ho's ugly head on a pike in the
town square, along with about twenty others. They
were the worse for wear—been out there since
October—but they were labeled. And being a dumb
shit sometimes, it occured to me to apply for a job.
I told them I'd been a sergeant here before, but quit
because I couldn't get along with Ho.

"To Bevins that was a recommendation, so he hired
me back as sergeant. I didn't realize what I was getting
into. The goddamn barracks was a zoo, and all Bevins
could do was wring his hands. I've heard since that
Alfred would have fired him—sent him back to
Hasty—only he didn't know who to replace him with.

"But I'd signed on, so I guessed I ought to stick
with it a while, see what happened next. Fellow
named Kirpal was sergeant major, a good man doing
his best, but too damned civilized. To run a zoo from
the inside, you've got to be the number one he-wolf.
He wasn't, and two weeks after I came on, the number one bully boy killed him. Kicked him to death."

Good lord, I thought, all in the name of mollification!

"So Bevins asked me to take the job. I told him
I'd be glad to. Everyone in the guard knew who'd
killed Kirpal; half of them saw him do it, but no one
was telling. As soon as word got around that I was
the new sergeant major, the guy stopped me in the
corridor and warned me not to fool with him."

Banda shrugged. "He had me by about thirty
pounds, four inches, and four, five friends, so I nodded.

Said I understood. Then got me a table leg and waylaid him in the messhall. Clubbed him to death in front of most of the guard. Blood and brains came out his ears.

"Then I told the main three in his little gang they had one hour to bag their gear and get out—out of town in an hour, out of the duchy in twenty-four. And if I heard of them again, I'd see their heads on pikes."

He laughed. "It's the sort of thing they understand. What surprised me, and shouldn't have, was that just about everyone else seemed to think it was a good idea, including some I'd never have expected it of. They'd been walking around scared to say or do anything that would get those four down on them.

"So here I am, Alfred Wiesendorf's sergeant major, his number two man—and I'd love to see him brought down."

He paused, then went on. "And while I'm talking, lemme answer some of your questions that didn't get answered earlier: The force at arms here isn't too bad, but it's not what it ought to be. As for its size, Alfred made it out to be three squads. I don't know what that's all about, but it's five squads, up from four in the old days.

"And the only thing that would get Alfred to send us anywhere to help against raiders is if Eldred Youngblood ordered him to. Meanwhile the rumor is, if a rebellion starts somewhere, we're to ride against Kato, fast as we can. Because Kato's the duchy that counts. Without it, no rebellion has a chance."

I told Banda to expect to hear from me again, with a proposition. One I thought he'd like. I'd expected it to be the following spring, and commonly my muse has pretty good timing, but there's always the chance of alternate vectors, and the odds . . .

Chapter 19
Ench the Dkota

After his uncle's outburst, Ench had determined to *be* a Dkota at any cost, and remain on Terra when Jorval left. Even if he had to hide out when the time came, though he didn't believe it would come to that. Despite his previous self-destructive behavior, he was quite intelligent. He understood from the first that to be a Dkota meant recreating himself, and almost as quickly that he could take little for granted. Thus he was quickly and increasingly alert to the clues in his environment.

He'd learned the household protocols without significant embarrassment. It had required noticing what others did, trying to copy them, and paying attention to their reactions. Almost at once he'd become comfortable eating with his fingers, and was learning the rituals central to Dkota life. Using a saddle, he could now ride at full gallop without falling off his horse. His first fall had shocked his young tutor, Franz-Goes-By-Himself, whose life had given him agility, balance, quick reflexes, and a deep sense of how horses behave. Fortunately, Ench's heavy-world heritage had given him strong bones and a compact, durable body.

His appearance was less adjustable. As gifts, he'd been given deerskin leggings, shirt, and moccasins that fitted, but in June, worn over his fur, they were too hot, so despite his furry appearance he'd settled for moccasins and breechclout.

He hadn't seen his uncle since he'd connected with Franz. Jorval knew where he was, of course. When Franz had asked his parents' permission for Ench to live with them, they'd gotten Jorval's approval through Mazeppa. In fact the horse Ench now rode was a gift from Mazeppa, who'd dismissed their brief confrontation, finding the Fohannid youth's ambition interesting and admirable.

Besides good starts on horsemanship and Dkota behavior, Ench, with Franz's guidance, spent a lot of time on archery. He was well coordinated and, like the Fohanni in general, strong. Soon he was shooting practice arrows into the vicinity of willow wreaths, and sometimes through them. Then Franz had him shoot from horseback, at first with the horse walking. As his horsemanship improved, he'd shot with the horse trotting, and finally galloping. To begin with, the arrows had no tips. Later they had tips, because with tips they flew differently, and at any rate they were generally recovered for further use. Soon he'd be taught to straighten and fletch shafts, flake flint points, hammer out steel points, and fasten them into place.

Many arrows—especially buffalo and war arrows—were made and prayed over by old men who no longer hunted, but every male child learned the skills.

Ench had also learned to pray to the spirit of the buffalo, deer, wild plum, camas—whatever was to be hunted, plucked, or uprooted—asking their agreement in advance to become food, hides, and other products. To give up their lives for human beings. In return,

the hunters promised respect and gratitude, in the
hunt, the kill, the cutting into parts, and the subse-
quent uses. Also Ench had learned to pray to the
Great Spirit, citing the need for food and hides, and
promising respect to the prey.

Actually Ench didn't truly pray, he recited, for
spirits great and small were unreal to him. What had
become real was that others believed, devoutly. And
as a side effect, he was learning respect for others,
and for the ecosystem.

If Ench fell well short of being Dkota, he was a
genuine and true-hearted apprentice, and now it was
time for him to kill meat. Small bands of buffalo had
arrived in the large, casually defined area called Many
Geese, though not near camp. Small parties had gone
out to kill a few, distributing the meat and hides to
their extended families. And to those who had no
family, for the Dkota were communal.

Even Franz had not yet been included in hunting
buffalo, though he expected to be that autumn.
Obviously Ench was far from ready for such dangerous
activities. So Franz, and Franz's younger brother Karl,
took Ench to hunt antelope. With Franz out ahead,
as scout, they rode for more than an hour before he
returned to them. He'd spotted a band of thirty or
so, over a low ridge. He told Ench to ride to a notch
in the ridge, half a mile west, with a copse of aspen
below it. There, on his pony, he was to position himself, screened by the slender trees. Franz and Karl
would circle around, undertaking to get on the far side
of the band, then try to drive one or more of the
antelope through the notch.

"Remember," Franz murmured, "it is common for
such hunts to go wrong. There are only the three of
us, and the antelope may scatter, with none of them
going in your direction."

Ench nodded. Then "Go," Franz said.

⊲⊳⊷⊶ ⊲⊳⊷⊶ ⊲⊳⊷⊶

The young Fohannu waited in the aspen copse for
what seemed a long time, hearing nothing except
meadow larks, the piercing "scree" of a high-circling
red-tail, and the faint rustle of aspen leaves, trembling
in the breeze through the notch. Waited with his ready
bow, an arrow nocked, wondering if the plan had been
aborted. He heard no shouts, no hooves.

Suddenly an antelope was *there*, through the notch,
running swiftly, low to the ground, in grass as high
as its back. Ench raised and bent his bow, released
the arrow . . . and saw the animal fall, bouncing,
cartwheeling. Two more antelopes followed, one
veering left past the fallen. The other veered right,
almost into the copse, passing within four yards of the
hunter. But buck fever had jerked Ench from his
focus. He hadn't reached back to bring forth and
notch another arrow, and the last prey scooted away
through the grass.

Only now did Ench hear hooves, as Franz and Karl
raced through the notch. Excitement swelled in the
young Fohannu, and he raised his bow, calling to
them. They slowed, and trotted down toward him.

"I GOT HIM! I GOT ONE OF THEM!" he
shouted exultantly, then quick-stepped his pony to
where the antelope lay. "RIGHT IN THE NECK!"

They rode up to him and looked down. "Good
shot," Franz said, then slid from his mount. Standing by the antelope, he began thanking it for giving
its life, that a young hunter would be able to bring
delicious meat and a soft skin to the people, that they
might eat, and be protected against the weather. "We
will treat your body with gratitude and respect, cut
it into the pieces, and in the order taught to our
ancestors by First Antelope. And we will remember
you while we enjoy the food, thanking you for what
you have done for us."

Ench looked on embarrassed. He'd forgotten what

he'd learned about showing respect to the animal he'd killed.

Franz continued. "White Bear is a new hunter, and you have helped him experience a successful hunt. As sometimes happens in a first hunt, he forgot, and shouted joyfully at your death. But he did not intend disrespect. Now he will speak his thanks and respect to you and to the Great Spirit."

Embarrassment warmed Ench's cheeks; Fohanni blushed too. Sliding from his saddle, he prayed as he'd been taught. Not verbatim—there was no verbatim prayer—but simply expressing respect and thanks in language much like Franz's. Then the two youths gripped each others' shoulders.

"You did well," Franz said. "Especially considering you have so recently learned to shoot. It may be Jesus has special things in mind for you."

Ench was no longer uncomfortable with praise or physical contact. He'd grown used to them, was warmed and gladdened by them. This was indeed, he felt, the life for him.

Chapter 20
Boat Ride

The princess had not been in a mood for talking, and Kabibi had been leaning back in her seat, mesmerized by the soft murmur of the river itself; the dipping of oar blades; the small swirling sounds of the eddies they made; the leisurely, rhythmic rubbing of oars against leathered thole pins.

Now Mary turned to her dark handmaiden. "What would you be, or do, if you could be or do anything you wanted?"

The unexpected question turned Kabibi's attention inward; it was one she'd never asked herself. After a moment she said, "My lady, what I would be is happy and useful. Just now I am happy, and I hope useful, overall if not at the moment."

"No, I mean—what *exactly* would you be or do?"

Kabibi answered indirectly. "In my family, the men were herdsmen, and the women were mothers and care givers. If a girl was not ready to be a mother, she might make use of what we learned from the Sisters of Learning, as I did. A person must eat, and have shelter and clothing—which means having something to trade, some skill or goods. So I would like to be someone who does something they like that others find good, but what that is can change with time." Her graceful hands gestured. "Just now I am happy in this boat."

She turned the conversation then. "What would you be or do?"

Mary frowned, looking even prettier than usual. "I was born a princess, and princesses are supposed to marry a prince, or the son of a duke or archbishop. Or become a nun. The alternative is to remain a princess all my life, which threatens to be deadly boring.

"On the other hand, as a queen, or duchess, or princess, one has certain resources: perhaps money, and the power to influence one's husband. Or one's sons in their time. And . . ."

She paused. "My mother died of a lung fever that killed scores just in Hasty. They coughed themselves to death. The Sisters of Mercy did what they could, but their hospital is small and their numbers few, and at any rate all they could do with such a plague was comfort and pray, and burn medicinal candles.

"And there are the cripples. Young boys playing can fall from trees, breaking an arm or leg that might not heal properly. A mother can cut off fingers splitting kindling. Workmen lose a foot or hand, and afterward do handcrafts if they can, or beg, while their wives take in laundry and mending, or do cleaning.

"So I would bring a famous healer to Hasty, the best I could hire."

Kabibi laid a hand on Mary's arm. "My lady, what a beautiful desire. Have you talked to your father about it?"

Mary nodded. "Yes, a few years ago. And he said what you just said: that it's a beautiful thought. But he also said true healers are few and expensive, and the sick and disabled many. And that too often even the best healers cannot help them.

"I believe he became cynical of healers when my mother died," she added quietly. "Our palace physician had apprenticed under a highly regarded healer in Sanlooee, yet he could not save my mother, his cousin. He's best at setting bones. Often, when someone's brought to him, he can only tell the family to keep them warm and clean, give them lots of water to drink, and food if they want to eat. And whiskey if the pain is bad, but not enough to make them sick. Koivun is a Lahti, so for some illnesses he prescribes a heat bath. The sweating draws out poisons. There are enough *Suomalainit* in Hasty that there are public sweathouses, as well as private."

Her hands gestured a graceful shrug. "Fortunately we're usually well, so Koivun spends most of his time helping servants and townsfolk. Father tends to be soft-hearted toward people, but he says Koivun is all we can afford toward public healing."

She sat quietly then, but Kabibi let be, aware that the princess was not done. After some seconds, Mary continued. "It seems to me that real healing is possible." Her tilted blue eyes, almost violet, held Kabibi's dark eyes. "One hears stories, but stories can be wishful thinking. When mother had the lung fever, Koivun could do little more than pray for her, he and father and Elvi and I. Pray and weep. And she died anyway." The princess sighed. "As did many others that winter."

Kabibi patted her arm. "I understand," she said. "My parents died, were killed when I was a little child, and some years later, so was my sister Jamila, whom I adored."

"Killed?"

"Murdered. Everyone dies of something, sooner or later, but they were still young. My mother was thirty-two when she was killed. And Jamila, when *she* was killed, was only twenty-two, as best I can figure it. She was also beautiful, and smart."

Mary's look of sympathy was genuine. Then Kabibi switched directions on her. "Have you ever considered becoming a healer yourself?"

"No. I've never felt the talent. And . . ."

"Yes?"

"The responsibility would be hard to bear."

Kabibi nodded. "I'm sure the best physicians can tell stories about that. But there's a holy order of nuns—the Sisters of Saint Althea—dedicated to healing. Their training is said to be the best."

Mary gnawed her lip. "It's only the wish I feel, not the talent."

"Ah. Could the wish be the talent trying to come out?"

She paused, to encourage a response. When none was voiced, she went on, following her muse. "There's an Althean hospital in Sanlooee, just two weeks or so distant by boat. I've heard you get much of the training during your novitiate, and until you've taken your final vows, you can leave if you like. And talent or not, you could use what you'd learned."

Mary gazed thoughtfully across the river, its ripples sparkling with sunlight. "I have heard of the Order of Saint Althea," she said at làst. "It's interesting that I never thought of this before. But I will now, Kabibi, truly I will."

Eight days later, Eldred reluctantly agreed to Mary's request, an approval quicker than she'd hoped. The archbishop had made the difference, saying perhaps the one thing that could have caused Eldred to "give up" his elder daughter so quickly: "If she feels the calling," Clonarty said, "and sincerely wishes to join the Altheans, it would be sinful to refuse her. The Altheans do much good, and are far too few."

So a week later, Mary was on her way to Sanlooee, with Kabibi and a letter of introduction from the archbishop. Along with a squad of picked armsmen to do the rowing, and make sure they got there safely. For there were four pairs of oars to help speed them southward, and buck the current on the trip home.

Chapter 21
The Collapse of a Time Table

Lemmi had left Mazeppa's tipi to use the trench, then "meditate a while" atop the low knoll nearby. It was the ploy he used for privacy, for his reports to Luis, Carlos and Tahmm. And Freddy in Moleen, so he'd be up to date if needed. Circumstances permitting, they conferred each evening.

He settled bare-legged onto the ground, wearing only a breech-clout, ignoring the bunch-grass humps and harsh stems. He'd gotten used to them. Switching on his com, he murmured instructions, then waited. Tahmm, still at his desk, was the first to respond. The others took a moment longer. When they'd all checked on, Lemmi began.

"Mazeppa's been in a strange mood lately," he told them, "and today he left the village with three of his 'close' men. Not hunting—he'd have invited me. They took remounts but no packhorses, like men in a hurry. I was sitting with the pastor in front of his tipi, getting instructed in "the web of life," when they passed a little way off, and I wondered out loud where they were going.

"Morosov said he didn't know, but it might have to do with one of the four, a man named Andre, of the Elk band. I'd met him earlier. Now Morosov described how Andre helped unite the Ulster with the Dkota. It was Mazeppa who'd lavished the Ulster with admiration, but Andre did the actual negotiating. Morosov called him the most persuasive man he'd ever known.

"Then he told me an interesting story. In early spring, Mazeppa had sent Andre off on some kind of mission—no one knew what—with two other men including another convincing talker, an Ulster warrior named Conrad, Gallagher's permanent envoy to Mazeppa. So 'in the time of mud, when the willow buds open,' as Morosov put it, these two, along with a famous scout, rode off westward with five pack horses and several remounts. Obviously they expected to travel a long way. But without lodgepoles, which meant minimal camps, and long days in the saddle."

Lemmi paused, giving the others a chance to ask questions. When they didn't, he proceeded.

"I'd met Andre right after he'd gotten back, apparently. He and Mazeppa had ridden off alone together, presumably to talk, but it didn't mean anything to me. Now I asked Morosov, and he just shook his head. The Dkota take a dim view of lying, but withholding is all right, and that's what Morosov was doing: withholding. Presumably Mazeppa has something he doesn't want known, or at least not talked about. But Morosov knows what it is, or thinks he does, and he's not telling."

"What do *you* think it is?" Luis asked.

Lemmi answered thoughtfully. "To the buffalo people, the buffalo are more than food. They're sacred, put here by God to sustain the buffalo people, who are 'to dwell in harmony with them, treating them with respect and reverence.' That's basic to their whole life. Before they go off hunting, for buffalo or anything else, they pray to God and whatever they plan to hunt, asking their help in obtaining food. Promising respect and gratitude. That holds for deer, wild plums, or water potatoes . . . but the *emotion* felt for the buffalo is way greater."

He paused, then spoke thoughtfully. "We know, and the tribes know, what happened, or almost happened to the original buffalo. My guess is that last spring, Mazeppa sent Andre and Conrad off with the tale of a dirt-eater plan to invade the Sea of Grass. To destroy the buffalo and subjugate the tribes. And Andre was to ask some other tribe or tribes to join in a preemptive attack on the neighboring dirt-eaters. The Sotans.

"To the Dkota at least, to destroy the buffalo would do more than wipe out their main food supply. It would be the worst kind of sacrilege. And one of the things I've learned from Morosov is there are two other northern buffalo tribes the Dkota consider potent: the Yellow Bears and the Wolves. And if their essential beliefs are like the Dkota's, Mazeppa would have a powerful argument, even though it's false."

"Hmm." It was Luis again. "And Mazeppa's new mood began after he talked to Andre?"

"Right. He's hung between eager and impatient now.

"If I'm right, this means more than a larger army for the Sotans to deal with. It means *we have a lot less time than we thought.* Because these people, for sure the Dkota, aren't much for long-range planning. Their lives are a response to nature—the weather, the grass, the buffalo . . . Most Dkota bands don't even garden a lot: some tobacco, some squash, some corn for flat bread . . . and medicinal herbs; that's about it. They might *think* a few years in advance, but to depend on tribes a few hundred miles west to join the invasion? If Mazeppa has an agreement with them, he'll want to do it this summer. Before something comes up to distract them, change their minds.

"And suppose the Yellow Bear warriors agree to join the invasion. When they show up and tribes camp near one another, there's a risk of insults or slights, and fighting, and Mazeppa can't help having that on his mind. So he won't want large numbers of outsiders living close to his people any longer than necessary. He'll make his move right away." Lemmi paused. "Assuming that's what's going on. I could be wrong, but I doubt it.

"It could even be—could very well be—that he and Andre rode off today because parties of these new allies have shown up in Ulster territory."

There was a moment of silence, then Luis spoke again. "Have you heard anyone there talk about this?"

"No one. Morosov's uncomfortable with the prospect of invading Sota. He intends to go along himself, but he's got misgivings. Something has him worried. He may realize at some level that the Sotans couldn't destroy the buffalo if they wanted to. In pre-Armageddon times, it was railroads, repeating rifles, and big industrial markets for leather that made it possible.

"And on a cultural level, a couple of days ago I overheard a deacon complain that Mazeppa takes too much authority on himself. Basically that he rules instead of presiding.

"So I believe Mazeppa intends to make war this summer, not next. The Dkota make their serious buffalo hunt in what they call 'the rutting moon,' call it October, putting down lots of meat for winter. So they'd have to get back home before then. No problem for the Dkota and Ulster, maybe, but the Yellow Bears and Wolves have a lot longer ride home."

"Any chance the council might veto Mazeppa's plans?" Freddy asked.

"There are no vetoes," Lemmi replied. "These people are as dedicated to free choice as the olden-time Dakotah. If the young men want to make war against the dirt-eaters, they can, regardless of the council. All they have to do is name someone their war chief, and go do it. And Mazeppa's their man; he has a lot of admirers. If the council disapproved, there might be fewer volunteers, but with defending the buffalo as the issue, I expect even the older warriors will go."

Briefly, Lemmi and Luis talked about their next steps. Tahmm was leaving the decisions to them. They were indigenes, he'd seen them in action during the Lizard War, and he'd supervised their education and training at the Academy. Lemmi'd been one of his best students, and Luis had what might be the strongest warrior muse he'd ever seen. So when they finished their discussion, that ended the conference.

❦❦❦   ❦❦❦   ❦❦❦

(Luis)

I'd been staying in a small cheap room in Hasty. When Lemmi disconnected, I told Carlos I was coming out to the brother house. Then I stowed my things in my saddlebags, told my landlord I was leaving, went to the stable where I boarded my horse, and rode out of town at a trot. Twenty minutes later I was at the brother house, where I went to Carlos's office.

"So you've got a lot to do and not much time, eh?" he said grinning.

"That's how it looks. How's Stephen coming along? There's something I need him to do for me."

"He's doing very well, actually. Says he doesn't need that sing anymore. Peng took care of his problem, and in the process his self-confidence burgeoned. He's way more mature than most novices are at first. More than I was." He raised an eyebrow. "What've you got in mind?"

"I want to send him on a mission to Big Pines, to his own people. He's green, but he's the only one here suited for it. I'd like him to leave early tomorrow, to talk to the chief and elders for me; set them up for me. What do you think?"

"It'll be good for him," Carlos said. "He'll be on his home ground, dealing with people he knows, within rules he knows. The processes Peng ran on him didn't turn up any hostility toward his people or his culture. He left home because his life goal is growth, and he needed to expand his experience." Carlos laughed. "He's certainly been doing that."

"Good. I'll get him back to you eventually, whenever that is. Meanwhile I have a lot of dukes to talk to, and I might as well start at Soggo. See whether the duke there is willing to send his militias out of the duchy. And Soggo's halfway to Big Pines, so afterward I'll go on north and see how Stephen's done."

The next day after breakfast, Peng sent Stephen to meet me in the small briefing room. I told him what I wanted, and he said he wasn't sure how much he could accomplish. The Sancroy Dinneh felt little connection with Sota's government or king, and hadn't even heard of the Dkota. I wasn't surprised. Big Pines was on the fringe of the northern wilderness, a long way from Dkota, and it was the baron in Sancroy who collected the taxes.

I told him if it didn't work, it didn't work, but if it did, it could help a lot.

After we'd discussed how he might approach the task, I told him to pack his gear and hit the trail, with a remount but no pack horse. Then I talked briefly with Donald, so he wouldn't think I'd forgotten him, stopped at Sugar Grove to ask Pastor Linkon some questions, and headed for Soggo, pushing my horses.

I didn't doubt for a minute that Lemmi was right, and that we needed to move fast.

I ate in the saddle. Deep dusk, which comes late

in that season, caught me at a crossroads village called
Los Abeduls, a good hour short of Soggo. Pastor Linkon
had recommended the hospitality of the Williamite
pastor at Abeduls, and I tested it. It was his bedtime,
but Pastor Pontedaro took time to tell me about the
duchy and its two rulers—the duke and the bishop—
while I supped on bread, cheese, buttermilk, and
warmed-over rhubarb cobbler, followed by wild plum
brandy. After a visit to the privy, I went to the guest
room, laid my com by the head of my cot, and went
to bed feeling optimistic. Lemmi hadn't reported yet,
but he'd been late before, and he was too sharp to get
in serious trouble.

⊲⊳-⊲⊳   ⊲⊳-⊲⊳   ⊲⊳-⊲⊳

Lemmi stepped outside to look at the sky. The last
faint wash of twilight was fading in the northwest.
Time to report, he told himself.

It was then Mazeppa rode up to the tipi. After he
and Lemmi had removed saddles and gear, Mazeppa,
with a word, started the horses trotting off to the herd
on their own. The two men carried Mazeppa's things
into the tipi, then sat down on the men's side.
Consuela and Trains Horses began to prepare a late
meal for their husband.

Mazeppa's strong face looked even more stoic than
usual, but his aura had expanded, full of power. For
several minutes, neither man spoke. It was Mazeppa
who broke the silence. "My son," he said, "I have
important things to tell you."

"Yes, my father?"

"I have spoken with Conrad's eldest daughter. She
is a good-looking woman of sixteen years, called Iris
because of her eye color. Her mother is Clear Voice
of the Branched Horn Ulster. For a time, Conrad lived
among us as Gallagher's envoy. Now he will return
to us with his wife and six children.

"Both he and his wife are tall and strong. And unlike

myself, prolific. For all my strength and two good
wives, my loins have given me no sons. This is the
means God has used to humble me. But my spirit will
have many children by my son-of-choice. Thus the
family of Mazeppa will be great in numbers and
strength, and all the world will respect it." He crossed
himself, something the Dkota reserved for profound
matters.

Now, briefly, his eyes found Lemmi's. "What do you
think of that?" he asked.

Lemmi met his gaze. "I am proud that my father
thinks of me in this way. God's will be done."

Mazeppa nodded. Taking his small pipe from its
rack, he packed it with tobacco and lit it with a coal
from the fire, then held it upward, offering the first
smoke to God. Next he offered it to the cardinal
directions, then to the lodge spirit, and finally to
Lemmi, who inhaled a single puff, held it, then let
it drift thinly from his parted lips before returning
the pipe to his father-by-choice. Again Mazeppa
inhaled the pungent smoke.

"I have other news," he said. "I have been to
Painted Rock. Gallagher had sent for me." He paused,
drawing again on his pipe, as if reexamining his news,
deciding how to tell it. "In the time of mud," he said
at last, "when the red shoulders had arrived from the
south on glossy black wings and the catkin buds were
opening on the willows, I sent Andre and Conrad far
west and north to the Yellow Bear people. Whose
great chief, Goyuk, is famous for his ferocity in
defense of his people's hunting grounds. Goyuk and
his council listened carefully, consulted, then fasted,
prayed, sweated, consulted further, then prayed and
sweated more. Seeking the proper decision." He
chuckled. "Andre wondered if they would seek till
summer. Finally Goyuk pledged to the Sun and the
Moon and the Buffalo that he would join the Dkota
and Ulster, to prevent the dirt-eaters from destroying

the buffalo. He would urge all his fighting men to ride with him, except the older, who would stay behind to protect the villages and women, and to hunt.

"When finally Andre and Conrad left the Yellow Bear people, they traveled south to the Wolf people, where much the same things were done. Taking even longer, till finally the Wolves too pledged themselves. Like the Yellow Bears, they would start for the tall-grass country when the horseflies appeared."

Briefly his eyes found Lemmi's again. "One cannot be sure of such things until they happen. When Andre and Conrad left them, people, especially the women and old men, would remember the arguments against the agreement. Sota is far away. Lesser tribes might learn of the warriors departing, and perhaps take advantage.

"And who could foretell whether, when finally the horseflies appeared, only a few tens of young men would take the warpath. Perhaps a hundred or two.

"I had no way to know. The horseflies have troubled our horses here for weeks, but I had heard nothing of any Wolves or Yellow Bears."

Mazeppa's back had been straight. Now it seemed even straighter. "Recently Gallagher sent a young man to the Big Ford of the Muddy, to watch. He had with him two strong horses. At last he saw warriors ride down to the water on the other side, and he met their scouts. They were Yellow Bears. So he rode hard all the way to Painted Rock, bareback for speed, and without stopping to sleep. He rode one horse to death. When he got to Painted Rock, Gallagher sent another rider on to me.

"When I reached Painted Rock, Yellow Bear scouts had already arrived. A thousand Yellow Bear warriors are on their way to join us! From there, guides will lead them to the village of the White Bull band, where they will camp till it is time."

"When will that time be?" Lemmi asked.

Mazeppa's lips thinned. "When the Wolves arrive. Or when I decide not to wait longer. It will be soon."

Mazeppa ate then, Lemmi keeping him company with a strip of flank steak. Afterward the young Higuchian left the tipi, going first to the latrine trench, then onto the knoll "to meditate and pray." Luis needed to hear about this immediately.

Chapter 22
Interlude at Big Pines

(Luis)

The country around Big Pines was different than anywhere I'd been before, and I caught myself distracted by my secondary muse, my nature-boy muse. There was a lot of forest, much of it running strongly to sugar trees, but there were also tracts of towering pines, some of them four feet through, with soft white-tinged needles five in a sheath. (Later I took time to examine some saplings, and counted.) It'd take a lot of time to chop one down, and you'd still have to cut it into logs, drag them up and saw out lumber. But other stands were of a short-needle pine, close-grown, straight and slender, just right for building logs.

I reached Big Pines Township in mid-afternoon. Dinnehville was at its north end—a settlement of scattered hamlets, each a cluster of farm houses and their outbuildings, surrounded by fields and pastures. More or less in the middle of the township was a market village, with a church, a smithy, a tannery (I recognized it by the smell), and a small inn. There had to be a sawmill around, because the larger buildings were of lumber. The homes, though, were of hewed logs.

Just about everyone had dark brown skin, like Lemmi and Stephen. The talking I heard was in a lingo—lots of country villages are like that—but when I asked where I could find the home of Stephen Nez, I was answered in Merkan.

The Nez home was back a couple of miles—I'd passed it without knowing—on a farm that looked typical for the locale. When I got there, his mother told me Stephen had gone "to town" to see the "headman," and wasn't expected home till supper. So I turned around and went back to the village.

The headman's home was no bigger than most— large enough to house a family. Built onto it was a shelter, the south side open to the day, where a woman sat at a thumping loom, while two girls sat spinning, one linen, one wool. A graying woman answered my knock. She recognized my collar, and when I asked for the headman, she called to him. Mostly in Merkan, out of courtesy. "Paul! There's a *belagaana* here looking for you. A churchman."

Paul Todachene was between middle and old age. "I'm Master Luis DenUyl," I told him. "I'm looking for Stephen Nez."

"He told me you would be. He was here a little while ago. When he left, he was going to the bachelors' lodge. You want to come in? My wife's got a pot of sassafras on."

"Thank you," I answered. "That would be nice."

A brick stove had been built into the wall, opening into both rooms, with the usual (for Sota) flues for heating. He gestured to a chair at a small table, both nicely carved. I sat. Mrs. Todachene filled two mugs with tea, then with a long-handled spoon, added honey from a crock, stirring it in. Her husband handed me one of the mugs, and sat down across from me.

"Stephen says he joined your Order. That he's helping you. And that some people out west might be going to make war, attack Sota."

"That's how it looks," I answered.

"He also says Lemmi Tsinnajinni belongs to your Order; that he's pretty high up in it."

"That's right. Lemmi and I trained together. Now he works among the Dkota, and I work in Sota."

"What do those Dkota people want to attack Sota for?"

"They don't seem to like the Sotans."

"Did we do something to them sometime?"

"They think so. Back before Armageddon."

Paul Todachene frowned. "That sounds crazy to me. That's why God shuffled the people after Armageddon, and made them forget. So they wouldn't hold on to old wrongs and hatreds. Don't they learn their catechism there?"

"A different catechism," I said. "The Dkota live a lot differently than we do in Sota. It's grassland there. They make their living hunting, mostly a kind of wild cattle."

Todachene considered that before replying. "Stephen says you want our militia to go and help defend Sota from the Dkota. But we don't have a militia anymore, and when we did, they belonged to the baron."

"I talked with the duke and the bishop yesterday," I said. "The king did disband the militia—but if the Dkota attack, the duke said he'll call them up anyway, as soon as he hears about it. And that I can have the Big Pines militia if I need them."

The Dinneh headman pursed his lips. "I no longer have anything to do with any militia. They are their own men now. If you ask them, or Stephen Nez asks them, they can decide for themselves."

He paused briefly, sorting his thoughts. "We Dinneh don't care who sits on the big chair in Hasty. The elders don't care, the young men don't care. But young men like something exciting to do. Clearing land, grubbing stumps, cutting and hauling hay and firewood and fence rails—those can be tiresome to the young, and tending cattle and sheep takes wolves or bears to make it interesting. So some of them may choose to go with you. Or with Stephen. That is their right, and they will come home wiser than when they left. Those who do not die."

"It's more than just being interesting," I said. "Those who go may save the Dinneh much grief and suffering, so I hope you and your people will give them your blessings and prayers."

Todachene considered that, then told me how to find the bachelors' lodge.

It turned out to be a longhouse, also of logs, with two rows of bedsacks on a plank floor. The sacks, Stephen told me later, were stuffed with dried sphagnum. Each had a striped woolen blanket folded on one end. Two young men were preparing supper while another watched. One of the cooks said that Stephen had gone to have supper with his parents. "His mother cooks better than we do," he added, and all three laughed.

"Are you going to talk to us about the militia?" asked the onlooker. "The rest of us will be getting here pretty soon to eat. You can eat with us, and tell us about this business with the buffalo hunters."

"Maybe later," I said. "I need to talk with Stephen first."

I left them and started back to the Nez farm. As I trotted my horse down the dirt road, I felt my com buzz; I'd turned audible all the way down. I took it off my belt. The call light showed Lemmi's quick-pulsing green, but this was way early for him. "This is Luis," I said. "What've you got for me, Lemmi?" I waited three or four seconds with no acknowledgement. "Lemmi?" I said, "are you there?"

The light blinked off, leaving me staring. *A mistake*, I told myself, but I didn't believe it. I wished I hadn't answered. How far away from his set might my voice have been heard? Three feet? Four? As much as ten, depending on the volume setting. It could have been activated manually, instead of by voice, in which case only I'd have been buzzed; I was his default recipient. Speaking brief code, I called Carlos. In a few seconds he answered. "What is it, Luis?"

"Did you get a call from Lemmi, half a minute ago?"

"No, I sure didn't."

"Uhm. I did. I'm his default connection. But when I answered, he switched off."

"What do you think's going on?"

"I hope nothing's going on. Meanwhile I'll leave well enough alone. The odds are, it was an accident." *If it was an accident, why didn't he answer? Maybe it wasn't safe to talk just then, and he had it on buzz mode, instead of audible. Maybe.* "I'm going to wait and see if he makes his evening report. If he doesn't, that still doesn't mean anything is wrong, but it's grounds for worry."

"Right. Anything else?"

"Nope. That's it. Luis out."

I didn't feel good about it at all.

Stephen's mother invited me to eat supper with them. After eating, Stephen and I walked down the Big Pines Road, south through forest, talking about how he might prepare a platoon of young Dinneh militia. He'd never yet commanded men, but his aura said he was meant to, and he'd begun believing it. Said it felt natural. After a bit the road curved past a mostly open swamp—exposing a pink and gold sunset. We watched without speaking. Gradually it faded to dusky rose and finally deep violet.

It was Stephen who broke the silence. "Master Luis," he said, "you're an example to the novices."

He took me totally by surprise.

"Master Carlos is very smart," he went on. "And wise. He knows more than seems possible for one man. And he says the right things, so the novices live in harmony with each other. While Master Peng has a different wisdom. With him, each action is correct, flowing from his muse.

"But you are different from both of them. Master Carlos told us what you did in the Lizard War, before you became a master. He says you have the greatest talent of all: you make very bad situations turn out well."

Which hit me right in the gut, because at that moment I realized that answering that buzz would have bad results. "Thanks, Stephen," I said. "But there are few guarantees in the physical universe."

As we walked back to the farm, it occurred to me that Carlos's praise, and Stephen having it fresh in mind, simplified something I needed to do. Some short-term spot planning. Though my muse wasn't really pushing it. Maybe the vectors and probabilities were too poorly defined.

"Stephen," I said, "I'm going to leave you here to recruit a militia platoon of your own, to be under your command. Your authority comes from Duke Noncheba. Recruit veterans so far as you can, and re-train them as necessary, keeping in mind what you've learned from Peng. Your muse will guide you.

"Now, two things to remember: First, my muse says you and your platoon will play an important role in this war. And the other is, I don't know yet what that role will be. But you'll hear when the war has started. Someone will tell you." I was talking off the top of my head now, and believing every word of it. "That's when you'll start south with your platoon, to Soggo unless it seems unsafe there. Otherwise to the church at Sugar Grove. Have you got all that?"

He nodded, looking at me intently. Peng did good work.

"If I can," I went on, "I'll try to leave instructions for you with the duke or the bishop, or with Pastor Linkon at Sugar Grove. But mainly you'll have to decide for yourself what to do. You'll be the boss."

I clapped him on the shoulder. It was as hard as Paddy Glynn's, if not so thick. "Now, tell me back what I told you."

He did, without a stumble.

"Stephen," I said, "you're going to be a very *good* Higuchian."

And it seemed to me he would, if he came through this alive. That's the part I wasn't sure about.

Chapter 23
Disaster

(Luis)

I spent that night in the loft above the Nez kitchen. At daybreak a robin gave hesitant voice, and within a minute or two the whole choir was in business: robins, orioles, wrens . . . I got up, pulled on my jacket, and with boots in one hand, went down the ladder into the kitchen. The back door was open, and I peered out. Emily Nez stood barefoot in the east yard, singing softly in the Dinneh language; a prayer no doubt. The sun hadn't come up yet, but she was facing where it would be when it did. Maybe singing it up. I turned around and soft-footed out the front door, where I sat on the stoop—sat on my feet in the Higuchian manner—and slipped into a trance.

I awoke again to the sounds of activity inside, and pulling on my boots, started for the stable to saddle my horses. Someone—Frank or Stephen, probably— had already forked hay into their mangers, and grained them. It was warm for the hour, the horseflies had wakened, sluggish in the coolness, but they didn't like the dim interior, so I left the horses where they were.

The house smelled of salt pork frying—crisp, with raised rye bread and butter, and a duck egg for each of us, fried in pork grease. And yesterday's buttermilk. I began by asking God's blessing on the food—it was expected from a churchman—and when we'd finished, offered thanks first to God, then to Emily and Frank Nez.

Afterward . . . I was already a little slow off the mark, so I shook Stephen's hand, grinned, wished him well, and said I'd see him when I saw him. Then I got my horses and left at a trot. Two miles south down the Big Pines Road, I came to the junction with the Soggo Road. There I stopped, took out my com, and with a twinge of discomfort, murmured the connection to Lemmi's. If he was still in the chief's tipi, the signal should be in buzz mode. He'd feel it but not hear it.

⋘∘⋙   ⋘∘⋙   ⋘∘⋙

Consuela, Mazeppa's senior wife, was a rare beauty. She'd been born a Sotan, and as a fourteen-year-old novice in a religious order, had been coerced and deflowered by a visiting bishop. She'd dared complain of it, which earned her dismissal for shameless behavior. However, the mother superior who dismissed her also believed her, and arranged a job and home for the girl with a (by Sotan standards) well-to-do merchant. She would be his clerk, for not only could she read and write, she was skilled with the abacus.

The merchant was little better than the bishop, however, and soon made her his mistress. In revenge, she seduced his fifteen-year-old son and ran away with him. This was on the marches, in the duchy of Oak Groves, and they encountered Dkota raiders. The boy was killed, and Consuela carried away captive.

Her beauty captivated the raider chief, and when they arrived at Many Geese, captivated the young, up-and-coming Mazeppa as well. He traded seven horses for her, and made her his wife. It then became her turn to be captivated, for Mazeppa was a talented and considerate lover who treated her well. She in turn applied herself to learning Dkota ways and skills, became an able and daring rider—and on buffalo hunts rode with the men!

A young soul and innate warrior, she was loyal in her friendships and adamant in her enmities.

Later, for political reasons and in hopes of a son, Mazeppa married Trains Horses. Consuela, a pragmatist, had adjusted well. She'd taken the new member of the household aside and they'd worked out a set of operating agreements.

It was Consuela who first suspected Lemmi of "treachery," and told Mazeppa of her suspicions. When the new *hunka* son left the tipi at night to visit the straddle trench, sometimes he didn't return for quite a while, and she didn't believe he was meditating or praying. So what *was* he doing?

Mazeppa considered. Lemmi's new wife hadn't arrived yet; perhaps he was dallying with someone's wife or daughter. If found out, it could embarrass his dynastic plans; even create enemies. So he called to him a famed scout and horse thief, noted for his silent, seemingly invisible approaches. Telling him what he knew but not what he suspected, Mazeppa asked the man to learn what was going on.

The next morning, Mazeppa ducked out of his tipi, pipe in hand, prepared to greet the rising sun with tobacco smoke and prayer. The first thing he saw was his spy waiting nearby, so he started toward him. The spy in turn moved to where another tipi stood between himself and the chief's. It was there they talked.

"What have you learned?" Mazeppa asked.

"He did just as he said; he went to the latrine and relieved himself. Then he walked up the knoll behind it and squatted on the top. Soon afterward he got up and returned to your tipi."

"There was no woman?" Mazeppa found himself hoping there had been.

"No woman. No person at all."

"Could he have seen you?"

The scout drew himself up even straighter. "I prayed to the owl. Fanned myself with an owl wing. Dusted myself with funeral ashes. Your son did not see me."

"How long did he squat up there?"

"Little more time than it took to climb it."

Mazeppa's eyes turned to the knoll. Somehow instead of reassuring him, the report had heightened his suspicion. "Very well," he said. "Tonight be on the top before him, near enough that you can hear him pray. If that's what he does. I want to know what he says."

"As you say, Mazeppa Tall Man," the scout answered, and left, disapproving of such deviousness.

Only now was Mazeppa really conscious of the sky. It was heavily overcast, but the breeze was cool. *It will rain,* he told himself, but it would not be a fast-moving summer storm that blows through flashing and crashing, passing quickly on. It would rain all morning and perhaps all day; unusual for the time of young ravens flying.

His prayer to the unseen sun was brief. Then he ducked back into the tipi, his mind on Lemmi's evening absences.

When Mazeppa ducked back into the tipi, Lemmi could see that something was troubling him. Usually, after Mazeppa returned his pipe to its rack, they went out together to run a few miles in the cool of morning, before eating, and swim briefly in a still-cold lake. Usually they'd see others running and swimming. But this morning Mazeppa spoke curtly to Consuela: he would eat now. A shoulder steak of buffalo had been roasting on a sharp stick beside the fire, for herself and Trains Horses. Now she lay it on a cutting block, and cut it into two strips, one for each man of the household. The two men prayed to the buffalo and to God, Mazeppa's prayer perfunctory, and it seemed to Lemmi that whatever troubled the chief had to do with him.

When they had eaten, Lemmi got the chief's leave and started for the pastor's tipi. Perhaps Morosov would agree to start his lesson early. Hesitant raindrops began, and within a minute or so became a light steady pattering. Lemmi would get his lessons inside the pastor's tipi, at least to begin with.

❧❦❧   ❧❦❧   ❧❦❧

Mazeppa's uncertainty about Lemmi didn't hold his attention for long. His mind turned to the warriors of the Wolf and Yellow Bear tribes. Two days earlier, at Painted Rock, he'd been exuberant to learn that a thousand Yellow Bear warriors would soon be there. Now he was asking himself how long was soon? And where were the Wolf warriors? How long would hundreds of Yellow Bear warriors be camped among the Ulsters waiting with little to do? He'd already sent well-mounted scouts west, to meet the Wolf warriors part way. To bring him word of them, and guide them to Many Geese.

But the waiting was hard, worse than it had been a few days earlier, when he'd known nothing for sure. When he'd wondered if he'd have to invade without the western tribes.

His thoughts were interrupted by scratching on the door flap. Then someone cleared their throat. "Who is it?" Mazeppa asked, for in his darker moods he could be rude.

It was Jorval. He hadn't visited for weeks, which had been fine with Mazeppa. But now the Dkota chief quickened, glad to hear the Sky Chief's voice, for he had something to ask. "Come in!" he called. The door,

east-facing, had been left unbuttoned, for the rain
blew from the west. Jorval ducked inside.

Mazeppa had gotten to his feet in welcome. Briefly
they shared smoke, and talked about the weather. Sky
Chief said something about a polar front moving
through, which meant nothing to Mazeppa. That it
would probably rain all morning, but maybe not hard,
which the Dkota chief had already surmised.

"When do you think the clouds will pass?" Mazeppa
asked. "I want to fly with you, and see from the sky
whether the Wolf warriors are coming."

Jorval was unprepared for this. He hadn't known
of Andre's mission, and the agreements he'd brought
back with him, so Mazeppa described them briefly.
Jorval could hardly believe his luck. "We can see them
through the clouds," he said. "Would you like to go
up now?"

They did, the scout flying through sunshine
above the bright white top of the vast nimbostratus
cloudscape. Mazeppa was awed, as much by the
beauty as by the situation—in the sky, looking *down*
on clouds. Incredible that clouds which looked slate-
gray from below should be dazzling white on top!

But his awe was brief. "How do you see through it?"

"Not through that," Jorval said, rapping on a window to indicate what *that* meant. "Look at this." He'd
been guiding on paired computer panels in front of
him, each showing the scout as a pointed cursor. His
right hand gestured, while surreptitiously his left
touched a switch. The featureless screen in front of
Mazeppa was transformed, seemingly by the gesture,
brightening abruptly into a duplicate of the two views
that Jorval watched. It captured Mazeppa's attention
totally. One view showed a perspective representation
of the ground below and in front of him—white and
pale green, overlaid with vari-colored lines and symbols:
the appropriate section of the planetary coordinate
grid, topographic contours, surface temperatures,

magnetic and gravitic data, a rough representation of
vegetation type, and selected other items of interest,
along with code. All technical, meaning nothing to
Mazeppa. The other panel showed exactly the same
ground, but looked like a full-color view through the
scout's forward window, except without clouds. For a
moment Mazeppa didn't realize what he was looking
at. The more bizarre-seeming of the pair, with its
inexplicable lines, symbols, tiny flashing icons had
trapped his attention.

Again Jorval's right hand gestured, and abruptly the
naturalistic view took over the entire screen. "There,"
he said. "That's what you'd see below and ahead, if
there were no clouds. And that"—the cursor brightened, began flashing—"that is the sky canoe, with us
in it."

Mazeppa stared, comprehension dawning. Saw
lakes, streams, hills and draws in three dimensions,
the program providing nearly natural color. He *was*
seeing through the clouds! During the next few
minutes he saw what he realized were bands of
buffalo, seeming no larger than ants. And a *train* of
ants moving eastward in single file. Jorval slowed,
then stopped the scout, and gradually zoomed in on
the marching ants. Which became a file of horsemen, growing till several of them took up the entire
view—men painted and equipped for war. In the
lead was a medicine chief, tall and lean, holding a
staff with the gray-skinned head of a wolf on its
upper end.

"Is that what you were looking for?" Jorval asked.

Mazeppa answered with a question of his own.
"How far is this from my village?"

"A hundred and fifteen miles."

"How far is that?"

"A rider in a hurry could travel that far in two
days." Sky chief had no experience of horses, but his
guess was good.

Mazeppa nodded thoughtfully. "Let us go on," he said. "I want to see if there are more."

So they went on, finding numerous similar parties, turning back only when it seemed they'd find no more. By then Mazeppa recognized Thunder Butte in the distance, and had counted some eight hundred horsemen. About a third had already crossed the Great Muddy River, the Mizzoo.

What he'd just experienced had both sobered and excited him. Lemmi's evening absences were forgotten.

❈❈❈   ❈❈❈   ❈❈❈

That evening, soon after dark, Lemmi went again to the straddle trench, relieved himself, and climbed the knoll. To sit on its brow and report. Having been closeted all day with Pastor Morosov, he hadn't heard about Sky Chief's visit, nor had Mazeppa mentioned it; he'd hardly said anything at all. So Lemmi's exchange with the others was brief and insubstantial.

The spy reported to Mazeppa after they'd greeted the sunrise. "Last night I lay less than a dozen feet from him," the man said. "There was no woman."

"And he prayed?"

The spy hesitated. "I'm not sure. He seemed to speak to an amulet he held in his hand, as if to a person he called 'Luis.' I could hear it answer in a voice too small for me to know the words. One of the invisibles; perhaps an evil spirit."

A wave of chills passed over Mazeppa. His son-of-choice wore a strange-looking object at his waist, and he recalled asking what it was. A religious amulet, Lemmi had said.

"Tell no one of this," Mazeppa commanded. He gripped the spy's shoulders with both hands. "You have done well."

When Mazeppa reentered his tipi, he said nothing about what he'd learned. Lemmi knew something was up, but let it be. The morning began much as usual. They ran, swam in Shell Lake, ate breakfast. Then Lemmi went to Pastor Morosov's tipi, where he heard of Sky Chief's visit, and Mazeppa's trip into the sky.

Lemmi's skin rucked with chills. It took a bit before he could get into his lessons. He wondered why Mazeppa had said nothing. Maybe it was time to leave Many Geese; too many things were going strange. But he couldn't just ride off. He was an excellent horse-man, but no match for most Dkota, and their trackers were superb. Perhaps that night he'd call Tahmm for a pickup. He could slip off to Coot Lake and wait. It was close and easily recognized.

After his lessons, he returned to Mazeppa's tipi. As he approached, he felt a strong sense of danger, but knew no good alternative to entering. Mazeppa was sitting against his backrest, trimming his nails with his knife. He looked up as Lemmi entered, and got to his feet. "Hello, son-of-my-choice," he said.

They'd been waiting for him, Lemmi realized. Mazeppa held his knife, and Consuela her short, strong buffalo bow partly bent, an arrow nocked and ready. Trains Horses stood to one side, a length of rawhide in her strong hands.

"I have seen how well you fight," Mazeppa said. "Now you will kneel, and Trains Horses will tie your hands. Afterward we will talk, you and I."

Lemmi knelt, holding his hands in front of him. With his free hand, Mazeppa waved Trains Horses back. "Hands behind you, son-of-my-choice. I will take no chance with you. I prefer not to spill your blood." Hands behind him, Lemmi knelt, felt Trains Horses wrap the rawhide around his wrists and draw it snug.

"Now help him stand," Mazeppa told her.

When he was on his feet again, Mazeppa took the com from Lemmi's belt and examined it closely, turn-ing it over. "A religious amulet," he said skeptically, and thumbed its knurled dial. Felt a perceptible click, and turned it till it would turn no more. A tiny red eye had opened; a tiny buzz sounded. After a moment a voice came from it, loud enough for Consuela to hear eight feet away. "This is Luis. What have you got for me, Lemmi? . . . Lemmi? Are you there?"

Mazeppa stared, then turned the sleeve in the opposite direction till the tiny red eye winked out. He looked at Lemmi. "I will keep this," he said quietly. "You and I will talk about it, but not here. Not now." He turned to his younger wife. "Trains Horses, bring a cane man."

A cane man; a policeman. "Mazeppa Tall Man," Lemmi said, "in this game there are players of whom you know nothing. It is Helverti Chief I've reported on, not you. Think before you throw away everything you have built."

Mazeppa's fist struck Lemmi hard between the eyes, driving him backward into darkness. Bitterly the chief rubbed his knuckles. This person had been sent by someone connected either with Helverti Chief or a rival. Someone who, despite his magicks, lacked the power to subjugate the Dkota. Otherwise why would they resort to such treacheries?

Perhaps the amulet would speak to him again, and he would learn more about it.

Meanwhile sleeping did not come easily that night.

<Ξ><Ξ> <Ξ><Ξ> <Ξ><Ξ>

(*Luis*)

I sat in my saddle at the fork of the Big Pines and Soggo Roads, the early sun behind my right shoulder, my com in my right hand. Its indicator light told me I'd made a connection. "Lemmi," I said, "this is Luis. Can you answer?"

A voice spoke. "I am not Lemmi. Lemmi is the snake at my bosom. I have not decided what to do with him yet. Perhaps I will tell you when I do, or perhaps

I will tell you afterward. Or perhaps . . . perhaps I will ask a favor of you. We will see."

Then the connection was broken. My short hairs prickled. Tahmm needed to know about this. There might be something he could do. As for me—all I could do was continue on my mission.

Chapter 24
The Situation Liquifies

(Luis)

The main reason I rode so hard to Soggo wasn't what Mazeppa had said—I couldn't do anything about that—but it had added a sense of urgency. I arrived at the Duke's mansion a bit after midday, to learn what steps he'd taken, and tell him time was shorter than I'd thought.

I turned over my horses to the stableman, who looked at their sweat-lathered hides, then disapprovingly at me. He shouted the stableboy from his lunch, and as I left, was telling him to water and grain them *lightly,* and rub them down "right now!"

The duke's secretary was eating at his desk while thumbing through papers as if looking for something specific. Duke Noncheba was away, he said. He'd left the day before to visit each barony personally, armed with his notes on my situation report. He could have sent couriers, ordering his barons in for a general meeting, but there'd have been delays and excuses, exchanges of messages, and general reluctance. By carrying the word himself, the hard-handed old warrior would simplify and speed things. He was a *big* man, with an aura and presence hard to stand against.

I arranged for an exchange of horses. To continue with the three I'd arrived with, riding them hard all the way to the brother house, might ruin them. So the secretary went to talk with the stableman personally, while I trotted a furlong to the bishop's manse, to see what progress he'd made.

Old Mtutuzela left his desk to pump my hand and clap my shoulder. He'd penned a short but potent sermon on the importance of defending Sota against the tribesmen and their pillaging, burning, raping and killing. By supper the day before, he'd had every literate person locally available, penning copies. I scanned one and winced. Strong stuff! We'd have to reeducate both sides after the war, but first we needed to win. Meanwhile, tomorrow morning, he and two deacons would ride out to visit every dean in the duchy, with copies to distribute immediately to each pastor in the dean's jurisdiction.

I asked for a copy of my own, that I could have copied in other duchies. He gave me three. Meanwhile I was looking at his wiry, well-grayed hair and wrinkled skin, thinking of the years behind them, and the long hours he'd be spending in the saddle.

He chuckled, as if reading my mind. "I'm no longer young," he said, "but as bishop I ride often, and sometimes long hours. So I'm up to it. And these—" he held up a copy of the sermon "—will be more convincing received from my own hand."

He and the duke were a matched pair in everything but age. I hoped things would work out as well with the other nobles I intended to visit.

Then, without taking time for lunch, I left Soggo with fresh horses. As I rode, I updated Carlos, Tahmm, and Freddy via com. Probably within a day or so, Eldred would hear what was going on in Soggo;

he almost surely had an informer there. Then he'd
put two and two together, and come after us, so we
needed to evacuate the brother house. Before next
daylight.

Carlos agreed entirely.

I pushed my new horses as hard as I'd pushed the
old, gnawing from time to time on a loaf of hard and
pungent rye bread from the duke's kitchen.

Blurry-eyed and rump-sprung, I reached the brother
house near midnight. I wakened the novice on stable
duty to see to them, then went to the house and wakened Carlos and Peng. They'd been sleeping fully
dressed, needing only to pull on their boots.

"How long will it take to evacuate?" I asked.

Carlos grinned at Peng. "What's your best estimate?"

Peng peered at the tall clock clacking in a corner.
"We'll be ready at two," he said. "Catch some sleep,
Luis."

We'd decided at Moleen that Sota was potentially
hostile, so during my trips first to Kato, then to Austin
and Nona, Carlos had made preparations for evacu-
ating quickly if need be. There were travel rations for
two weeks, including oats for the horses. Pack saddles
had been lashed up, and stashed in an empty stall.
Each brother and novice, as well as their two masters, had hooks by his bed, with civilian riding clothes,
hooded oilskin cloak, saber, knife, longbow and quiver.

Horses had been assigned. Not all the novices had
arrived as able horsemen, but since being recruited
they'd ridden almost daily, often fast, on roads, trails,
and in untracked woods.

"Do we have a guide?" I asked.

"In a guest room: a deacon from Sugar Grove. I
sent for him this noon. And we have Tahmm's maps,
and the royal list of nobles by duchies, annotated by
Pastor Linkon."

"Good," I said. "I'll need fresh horses. The three I arrived with can follow along unburdened. They'll have to recover on the go."

I pulled off my boots wondering if I'd lie awake, and fell asleep so quickly, that even with the verikal, I don't remember lying down.

It was Peng who manhandled me out of bed, and once on my feet I was functional. As we rode quietly down the night-bound road, the three of us counciled, with Donald at my side. I intended to involve him in every discussion allowed by policy. Before long he'd need to operate independently of me, talking to hardheaded nobles and bishops on his own, getting them to do what was needed.

We'd ride first to Cloud, to rouse its duke and get its militias mustered. The molli king and archbishop would try to destroy the whole effort. And we? We would convert any king's men we could to our side.

⋘⋙   ⋘⋙   ⋘⋙

"Your Majesty?"

The lunch nook was small and private, and the voice from the door an unwelcome intrusion. Both the king and Elvi turned frowning. Mary's departure had left Elvi at loose ends; she missed her twin more than she or their father had expected. They lunched together regularly now, and interruptions were not appreciated.

"Yes, Brookins?" he said, more severely than he'd intended.

"Your Majesty, Mr. Rodney Sipliwo is here to see you, from Soggo. He says his business is quite urgent." Sipliwo was Duke Nonchebe's "expediter"—and the king's ears in Soggo. That he had come here himself was more than remarkable, suggesting something too important to send by post rider.

"Thank you, Brookins, I'll see him shortly. Just now I am lunching with Princess Elvi."

Brookins bobbed a bow. "Of course, Your Majesty," he said, and left the room.

Eldred turned his attention back to his daughter. "You were telling me of your sword drill," he said. She'd finally tired of being his "deputy," and returned to her earlier game of armsman. In a prepubescent child there'd been a certain charm in it, but in a princess nearing her eighteenth birthday? Well, she was the way she was.

"Yes, father," she said. "Halldor and I need instruction. By one of your better men. We've gone as far as we can with our old drills."

She had not wheedled. Her tone and expression were of someone stating an undeniable and important truth. He sighed inwardly. "Of course. I'll talk to your uncle Jaako. He'll know who best to assign."

"Thank you, father, you're a dear." She got off her chair and stepped around the table to kiss his forehead. "I must go now. To the . . . you know."

"Of course. And my dear, as you leave, tell Brookins I'm on my way." He watched her depart. Apparently she'd been spending substantial time with a young man new in his court, a well-mannered and rather good-looking lad, but empty-headed. His father was Halvor Eriksen, Baron of Floren. At their age, the two young people might develop a *serious* interest in one another. Eldred decided to learn more about the young man.

Brookins himself ushered Sipliwo into the small audience chamber, a gangling, disheveled black man who walked with evident discomfort. Eldred wondered if the man had been beaten. His face wasn't swollen.

Brookins bowed. "Your Majesty, this is Mr. Rodney Sipliwo. He brings urgent news from Soggo."

Eldred nodded acknowledgement. "So, Mr. Sipliwo, what is this urgent news?"

Words tumbled from the man's mouth. A Higuchian,

a "Master Luis," had arrived at the duke's manor with rumors of a Dkota invasion expected soon. There'd been a conference, with Bishop Mtutuzela taking part. Questions were asked and answered, plans made, and actions begun.

Unfortunately, Sipliwo had had no opportunity to contact either of his sometime couriers, for the duke had kept him at hand, and when he'd left Soggo, had taken him along. Not till the night before last, in Riverton Sancroy, had a chance shown itself. Armed with a false oral "message from the duke to the bishop," Sipliwo had wakened the baron's stable master, gotten his horse and left. He'd ridden most of the night and till noon, almost without a break and entirely without eating, until "now I can scarcely walk."

Eldred was outraged. "Brookins," he snapped, "send for the archbishop! And Jarvi! I want them here at once! I will put a stop to this treachery in such a way it can never recur!"

In the real world, every action takes time. In this case beginning with a constipated archbishop who resisted being hurried, but finally came away with his mission incomplete. Still, seventy-six minutes after Eldred had risen angry from his throne, he, along with a dismayed Clonarty and a grim Jaako Jarvi, were in the saddle, jogging down the road toward the Higuchian brother house, followed by a platoon of armsmen.

Jarvi was an old warrior nearing sixty, a kinsman of the late queen, thought of as an uncle. The king trusted and relied on him. But even if Eldred hadn't invited him—ordered him actually—he'd have been there. He knew Higuchian military prowess from the Anti-Pope's War. Locally the brothers were too few for meaningful resistance, but there'd be the problem of rounding them up, if they scattered.

Jarvi had the true warrior's innate sense of loyalty.

But his loyalties were various—to family, kingdom, monarch, God, and his troops. And the Church! And there were levels, and priorities. To his mind, at the spiritual level the Church was second only to God. But at the same time, a good and just king acts on lives at a very basic, material level, and good rule was essential to the welfare of kingdom and people. While the Church, with its saints, angels, pope . . . acted on a less material, less immediate level. But men erred, and both king and pope were men. Jarvi had pledged his loyalty to both, but for years he'd lived by the king's dollar.

They reached the brother farm and school to find them abandoned. Furnishings and tools remained, but no people—not even servants.

Now Jarvi took over. He sent two squads, each under a sergeant, to visit neighboring farms. They were to learn what locals the Higuchians had employed, and when the exodus had taken place. And to bring in any employees they found, for further questioning. Two other armsmen, who as youths had been hunters and trappers, were ordered to determine by tracks whether the Higuchians had headed west or south.

On the farm across the road, the armsmen found a woman who admitted to cooking there, she and her lame adult daughter. A son, also lame, had worked there as a handyman. They'd been wakened the night before and told not to come again till asked, she said, and referred the sergeant to another neighbor, Milo Bambino, who supervised the actual farming for Master Carlos.

Bambino admitted taking in the brotherhood's livestock. Master Carlos had asked him to, telling him to treat them as his own until notified otherwise. Early that morning he'd gone to check on them. All the cows and calves had been there, but of the horses, all that remained were the foals, two pregnant mares, and two heavy draft animals. The pigs seemed to have been let loose to fend for themselves. There'd been no goats or sheep. He and the missus had rounded up the ducks, along with the truculent old gander who guarded against weasels and the like.

The king was disarmed by Bambino's volubility and seeming artlessness—that and his not working in the brother house, where he might have overheard things—and he was one of those released. Several were taken to Hasty, herded on foot—"for further questioning." The two lame young people were helped to mount behind soldiers.

Chapter 25
Pursuit

With the first faint wash of dawn, an elite platoon rode out of Hasty northwest up the Cloud Road, commanded by Captain Kaarlo Horn, a kinsman of the late queen and General Jarvi. Eldred's orders to Horn were to *capture* the Higuchians, killing only in self defense—a reluctant concession to Clonarty and Jarvi, who were strongly against killing churchmen.

By the time Horn's platoon set out, the Higuchian refugees had been gone more than twenty-four hours, but as Jarvi had pointed out, it was not a twenty-four-hour lead. The Higuchian horses would have been resting part of that time, and the Higuchian stable had lacked horses enough for remounts, so they couldn't keep the pace Horn would.

Jarvi had pointed out that to accomplish much, the Higuchians would have to get the dukes to rebel, which meant stopping long enough to convince them. Their first target for subversion would be the Duke of Cloud, and by the time they reached him, Horn's well-mounted force would be close behind. And if

Horn caught them still in Cloud, the duke could hardly protect them.

Jarvi had talked Eldred out of sending a full company to chase them. A platoon, he said, was enough to intimidate a duke. As for the Higuchians—most were novices, and not dangerous, nor would the nobles readily embrace the cause of fleeing refugees. In fact, he said, Horn's task was less military than political: he'd remind the nobles where the real power lay.

Eldred had already considered the Duke of Kato the main danger. Edward might be frail, but both king and general believed his ambition had survived his accident, and that his injuries had probably been exaggerated. In the back of Edward's mind would be a vision of his son Donald on the throne in Hasty, with himself the power behind the throne, and Keith Frazier as military commander. Edward would know the prospects were poor, but Higuchian support might fan his flame and heat his dynastic ambition.

To quench that flame, Jarvi proposed leading an overwhelming force to Kato. Edward had never been self-destructive. A bit reckless, but not self-destructive. Confronted by sufficient force, he'd back away, and renew his oath of fealty.

Eldred and Jarvi were operating on a faulty premise: that the Higuchian's central goal was rebellion. Eldred was convinced this was the opening act in a factional schism between the peaceful Carlians and a power-grasping faction led by the Higuchians. The invasion threat was a ploy for support.

Jarvi wasn't convinced by Eldred's case, but clearly the Higuchians were inspiring insurrection, which had to be prevented. Their first stop would surely be at Cloud, whose Duke Jonas Duonelaitis was a long-time friend of Edward's. And if they got safely away from Cloud, Jarvi believed they'd ride west to make their case at Zandria, on the prairie marches. Its Duke Marcel Boileau, his duchy wounded by past Dkota raids, might well be susceptible to the Higuchian story of a new and greater Dkota threat. From Zandria, they'd no doubt ride south to Grove Falls, with its own unfortunate memories of Dkota raids.

But a powerful royal army in Kato would effectively deter rebellion in either Zandria or Grove Falls. And when Jarvi had finished laying out his strategy, Eldred couldn't imagine a rebellion succeeding. All that was needed was hard pursuit of the Higuchians, and a royal army occupying Kato Town.

∙∙∙ ∙∙∙ ∙∙∙

As an eleven-year-old captive boy, Gavan Feeny knew the Dkotan legend that pre-Armageddon dirt-eaters had conquered and humbled the buffalo peoples. It was a minor part of Dkotan lore. Little had been made of it by the teller, his foster grandfather. Armageddon and the Shuffling had neutralized old wrongs.

Much more recently he'd heard that the dirt-eaters intended to repeat the performance, and that Mazeppa Tall Man wanted to launch a great war to drive the dirt-eaters far away from the grasslands. Gavan had talked to Pastor Morosov about that. He didn't believe that people like his birth parents had designs on Dkota land. If for no other reason, how could they farm it? There was too little forest to provide fence rails and firewood and building logs. Nor would his mother, nor Sotan women in general, be willing to live in a tipi or soddy, with only hanging racks and back rests for furniture.

Morosov had pointed out that the choice to take the warpath was the individual's, not Mazeppa's. If Gavan didn't wish to go, he was free to stay behind as a hunter and safeguard. But Gavan was not relieved. He'd long since come to think of himself as Dkota, rather than Sotan. Not that he felt animosity toward his origins; he simply preferred the Dkota way of life.

But now he lived in a bachelor lodge with other

youths, most of them excited at the prospect of war, and when he'd shown no enthusiasm for it, they'd questioned him. Yes, he'd said, if the Dkota took the warpath, he too would go, but he hoped no harm would come to his birth-father and small nieces.

His reply had satisfied his questioners, but not himself. For it seemed to him he'd lied—a sin considered more serious among the Dkota than among Sotans.

If Dkota youths were unanimous, or nearly so, in their eagerness for this war, Gavan was aware that many grandfathers felt differently. A chief had no authority to make such plans for the people. Old Standing Bear said openly that the whole idea had come from Sky Chief, and that Sky Chief had been sent by Skunk Bear, Satan, to trick Mazeppa.

But it was the young men, not the grandfathers, who would take the warpath. And even most of the able-bodied older men would go, because the story about the dirt-eaters' plans was widely accepted. Besides, with emotions as they were, it was easier to go than to stay.

Gavan's frame of mind had worsened when Mazeppa said the Wolves and Yellow Bears were coming to join them on the warpath, and already had entered the land of the Ulsters. Together, the tribes would drive out the dirt-eaters, and become masters of the Misasip. Then they would set fire to the forests as often as needed till Sota was grassland, fit for buffalo and the buffalo people.

Finally Gavan had stood with other youths, watching four chiefs of the Wolves ride into the hoop to pay their respects to Mazeppa. The rumor was, a hundred Wolf warriors were setting up war camp only a mile west—no tipis, only travel shelters—and that hundreds more were coming.

On the evening of that same day, Gavan took his bird spear, making sure he was noticed, and trotted off on foot as if going fowling. As he left, grief blurred his eyes, but he would not turn back. His decision was made.

He trotted not east toward the Sota River, but north, toward Lake-With-Floating-Shores. Bordered on the long, far side by floating bog, it was used by countless geese, ducks and swans for nesting. Small fowling rafts made of cattails were stashed along the near shore. His plan was simple: a drifting raft carrying a dead goose, a duck impaled by a spear, adrift with its bladder floating, and carved with marks identifying it as his . . . Cramps happened, and young men's bodies were not buoyant.

That night he'd steal two horses from the herd, sneak off southeastward, then ride hard to Kato, where Captain Keith would know what to do. Gavan had grown up Dkota, needing neither saddle nor bridle. Nor food, for the time it would take. And the ponies he'd ride were strong, fast, and tough.

He would be there before the fourth day.

❦❦❦   ❦❦❦   ❦❦❦

(Luis)

I'd left Peng hidden in the woods a few miles south of Cloud, to watch the road. The choice had been Peng or Carlos; none of the brothers were approved to know about coms, short of serious emergency. My muse hadn't been fussing at me about pursuit, but I was pretty sure Eldred had sent armsmen after us, and I wanted to know if they were catching up. It depended mostly on when they'd started. Eldred *could* have gotten word from Soggo the same night I got back to the brother house, or sooner, though that seemed unlikely. If he had, we'd already have seen pursuers.

It appeared they hadn't gotten away from Hasty much before noon of the day we left, but they'd have remounts, and if they pushed hard . . . I didn't realize how long it would actually take them to start.

I found Duke Jonas Duonelaitus a rough old warrior, with no use at all for Eldred or any other mollies. To begin with, he didn't take the Dkota threat seriously. He was just happy to see Donald—"the new Donald," as he told Peng later—and to hear that Edward was mending.

Eldred's savage revenge at Austin and Nona may have sobered would-be rebels, he said, but the king no longer had any support among the dukes except at Nona and Austin. Like Keith Frazier, he'd fought in the Anti-Pope's War; involvement by the Order, he said, would make the nobles bolder. And when I insisted the Dkotan threat was real, he actually brightened! Mobilized to defend the kingdom, the militias might afterward be marched against Eldred.

I pointed out that we needed to stop the Dkota first, and Jonas gave me his firm agreement to set up a defense, to blunt and bloody any Dkota move east toward Cloud.

All this took place with my com on, so Peng heard it all; Peng and Tahmm. Duonelaitis would have fed us, but we needed to be on the road. Peng would arrive soon after we left, and stay with the duke as my liaison, dressed as a duke's man. Unless the king himself was leading the pursuit—and he almost surely wouldn't—Peng wouldn't be recognized as Higuchian, even if seen. Peng and I would keep each other informed by com, as necessary, though of course Jonas couldn't know that.

Regarding Peng's liaison role—ever since the Saint's time there'd been stories that Higuchians could communicate mentally with each other, even when the Higuchians hadn't heard of radio. And most people had heard such stories, whether they took them seriously or not. With Peng as liaison, Jonas would start believing, to account for what Peng knew about what was going on in Kato and Zandria, and wherever else.

For some of us—though not me so far—explicit

mental communication did happen occasionally, but coms almost always worked.

When we left the duke, we headed west toward Zandria. Cloud had been a good start. And our pursuers would almost surely pause at the duke's manor; Peng could let me know how far they were behind us.

He let me know sooner than I'd have liked. We'd been traveling at a brisk trot, when I slowed to a slow trot, dropping back. Carlos realized why—he'd felt his com vibrate too—and held to a brisk trot, taking the others with him and leaving me behind. A platoon of kingsmen, Peng reported, had galloped up to the duke's manor some five hours after we'd left. The duke offered to feed them and grain their horses, but the officer in charge—a Captain Horn— wasn't interested. He was hot to catch us. His only questions were if we'd been there and when we'd left. The duke told him, adding that I'd warned him about a Dkota invasion. He also told him our horses looked pretty well used up, which was only half-true. We'd been rotating our several remounts.

Horn demanded a one-for-one horse trade—worn-out horses for fresh. Acting for the king in hot pursuit, he had the right, and besides, his platoon outnumbered the duke's. But Duonelaitis was allowed to hold back his own personal favorite. He was as slow about the exchange as he dared, but Horn rode out of there maybe half an hour after he rode in.

Not long after Peng reported, there was another call. I ordered a break, and the men dismounted to relieve themselves, while I walked on ahead a little, to handle the call.

This time it was Tahmm. I got a big twinge—part hope and part anxiety—that he had news about Lemmi. No such luck. He was out in a courier, scouting the Many Geese region from above. There was a large temporary encampment near Mazeppa's hoop, and a sweep to the west had found sizeable groups of men riding toward it, armed and painted for war. The closest thing to good news was Tahmm's estimate that some of the groups were still three days ride west of where the armies were gathering.

I suspected his main reason for being out there was to make sure the Helverti weren't flying air support for the Dkota. If they did, or if they attacked his courier, a marine detail would fly in from the Belt and nail them.

As I ordered my people to mount and move out, it occurred to me to wonder if Mazeppa had maps. Probably. The Helverti's shipsmind could make them, just as some COB computer had made ours.

From time to time we passed someone traveling east. Or west as we were, but more slowly. Horn could ask them about us, and with his platoon of armsmen, anyone he questioned was bound to be intimidated. Probably even Duke Jonas was less enthused about rebellion just now, which was fine by me, as long as he took the Dkota threat seriously. Anyway Horn would get occasional position checks on us. So it was time for a change. Our horses weren't getting any fresher, and the men dozed in the saddle. Riding at a trot, as we were mostly, falling off your horse could cause serious injury, especially if you got stepped on.

On the move again, I made another decision, because I really needed to have someone at Kato with a communicator. That was one of the reasons I'd been keeping Freddy up to date on the project. And now was the time. So again I dropped back, and called Tahmm.

Yes, he said, he'd provide transportation for Freddy. So I called Freddy, who said he'd been looking forward to the call. Tahmm arranged to pick him up at

Moleen as soon as it was dark enough, and drop him off in Bishop Joseph's pasture outside Kato. I felt really good about that, probably from something my muse knew that the rest of me didn't.

Meanwhile the sun had set and it was getting dark. I wanted to leave the road, find a safe place to sleep, where our horses could graze and rest. Shortly I saw a stretch of rolling prairie ahead that might fit our needs, so one at a time we left the road, entering the forest. From there we rode to the prairie edge, and along it three furlongs or so, to bed down behind a little rise, out of sight from the road.

Then shouldering my bedroll, I hiked back, lay down in the woods a few yards from the road, telling my muse to wake up if anyone came along. By that time it was so dark back in the woods, I couldn't see to pick my nose; way too dark to be seen by anyone riding past. It took me two or three minutes to get comfortable—pick the sticks and stones out from under me—and only one or two more to go to sleep.

I woke up twice to a late traveler riding by. The second time, dawn was silvering the northeastern sky, and our pursuers hadn't shown up. I used my com to call Carlos. He'd already wakened, and had the others out rounding up our cross-hobbled horses. We agreed our pursuers must have camped too, hopefully not close behind, that it was time for the fox to stop running, and use his wits, and we discussed what I had in mind. Then I walked to the prairie's edge to wait for him, and listened to the birds wake up. Soon our crew arrived, Carlos leading my horse. We started down the road, and when it was light enough, I got out my mapbook. I didn't know exactly where we were on it, but not too far ahead was a village, Novo Cechov. From there, a substantial road wound south through country rich in lakes.

A night of rest and grazing had helped the horses, but it would take days to renew them entirely, so I kept the pace moderate. We reached Novo Cechov about two hours after sunup. The junction with the south road was in front of the general store, where loafers on a bench eyed us warily, curious about so many armed men. We gathered in the middle of the junction, in a tight circle, and I murmured brief instructions. Then we turned south and rode out of town at a brisk trot. About a mile south of town, the road topped a ridge, and we stopped to look back. I could see the Zandria-Cloud Road disappear over a hill a mile east of town. There was no sign of the dust cloud a platoon would raise.

We continued south at an easy trot, Carlos beside me, and entered an area of forest and lakes skirted on the east by the road. Ahead the road curved west around a hill, past a small marsh-ringed lake. The lake was fed by a small creek that crossed the road.

"That's it," I told Carlos. "Donald, you and I will take to the creek."

"Stay with me!" Carlos called to the others. "Luis is turning off here." Donald and I stopped at the creek while the others trotted splashing across, then we walked our horses into the foot-deep water and turned downstream.

After seventy or eighty feet, the creek slowed, entering the marsh. There we left it, slopping through cattails, and entered young aspen forest, our horses walking. We stayed near enough to the edge toward the lake, we could see the road curving round the hill.

"Where are we going?" Donald asked.

"I'll tell you pretty soon."

When we reached the far end of the lake, we stopped and tied our reins to slender aspens, then sat within the edge of the trees, gnawing on hardtack and watching the road six furlongs away, my spyglass ready on my lap.

It was time for a quiz. "Why did we leave the Zandria-Cloud Road?" I asked Donald.

"Because the kingsmen were gaining on us. But . . ."

"Right. You and I are going on to Zandria, while hopefully the kingsmen follow Carlos and the others. Just now I'm watching the road back there, so we'll know for sure if they're following, and that they don't notice we left the others."

I paused. "Why did we stop in the middle of the junction in Novo Checov?"

"To tell us we were turning south." Even as he said it, Donald realized that wasn't it. All I'd needed to do was turn. The rest would have followed.

"No, we stopped so the men hanging around there would get curious and pay attention. They probably would have anyway, because we're well armed, but that assured it. When Horn and his men reach the junction, assuming they haven't already, he'll question any loiterers, to learn we turned south."

"Then they'll still be following us."

"They'll still be following Carlos and the others, not you and me. Hopefully. That's why we're sitting here watching; to make sure. If Horn's as good as he should be, his scouts will be watching for sign of anyone leaving the others. And maybe the current, and sediment, haven't smoothed our tracks out below the ford. We'll see."

"What about Carlos and the others?"

"We're not entirely sure, Carlos and I. That's another reason you and I are sitting here watching." I gestured at the ground. "Take a nap if you want. You might as well."

A while later I suggested it again, and that time he did. I spent another hour watching before anyone showed up. "There they are," I said sharply, nudging Donald awake, and picked up my spyglass. The armsmen trotted across the ford without pausing. Their guidon was the royal standard; kingsmen for sure.

"I thought there'd be more of them," Donald said. Our eyes followed them out of sight around the swell of the hill.

"There were."

"How do you know?"

"Good question."

I laid down my spyglass, but still watched the road in case other kingsmen came along. Then I took my com from its belt holster, for Donald to see. "Each master carries one of these," I told him. "If anyone asks, it's a religious amulet, very personal. We call them coms, or radios. Ordinarily you wouldn't learn about it. They give the Higuchian master an important advantage, and if the world finds out, a lot of that advantage will be lost." I glanced at him, then turned my eyes back to the road.

"You're not supposed to know about coms, but this is a special mission, and you're a special part of it. Now watch and listen." Raising it near my mouth, I switched it on, at the same time thumbing the sound up so he could hear it when Carlos answered. Carlos's com was my default setting now. "Carlos," I said, "this is Luis." To Donald I added, "his com will have buzzed. He can feel it. He'll drop back, to answer without the others knowing."

Donald's eyes widened, remembering. Seconds later we heard Carlos. "What have you got for me, Luis?"

"Twenty-four kingsmen just crossed the ford at a brisk trot. They didn't notice a thing. You're still two hours ahead of them. Donald and I will stay where we are awhile longer, to see if the rest come along. I'll let you know if they do. Anything I need to know?"

"Nope. Thanks, Luis. If you're done, I am."

"Fine. Luis out."

"Carlos out."

I gave Donald another glance, grinning now. His mouth still hung open. I gave him a closer look at the com, indicating the tiny clock. "And that," I told him, "tells us what time it is. Just now a quarter past ten."

"Good lord," he said, hardly more than breathing it.

Then I told him about Peng, and how I knew there were two more squads. And what he and I would do next, unless something happened during the next hour to change my mind.

Now Donald asked another question, a bit hesitantly. "How will Carlos and the others keep ahead of the kingsmen?"

"They won't. They'll split off two at a time, wherever it won't be noticed. Like creeks and well-tracked crossroads . . . Carlos will ride alone to Hasty. The others will work their way back east and north, and join Peng at Cloud."

After another hour, no other armsmen came by, so Donald and I rode off west through forest, and after a time, prairie. A country lane took us north to the Cloud-Zandria Road. Several hours ahead of us should be another twenty or so kingsmen riding west toward Zandria.

The only loose end I knew of was the two squads chasing Carlos's folks. When they lost them, their commander would most likely return to Hasty, to report that the Higuchians had scattered on the back roads north of Kato. But they might go on to Kato themselves; I'd call ahead and warn Freddy, just in case. An unlikely third alternative—the one I liked least—was, they might ride back to the Zandria Road and arrive at Zandria behind us.

Chapter 26
Gavan Feeny Debriefed

"Thank you, Jamie," Frazier said, and sent his page back to the orderly room. Then he turned to the visitor the boy had brought, a man dressed in Higuchian travel habit. "Master Freddy," Frazier said, "I am Captain Keith Frazier." He motioned to a chair, and both men sat. "Thank you for sending word of your arrival. I trust you slept well after your long day in the saddle."

Freddy did not correct him. "I slept quite well, thank you captain. Your page said you had someone you wanted me to meet."

"I do: a young man from the Dkota, Gavan Feeny. He was born in the duchy, on a farm west of here in Killibegs, in the barony of Tasnad. He was stolen by Dkota raiders at age eleven; he'd made a good impression on the raid leader by trying to protect his mother." Frazier grimaced. "She in turn was killed trying to protect him. One might wish our king had been there to witness it.

"From that point Gavan was brought up Dkota, and with kind treatment and youthful resiliency, became

Dkota himself in every way—except for his early memories. So at age fifteen—with his foster father's approval, I should add—he came back to see if his younger sister had survived. Then, preferring hunting to farming, he returned to Many Geese.

"Yesterday he returned to us again, with *very* troubling news. And since you've come as Master Luis's deputy, you need to hear what the boy has told us."

"You have my attention."

"The kernel of his message is that the Dkota and Ulster have formed an alliance with two buffalo tribes from farther west—from what Gavan calls 'the red grass country.' Allied warriors from those tribes had begun arriving at Many Geese—and that was four days ago—to take part in an invasion of Sota. And I do not say 'invasion' carelessly; Mazeppa's stated purpose, Gavan says, is to drive us 'dirt-eaters' out of our country. One might be excused for wondering if we can withstand such an attack, weakened as we are by a molli king who doesn't believe in self-defense."

"Indeed."

Freddy's one-word reply reminded Frazier. "But of course it's Gavan you want to hear." He stepped to the door. "Jamie, tell Gavan I'd like to see him, please." He turned back to Freddy. "During Gavan's earlier return we talked at length, and he told me much about the Dkota: among other things, that they consider it rude to order or interrupt. As a people, it seems they are generous, not demanding."

"Thank you, captain. I'll keep that in mind."

A minute later the page was back at the door, followed by a tall, strong, sun-darkened youth. Freddy had been expecting someone smaller, more vulnerable seeming. He got to his feet, and Frazier introduced them. Gavan met Freddy's extended hand, his own hand firm but mild, not squeezing.

Briefly Frazier took charge, not launching into what was wanted or needed, simply telling the youth that

Freddy was from Ilanoy, far to the south. That he was a warrior and churchman who'd ridden (Frazier assumed) a long week or more to reach Kato, and that he'd come to aid in the defense of Sota.

Then he invited the young man to sit, and tell what he knew about Mazeppa's plans. Freddy sat again to listen, backward on a chair, thick, pale-haired forearms resting on the chairback, pale gray-blue eyes resting so mildly on Gavan, the boy was not put off despite his Dkota upbringing.

Much of what Gavan told, Freddy already knew, from Frazier's summary and Lemmi's reports—most importantly that the Wolves and Yellow Bears were arriving, and that surely the attack would follow soon.

When Gavan had finished, Freddy thanked him. "I appreciate all you've told me," he said. "It's the wish of the Church that this difficulty between the Dkota and the Sotans be settled without fighting, if possible. I can also tell you that the kingdoms along the Misasip have no intention of killing the buffalo, or invading the buffalo people. The old stories are true—the eastern people did those things before Armageddon. But God *undid* them, and the Church will not let it be done again, even if the kingdoms become able to.

"And the Church has another concern in this. Many people will die if this war takes place, and such killing can poison the minds and souls of farmers and buffalo hunters alike, leading to hatreds and bloody vengeance for years to come. So if the Church cannot prevent the war, it will try, so far as possible, to let the invaders do the dying, instead of women and children. The more decisive the invaders' defeat, the less will be the Sotan wish for revenge. While being the invader, the Dkota can more easily blame themselves.

"It remains to be seen how successful we will be.

"Now I have questions to ask, that I hope you will answer. They may help us.

"Tell me what the Dkota do to wrongdoers among them."

For just a moment the question knocked Gavan off his center. Then he answered. "Someone, usually someone who has been harmed, complains to the council of elders. Then the cane men—the constables—are sent, and the person accused is brought before the elders, who listen to both sides, and question others who may know something about it. Afterward they decide if any wrongdoing occurred, and what restitution must be paid. Also what penance the wrongdoer must perform to be in harmony with the people again. If the wrongdoer refuses, he must leave the tribe, to live alone or with outsiders. The newscarriers make it known throughout the people. The wrongdoer is no longer Dkota, and is not to be helped in any way."

Freddy nodded. "Um-hm. Last autumn the Church heard whispers that Mazeppa wanted to attack Sota. That he had been lied to by a chief who looks like a white bear, and rides in a sky canoe, an evil person who wishes all people ill. So the Church sent a man among the Dkota to learn what was true in these stories. We hoped he would have returned to us by now, telling us what he'd learned." Freddy paused. "The churchman's name is Lemmi. He has a dark skin, and speaks Dkota. What do you know about him?"

As soon as Freddy said the name, it was clear that Gavan knew something, and when he answered, his voice was soft.

"In our hoop, everyone knew him. He was adopted into the Dkota, and named Mazeppa's son-of-choice. But later Mazeppa announced that his son-of-choice was a traitor to the Dkota."

"Ah. And what is done with traitors?"

"Only the oldest of the elders could remember the last traitor. Now I too am a traitor; I could not be true to both peoples. But Mazeppa does not hold me in his hands.

"The oldest grandfather said the last traitor had been executed by the chief cane man. The bladder of a buffalo was tied over his head so he couldn't breathe, and left there after he was dead, so his soul couldn't get out. Then his body was put on a pyre and burned to ashes, to destroy the evil in him, and the ashes spread to feed a tobacco patch, that in death, the evildoer might provide good to the people."

Freddy nodded, his lips pursed. "And was this done to Lemmi?"

"No. Pastor Morosov is our spiritual leader, and he said Mazeppa had not proved Lemmi's treason. The elders agreed. So Mazeppa said he would keep him where he could do us no harm. And the young men backed Mazeppa, so the elders gave way on this."

"Keep him where?"

"In times past, many Dkota lived in soddies in the winter, north of the great hoop. Some bands still do. It is believed that Lemmi is kept in one of the soddies, guarded by cane men."

Freddy's gaze was calm. "Gavan," he said, "you have helped both your peoples: the Dkota and the Sotans. More than you can know yet."

He got to his feet, Gavan rising with him. "It is clear the Dkota are a good people," Freddy continued, "but misled now by the white bear chief. I will want to talk with you further. Your knowledge will help us understand what the Dkota consider justice, so we can be just to Mazeppa and his warchiefs when the fighting is over. Those who do not die in the fighting."

Freddy crossed himself. "I can hear confessions, and even a person with nothing to confess may want to talk about things that trouble them. I expect to be in Kato for some time, staying with the bishop. Any time you wish to speak with me, send word. I'll come if I can."

He turned to Frazier. "Captain," he said, "I would like to meet your duke now."

That was both the truth, and a good way to dismiss Gavan. Frazier called Jamie in and told him to continue working with Gavan on reading and writing. "If Gavan is willing," he added.

Gavan nodded, and left with the page. Freddy recognized a troubled soul when he saw one, but this was also a strong soul.

As the two men walked to the duke's apartment, Frazier asked a question. "What was that about a sky canoe and a white bear chief? He hadn't mentioned them to me."

"I suppose it didn't occur to him when you talked yesterday. We've heard of them before, the man and the sky canoe. Stories travel. We may know more later."

The captain didn't know what to make of that reply, and let it pass. "Do you think we can win this war?" he asked.

"Sooner or later," Freddy replied, "Mazeppa will lose. The sooner, the better, to reduce the demands for vengeance, that generator of further hatreds, self-perpetuating spiller of blood."

The Higuchian's gaze was mild but firm. "The Order is involved in this for only one reason: to prevent that deadly cycle. And it has ordered five of us to see to it. Obviously our five swords can't win it, so it will have to be yours—Sotan swords and Sotan resolve—with our guidance."

Frazier nodded. He'd hoped for more, but what the Higuchian said felt right to him.

Chapter 27
The Road to Zandria

(Luis)

Donald and I reached the Cloud-Zandria Road again and continued westward. Near evening, off the road a bit, we saw a stockade, a village, and a baron's manse. We turned off there, and still wearing civilian garb, I asked the baron whether he might trade horses with us—good horses, fresh, in exchange for road-weary. Ours were visibly of good breeding, but worn out, and it was our need, so it was he who offered terms. I countered them, and after the second round he stopped.

"If I'm to bargain with a man," he said, "I should at least know his name. Also, 'twould be a shame if animals like these"—he gestured at the horses I wanted— "were to be used as hard as those you rode in on."

"Ah." I decided to take a chance. I liked this baron's aura, and what he'd said, and maybe my muse was nudging me. "Did you have visitors earlier today?" I asked. "A dozen at least? Likelier twenty? Headed west?"

He grimaced. "And demanding the king's hospitality? I have. As for which direction they were going . . . I didn't see. We're a furlong from the highway here."

"How did their horses look?"

"They'd been ridden hard, but not so hard as yours."

"That's because they had remounts. Did they ask whether you'd had guests within the past few hours? Probably more than just the two of us."

"Their leader did."

"Did he mention why they were interested?"

"No, nor did I ask. But I can tell you this: when I answered, they seemed . . . not surprised."

"Let me do you a favor," I said, "whether or not the two of us do business. The next large party of armed men through here will be headed east, not west, and there'll be a lot more of them. Counted not on the fingers, not even showing them twice—unless each finger stands for a hundred. And it's not the king's hospitality they'll want, but anything they see and can easily carry. The rest they'll kill or burn."

I extended my open hand then, and slowly, uncertainly he met it. "I am Master Luis Raoul DenUyl, of the Order of Saint Higuchi," I told him. "And my comrade . . ." I turned to Donald. "Would you care to identify yourself to the baron? He appears to be a man to trust."

Donald reached and also shook the baron's hand. "I am Donald Edwardsson Maltby, of Kato. Our horses look as they do because we were pursued, without remounts, all the way from Hasty. We threw off our pursuers by baiting them south out of Novo Cechov, then circling back. It was Master Luis's ploy." He gestured toward me. "Just now I'm . . . his apprentice. I'm learning a lot from him." He laughed. "And so are the kingsmen, though they don't yet know what."

We were there another twenty minutes or more,

answering the baron's questions. Then he exchanged horses with us, a straight trade, throwing in a five-pound cheese, two long loaves of rye bread, a gallon of beer and his good wishes. When we left, he was getting ready to warn his people, summon his old militias, and prepare his stockade. He wasn't waiting for word from his duke, Marcel Boileau of Zandria. He considered Marcel a good man, but one who might soon have kingsmen lodged with him.

We didn't want to catch or overrun the kingsmen, so Donald and I laid up early in the edge of an aspen grove. Before we slept, I made a conference call. Carlos was in the southeast of the duchy of Zandria, or maybe across the line in Cloud. Freddy was in Kato, Peng in Cloud Town, and Tahmm wherever. Carlos had dropped men off by pairs as he went, at crossroads and junctions, to pick their way back to Cloud. Carlos himself was alone—"hard at work growing a beard"—and expected to be back in Hasty in a few days, where he'd do whatever seemed productive. Peng said Duke Jonas had had a planning session with his engineer, who was now working west of Cloud, marking areas of forest for felling abatises. "Interesting patterns," Peng added. "The man is a strategic genius."

But it was Freddy's news that interested me most. A young Dkota named Gavan Feeny had arrived at Kato Town. I remembered Keith telling me about him before. He'd verified that allied tribesmen were arriving at Many Geese for the invasion. And most important, he believed Lemmi was still alive, a prisoner.

Donald listened to all of it, intently, soaking it up.

Again we were awake at first dawnlight, and in the saddle by sunup. This was prairie land, with aspen groves and scrub. Pleasant enough country, except it hadn't rained for two weeks, and the road dust was bad.

An hour later, from a high point on the road, we saw a village ahead, of maybe three or four hundred people, and beyond it a dust cloud I felt pretty sure was raised by the kingsmen. Donald had the same idea: "I'll bet that's the other two squads," he said pointing. "There's probably an inn there, where they claimed king's hospitality last night. They've given up on us."

"I'll bet you're right," I told him.

I decided to close the gap enough to keep track of them. We speeded a bit, but slowed when we reached the village. Now I realized there were two inns, one fairly large, the other small. Not too surprising on an important road with villages far apart.

Seventy or eighty yards ahead, two riders pulled onto the road from the smaller inn, *both dressed as kingsmen!* That took my interest. "Donald," I murmured, "let's stop here and water our horses. When I ride on, you hold back till you're a hundred yards behind me." I indicated the couple ahead of us. "There's something peculiar about those two. I want them to think I'm alone."

He nodded. I'd sparked his curiosity too.

The two armsmen had remounts trailing, but no pack animals. And even at a distance, neither really looked like an armsman except for the uniform. As I drew nearer, one seemed too small, like a fourteen-year-old. The other was tall but slim. They were trotting their horses at an easy pace, and I gained on them. We were well away from town before they looked back. I wondered if they'd speed up to avoid my dust, but they didn't. Experienced travelers, I supposed, not wanting a race.

At twenty yards the smaller glanced back again. *A young woman!* What was she . . . Then I realized. Princess Elvi! Pastor Linkon had told us that when she'd been younger, she'd played soldier: even had her own small hauberk. And what came to me was, she was following the armsmen, hoping to join them in the capture of the evil Higuchians.

But not yet riding with them; they'd have sent her home under guard. Maybe the armsmen had stopped early, at the large inn, and having caught up inadvertently, she'd stayed in the other.

Coming even with them, I slowed, and tried out my Swedish accent. "Good day, good sirs," I said. "Can you tell me how far it is to Zandria?"

It was her squire who answered. "*Goddagen, herr landsman.* "*Jeg kjenner deg ikke. Er du fra Floren?*"

A Swede! He'd expect me to answer in Swedish![3] I drew my saber, at the same time crowding him, and slashed his arm, then knocked him from the saddle. For just a moment Elvi froze, then went for her blade. I slammed her helmet with the back of my saber, and she let go of hers, grabbing at her saddle pommel to keep her seat. I jabbed her horse in a haunch; it reared, and Elvi fell, already half stunned. The horse ran off.

Meanwhile Donald galloped up. Seeing no witnesses, we tied their wrists, lashed the two across the back of her squire's horse, and hauled them to a thick grove of aspen two furlongs from the road. There, in the middle of the grove, we sat them down, tied them to trees, and I bandaged the squire's wounded arm. He'd lost a fair amount of blood.

That done, I took Donald aside and told him who the girl was. He was dumbfounded. "She may prove useful before we're finished," I went on. "Meanwhile I don't want her to know that I know who she is."

Leaving them in Donald's care, I rode off to catch Elvi's saddle horse. It wanted nothing to do with the guy who'd jabbed it, so I hazed it away from the road,

---

[3] Actually, Halldor Halvorsen had spoken a dialect of Norwegian

out of sight behind a hillock, and drove an arrow behind the shoulder. It fell dead. I stripped it of everything that might identify it. As for the remounts, they'd been without saddles, and had already trotted off toward town. I'd have to let them be.

After that I radioed Freddy, Tahmm, Carlos and Peng, and told them whom I'd just caught.

Back in the aspen grove, Elvi told us who she was, and what her father would do to us if we harmed her. I slapped her hard on the side of the head, bringing tears. Skipping the accent, I told her she was no princess. "A princess wouldn't be riding down the road dressed like an armsman's hoor. Whaddya take me for, a fool?"

At that she shrieked such obscenities, I gagged her. This enraged her squire, so I gagged him to. Then I told her I could easily sell her to the Dkota for ten good horses. "They enjoy owning Sotan women." I laughed then. "They might even throw in a cur dog for your lover."

After a breakfast of rye bread and cheese, I announced I was leaving them in the aspen copse and heading on west, to see about hiring a covered cart to haul them to Dkota. "Watch them," I told Donald, "and don't no way untie them. They're worth a lot to us."

I arrived in Zandria at first dusk and stopped at the inn, where I had a beer with a pair of locals. They told me two squads of kingsmen had arrived that day. It was the talk of the town.

"Kingsmen? I'll be damned! Why are they here?" The locals didn't know.

"What's the chance of me hiring on with the duke's force at arms?"

"No chance at all. They've got a waiting list."

"Then who should I see about joining the militia?

Or whatever you call them these days. It ought to be easier to find work if a man's in the militia."

One just shook his head. The other gave me a couple of names, and where they might be found. One was a tapman named Vito, who worked days right there at the inn. He lived down the street, and was probably at home.

He was, and he was also a man glad to talk to me. An ex-guardsman, he'd lost his place as part of the reduction. What did he think of the Dkota threat? He took it very seriously. What did he think of the king?

Vito was instantly suspicious. "Why do you want to know?"

"I'm a friend of Duke Edward."

"Of Kato?" We talked some more. By reading Vito's aura, I could say things that kept him going. According to him, the duke's armsmen considered Eldred a dangerous fool.

Zandrians, it seemed, were a little like buffalo people: many of them herded unfenced cattle, could ride and rope, and were generally tough. Vito had grown up a herdsman, then spent two years in the northern wilderness before becoming an armsman. Yes, they'd kept the militia going, sort of. In fact, he was a militia sergeant.

Then I told him who I was, and what I had in mind, and he agreed to help. Within three hours he had twenty others, each with a saber at his side and a bow in its scabbard. We left them in a belt of cottonwoods near the river, while Vito and I slipped through the shadowed night to an unguarded entrance that's "the best way to get into" the duke's mansion. He also knew, he said, what room the commander of the kingsmen would be sleeping in.

He was right. We slipped silently down the hall, entered the room, and found the lieutenant asleep, reeking of whiskey. Not wanting him awake yet, I pressed on his phrenic and vagus nerves, then tied and gagged him, wrapped him tightly from neck to foot in bedding, and stashed him in a closet.

"Looks like a damn cocoon," Vito murmured.

Then, as agreed, he showed me which room was the duke's. "But don't do anything to him," he whispered. "He's a good man, and I don't want to have to kill you."

I chuckled just loudly enough for him to hear; it was too dark to see a grin. "I want his help," I reminded him. "If he's not willing, I'll have to knock him out so I can get away, but that's the worst I'll do to him."

Vito wasn't comfortable with that, but there he was, cheek by jowl with a man he'd helped break in, a man who'd assaulted a king's officer, so he muttered, "All right, let's do it."

I was the one who knocked at the duke's door: softly, with fingertips instead of knuckles. It took a minute for the sound to waken him. Then, muzzy and grumpy, he asked who was there. I knocked again without speaking; I needed him close, so Vito wouldn't have to talk loudly. After a moment he asked again, this time from just the other side of the door.

Vito answered as agreed upon: he had a messenger from Edward Maltby. The door opened, and the duke let us in. When he'd closed it, I told him who and what I was. That Edward had had a spy among the Dkota, a Sotan raised by them from age eleven. And that Mazeppa had not only united the Dkota and the Ulster; he had an alliance with the Wolves and the Yellow Bears. That he was set to invade Sota with two armies; one rampaging down the Sota River, aiming at Grove Falls and Kato. The other would attack Zandria and Cloud. Then both would ride on to Hasty, where they'd no doubt burn the town and massacre the population.

I also said the Church had a plan. That I had the commander of the kingsmen bound and gagged in a closet, and held Eldred's daughter Elvi captive, with Donald Maltby guarding her a few hours away. And finally I asked him if he could turn the kingsmen; that if turned, they'd make a difference in defending his stockade.

Half an hour later, the duke's men were awake and armed, and Vito had brought the militia into the duke's yard. That done, it was I who wakened the kingsmen.

I identified myself to them, then told them Mazeppa's plan, and that Eldred refused to believe it. Had even tried to have the pope's representatives captured or killed. "You'd know which," I added. "It was you, Horn's platoon, he sent to do it."

It was then I told them I held their commander captive, and Elvi hostage. And that one Dkota army was positioned to move down the Sota River against Oak Lands and Kato, while the other would attack Zandria, then go on to Cloud.

"So what I need you to do," I went on, "is stay here with the duke's force at arms until the Dkota arrive. Men like you can make an important difference. Meanwhile I'll send word to Eldred that I have Elvi— send word and her hauberk, helmet, and saber. There's not another set like them. She was playing soldier when we caught her."

They knew Elvi's penchant for "playing soldier," so that got them as convinced as they were likely to be, short of seeing her.

"And if any of you are worried about the Church— Clonarty won't be archbishop after this." I paused, then went on. "But what happens to Clonarty, or even the king, isn't as important as what happens to Sota."

"What's the lieutenant say about this?" one of them asked. He was troubled at breaking his oath to the king, and looking for more highly ranked support.

"He's all right, but bound hand and foot," I said. "I didn't know if I could trust him."

The kingsmen split. About half agreed to remain at Zandria and help the duke's forces defend the stockade. The rest said they'd do whatever their lieutenant said. So accompanied by the Duke and Vito, I got the lieutenant out of his closet, took out his gag, and went through it all one more time. "If you sign a warrant to defend Sota against the Dkota," I finished, "and if the *duke* trusts you, *I'm* willing to trust you."

I'd read his aura while I talked to him. I read no sign of trickery in his mind.

"Yeah," he answered, "I'll sign that warrant. The reason I got drunk tonight was, I didn't like my orders. I never trusted Eldred's treaty, and this mission went against my grain."

I got a few hours sleep, then rode out of Zandria at first dawn, trailing a horse for Elvi. While I rode, I radioed Freddy in Kato. He talked first. Tahmm had reported that Mazeppa's allies were mostly all gathered. They'd probably leave Many Geese within a few days.

Then I told Freddy what had happened in Zandria the night before. "Meanwhile what really troubles me is Lemmi."

"Luis," he interrupted, "let's not worry about Lemmi yet."

"Why? What do you know that I don't?"

"Probably nothing, but I'm not worried about it, so it seems to me my muse knows something."

I wonder if that means Lemmi's already dead, I wondered. If he was though, it seemed to me I'd know "All right," I said, "I'll go with that," and we disconnected.

About noon I reached the grove where Donald watched our captives and fought sleep. I took him aside, and reran the night's events. When I finished, he laughed, shaking his head. "Luis," he said, "I wouldn't have imagined even *trying* all that. Blessed lord! The world's a good place after all."

I let it stand at that. We'd won this little tilt, but the actual war hadn't started yet. Removing the squire's gag, I gave him water and food, then gagged him again. When I removed Elvi's gag, she tried to bite me, so I slapped the side of her head again, stunning her. Then I gave her water and bread, and when she'd had some of each, I gagged her again. After letting them relieve themselves, we retied their hands in front of them so they could hang onto their pommels, hoisted both Elvi and her squire onto their horses, and led them down the road toward Zandria.

We'd hardly gotten started when my com buzzed. I dropped back and checked in. It was Tahmm.

Donald was right. The world *is* a good place. And it would be better when I'd had some more sleep.

Chapter 28
Smooth and Bold

Master Freddy had replayed his session with Gavan Feeny for Tahmm, who'd then taken off for Many Geese, with two men in an armed scout. En route he'd spotted a sizeable party of braves riding east to join Mazeppa, but that was not what he'd come for.

Now, hopefully, he'd found the site. From 10,000 feet, the old soddy winter villages were clearly discernible on the green early-summer prairie. The weather had been dry enough that the roof grass on the low huts had died back. The village Tahmm examined held some thirty huts, but the grass and ground around them suggested they hadn't been occupied for two or three years.

What had taken his attention, via scanner, was a man lying on one of the roofs, perhaps asleep, his face shaded by a broad-brimmed grass hat. Two horses grazed nearby; apparently the man on the roof had a partner inside. Tahmm locked on a gravitic vector that intersected the surface thirty yards in front of the soddy, and rode it down, decelerating smoothly the last hundred yards, stopping inches above the ground.

The man on the roof sat up and slid off the mound-shaped soddy, landing lightly on moccasined feet, watchful, strung bow in one hand, an arrow nocked. Another man pushed aside the buffalo-hide door flap and came out, also with bow in hand.

Tahmm extruded the ramp and stepped out, a hand raised in greeting. "Mazeppa has asked me to bring his troublesome son to him," he called. "To answer questions."

The Fohannu had left his cap inside the scout, exposing his white cranial fur. He resembled a burly human with prematurely white hair. Presumably these particular two Dkota had never seen "Sky Chief" close up. At any rate there should be some of the cult they didn't know.

The two Dkota looked at each other. Tahmm started toward them. "Leave him bound," he said. "It will be safer."

The senior guard nodded, and they ducked inside. A minute later they reappeared, supporting Lemmi between them. The Dinneh's brown face was gray-tinged, swollen and cut. His feet dragged. His wrists had been freed, the cord cut.

Tahmm gestured. "Bring him," he said. Together the two Dkota half carried, half dragged their prisoner. Tahmm's copilot emerged watchfully. At the ramp, the two Fohanni took over from the guards. Lemmi seemed comatose, even moribund, his body aura on the verge of disintegrating. But his spirit aura was—not strong, but aware, connected

"Lemmi," Tahmm murmured, "hang on. You can make it."

When they had him secured on the stretcher, Tahmm returned to the hatch and looked out. "Thank you," he called to the guards, then stepped back inside, and the hatch slid shut. A minute later his healing hands were busy with Lemmi's aura.

⋘-⋙ ⋘-⋙ ⋘-⋙

The guards watched the scout rise, shrink skyward and dwindle out of sight. "He will answer no one's questions," said one of them. "I should have gone to Mazeppa yesterday, when he first had convulsions."

The other didn't answer. They'd followed orders. Mazeppa had beaten the prisoner badly, probably ruptured something in the man's belly.

Chapter 29
Jarvi Marches

Jarvi's orders were simple and explicit:

- Occupy the stockade and palace at Kato
- Arrest the Maltbys, father and son
- Arrest Captain Keith Frazier
- Send the three of them, in chains, to Hasty for trial and punishment
- Remain at Kato at the expense of the duchy, holding the palace and stockade until otherwise notified

And unwritten but understood; remind the nobles everywhere of the royal power.

Simple and explicit, but not easy. First it was necessary to *get* his force to Kato. It consisted of four of his five companies of mounted infantry (bowmen), one of his two rifle companies (also mounted), and two batteries of light field artillery. For the mounted infantry this came to 480 men plus officers, and 20 wagoners and their draft horses. For the rifle company, 120 men plus officers, 5 wagoners, and draft horses.

For the artillery, 56 artillerists, 16 gun teamsters, plus ammunition wagons and 80 horses. While attached to the command section were kitchen wagons, blacksmith wagons, haywagons, officers' baggage wagons, all their horses, teamsters, helpers. . . . All told, including remounts, replacement horses, and horse tenders, they came to some 950 officers and men and over 1,200 horses.

The mustering had taken place on the royal military reservation four miles north of Hasty. The army didn't have most of the wagons, carts, and draft horses necessary. They were hastily requisitioned from farmers, draymen, etc. for miles around, as was much of the hay.

Four extremely busy days after the Higuchian flight, the army was ready to leave, an accomplishment of which General Jarvi was justly proud. Eldred, of course, had been complaining about the delay half a day after ordering the movement, so Jarvi, gruff old warrior, had taken him aside and begun going over with him all that the job required. After twenty minutes of that, a sobered Eldred begged off and returned to the palace, where he bragged on his general as a genius.

With the army finally mobilized, the next day was spent moving it eight miles to the North Landing ferry dock. All the oared ferries of useful size had been gathered, for miles along the river. The next day and much of the following night were taken up with ferrying the army, its men, horses, wagons and field guns, across the river.

Once across, the artillerists, who marched afoot, and the more heavily loaded wagons, set the pace. They made three miles per hour—when moving. The officers and mounted infantry could easily have traveled twice that fast, but that was not an option. And there was, of course, the time spent breaking camp in the morning and setting up camp in the evening.

At least, Jarvi told himself, the road was dry. Dust was preferable to mud.

On the third day after crossing, the lead scouts heard the sound of axes ahead, and trees falling, and discovered a large party of axmen felling trees on both sides of the road. They hurried back at once, to inform the general. Soon afterward, a scowling Jarvi approached the work at the head of a company of mounted riflemen. At sight of them, the axmen rested their axes and cheered lustily. One of them, presumably the foreman, came forward grinning.

"What," Jarvi asked, "are you people doing?"

The foreman had swept off his hat, exposing a long, ruddy-brown face and white forehead. "Why sir," he said, "we are felling an abatis. On the duke's orders sir." His accent announced French as the language of his community.

"The duke? You're on the Royal Domains here! The duchy begins at Ville!"

"Yessir, begging your pardon sir. We are from Ville. But this is a very good place for an abatis." He waved an arm. "When the Dkota get here . . ."

Jarvi realized now, from the direction these people were felling trees: they were to stop an enemy riding along the Sota River toward Hasty, not to stop a royal army marching on Kato. And the axmen had cheered his arrival! These people *believed* the Dkota were coming, as seemingly must Edward then, and his commander at arms, Keith Frazier.

"Very well, m'sieur," Jarvi said. "Rest while we pass, then continue as you were."

As he led his troops past, he looked the peasant axmen over, shirtless, their torsos slick with sweat. They'd accomplished a lot, and believed in what they were doing, he did not doubt. He'd swear they had no notion he'd been sent to arrest their duke and take him to trial at Hasty.

And now he felt ill at ease with those orders.

Chapter 30
Jorval Rebuffed

Notes Toward An Analytical
Compendium of Chaos Cults
ESS Office of Technical Studies

The term "Commonwealth of Homid Worlds" is a translation from Xioxa, and "homid" a Terran word of Indo-European origin meaning any sapient, mobile, limbed and usually bipedal lifeform that manipulates its environment.

The Commonwealth originated as a logical effort to keep peace in the Xiox section of the galaxy, to regulate commerce and adjudicate controversies. It evolved as (1) the result of Xiox socio-philosophical evolution, (2) the hazards of shared existence, and (3) the impulse to nurture other sapient homid life forms through the minefields of technological and philosophical evolution.

Chaos cults are a reactionary fringe phenomenon, decay products of abandoned cultural values. The Xiox themselves have had chaos cults, have survived and outgrown them, by learning to tolerate them within limits, and excising (with minimal force) only the dangerously destructive. Tolerance, compassion and inclusiveness had been the keys. Those and patience. It had not been easy.

The Helverti result from the Fohannid culture's absorption into the broader and more mature Xiox culture. They are an ill-defined set of individuals unhappy with the direction their species had chosen. A sort of cultural foam, self-skimmed from the kettle of change. Their adherents were sparse, a network without membership rolls, ranging from wealthy to indigent, professional to unskilled, sober to addict, affable to hair-triggered. A few are scions to fortunes, others to misfortunes.

But in general they share a need to contact others similarly disaffected. And what defines them is their attraction, at some level, to chaos as a response. Most are relatively benign, the basic difference between the benign and the malignant being zealotry. . . .

Most Helverti are not zealots. They simply seek connection—on the broadest level electronic—with others similarly disaffected. Groups grow out of those contacts—groups and sometimes chaos projects, clandestine, more or less haphazard, and often self-aborting.

The Fohannid cultists led by Charconvera Jorval were a mixed group. Jorval himself had good intelligence, some management talent, and considerable if low-key magnetism. He'd been born wealthy but not extremely wealthy, been well-educated, and employed in the family enterprises. Deemed lacking in judgement by his seniors, his had been staff positions, which he'd filled with as little diligence as the family would accept. Basically he was self-destructive (a common feature among chaos cultists), and at some level was aware of it. Thus at critical junctures he tended to back out of situations. But some situations are difficult to back out of.

⋖⋗⋖⋗ ⋖⋗⋖⋗ ⋖⋗⋖⋗

From four miles up, it seemed to Jorval that Mazeppa had done remarkably well, given the scattered people he worked with, and their independent nature. They appeared to be fully gathered now, needing only to mount and ride eastward. He realized his major role in this had been to provoke and justify the war, and that fighting it was entirely in Mazeppa's hands. The only reason to stay—a very compelling reason—*was to see it happen.* Then he'd pick up Ench and return to the shuttle.

After taking Mazeppa up in the courier, some days earlier, and showing him his approaching allies, the chief's appreciation had warmed Jorval's heart. Which had surprised Jorval; he'd never imagined that appreciation would mean anything to him. Now he wanted more of it. So he'd had the shuttle's shipsmind create and print out detailed maps to facilitate the tribes' military operations, and had flown to Many Geese to give them to Mazeppa.

Mazeppa had frowned. "What are these?" he'd asked.

Maps were familiar to the Dkota, scratched in soil with a stick, or made with paint on leather. But what Jorval had given him were so loaded with arcane detail, Mazeppa hadn't recognized what they were. He should, Jorval realized, have foreseen the problem. So he'd explained, which by itself tarnished the pleasure of giving. "Maps," he'd finished, "are a means of knowing where you are, and finding places."

Mazeppa had shaken his head. "My people know

where they are," he'd said, "they know where they are going, and what they are to do. In the greening month, Gallagher and I sent scouts—truth tellers in dirt-eater clothing—to scout the way. They fasted, purified themselves, prayed to the Great Spirit, Mother Earth, the four directions. Then they rode separately all the way to Hasty, looking about them. Every brave knows that water flows downhill, that the streams gather, that the trails of men come together, separating from time to time, and end, and that the great trails lead to the principal places."

He'd handed the maps back to Jorval. "These can only mystify and distract them."

From the Fohannu's expression, Mazeppa had recognized his disappointment. So he'd reached, grasping the sky chief's thick shoulders in friendship. "My people are unlike your people," he'd said, "but we appreciate our friends, and Jorval is truly my friend. When my spirit sagged, he lifted it. He showed me the coming of the Wolf warriors. I will not forget that."

So Jorval had departed feeling . . . not so badly. And with a new understanding of Mazeppa and his people, who were not so primitive after all. This morning he was revisiting Many Geese for one purpose: to congratulate Mazeppa on his armies. He felt a bond between the two of them, and this congratulation would validate it. Also, his visit would boost Mazeppa's stature among any non-Dkota there.

It took a while to locate the chief from the air, for Mazeppa was not at his hoop, but with his southern army, mustering to march. When Jorval located him, he landed at once. The chief was at the ramp before Jorval stepped out—and stunned him with a bitter and unexpected indictment! "You stole my son from me!" His voice was hard, hard. "Why?"

Jorval stammered his reply. "Stole? Your son? I've never even seen him!"

Mazeppa told him of his foster son's treachery, and

what the guards had reported: that Sky Chief had taken Lemmi away. Jorval shook his head. "It's not true! They lied! Why would *I* want him? He's your son, not mine. Maybe—maybe his guards treated him roughly, and he died, and they buried him. I don't know!"

Mazeppa was not touched by his denial. "He is yours now," he said. "I give him to you. I do not want him back. But you stole him from me. I will remember that."

He turned and stalked away then, leaving Jorval deeply shaken by the unjustness of the accusation—and by the focused anger of such a powerfully charismatic personality.

Then, abruptly, Jorval realized: for whatever reason, the COB had done this thing. The guards had never seen him personally, certainly not close up, but they'd have heard him described. And to the Dkota, no doubt all light spacecraft would look alike.

He was so shaken, it was difficult to climb back aboard the scout. The indigene Mazeppa called his son was a COB agent. Had to be. And they'd rescued him without compromising their secrecy.

It wasn't fair! He hadn't deserved this! He'd played within the bounds!

But the COB had touched him, even though indirectly, and he knew the taste of fear.

Part Four

WAR

Part Four

WAR

Chapter 31
The Bowstring Released

For days, couriers had ridden from Mazeppa to Gallagher and Gallagher to Mazeppa, with questions and updates. That nothing was written was not important. Non-literate peoples, or those with limited access to writing materials, tend from childhood to develop good recall of details. And for couriers, their leaders tend to choose from among the better of them.

That morning Mazeppa mounted his best horse. At midday, the army would start eastward as planned. All the chiefs were prepared. All knew.

As the sun climbed, the braves gathered. There were no MPs to direct traffic, nor did the war parties muster in ranks for pre-departure roll calls and inspections. There was no last minute checking of maps, rolling stock, order of march. The entire plan consisted of what army went where. Once launched, speed would be of the essence.

That spring, scouts dressed as dirt-eaters had explored both routes, learning the main roads, the countryside, place names . . . Food would be no problem. Everywhere were bands of the dirt-eaters' spotted buffalo, stupid, easy to kill.

The northern army, led by Gallagher, consisted of some 800 Ulsters and 500 Yellow Bears—1,300 fighting men in all. The southern army, led by Mazeppa himself, numbered 1,200 Dkota, 1,000 Wolves, and 300 Yellow Bears.

The chiefs didn't worry about coordination. Their braves knew how to ride, to camp, to fight. They would, more or less, follow the directions of their leaders. And these rules: "Move, don't linger; burn all the hamlets and villages you come to; kill all male dirt-eaters you encounter, man and boy, but don't waste time on long pursuits. Nor on pillaging or raping; wait till the war has been won. Burn the palisades, where it can be done quickly, otherwise pass them by; but if they take fire, kill the male dirt-eaters when they come out. Move swiftly till you reach Hasty. Then all the braves will rest outside the stone walls, eating spotted buffalo and enjoying Sotan women and girls, while the Sotan fighters starve inside their fort."

It wasn't necessary or possible to tell his braves how to do those things. They'd see, and seeing, they would know.

That's how it would be done.

At the two camps, some sixty miles apart, the sun reached the meridian at nearly the same moment. Hardly a minute apart, the two principal war chiefs made a loud cry, and their armies set out at an exuberant gallop. They'd slow quickly enough. They knew horses, and how to treat them.

❦ ❦ ❦

(Luis)

At Zandria Town, Donald and I had gathered several excellent riders as couriers. Then we set out for the baronies in southern Zandria and northern Kato, to explain the situation and strategy to the barons and their local headmen. And to suggest tactics. We needed to do at least two baronies a day if we could. Hard on horses. Hard on us.

Marcel and his captain would educate the baronies farther north and west.

At our first stop, we generated less than certainty about the situation, but enough concern that the baron promised quick action. The stockades would be resupplied—mainly with food, water, arrows and fodder, depleted since the peace treaty. It was interesting that no one had really believed in the peace treaty, yet they'd used it to rationalize letting supplies get low, and to not seriously push militia training as a volunteer activity.

On the second morning we arrived at the baronial seat of Ronglue Lumthan, and met with the baron, his captain, and a local headman. I described the strategy: supply the palisade, muster the militias; and get the women, children and elderly well away from the Zandria-Cloud Road, with older men to guide and assist them, taking only a few milk cows per group. Drive the rest of the cattle eastward to more extensive forest.

The baronial armsmen and part of his militias were needed to help fell and man abatises at the most strategic sites, well to the east, toward Cloud, where there were sizeable areas of forest. "Abatises to bleed the Dkota, stop them and send them back to their grasslands."

My com buzzed, and without explaining I excused myself, to receive the report in the shade of a yard maple. It was from Tahmm: the invasion had been launched—something like twenty-five hundred headed southeast for the Sota River Road, and maybe twelve hundred headed toward Zandria.

I returned to the meeting and gave them the news. They looked unsure. How could I have learned such a thing? In a few days, when my news was verified, the Order's reputation would be enlarged.

<≒≺-≺≎≻   <≒≺-≺≎≻   <≒≺-≺≎≻

That night we had another conference call, sharing what we'd learned. There were four masters actively involved, not counting Lemmi now, plus Tahmm, our eye in the sky. Carlos, who'd grown up bilingual, was back at Hasty already, using a Spanish accent as part of his disguise. He'd rented a room in a house where Spanish was the language, and played an occasional game of checkers with the grandfather there to brush up on the language.

He was looking for a job that would get him into the palace, a delivery job, he thought. He had a ten-day growth of black beard that covered him from the eye sockets south. A few more days, he said, and Eldred wouldn't recognize him if he had five guesses.

As for Peng, he'd told Duke Jonas, at Cloud, that Mazeppa's armies were on the move, also their size and where they were headed. Jonas had asked how he knew. Peng answered that Higuchian masters had ways of knowing things.

Freddy and I had made our coms known to Donald and Keith Frazier, violating major policy in this very first masters' operation. But Donald and Keith were key actors in this, and responsible men. We needed them, and they needed confidence in us. Tahmm had done the same with Lemmi and me when we were brothers, but Tahmm is Tahmm, the COB's director of operations in North Merka. When it was over, we'd have to defend our policy breach to Dzixoss. But according to Tahmm, if you followed policy slavishly, you had no business being on the job. It's almost as bad as ignoring policy.

Until the call was nearly over, Tahmm said nothing. It was our mission, not his, and he wouldn't put his oar in the water unless he thought it was vital. The problem was knowing what was vital before the fact. But the high point was when he put Lemmi on, from the clinic at the Academy. Lemmi sounded heavily medicated—slow, muzzy, groping—but alive and able to talk. He was being treated mainly for internal injuries, he said, and looked forward to getting back to us.

I didn't feel too kindly toward Mazeppa just then.

I spent the night in the rectory at Satomomiji, a baronial seat in the south end of the Duchy of Cloud. I didn't go to sleep right away; I was reviewing mentally. We didn't have much time—the tribesmen weren't riding turtles—and there were things I'd neglected. When I'd left Austin, I'd had the notion (my muse again) that Sergeant Major Banda would play a role in this. So I decided that in the morning, Donald and I would split up, take two different routes to Kato. We'd handle the barons along the way single-handedly, and push hard to get there in two days. The Dkota wouldn't be there that soon. Then, from Kato with two fresh horses, I'd head for Austin.

❖❖ ❖❖ ❖❖

At various points along the River Road, Jarvi and his army had come upon, or heard, companies of peasant axmen felling abatises. They'd left most of the roadside trees standing for now, trees typically coarser and heavier, with the limbiest tops. They could be felled later, as necessary, to close the road. Every group of axmen he'd talked with had been enthused to see him. Twice, foremen had told him they'd known all along that Eldred wouldn't abandon them to the Dkota, and Jarvi hadn't corrected them. Which was unlike him, but what could he say?

Late spring and early summer had been dry and clear, but this morning had dawned on puffy cumulus that grew quickly, riding the wind eastward. Jarvi kept glancing upward, concerned. Being near the river, the road burrowed through forest, mostly, but occasionally the general was granted a larger view. Far to the west, clouds had built high, and flattened. The troops saw what Jarvi saw, and knew as well as he what it meant: storms, big ones. By late morning, thunder muttered in the distance.

Accompanied by an aide and three horsemen, Keith Frazier arrived to meet the general before noon. Two of the newcomers hurried on northeastward. Frazier, his adjutant and an aide stopped, then fell in beside the general. The "adjutant" was Freddy, dressed as a Katoan ensign. By that time the thunderclouds were close enough that only their dark blue-gray undersides could be seen. The treetops had grown restless, and the distant muttering had become rumbling, with occasional rolling booms. As the two seasoned warriors shook hands, Frazier wondered briefly what Jarvi would think—or do!—when he heard what he'd hear.

Just now, Jarvi's mind was on the looming storm. "Did you bring this?" he asked half humorously, gesturing upward with a thumb.

Frazier laughed. "It's you, not me. It's come to greet you; meet you halfway."

The general ordered a halt, his trumpeter bleating it northeastward, others passing it on. The riflemen reslung their rifles with muzzles inverted; the artillerists covered the mouths of their guns with leather caps, and the teamsters their cargoes with oiled, tightly woven canvas, lashing it snugly against threatening wind. Everyone donned their oilskins.

Now the treetops began to wave, bob and bend, a great leafy thrashing. The thunder was near, and the wind suddenly cold. Men, horses, the forest, seemed to draw in on themselves against impending violence. Then they heard the hail, wind-driven, galloping—stampeding!—across the forest roof. Teamsters and artillerists crawled under their wagons. Men on horseback left the road for the shelter of the forest eaves. Lightning flashed, thunder *crashed* deafeningly. The horses started, some rearing. Then the hail

arrived, the first raising puffs of road dust. Within
a minute the road was blanketed thickly, some of the
stones an inch through, clicking, snapping, clattering,
bouncing high in all directions like round white
drunken grasshoppers. Leaves and twigs rained down
from battered treetops. Lightning flashed and pulsed,
accompanied by crashing rolling thunder. Near the
column, several trees split, tops plunging to the ground
with shocks the men could feel.

Then came the rain, displacing the hail, pelting
almost as hard and cold, and more thickly. The forest
roof leaked like a sieve now, the leakage gentler than
the rain, but thick.

Frazier traded exhilarated grins with Jarvi.

It was a strange conference they held then, talking
loudly to be heard. Frazier's news was biggest:
Mazeppa had begun his invasion with two armies,
the collected braves of four tribes. No mere raiders
these. The northern force was riding eastward toward
Zandria, the other southeastward toward Grove Falls
and Kato.

Frazier didn't say how he knew. Jarvi assumed spies
galloping headlong to report, while the tribesmen
mustered, preparing to leave Many Geese.

That first squall line passed in half an hour, moving off eastward, the thunder mere grumbling now,
the rain only heavy, not torrential. Jarvi contemplated
a new set of circumstances. The kingdom was being
invaded, and time was short. At least so Frazier
claimed, and for as long as Jarvi had known him—
twenty years—Frazier'd had a reputation for integrity.

Meanwhile the road was muddy, which would slow
his army. If he turned back, would he reach Hasty
before the Dkota did? Kato was considerably nearer,
but could he get there before the Dkota?

"Keith," he said, "when will the abatises be closed?"

"When I send word."

"What will the road be like between here and Kato? For wagons, and the guns?"

"In places not too bad. In others . . ." He shrugged. "It's been dry enough that if the rain stops soon, the excess should drain fairly well. But if it keeps up all day—" he waved a hand to indicate the steady rain "—it'll be hard slow work getting them through."

Jarvi contemplated. "In the stockade at Kato," he asked, "are the runways strong enough to accommodate artillery?"

"Neither strong enough nor wide enough."

"Umh." Again the general thought, a long silent minute as they rode. "I'm going to send the artillery back to Hasty, with the rifle company, and their wagons, of course. The rest of us will go on to help stop the Dkota at Kato, God help us. How's your fodder supply?"

"You're bringing a lot of horses with you. Until the Dkota get near, you can graze your stock in local pastures, but once inside the walls, the hay will disappear fast, and it'll be seriously crowded."

Jarvi glanced at the sky as if hoping for a sign that the rain might stop soon. The undersides of the clouds remained dark blue-gray, still tall and full of rain.

He turned to his executive officer. "Major, tell Stolz and Koskela the Dkota are on their way." He turned again to Frazier. "About two thousand of them, is that right, captain?"

"About twenty-five hundred on this road, and twelve hundred more on the Zandria-Cloud Road. That's the word."

Jarvi looked at his executive officer again. "Tell them that. Tell them they're to take their people back to Hasty to help defend it. I'll lead the rest on to Kato, to delay the Dkota. To . . . " He paused, took a deep breath. "To give His Majesty time to come west, or send an envoy west, to negotiate with Mazeppa. Go now."

Briefly, glumly, he watched the major turn his horse

and trot back down the road. Wondering how close those estimates were. Twenty-five hundred. Twelve hundred. Their precision generated skepticism. He'd feel happier with rounder numbers—two thousand, one thousand—but let it pass. The Dkota had mustered two large armies; that seemed to be the reality.

He looked at his adjutant. "Captain Piper, repeat to me what I just told Major Fahzi."

The captain repeated it, adding nothing, leaving nothing out.

"Good! You will ride back to Hasty as fast as you can, with a good remount but no baggage. *That's as fast as you can.* And report it to the king."

The adjutant looked stricken. He couldn't *imagine* His Majesty accepting such a message. He'd be outraged! Nonetheless he saluted. "Yessir!" he said, then wheeled and galloped off northeastward, skirting the stopped wagons, hooves splashing mud.

The old warrior watched him go. He couldn't imagine Eldred accepting it, either; the king would deny the facts rather than change his philosophy. He turned to Frazier. "Captain," he said, "your report had better be true." But there was no edge to his words. He'd been uncomfortable with the treaty from the start, but had swallowed his mistrust.

He'd sworn two oaths—one to the king, and one to defend Sota. Now it seemed they were incompatible, and he'd been forced to choose in the saddle.

Again the mounted infantry took up their march toward Kato. After a bit the rain eased, and Jarvi suffered pangs of uncertainty. But the road *was* bad in places. In some the troops had needed to uncoil ropes and take up pry poles to get the wagons through mudholes. And when a new phalanx of thunderheads rumbled to the west, his uncertainty eased. Eldred would still hate him for what he'd done, but he'd stand by his decision.

Chapter 32
No Longer Theoretical

There were always rumors in Hasty; it went with being the king's town. King's towns get more than their share of travelers, and the tales told and heard tend to be more interesting. Recently, more than one rumor from Soggo had dealt with supposed activities of the duke, the bishop, and a Higuchian master. Also a great invasion was soon to be launched by the Dkota chief, Mazeppa, who'd tricked the king into a false peace treaty. And not only the Dkota, but half a dozen other buffalo tribes, sworn to kill all the Sotans they could lay hands on—after raping the women and girls—and drive the rest out of the kingdom.

Before Jarvi left with his army, everyone in Hasty had heard the stories, variously embellished. Meanwhile the Higuchians had abandoned their school and farm. (They'd said they'd return, but who could know for sure?) The neighbors speculated among themselves, and inevitably, on visits to town, dropped a few comments to friends.

A few days later, a rumor whirled through that Jarvi was preparing to leave with his army, to stop the invasion if he could. By that time it was generally known that Captain Horn had galloped off up the Misasip toward Cloud, at the head of a company. (A platoon wasn't interesting enough.)

Later, part of Horn's so-called company, a "remnant," rode into town and disappeared into the palace grounds. From this grew four rumors: one, they'd brought Higuchian prisoners; two, they'd brought dead Higuchians; three, they'd come back bringing their own wounded; and four, only a handful of the "company" was left.

Meanwhile some of the more affluent and prudent burgers bundled up valuables and carted them into the countryside by night, to bury them, and by dawn's light make a map of the site. Others at least boxed or bagged theirs, and perhaps rode out to find a good location. Still others, even more covertly, picked someone to spy on. People on one or another such errands even disappeared, though their bones might eventually turn up.

The process accelerated when travelers from Kato reported hundreds of militia out felling abatises in an effort to protect Hasty from the invaders. At this, some of the less affluent townsmen began not showing up for work. Employers checking on them discovered their lodgings abandoned, stripped of anything they could hike away with. "Off to Skonsin" was the guess.

The last to hear of these things, of course, was the king. When finally he did hear, he sent out criers, with trumpeters and guards, to announce there was nothing to it, and forbidding anyone to leave town without a pass signed by a royal warden. This slowed the exodus, and encouraged those with suitable penmanship to try their hand at forgery.

Carlos, when he arrived, heard much of it himself, and passed it on to the others during their evening conferences.

⊰※⊱　　⊰※⊱　　⊰※⊱

At Duke Nonchebe's residence in Soggo, they'd heard nothing new and reliable about the developing situation. Then, one morning, a courier rode up to the duke's residence on a lathered horse, bringing a packet from Peng, who'd recorded and copied a message from Luis to Nonchebe, signing it "signed for Luis." With it, at Luis's request, he'd cut and sent two pages from his own mapbook. All to be given to Stephen Nez.

Nonchebe looked it over. The key information was that Mazeppa had launched his two invasion armies, one toward Kato, the other toward Cloud, with Hasty as their ultimate target.

He at once sent off a courier to Big Pines. Without the dispatch or maps; he wouldn't risk their loss. Within an hour the courier was back. He'd run into a platoon of Dinneh on the road, with Stephen in command, in Higuchian uniform.

The duke stepped out on his wide veranda and met the young Dinneh as he rode up. "I have a message for you from Master Luis," the duke said, and led Stephen to his office. "It arrived an hour and a half ago. If I'd had any doubt before about why he is called 'master,' this dispels it." He handed Stephen a rolled sheet of paper. "I've read it," he added, "in case anything happened to it." Then he handed Stephen the map sheets, which had begun as selected high altitude recon photos of the northern Royal Domains and adjacent Soggo, and been enhanced by a photo interpretation program in the courier's shipsmind. Inked on one of them was a small rectangle through which ran a segment of the Misasip. The rectangle had been enlarged on a page of its own. Luis's message, in small neat script, told what was needed and wanted, with an addendum signed "Peng."

Stephen looked, studied, and considered. As a novice, he'd been introduced to contour maps. Finishing, he whistled faintly.

"It will take much doing," the duke said. "I can let you have some militia. Otherwise I'll send them to Cloud."

The young Dinneh shook his head slowly, eyes thoughtful, attention on this new task. "No," he answered, "I have nearly forty men of my own. What you *can* give me is written authority to recruit laborers."

Without hesitating, Nonchebe lay a piece of paper on his desk, sat down, dipped his pen and began to write.

Actually, the job as Stephen saw it was greater than Luis had envisioned, and with greater potential benefits.

But he'd overlooked the main obstacle entirely. And he didn't see auras.

❦❦❦   ❦❦❦   ❦❦❦

If he'd learned nothing else from all this, thought Halldor Halvorsen, he'd learned not to trust love.

In fact, Elvi had never been "in love" with Halldor. She'd been looking for some young noble who'd do her bidding, someone suitably good looking, and he'd met her criteria. As for him, he'd dreamt of marrying into the royal family—Princess Mary, actually—but she'd gone off to a nunnery, which left Elvi.

Then, one breezy afternoon while sparring, Elvi had decided to find out what sex was like. With unremarkable ease, she'd enticed him into her room, and discovered she enjoyed it greatly. Coupling was one thing Halldor was well suited to. At age fourteen, in his father's manse, he'd been seduced by a serving wench, an experienced woman of seventeen. (Not all noble seductions were of the help; it could work both ways.) Actually his skill was limited—he was too self-centered—but he had a large capacity for it.

Elvi had coupled with him in the palace a number

of times. On her initiative—she was the princess, after all—and they'd never been caught. (As a child she'd been a clever, sometimes daring explorer, and knew most of the palace's concealed nooks and passages.) And along the road, they'd coupled in every inn and hayshed they'd stayed at, along with a couple of shady nooks in forests. If that wasn't love, what was?

But in Zandria, in protective custody, she wouldn't even talk to him, except to upbraid him for "letting me be humiliated by that arrogant bully on the road." And for Elvi, sex was less compelling than what she thought of as principle, which was whatever aberration currently gripped her. In this case she couldn't have defined it.

Actually, defining was something she seldom did, even to justify her wishes, because justifying was another thing she seldom did. She didn't need to. She was her father's daughter.

At any rate, she'd dropped Halldor like a hot stone.

So he felt sorry for himself. He had no horse, and his father's barony—one of the Royal Domains—was a very long way to walk. Especially with a Dkota army on its way. He'd never disbelieved in a "Dkota" invasion, but it had never seemed very real to him either. Now it was beginning to. And while he'd like to revenge himself on Elvi for cutting him off (he'd fantasized several versions), his overwhelming desire was to escape before "thousands of screaming tribesman" came to destroy Zandria and the stockade, and kill everyone there.

Thus one night he dressed for the road, tossed a heavy brass candleholder out his second-story window, then let himself over the sill, from which he hung by his fingers as long as he could before dropping. It took him a long uncomfortable minute to find the candleholder, then he walked quietly to the stable.

He knew the layout; he'd visited it earlier that day

to "admire the horses." In the process he'd seen where the tack was kept, and the empty stall that served as the stableboy's bedroom.

The stable door had been open during the day. Now it was closed. Carefully and almost soundlessly he raised the latch. The hinges were less than soundless, but he heard no response from the stableboy.

Unexpectedly, the oil lamp inside was lit. Was the boy awake? Apparently not. Hmh! He deserved to be sacked, but meanwhile his failure simplified matters. Halldor closed the door, slunk to the boy's stall and peered in. He smelled whiskey; that explained the unsnuffed lamp. But still—how deeply was he sleeping?

Halldor hefted the candle holder. Very little light found its way into the stall, and he could barely make out the lad's form. By daylight he'd looked pretty well grown—a husky sixteen-year-old, he'd guessed. He got the lamp, brought it to the open end of the stall and set it on the floor.

One chance. He knelt beside the boy's straw-sack bed and raised the heavy candleholder, telling himself silently, *do not close your eyes*. Then he swung, *hard*, felt the impact—and realized his eyes were shut. They popped open. The boy's head was a mess, the candleholder a mess. Halldor fought down the contents of his stomach.

Fear helped, for he had no doubt that now, if he was caught, he'd be hanged. Shuddering, he wiped his bloody right hand on the boy's trousers. Thoroughly.

Surely the horses would smell the blood and ooze of brains or were they war horses? Hunters maybe. At any rate he needed to hurry, saddle the horse he'd selected earlier, lead it outside and silently ride away. But first he needed to cover his crime, and overhead was a loft half full of hay.

When his mount was bridled and saddled, he took

it to the end of the barn that faced away from the
house, opened the door and led the animal to the
hitching rail there, looping the reins around it. Then
he went back to its stall and carried a armful of hay
from the manger to the stableboy's room, piling it on
the foot of the straw-sack bed, next to the wall. Almost
frenzied, he added another armful, and more. The
other horses were awake and restless now, nervous
hooves hammering the floor.

Finally he tossed the oil lamp onto the hay he'd piled
up. Flame flashed, and he fled. Outside, his hands
shook so, he had trouble freeing the reins. The other
horses were snorting and stamping, and swinging into
the saddle, he rode away. But somehow not at a gallop, not yet. A trot. And not into town nor past the
stockade, but across a pasture where the armsmen's
horses, some distance off, raised their heads to watch.

Burn! he thought urgently, backward toward the
stable. *Burn!* Now he speeded his mount. In the
stable, the horses would be frantic by now, whinny-
ing, kicking the walls of their stalls, and wakening the
duke's palace, where they'd be wondering if the Dkota
had already arrived. Then they'd see the light from
the fire. First one, then another, would run out to
free the horses and lead them from the stable. Would
they discover the dead stable boy? Get all the horses
out and discover one was missing? Or would the fire
grow too quickly? Had he remembered to close the
door he'd left by? If he hadn't, they'd surely know,
know someone had left by it, know what had happened.

In the excitement, would someone think to check
his room? Or would they not miss him till morning?
Fool! he thought. *What made you so sure the Dkota
would come? You'll have the duke's men on your trail.
They'll beat you up and drag you back behind a horse.
And then, if you're still alive, they'll hang you. If
you're lucky.*

Looking back over a shoulder, he could already see flames.

Gradually, riding calmed Halldor, and he slowed his mount to a canter. He'd intended to flee to Hasty by way of Cloud. Should he take lesser roads instead, south, then east? Which would they expect, back in Zandria, when they decided what had happened? And he couldn't drive this animal at a canter all night. *Fool, fool!* echoed in his head.

An idea struck him then—stop at the post station in Chita, tell them he carried an urgent message from the duke to Cloud. Snatch a bite to eat, a drink of water, get a fresh horse. Did he dare?

At Zandria, practically everyone under fifty years of age came to watch the fire. Andre and Jason had entered the burning barn and managed to rescue a single horse each. The animals were terrified and dangerous, almost impossible to control. The fire, Andre reported, seemed to have started in Pierre's room. It was an inferno, and they'd seen no sign of the lad.

Nor would they, the duke thought. He might have run away, of course, but he doubted it. When the hayloft floor had burned through, the whole mow of hay had fallen onto the level below. Such a mass of it would smolder all the next day, too hot to approach. Pierre was almost surely under it.

He should have sacked the boy when he'd been caught drunk on duty. But mostly he'd been a good lad, and his widowed mother worked in the kitchen, so the duke had heeded his pleas and promise, and kept him on. As for how the fire had started—he'd probably taken the lamp into his room.

Not till young Halvorsen failed to show for breakfast was another explanation offered, and it was Princess

Elvi who offered it. "It is," she said, "the sort of thing he'd do."

Perhaps, the duke thought, but if so, the young man had a ten-hour head start, and there was no way of knowing what road he was on by now. Meanwhile he himself had things to deal with that outweighed even the crime young Halvorsen stood accused of.

⊰⊱⊰⊱   ⊰⊱⊰⊱   ⊰⊱⊰⊱

The northern invasion route ran through the center of the Zandrian barony of Grande Prairie, where an extension of the Cloud-Zandria Road petered out a little west of the village of Ellbogen. From there it continued as the Grande Prairie Trail, much-used for driving cattle. But it seldom knew a wheel, or even a travois.

With the treaty of Kato, cairns had been raised to mark the border at major crossings, and the Grande Prairie Trail was one of them. The cairns had been raised on order of King Eldred II; Mazeppa had agreed to their locations. The chief considered them a sham, a sop to the Sotan king. So did Duke Marcel.

Ellbogen was not the seat of the barony, but being on its western fringe, and subject to past raids, for forty years it had had its own small stockade. A nearby chain of lakes was bordered largely by tamarack swamp, whose straight durable conifers provided excellent poles for the walls.

Recently—and earlier on occasion—scouts had patrolled the boundary, small wiry young daredevils mounted bareback on the fastest horses in the barony. They'd grown up herding cattle, and as riders were near enough to Dkota quality that the difference would be of no consequence in a race.

And they didn't need to *carry* the news. Also along the boundary was a series of pyres, like chest-high tipis roofed with birchbark. The scouts were never far from one. The pyres were of tamarack or jack pine—pitchy

wood easily ignited—replaced every other August. A
costly task, because except for tamarack in places, it
was brought from scores of miles away. Here the
scattered upland woods were of aspen, or burr oak,
and along the streams, cottonwood, silver maple, ash
and boxelder . . . that didn't smoke as abundantly and
darkly. And elm, which hardly burned at all.

Those pyres were Zandria's early-warning system—
the pyres and the expensive fire starters the scouts
carried. Fortunately the massive storm, that had
dropped nearly seven inches of moisture on Kato, had
passed a hundred miles south. These pyres hadn't
known rain for more than two weeks, in what normally was the wettest season of the year.

The Grande Prairie Trail was the invader's point
of entry. Twelve minutes before they reached the
border, a scout, Dieter Dietrich, had spotted them and
lit a pyre. Seeing the smoke column, the braves
speeded their mounts, and entered Sota at a gallop.
The invasion was no longer theoretical.

It was afternoon when word of the attack on
Ellbogen reached Duke Marcel at Zandria, carried by
Dieter Dietrich himself on his third horse. His last
look back at Ellbogen, Dietrich said, had shown him
a large column of smoke; the invaders had succeeded
in setting fire to the palisade.

Marcel sent a fresh courier on a fresh horse eastward toward Cloud, and others to his barons—all but
Baron Thibeau at Grande Prairie, where Dietrich,
while changing horses, had already raised the alarm.
That done, Marcel ordered the remaining townsfolk
and his own household, Elvi included, into the stockade. It was then the duke thought again of her lover—
he had no doubt that's what he'd been. The scoundrel
had abandoned her. As for himself, the princess was
not a person he could like, but still, how must she

feel, abandoned and with her father's philosophy utterly discredited?

And while occasionally she said something remarkably odd, even stupid, this changed when she asked about the management of duchies. Then she could sound knowledgeable, even astute.

He would, he decided, watch for something she could do, something worthwhile with which to busy herself.

❖❖❖   ❖❖❖   ❖❖❖

Meanwhile the northern army, having so easily destroyed the Ellbogen stockade and the people inside, had dashed on to the baronial seat at Grande Prairie. The baronial fortress was unique, built of sun-baked bricks and well defended, so the invaders paused only long enough to set fire to the village before storming off again. The next village, Lago Preto, had been abandoned; again the invaders set fires before swirling off once more toward Zandria.

It lost the race to a squall line that, booming and flashing, thrashing and gusting, drenched the grass, aspen and oak savanna. Cattle stampeded, then surrendered, backs hunched, water streaming from their flanks.

The braves arrived at Zandria lashed and soaked by icy rain, shivering, teeth chattering—and took shelter in the abandoned town. They never thought of attacking the stockade. The only fires their numb, barely functional fingers made were in fireplaces, and those with difficulty. Then, glum and thoughtful, they huddled there till morning, which dawned chill through broken clouds and fitful showers.

Because the day before had been long, they made the new one a day of rest and recreation, butchering and feasting on cattle, sheep and swine, not much disturbed by occasional spatters of rain. Not till nearly evening did they feel out the stockade's defenders, finding them alert and able. The attackers backed off, serious assault dismissed.

At dawn of the second morning, the Ulster and Yellow Bear braves torched most of the town's buildings on the inside. Then they mounted and left, trotting eastward without enthusiasm. It was still cold, and raining again, not hard, but as if to continue all day.

On the stockade's defensive walkway, Duke Marcel and his bishop stood in woolens and slickers, the wet stink of smoldering wood and thatch ugly in their nostrils, watching and listening as the invaders rode away. As if in truce, without a farewell flight of arrows from either side.

The two noblemen watched them out of sight. Then Bishop Loudun lowered himself onto aging knees, pressed his palms together, raised his eyes to heaven, and recited a prayer of thanks to God, in French. Duke Marcel turned his eyes to the courtyard and called to his marshall. "Charles!" he shouted, "organize crews and lead them into town to put out the fires, while the rain is still with us. God willing, the devils will not return this way."

⬦⬦⬦   ⬦⬦⬦   ⬦⬦⬦

Two days later, Elvi, wearing new traveling clothes, went to the fort's stable carrying two sheets of paper. One was folded, sealed, marked with the ducal signet, and featured the word "SECRET." The other—the most important from her point of view—was a brief order signed by the duke.

Or so it seemed. She'd acted as his scribe on several instances. And because most of the duchy was not French-speaking, the duke had followed the usual procedure for government business: he'd dictated them in Merkan. So she'd gotten a sense of how he worded things, and by now her handwriting was familiar to the fort's dispatcher.

Also she'd salvaged a message he'd signed, then changed his mind about and thrown away. And by lamplight had practiced his signature in her tiny room, first tracing, then free-handing.

The upshot of all this was, she rode out of the stockade claiming to be on a ducal errand: to personally deliver a sealed message to Duke Edward Maltby.

That the "message" was blank seemed unimportant; she had no intention of opening it for anyone. She'd even taken advantage of another opportunity, when the duke had gone to the latrine, leaving his signet on his desk.

Chapter 33
The War Unfolds

(Luis)

I learned about Keith meeting Jarvi the night after it happened. I was sheltering at a rectory a few hours north of Kato. Rain lashed the shutters, wind hooted, thunder rolled and boomed, but I was snug and comfortable, my clothes, boots and gear drying before a fire.

Freddy and Keith, along with Jarvi and his headquarters section, weren't *that* well off, but at least they were out of the weather, bedded down in an abandoned house. There was hardly a pane of glass in the entire hamlet, Freddy told me—too poor—and where people hadn't closed the storm shutters before they'd left, the place was cold, and the floors and hay-stuffed mattresses more or less wet. Armsmen filled every building larger than a privy and warmer than an icehouse, with orders to build no fires except in fireplaces or on dirt floors. Haylofts and haysheds were popular, dry and warm if you buried yourself in the hay. Freddy stayed by Keith and his aide, except when he went out to the icehouse to "pray." Report.

Keith, he said, hadn't been surprised at Jarvi's easy conversion, and now we had four companies of disciplined, well-trained kingsmen to help defend the Kato stockade. Keith figured another two days would bring them all to Kato, unless the river blocked the road. If that happened, they'd have to abandon the wagons or take a long way around—or wait for the river to go down. *That's all we need,* I told myself, then decided if Freddy wasn't worrying, I wouldn't.

The river was out of its banks in places, but the road had long-since been relocated to bypass those places, so three companies of Jarvi's army reached Kato in three days. The fourth, escorting the wagons, arrived about thirty hours later, helped by extra draft horses sent from Kato.

I reached Kato the day after learning of Jarvi's conversion, and spent most of the day getting familiar with the defenses.

I also had a long lunch with Edward. I doubted he'd don a hauberk or draw a bow again. He was still somewhat hunched over, and couldn't turn his head very far, but he'd gained flesh and strength and self-assurance. He was going up and down stairs pretty well, and without getting particularly winded; even drilling with a practice sword for the exercise. Ruefully he told me he'd never again be worth his salt as a fighting man; he lacked the flexibility.

Sara Sanders had been treating him, applying what I'd taught her, and though she couldn't see auras, she could feel his energy foci with her hands. Which helped. And Freddy, since he'd been there, had given him a session a day.

I couldn't help wondering what the wizards at the Academy's infirmary might have done for him, but they had limited personnel and facilities, and policy restricted who and what they were allowed to treat.

Sorry. I ramble. Blame it on the verikal.

Edward asked no questions about Donald. He wanted to, but he was leaving it for me to bring up. So I told him Donald would arrive in a day or so—that he was out dealing with barons. I didn't say dealing on his own; I wanted that to seem like a given, something taken for granted.

That afternoon, Donald rode in. I took him to my small office-sleeping room and debriefed him. None of the barons he'd met with had challenged him or acted unwilling. He already knew about Eldred sending Jarvi off with orders to subdue and occupy Kato. Now I told him about Jarvi's conversion. After we were done, he went upstairs to see his father. Privately of course, and confident, cheerful. At the brother house, Peng had bled off the old resentments, hurts, angers and griefs.

When he returned to my room, he was thoughtful but not troubled. I'd half expected him to say something about the meeting, but he didn't, which actually was preferable. I invited him to sit, then poured two small glasses of watered wine, handed one to him, and sat down with the other. "To the future," I said, raising my glass.

Nodding, he raised his. "To the future." Then added: "What next?"

"Remember I said I was going to Austin?"

"Yes."

"I've changed my mind. I'm sending *you* to Austin. I'm staying here, at least for now."

He frowned, thinking, then nodded. "All right. What do I do there?"

"You find a man named Banda. Sergeant Major Banda of the ducal force at arms. Tell him I sent you, and that I want him to come north with you, bringing his armsmen, and as many militia as he can round up. He may have to overthrow the duke's captain to do it, and Duke Alfred himself. He'll be glad to.

Alfred knows the invasion's started—Keith sent word—and stories must have reached there from the marches.

"From Austin, I want you and Banda to head north with his men up the Fairbow Road, recruiting ex-militias along the way. You're to deal with the barons. Especially at Fairbow, because it's a Royal Domain. One or another of them may want to arrest you. Make sure they don't. Point out that you have a larger force than they have. Tell them you want their armsmen for the defense of the kingdom, and you're already recruiting their ex-militias. Tell them all you want from them is agreement, and you don't *need* that.

"*Leave the barons behind.* Otherwise they'll be a nuisance, bypassing you, giving orders." I paused to grin, setting him up. "Telling you what to do is my job, not theirs." Then I turned serious again. "No one knows what'll come up during the next two or three weeks, so you'll be on your own."

I opened my map book. "There's a village here called Dindigul." I pointed to a tiny circle well north of Fairbow. "A baron's village about as small as they come. I've been by there on my way from Austin to Hasty. The stockade is right next to the Fairbow Road, and the village a furlong or so north. I suspect you'll need to make a decision there. Either to turn west to the Sota and help man the abatises, or ride north and block them on the Causeway Road. Or something else; you'll know when the time comes. Just . . ."

I paused. "We don't want civilians massacred. So far as possible, let any blood shed be the invaders', and any Sotan blood be that of fighting men. This is more important than you may have realized. It will make the future far easier to live in than it would be otherwise, because combat is a very different matter from the massacre of noncombatants. They leave very different wounds, very different scars. Understood?"

"Understood, sir."

"Good. Now, I've put you in charge because you've had a military education, and because I believe in you—and because *it's the best way to establish yourself as an accomplished leader with an important future in Sota*. But Sergeant Major Banda has spent years as an armsman, he's smart, had a lot of experience at commanding men, and he's tough. So ask his advice and listen to it—listen to it even when you haven't asked for it—*then make your own decisions*.

"I've written a letter to him, for you to deliver." I handed it over. "Read it; then I'll seal it."

He read it and gave it back, looking very sober. "I'd better leave today," he said.

"Absolutely. Any questions?"

"Does my father know about this?"

"No," I answered, folding the letter. "And neither does Keith. Not yet." I dripped sealing wax on it. "I'll tell Keith when he gets back, and then I'll tell the duke. I've taken charge of this operation on behalf of the pope. It's importance goes far beyond Sota, let alone Kato, believe me." I pressed my signet into the wax and handed the letter back to him. "And when you say goodbye to your father, just tell him you're off to raise more militias."

"Yessir," he said nodding.

I'd given him a lot of responsibility, for someone not ambitious for power. But then, I wasn't ambitious for power either.

❖❖❖   ❖❖❖   ❖❖❖

Few Dkota youth thought in terms of conquest. To most this was a great raid, indulged in mainly for excitement and reputation, though its stated purpose contributed. The dirt-eaters wouldn't want any more war with the buffalo peoples after this.

For Ench, though, it was a matter of *acceptance*; *belonging*, something he'd never had before. So far as he knew, he hadn't killed anyone yet, but he might have, for with others he'd shot arrows over stockade walls. The few bodies he'd seen had been Dkota, because the dirt-eaters, those who hadn't run away, stayed inside stockades, or behind tangles of fallen trees. He hadn't much understood what was going on, it was all so—chaotic.

His band saw some dirt-eaters ride out of the riverside woods, and whooping, chased them back in. Then an arrow struck Franz's horse in the eye. It fell headlong, throwing its rider, leaving him stunned and unmoving. Brandishing a hatchet, a red-haired dirt-eater darted out at the fallen Dkota youth. Ench nocked and released an arrow in less time than it takes to say, but the red-hair had swung his weapon before Ench's arrow struck him in the neck.

Ench ran to the two fallen youths. The red-hair was bleeding to death, choking on his own blood, but Ench hardly noticed. It was Franz he stared at. Dropping to his knees beside his friend, Ench wept for the first time he could remember. In his grief, he would have wrapped his arms around Franz's body, but it was too horribly dead—slick with blood and brains. He couldn't touch it.

After being repeatedly sick, he pulled himself heavily into the saddle. Within the woods he heard occasional shouts, yips, war cries, but he did not join them. Instead he rode back to the road and attached himself to a passing war party. They weren't of the Beaver Band, but that made no difference now. He stayed with them.

Mazeppa, his close men, and a whole fraternity of cadre men had stayed on the river road pretty much all day. Actually, on that stretch, there were two river roads, one on each side, mostly far enough from it to lie outside the woods. For the most part his army simply traveled, with pauses to burn out farmer hamlets, and longer pauses for the occasional village. In some places where the road passed through forest, dirt-eaters had felled tangles of trees, and sometimes from their cover, his braves had been ambushed. The dirt-eaters were good bowmen; braves had been wounded and killed.

Clearly the Sotans had known he was coming, and the only explanation was that Sky Chief had warned them. Evil! Treacherous! But there was nothing to be done about it except continue. And with so great an army, it made no difference. He would conquer; he did not doubt it.

With an army so large, there was no way to direct it. But by staying near its head, as often as not he was one of the first to see a new hamlet, new village, or the occasional tangle of felled trees. And from there, if some party acted sufficiently counter to his policies, he could send his cane men to discipline them.

On his orders, foraging parties swept the land to the north and south, three miles or more from the river, gathering livestock the dirt-eaters had failed to drive away. His braves had to eat.

More tempting, as a delay, was the infrequent stockade, fiercely defended and costly to attack. Given a few more sunny breezy days, the stockades would be flammable. Then hay carts, pushed against the palisades and torched, would burn them out. The killing that followed, and the cattle and sheep inside, would raise his braves' morale. But for now, mostly he bypassed them.

He knew that as forest increased eastward, so would the tangles of felled trees, too green to burn and too thick to fight through. They wouldn't be flammable till the yellow-leaves moon. If one was patient, the tangles could no doubt be solved, but that would cost time, and the lives of braves.

So he'd spread the word to bypass the tangles, so far as possible. He had not, however, fully realized how tricky that could be. The invader was *expected* to bypass them, and blunder into dead ends, or traps.

Meanwhile his army had already come far, and at little cost.

❊❊❊   ❊❊❊   ❊❊❊

While leading his platoon southward from Soggo, Stephen Nez recruited all the way. When riding through villages and hamlets, he was usually met by citizens or militia eager with questions. To the militia, his answer was "follow me." And when he *wasn't* met, he'd shout in a bellow astonishing for a Dinneh, ordering everyone out in the name of the duke. Then, at the village square, he'd summarize briefly the situation and the duke's order, before showing the duke's message and reading it aloud: "I herewith order you . . . this Higuchian brother . . . at all costs."

Then he'd hold up the map, and invite whoever seemed to have authority to look at both map and message. Usually it was a militia officer or sergeant— a veteran armsman.

When worried people don't know what to do, someone who'll tell them is often welcomed, especially if he has presence, and carries authority, secular or religious. The responsibility laid on Stephen had triggered his latent presence, and the marvelous map, the duke's written order, and the Higuchian reputation provided authority. Perhaps most of all the map, on paper that gave an impression of being indestructible—strange and smooth, with hair-fine grid lines, curves of black, blue, red, brown, forests shaded thinly with green. All replete with tiny numbers and labels . . . and blocks of neatly printed words and symbols on the margins and back. It seemed to bear power of its own, a sacramental formula for victory.

And the thirty-some armed Dinneh militia provided the reality without which some would not be convinced.

The Higuchian "brother" didn't wait for his recruits

to get ready. Didn't even take names. He simply showed the duke's authority and the map, and gave orders, telling them where to go. Then he moved on, he and his militia, trusting them to follow. Most or many did.

On the high bank, high above the river terrace, the Soggo Road met the Hasty-Cloud Highway just south of the village of Teng-Xian. Met it, then slanted down the wooded slope to the flood plain and the local ferry dock. And the Lower River Road, sandy, favored by local traffic except when flooded.

This was the mighty Misasip, a very different, far greater river than the Sancroy or Sota.

At Teng-Xian, Stephen recruited more axmen before once again reviewing the plan with his platoon. That done, he left the local sergeants in charge, with orders on handling further militias and laborers as they arrived, and requisitioning food for them. Then he rode off with his platoon sergeant and squad leaders, to examine the most critical sites on the ground, and with hatchets, mark in detail what he wanted done.

They spent two days deciding on wheres and hows, and blazing guide lines with their hatchets, Stephen impressing his sergeants with the importance of doing the job right. They worked despite the great storm, his maps shedding water as if charmed. By the time he turned the job over to his second in command, a hundred axmen were already at work.

Now he started off alone to Hasty, where a vital part of the project awaited him. A part overlooked by Luis and everyone else. The part that was truly his own. For it seemed to him he knew Eldred Youngblood better than Luis did, or Carlos or Peng. He'd known and liked the king, and had felt that liking mutual. He'd stood beside him, guarding his life, had seen him listen patiently, and for the most part courteously, to the problems of tradesmen and artisans, nobles and farmers and laborers, acting as justly as he knew how. Stephen expected to find it so with his own request, for with Dkota invaders galloping the kingdom's roads, His Majesty would understand the need, and take action.

Which would be to send his rifle companies and artillery to the positions Stephen was having prepared.

Chapter 34
The Man Behind the Throne

Riding southeastward toward Hasty, Stephen Nez kept his mount mostly at a trot. But from from time to time he dismounted, leading it loose-reined along the road's edge, where it snatched bites of the grasses and forbs that flourished there.

This was well-settled country, the farmsteads not concentrated into hamlets, but dribbled along the highway in twos and threes. Often the road was bordered by woods, tended more or less for the production of firewood and fence rails. But even more it was edged by pastures and fields, with a row of sugar trees on the road's west side for afternoon shade. Most bore the marks of spiles, used to tap the sweet sap in early spring. The maize, inspired by recent rains, was nearing knee high, and farm folk wearing broad-brimmed straw hats, the products of long winter evenings, were out with busy hoes, chopping weeds. The rail fences wore thorny skirts of raspberry and blackberry cane, their fruit bringing hungry birds. Bees and hornets zipped and hovered, probing, drinking deeply of the nectar.

There was more traffic, here on the Hasty-Cloud Highway, than Steven was used to. Often he met wagons, carters and horsemen on everyday errands. But more than a few were clearly refugees, Hasty folk presumably, returning to their rural roots, their belongings stacked behind the seat. Or trudged on foot, with bags on backs or heads. Most looked neither to right nor left, their thoughts—on what?

Often Stephen slowed at their approach, to tell them in passing that there was work for them farther up the road, felling trees at the Knees of the Misasip, work that came with food and protection.

But mostly he held to his brisk pace, and arrived at Hasty that evening. There he found lodging with a Dinneh couple he knew, who made leather goods. They didn't plan to leave, they told him. They were too old for a refugee's life, and content to die when the time came.

◁▷◀▷ ◁▷◀▷ ◁▷◀▷

Master Carlos Del Passo left his push cart at the tradesmen's delivery entrance, and hoisted the heavy quarter of freshly butchered beef onto his shoulder. The 4th usher was in charge of dealing with delivery men, and recognizing the cart, and recently Carlos, as legitimate, opened the door to him. The usher's breath smelled of whiskey. *Early in the day,* Carlos thought.

"Looks heavy," the man said, eyeing the haunch. He didn't sound under the influence, but neither did he look too well. Recovering from a hangover, Carlos decided. "Any bigger," he answered grinning, "and it would carry me."

The usher laughed, then led him down a now familiar corridor to the staff kitchen, and left him there. The chief staff cook had Carlos lay the meat on a platform scale, placed weights on a counter-beam until it balanced, and examined the invoice Carlos handed him. The readings agreed closely enough. He initialed both copies with a graphite stick. Carlos counter-initialed them and pocketed his copy. Only then did they exchange chitchat, Carlos commenting that if staff ate as well as it seemed, he'd like to get a job there.

The cook laughed. "Be careful what you wish for," he said. "You might get it." Then more seriously, "We had people who didn't come back to work after last payday; afraid the Dkota are coming. So if you're serious about working here, this is a good time to apply."

"Quit, eh? I'd think if the Dkota arrive, the best place to be is inside these thick stone walls."

"Yeah, if you live in. But few do, except guards."

"The town is walled."

"Walled, sure. But think of all those thatched roofs just waiting for fire arrows. It won't come to that, of course, even if the Dkota *are* out raiding. They'll burn a few villages out in the marches, steal some horses and girls, and gallop off home like before."

"Who do I talk to about . . ."

A man interrupted, bursting wide-eyed and excited into the large kitchen. He was visibly shaking. "There's fighting upstairs!" he squawked. "Shouting, and swords!"

<>-<>   <>-<>   <>-<>

Eldred sat in his lesser audience chamber, twenty feet long and fifteen wide. As for "audience"—that referred to the listening king; there were no spectators. The room held only His Majesty; two large bodyguards, each with a sword held at "order arms"; another by the door; and the inner bailiff, wearing a dagger at his right hip, and carrying a ceremonial but deadly mace in his left hand. His function was to receive persons at the door, and on command, escort them to the low railing before the king, where they would speak. And finally the king's executive secretary, a nobleman of years and dignity, learned in the law and human behavior. He sat to one side, at a writing table on line with the railing.

Ordinarily, Eldred heard petitioners two mornings a week, from 9:00 o'clock till 11:30. They were not plaintiffs bypassing the courts, simply persons asking favors or other considerations of the king. Such hearings were an important reason for Eldred's popularity—the hearings, and Eldred's usual affability.

But today he was not his usual self. For one thing, he'd been abraded by the rumors rampant in his capital. Not that he believed them; he rejected them utterly. What bothered him was their insolence, and their effects on the people. The Higuchians were to blame, he did not doubt, disrupting order and the peoples' trust. But more personal than the rumors, more painful, was the disappearance of his daughter Elvi, with her brainless "squire," young Halvorsen. It cost him sleep.

He did not let such matters interfere with duty though.

A guild master, representing the glue makers, had just been heard and led out, when the palace's senior usher hurried in, an unusual interruption. "Your Majesty!" he said, "a messenger has just arrived, with urgent business! You may wish to hear him out of order."

The king frowned. Usually Arpad would identify the matter. Well, Presumably he had a good reason. "Bring him in," Eldred said.

The usher went back into the antechamber, returning a moment later with a man wearing the uniform of the royal postal service, and carrying a bulky package. No petitioner, apparently, but standard procedure held; the inner bailiff led him to the railing.

"What have you brought, my good man?" the king asked.

The messenger kept his eyes averted and his voice soft. "Your Majesty, a package from Zandria. With a message from Lieutenant Mitchell, commanding a royal force at arms there."

Eldred felt his hackles rise. "You've seen the contents?"

"No, Your Majesty. But the letter was read to me before it was sealed, in case something happened to it."

In case something happened to it? What in God's name is this about? The king snapped his fingers in sudden impatience, the sound loud and imperious in the otherwise quiet room. "Open them! And give them to me!"

The messenger's hands shook so, he cut himself trying to sever the strings that wrapped the bulky package. Brookins took it from him, then handed the folded letter to the king, its seal unbroken. The king left it that way, laying it on his lap. It was the package he would deal with first, for he feared it most; it seemed to him it held a human head, bundled against seeping blood. Again he snapped his fingers, demanding haste. Brookins stripped away the severed cord, leaving the gob of imprinted sealing wax undisturbed on the knot, then placed the package in Eldred's hands. Fierce-eyed, the king opened it. Instead of a head, it held a light hauberk, and wrapped in it a helmet, all in the style of the royal guard. But too light to be effective; a costume.

Who'd worn it was beyond doubt. The king went pale, as if he might faint and fall from the throne, but he gathered himself. Opening the lieutenant's letter, he began to read. She was alive, or had been when it was written. And it *was* Halldor Halvorsen she'd left with, to follow the armsmen, intending to join them when they caught the Higuchians, and take part in the fighting. Finally she'd caught up with them at Zandria; Lieutenant Mitchell had her in his safekeeping. He'd bring her with him when he returned to Hasty.

Eldred contemplated what he'd read. Something was terribly wrong here. Why send the messenger? Or her armor? If the lieutenant and his men had reached Zandria, why hadn't they come back, bringing her with them?

And why hadn't Elvi sent a message of her own?

Of one thing he was sure: the Higuchians were behind it, and they would pay. With the first installment today, because he knew who was next on his audience list. As soon as he'd seen the name, he'd remembered, and had him moved up. God was good.

Now, turning hard dangerous eyes to the inner bailiff, he gestured toward the messenger. "Have this man taken to the guardhouse and held there securely till I have time to question him more thoroughly. I'll be along soon." And to the messenger, "Go now. If you answer my questions, you have nothing to fear."

He handed the bundle and letter to Brookins, who lay them on a corner of his writing table. Meanwhile it was not the antechamber door the bailiff took the messenger to, but a door in the back of the room, concealed by one of the velvet wall hangings. It opened into an ill-lit passageway, where instead of an outer bailiff, there waited two guardsmen, rarely called upon. Until they heard the door latch, they'd been on their knees shooting craps with practiced silence. They were on their feet as the door opened. Stepping into the audience chamber, they received custody of the messenger, and gripping his arms firmly, led him into the passageway. The bailiff closed it behind them, then covered it again with the hanging.

Before receiving his next petitioner, Eldred sent the inner bailiff hurrying to the royal apartment to fetch a bottle of whiskey, an unprecedented request. The bailiff returned quickly, the bottle in his blouse, and ignoring appearances, Eldred downed a stiff drink.

When he'd recovered his breath, he ordered the next petitioner brought in.

Having been one of the king's throne guards, Stephen knew the procedure. What he didn't know was the situation. His saber and belt knife had been taken in the vestibule, but they'd be returned when he left. And as he entered, it seemed to him the king would remember him, perhaps greet him in a personal way.

But being led the few yards to the petitioner's railing, he began to realize something was seriously wrong. The inner bailiff's grip was tight, and the king's gaze hard and grim. They numbed him so, he hardly heard the bailiff speak his name. Then it was time, and he began his recital, the king listening, gaze cold as a snake's. Even so, telling it steadied Stephen. He summarized what was underway, then asked the king to send his rifle companies and artillery. "I believe we can break the invaders there," he finished.

The king continued to eye him, and Stephen's apprehension re-congealed. Finally Eldred spoke to the corporal of the watch. "Corporal Glynn," he said, "put this traitor to death! Here and now, while I watch!"

Stephen was rooted to the spot.

Being left-handed, Corporal Paddy Glynn's position was a step behind the king on *his* left, his ceremonial but very sharp two-handed sword unsheathed at order arms. Now Paddy raised it to present arms. "As you order, Your Majesty," he said calmly, then turning his gaze to the petitioner, boomed "Prisoner! On yer knees!" Paddy knew no precedent for this, no set phrase, but he'd ad-libbed it nicely. All attention, most intensely the king's, fixed on Stephen Nez, whose brown face had grayed and turned wooden. But Stephen's knees did not buckle. Slowly he knelt, the act breaking the bailiff's hold.

Paddy stepped forward—and without the least

forewarning delivered a right-handed side-fist to the
king's forehead. As Eldred slumped unconscious,
Paddy pounced from the dais, and sword ready, spoke
sharply to the other guards: "Michael! Arturo! It's now
or never! Are ye with me?"

On the other side of the throne, a shocked Arturo
husked out "I am!" Michael was already advancing on
the inner bailiff, great sword threatening. "And I!" he
said. The bailiff froze, and his mace thumped to the
carpet.

Now Paddy's voice turned soft. "And you, Sir
Lawrence? Are you with us?"

"God's mercy, I cannot help myself. For I fear the
king is mad, and I do not doubt that the Dkota threat
is as real as bloody death."

In the palace, the fighting was sporadic and reluctant, because the adversaries felt themselves brethren at arms. At first, loyalists controlled the corridors.
But the rebels threw words before blows. They all
knew the rumors of invasion, and had serious misgivings about Eldred. Thus some were quickly turned,
and within the hour the rebels held the palace.

The king was locked in the dungeon, for a mutiny
was liable to be followed by a counterstroke, certainly
when the deposed ruler had been popular. And many
in the guard looked at him as a bargaining chip, to
be held secure.

No one was being let in or out of the palace.
Things were chaotic, and a new kind of rumor and
fear abounded, of coats waiting to be turned, of
conspiracies to take command and execute the guard.

Carlos, his ears and eyes open, was happy to remain
inside, a friend of the chief staff cook. And one thing
he could not miss: *Corporal* Paddy Glynn was said to
be in charge.

But not, Carlos thought, the ruler; no one actually

ruled. The guard held sway, but no formal directives or policies were being issued, because none of the royal guard *knew* what needed to be done. Paddy gave orders when he saw the need, trusting they'd be followed. The preexisting bureaucracy could keep things running, more or less—the kitchen staff, for example, still prepared food—but there was no mechanism of command, no oversight, evaluation or enforcement.

In fact, the mutiny had been impromptu: Paddy had acted to save Stephen Nez. But once he'd had Eldred manacled and the key in his own pocket, he knew very well what it meant.

So now, with the palace more or less secured, who might he turn to who had the authority of class, position and experience to be recognized as regent? Someone in the palace or at the military reservation, whose authority would be accepted by the troops. Someone who'd defend Sota.

Paddy saw the need as urgent. He had no authority over the forces at the military reservation, and he needed the rifle companies and artillery *sent as quickly as possible* to man the ambush under construction. Meanwhile, if artillery showed up outside the palace gates, things would get desperate. And if Eldred was returned to the throne, he'd surely execute the rebels.

Paddy had already attached the royal pages as his own. Now he sent two of them running off to Lord Brookins' room. Between himself and the king's secretary, they might interest an acceptable royal in-law to rule as regent.

By that time, of course, Carlos had found an unoccupied room from which to notify Luis and the others of what had happened.

Chapter 35
The Battle of Kato

Encyclopedia of the Holy Church

The Kato stockade is one of the finest timber forts known, as well as one of the larger, being 150 by 130 yards in size. A blockhouse stands at each corner, and one midway of each wall, and from these, bowmen can shoot at attackers along the base of the walls. Thatched roofs are not allowed. Instead, all buildings are roofed by shakes, rendering them less susceptible to being set alight by fire arrows. The shakes used to roof the primary buildings are split from black walnut or white oak, because those species are slow to decay, yet readily split. Shakes for outbuildings are most often silver maple, green ash or basswood. Although they decay readily, they are even easier to split, and locally more abundant.

The individual timbers of this stockade are of either white oak, burr oak, or black walnut. These species are relatively durable when set in the ground. They can be left in place several times as long as timbers of other local species before needing to be replaced. To improve that durability, the trenches in which the cants are set are then packed with coarse sand and small cobbles, to improve drainage.

Timbers are transported in winter, on large sleighs for distances as great as 25 miles, then sawn by a water-driven circular saw into cants 15 inches on a side and 25 feet long, all sapwood being removed in the process. After squaring, the timbers are set 10 feet into the ground. While being set, every third and fourth timber has 3 feet cut from the top, to provide an "archery notch" through which a defender can shoot at attackers.

Happily, the Kato stockade has never been attacked. It is regrettable though, and to the Church embarrassing, that such fortifications are needed. For the Church has been charged by God to improve human justice, tolerance and harmony, and to increase unqualified love and compassion, so that fortifications are no longer needed, and become curiosities for future generations to read about.

From the back of his favorite horse, Mazeppa examined the stockade. It was built on high ground above the river. He'd ridden around it on three sides, and swum his horse across the river to examine the fourth side from there. His braves had occupied the nearby town, well-sheltered from further storms, but it would not suit them to stay there long with nothing to do.

Several war parties had not yet arrived. Meanwhile Mazeppa needed to decide: (1) to attack, or (2) to bypass Kato, and proceed downriver to the Misasip, and the King's Town. But if he allowed himself to be deflected by Kato's wooden walls, what would his braves think when they saw Hasty's high stone walls? While to destroy Kato and its people would add to their confidence. They were willing—eager—but it would not do to squander them, so he looked for vulnerabilities—means to victory at the least cost of lives.

From raids in the past, his people had learned ways of attacking stockades. Thus he'd sent parties to bring in wagons and carts loaded with hay, to be pushed against the stockade and set afire. Meanwhile, in town, doors had been taken from doorways, and fitted with scavenged ropes and straps to make large shields. Behind these, braves could approach the walls sheltered from Sotan bowmen.

The scouts he'd sent that spring had seen from inside what could not be seen from outside. Large water containers called "cisterns" had been built partly below ground, and walled with cemented stone. The dirt-eaters kept them filled with water. And the walls had walkways from which bowmen could shoot. Also, on the walkways, they could strike with their long knives—their "sabers"—at attackers climbing over the walls. Inside the enclosure were many houses, some backed up against the walls, others standing free. In these the dirt-eaters could take shelter from arrows shot over the walls.

But except for the cisterns, all of this was built of wood, and it had not rained for several days.

As for food . . . no doubt most of the townspeople had fled days past, warned by the treacherous Jorval. And he could hear the bawling, bleating, barking and squealing of animals inside. His braves would grow restless long before the defenders could be starved out.

The fort's most promising vulnerabilty, it seemed to him, was its flammability. So. He'd prepare several modes of attack, feel the defenders out, examine their reactions, then decide what to do next.

His options shrank, however, when the parties sent out to bring wagons and carts failed to find any. They found wagon *beds*, and cart beds, but the wheels had been taken away, or broken up with axes. The dirt-eaters too had learned from past raids.

In the fort, a short section of the south-side walk-way was being used as a command post. General Jarvi was the senior officer and had brought the most fight-ing men, but he'd deferred to Captain Frazier, who knew the enemy far better than he did.

At the moment, Frazier was sweeping the edge of Kato Town with his spyglass. *It was crawling with Dkota;* had been since well before noon. Some were carrying doors and shutters; he knew what that meant. A little later, some approached driving cattle with them. Foragers. He saw butchering. Cookfires were lit, mostly outdoors, but some chimneys began to smoke. Near the fires, tribesmen stood or squatted, or sat crosslegged, but to send a mounted platoon charging out to scatter them would be insane. These walls were the place to fight from; here he had the advantage.

Frazier wondered what Luis was doing, and how far he'd gotten on his trip to Hasty. He'd left two days earlier, with the messengers who'd gone to order sections of road closed. He'd never made clear why he was leaving, but he'd get there today; he'd been well mounted.

Before the Dkota had arrived, Jarvi and he had agreed on the watch schedule. Two hours on, six off. Each duty watch was to be preceded by a standby watch, napping on the walkway. At least resting. The off-watches were to rest in their crowded barracks, hopefully sleeping, so they'd be fit to stand watch later.

When the Dkota first arrived, all the men had wanted to be on the walkway watching: kingsmen,

dukesmen, militia . . . and briefly Jarvi and Frazier had
allowed it. Then they'd cleared off all but the duty
watch and standbys, and the duke, who'd promised
to take cover in the blockhouse during the fighting.

Jarvi wasn't happy about the duke's presence, a
hangover from the king's attitude, but he didn't object.
There were enough enemies outside; no need to make
any inside.

In the latter part of the afternoon, some mounted
Dkota moved in to about a hundred fifty yards, and
began haphazardly and almost casually shooting arrows
over the wall. For their bows it was well beyond
serious killing range, but even so, you wouldn't want
one of their arrows to hit you. They arced high, easily
clearing the walls, and caused a lot of milling around
in the bailey. Two people and several animals were
hit. The Sotan bowmen answered, and with visible
targets, and the greater power of longbows, they
backed the Dkota away.

Why the devil did they do that? Jarvi wondered.
He was annoyed at what he considered gratuitous
nonsense.

It was Freddy who answered, at the same time
keeping his eyes on the enemy. "I suspect they plan
something more energetic in a few minutes, and want
us ready."

Jarvi scowled. "That makes no sense. If they're
going to attack, they should prefer us off guard."

"They want to test us before they attack all out.
To see how we react. If we respond weakly enough,
the test may grow into the real thing. Otherwise they'll
probably back off and consider alternatives."

It was Frazier who replied to that. "Freddy, I
hesitate to argue tactics with a Higuchian, but I've
never seen or heard of Dkota warriors doing something as indirect as that. Or backing off to think about
anything."

Freddy answered, his eyes still on the Dkota.

"Those earlier attacks weren't war. They were raids by young bucks out for excitement. Now they're led by a shrewd, mature chief, a man with a mission." He paused, letting the word "mission" hold their attention. "A mission to destroy the kingdom of Sota, and drive out or kill its people."

Even as he said it, men on horseback began riding out of the streets and lanes of Kato Town, into the open ground separating it from the fort. There they began riding in flat loops, yipping, whooping, shaking bows and hatchets overhead. They did this till two or three hundred horsemen were demonstrating opposite the south wall, from which the fort's commanders watched. Probably, Frazier thought, there were similar demonstrations on the east and west sides.

They kept it up, gradually encroaching on the open space, and Frazier murmured to Jarvi, who spoke to his trumpeter, who sounded the command to nock arrows. At a hundred yards he ordered a single flight launched. Across the field, the yelling swelled. Horses reared, men fell to the ground, and a return flight of arrows, ragged but thick, was launched toward the fort. From the walkway, and the bailey inside, came scattered human cries of pain, and bellowing and bleating by wounded livestock. People headed for the shelter of buildings.

At the same moment the circling warriors ceased firing, and about half charged the stockade, lariats whirling. The defenders fired at will. Few had time to loose more than a second arrow before lariats were settling over the merlons that separated the archery notches. On the walkway, defender bows were set aside then, and sabers drawn, though from the blockhouses, the archery intensified. Warriors scrambled hand over hand up the ropes, some with knives in their teeth, moccasined feet scrabbling on the timbers. Some fell back, their ropes severed by sabers, but others reached the top, painted faces and sinewy arms struck at by sabers. Some made it onto the walkway, and were struck down.

As suddenly as the attack had begun, it ended, horsemen galloping back to safety, some after dismounting to load a wounded warrior across a horse. Perhaps a minute after the charge had been launched, the field was empty of attackers, including most of the fallen. Bodies were thrown over the parapet now, to thud down from above.

The defenders had lost two dead and four wounded by Dkota arrows; excellent archery at that range, with the targets largely protected by the parapet. A few others had been wounded or killed by hatchet or knife. In the bailey, several people and animals had been wounded. There'd been no time for a count of Dkota casualties, but observation suggested twenty or more had been killed or wounded.

All on the south side, the only side actually attacked. Almost surely, Master Freddy's prediction had been correct; the attack had been a test of the defenders. It seemed to Jaako Jarvi that Mazeppa could not be pleased.

As for Duke Edward: with the first exchange of arrows, he'd gone to the blockhouse as promised, keeping his mouth shut, and staying out of the way. Jarvi felt somewhat mollified by that.

Mazeppa Tall Man had watched from his saddle, his hunter's eyes registering everything they looked at. The dirt-eaters had shown themselves alert and quick to respond. And it seemed to him he'd squandered his option to bypass, for the dirt-eaters had more than passed a test. They'd bloodied his braves.

That night, he promised himself, would be another matter.

Night *was* another matter, but Keith Frazier was

a creative planner with a mind for details. Among other things, he'd had sconces built years in advance. With the prospect of war he'd had them fastened to the outside of the merlons, and with the Dkota rampaging through the marches, a torch had been put in every sconce. This evening they'd been lit. And while their combined light had little effect beyond fifty yards, it was a very important fifty yards.

Among Kato Town's buildings however—none having been built within two hundred yards of the stockade—darkness hid the Dkotan piling of flammables: window shutters, furniture, straw-filled bedsacks, blankets piled with hay and kindling . . . And behind buildings, small fires had been lit, not directly visible from the fort. Mazeppa did not supervise the work; his warriors knew what was needed. Instead he sat his horse, watching the stockade, where just now the only visible movement was torch flames. From time to time, he looked westward at the waxing moon climbing slowly down the sky.

Now it was only two fingers above the seen horizon. Soon it would be out of sight.

When it disappeared, the darkness intensified, but still Mazeppa waited till the refracted moonlight had faded in the west, and only the stars and God's snow trail remained.

Then, face raised, he spoke to the sky in the voice of the old he-wolf, and from east and west was answered by other "wolf voices," alerting both attackers and defenders. From the three directions, men moved quietly, slowly forward, carrying flammables, and shielded by other warriors bearing doors. The first arrows met them about seventy yards from the stockade. At once, Dkota bowmen returned the archery in volume, aiming at the archery notches, marked by the torches beside them.

The fuel bearers and their shield bearers promptly

broke into a trot. A few were shot down, but most were not. They placed their burdens against the wall, providing a focus for others, who added to the piles.

Then armsmen on horseback streamed from the sally ports to cut down or drive off the fuel bearers. They were expected, and as soon as they appeared, Dkota bowmen sent swarms of arrows at them from eighty or ninety yards. Then, from deeper in the darkness, Dkota horsemen charged, not with bows but with buffalo spears. As soon as they were seen, trumpets sounded from the walls, and the Sotan horsemen, most of them, made it back inside, while Sotan arrows struck their pursuers fiercely. A few Dkota horsemen got inside, but despite the confusion, died before they could prevent the gates being closed.

Meanwhile more Dkota horsemen had raced onto the field, these bearing torches to light the fuel piles. Within a minute, all the piles were burning. More Sotan horsemen, not in numbers now, charged from the sally ports, some with grapples on leather ropes, throwing them into the burning piles to pull them apart. Others followed with hooked poles to help them. Dkota horsemen charged again, rushing toward the grapple men. But fires lit the field now, and Sotan archery was rapid and aimed. This time all their own horsemen made it back inside, abandoning some of their grapples and hooks, but leaving most of the fires pulled apart. More than a few Dkota horses and riders were shot. The rest turned back into the darkness.

At once, Sotans emerged again to further scatter the piles. The invaders did not rush back to attack them. This was not the kind of fighting they'd known in the past, and they weren't ready for it. Meanwhile the burning fuel lay scattered, mostly away from the wall. The heavy timbers had been scorched, but had not taken fire.

The night was still early, and the men at the archery notches stared once more into darkness.

❦❦❦   ❦❦❦   ❦❦❦

Mazeppa let the defenders wait while most of his braves slept. His clock was the sky, and when the Great Bear stood below the Star That Does Not Move, he made the call of the walking dog, the coyote; yipped four yaps, then keened, then five and keened again, the note wavering. It was answered from both east and west, in the same sequence, the responses overlapping. He did not suppose it would pass unnoticed in the fort. They would suspect, but it would not wake the sleeping nor raise an alarm.

Freddy heard, wakened, got to his feet. Crouching, he shook first Frazier, then Jarvi and his trumpeter. "Something's going on out there," he said. "We need to be ready."

It took the general a moment to clear the sleep from his mind. "What?" he said.

"They're signalling back and forth. Making coyote calls. And some of the duty watch is probably asleep." He was looking through an archery notch now. "And they've fed their fires again. Behind buildings, but I can see the glows here and there."

Jarvi grunted, got heavily to his feet, and nudged his trumpeter with a boot. "Erkki," he growled, "sound 'prepare to repel.'"

The young trumpeter had remained curled on his side, hoping against hope nothing would come of this, and he could go back to sleep. Now he got to his feet, much more nimbly than his commander. "Yessir," he said, and raising his instrument, blew a short patter of notes, loud and bright in the darkness.

Within a minute or two, in the near distance, braves with torches trotted from the shadows of buildings. After the previous assault, numerous small fires had been laid but not lit in the open, some hundred yards from the stockade. Now the torchmen lit them. By their small light, Freddy could see braves dip long arrows into the fires, then step aside, a rank of small flames in the darkness. Then, each nocked arrow tipped with flame, they waited for a signal that must come quickly.

Frazier spoke the first order directly to Erkki: "Fire at will!"

Another patter of notes, and hundreds of Sotan arrows took flight. Not as accurately as by day, though the targets were apparent, but braves fell nonetheless.

Now the braves began to shoot, flaming arrows arcing over the walls. Stricken livestock bawled and bleated. Human voices screamed with pain. Arrows struck roofs and walls. Commands were shouted. People had slept in their clothes; now they poured from doorways. Frazier had foreseen this too, and the people had drilled it. A ladder leaned against every building, and boys scrambled up. Voices called "here! here!" and bucket lines formed in response, from cisterns to ladders, with the speed of deadly urgency.

Meanwhile the fire arrows kept coming, while archers on the walkways shot back.

Then tribal horsemen charged out of Kato Town, again with lariats, and this was no test. Toward each wall they came by the hundreds, shouting war cries. Some merlons had two lariats over them. The sally ports didn't open; it would have been suicide. Braves yelled war cries. The defenders too were yelling. Sabers cut lariats. Hands, arms, shoulders, heads were sliced, even severed. Hatchets chopped, knives struck. The walkways were quickly slick with blood. Men slipped in it, or stumbled on the fallen. Bodies fell or were thrown from the walkways, some out over the merlons, others inward, into the bailey.

And increasingly there were braves who jumped from the walkways into the bailey to extend the violence. But squads of militia had been kept on the ground, between buildings, ready, their orders not to involve themselves with fires or bucket lines, nor climb to the walkways unless ordered. Quickly, savagely, they attacked any invader who jumped. Scattered, outnumbered, disoriented, those who jumped could do little but die defending themselves.

Outside, more and more attackers jammed up along the walls, the focus of bowmen in the blockhouses. And some, instead of waiting to throw their lariats, turned back. Watching intently, Mazeppa saw the attack stacking up, but waited, giving it a chance. As more braves turned back, it was clear the assault had spent itself. He snapped an order to two of his next men, and they separated, angling toward the stockade at a gallop, one eastward, one west, bellowing *"Break off the attack!"*

It was already foundering. What he'd done was give his braves justification: they quit because they'd been told to. Meanwhile bile rose in Mazeppa's throat; it was all he could do to fight it down.

Almost at the beginning of the attack, Freddy had seen something totally unexpected. He'd known Fohanni from the time he'd been selected to the Academy, where Fohanni made up much of the faculty. And out in the melee he'd seen another, charging the stockade, his white body distinctive. Saw him dumped, bouncing, when his horse had fallen. But the field outside the wall had teemed with charging tribesmen on horseback. It would have been suicide to go out and investigate.

Brief minutes later—it seemed longer—the attackers had withdrawn. Now Freddy slid down a pole to the bailey, ran to the nearby sally port and demanded to be let out. Reluctantly the sergeant in charge opened for him.

A lot more bodies lay strewn on the field than when he'd seen the Fohannu dumped from his horse. Some had obviously been trampled. Freddy trotted unerringly to where the Fohannu had stopped rolling, and kneeling, examined him. His aura indicated life, a concussion, and a neck injury that was not a fracture. With an effort, Freddy hoisted the limp form onto his shoulder and carried it back through the sally port.

Helverti, he thought, *unless the COB has something going we don't know about*, and that he very much doubted.

The fort "medical facility" was primitive, but it did have beds—sacks of straw on a plank floor—and he lowered Ench onto one of them. They were filling fast.

Freddy talked to the surgeon in charge, identifying himself and claiming ownership of his "foreign prisoner." "Norlins will want him," he finished.

Kneeling, the surgeon examined the Fohannu, feeling for fractures, turned him over looking for wounds. He got up shaking his head. "That's about as foreign as a man can get," he said. Thinking about possible bestiality between humans and—what? "He's yours, but if he makes trouble, I'll call the dukesmen to deal with him."

Then the surgeon went to another man newly brought in, and Freddy left, looking for privacy. He needed to tell Luis and Tahmm what he'd found. It seemed to him Tahmm would want to pick the man up. Or the boy. His own experience with Fohanni had been limited to mature adults. This one, he suspected, was an adolescent.

Whatever; he hoped the Fohannu survived, entirely aside from the value he might have for Tahmm and the ESS. It would be nice to know why he was here at Kato, riding the war trail with Dkota warriors.

For a short while, Mazeppa's braves kept up a rain of fire arrows, partly from resentment, but still hoping to burn out the defenders. Their supply of fire arrows was limited, however, and war arrows were too short to serve, so Mazeppa ordered them to stop.

He knew what he needed to do. He didn't like it, but he knew. The Sotans, here at least, were better fighters than he'd expected. It was time to leave this place and ride on to Hasty, ravaging lesser places as they went. And then? Burn it. Stay in Sota till September, burning towns and villages, killing their people. Afterward he would send emissaries to every buffalo tribe in the north, and come back next year.

In the growing dawnlight, the smell of wet char found Mazeppa's nose, but he saw no columns of smoke; the Sotans had put out whatever fires his people had started. The extent of his own losses were clearly visible. The Sotans had dragged numerous dead braves outside and laid them in a line, on their backs, legs straightened, hands crossed on their chests. They contrasted with the much greater number sprawled helter skelter where they'd fallen.

He and Pastor Morosov led a large party of braves, with horses drawing travois, to where the dead lay. Some of his braves were nervous about exposing themselves to Sotan bowmen, but Mazeppa knew the Sotans wouldn't shoot. That they'd given back his dead from inside the walls told him that. When his people began loading bodies, a Sotan stood up in an archery notch, to call that there were sixteen Dkota wounded inside, some severely. Mazeppa could have them now, or they could be sent back to Many Geese after they'd healed or died.

Mazeppa didn't hesitate. "Those who can ride," he shouted grimly, "I will take away with me. Those who can't can go home later."

Freddy nodded, crossing himself. He did not mention the Fohannu he had in custody.

The Dkota worked carefully but quickly, taking bodies away. Not only the 38 brought out of the fort, but 317, many still alive, who lay on the killing ground outside the stockade.

Chapter 36
Episodes

When Halldor Halvorsen arrived at Cloud, he rode at once to the ducal palace and asked to see the duke. The usher offered to take him to the major-domo instead. And Halldor, being *very* hungry, agreed, following him down a hallway to a closed door. The usher knocked.

"Who is it?"

"Franklin, sir. I have a gentleman to see you, asking Noble Hospitality. He says his father is Baron of Floren."

Noble Hospitality—meals, conversation at the ducal table over wine, and a guest room for the night. It wasn't law, but it was custom. "Show him in," the major-domo answered, getting to his feet.

Halldor entered straight-backed and tall, displaying his nobility, but the major-domo saw a youth with grimy face and unkempt hair, wearing filthy clothes of inexpensive cut.

"How did you come here?" the major-domo asked.

"From the west."

"I suppose you noticed the activity in the forest."

"One could hardly miss it. It's noisy enough, and in places trees had fallen into the road."

"The men who work there get all the food they can eat, and shelter, with blankets furnished. Ask for the supervisor. He'll put you to work."

The major-domo turned away then, sitting back down to the records he'd been examining.

Halldor left the palace indignantly, but went no farther than his horse. He, who'd been welcomed by the king, allowing himself to be dismissed by a ducal servant? And had actually considered accepting common labor, just to feed his belly? He retained an image of the work crews: peasants with axes whacking away at trees, while others, with long pike poles, pushed strenuously to ensure the trees fell in the desired direction.

Abruptly he turned, climbed the veranda steps and knocked again, the heavy brass knocker clashing imperiously. Again the usher opened to him.

"What is it this time?" he said.

"I will not allow myself to be turned away by a servant!" Hallvor answered. "I demand to see the duke!"

"The duke is busy, and the major-domo was well within his authority to turn you away." The usher's hand went to a bell cord. "I suggest you leave before I summon . . ."

"What's this about, Franklin?"

"Oh! Your lordship! This young man came asking Noble Hospitality. Algis directed him to the work crews felling abatises, but he insists on Noble Hospitality."

Jonas Duonelaitis had been on his way out with a guard officer. He examined the grubby Halldor. "Introduce yourself," he said. Ordered.

Halldor managed to pull himself a little taller, a little straighter. "I am Halldor Halvorsen i Floren. My father is Baron Halvor Eriksen i Floren."

"Ah! And how do I know you are who you claim to be?"

It was like a slap in the face! What kind of duke was this who wouldn't take a fellow noble at his word? "Sir, I have never been asked such a question before," said Halldor stiffly.

Jonas accepted the reaction calmly. "Perhaps you haven't traveled before to where you aren't known. Here we haven't heard of Floren. Meanwhile we're at war. The kingdom—and your father's barony—are direly threatened. You've seen some of the defensive works being built. It's my purse that feeds the hundreds of men working on them, and my resources are severely strained."

Without taking his steady eyes from the youth, the duke's right hand fished in a trouser pocket and came out with two silver dollars. "This is not a loan. It's a gift," he said, extending his hand.

Halldor took the two coins, staring down at them. Six meals, if he ate cheaply, and two nights at inns, if he was willing to share a bed with vagabonds. He didn't thank the duke, but neither did he reject the coins. He simply turned, and straight-spined, head erect, strode to his horse. *Let this miser recognize the kind of man he insulted.*

The duke and his guard officer watched him ride away, then Jonas looked at Peng. "I wonder what his father thinks of him. If he is who he claims to be."

Peng smiled. "I believe he is. He was at Eldred's court."

"You know him then?"

"I know *of* him, and his attitude here is not at odds with what I've heard."

Peng looked forward to talking with Carlos and Luis that evening. The last they'd known, young Halvorsen, with his lady love, had been under detention in Zandria. But he kept that to himself, as of no importance to the duke.

❦❦❦   ❦❦❦   ❦❦❦

On the third day after that, Halldor reached Hasty, hungry, well-chewed by bedbugs, and host to head and body lice.

By then he had no doubt at all the Dkota were coming. Rumor had it they were on their way. But more convincing, he'd seen abatises being felled around Noka, nearer to Hasty than to Cloud. And on the Great Knees of the Misasip, just a day's ride from Hasty, whole tracts were being totally cleared! No one would undertake such expense unless the reports were real.

He'd thought to stay in Hasty only a day or two—borrow money, rest, eat his fill, then ride home not looking like some kind of fugitive. But home was south, and rumor had it that a second Dkota army was expected via Kato. General Jarvi was said to have taken his army there to whip the savages and send them home with bloody noses, but who knew, really, who'd win?

So he decided to stay in the shelter of Hasty's stone walls till the war was over, and for that he needed money for lodging and food. But to receive—or really to benefit from acceptable lodging, he needed to rid himself of vermin. His twitching and scratching were beyond control. For his last half dollar (he'd stayed only one night in an inn), he was accepted in a public bath, where his clothes were boiled and beaten, his hair shaved to the skin, and his groin and young beard lathered with soap so strong, he'd feared he'd blister. Then came a soak in scalding water, shared with several other men, and finally a quarter hour in a sauna and a plunge in a cold tub. When it was over, he felt renewed—and ready after all to seek work.

He got a job on his first try, delivering produce for a grocer, starting at once with an order to the palace. And yes, considering his need, he'd be paid when he returned with the signed invoice.

He was shocked to discover he was to deliver it with a push cart. A noble pushing a grocer's cart! By the time he arrived at the palace, he hated both the cart and Hasty's cobblestone streets. But he was grateful for his thin young beard, and the dingy white baker's cap pulled down to his eyebrows. He didn't want anyone to recognize him, to see how low he'd fallen. And *especially* he didn't want to be recognized as the man who'd run off with Elvi, for that, conceivably, could cost his life.

He didn't hear, that first day in town, that Eldred had been overthrown and locked in the dungeon. The mutiny had been displaced, in public attention, by rumors of Dkota armies thousands strong, rampaging through the marches. Where might they be rampaging now? Reports carried by the best riders on the fastest horses, took two to three days to arrive from Zandria or Grove Falls.

Meanwhile Hasty's streets, shops and markets had fewer people than he remembered from before. Even the taverns had fewer people. Not that he had money to spend in them, but he looked. And commenting, was told sourly that "the damned Dkota," were to blame, because Jarvi's army had gone to stop them.

Not until his second day did he hear of Eldred's fall. That too troubled him. It made his *immediate* situation seem much less dangerous; he'd dreaded what Eldred might do to him if he were recognized. But on the other hand, his father was Eldred's man, promoted by him when the old Baron, Karl Sivertsen i Floren, had been hoisted for false reports, evasion of taxes, and to cap it off, the "accidental" death of a king's investigator.

In fact, in the Royal Domains, barons were totally dependent on the throne, being little more than the king's tax collectors and enforcers.

There were those who said old Sivertsen had been
the victim, not the originator of false reports, and with
Eldred in the dungeon, the Sivertsen clan might well
decide to throw off what they no doubt thought of
as the usurper.

In fact, that danger seemed to Halldor more threatening than the Dkota. If the father fell, the son had
no safe harbor. So he'd keep his ears and eyes open
for opportunities.

❧❧   ❧❧   ❧❧

Carlos had been given a pass signed by Paddy Glynn.
Sergeant Major Paddy Glynn, a promotion bestowed
on him by himself. The authority he wielded was dis-
proportionate even to his new rank. Colonel Arvid
Bonde (another self-bestowed promotion, from major),
ruled the government, so far as anyone did. And it
was Paddy who'd installed him, on the advice of Lord
Brookins, based on Bonde being the senior military
officer after General Jarvi, and cousin to both Jarvi
and the late queen.

Bonde in turn was uneasy about Glynn, who ruled
the palace guard, but for the time being it seemed
best to let be. Clearly the sergeant major understood
the need for a legitimate regent, but he'd also tasted
power, which made him dangerous.

The real problem was, getting rid of Glynn might
spark a new uprising by the guard, and Bonde couldn't
be entirely sure of his own troops just then. For his
forces and the palace guard were brothers in service
and restlessness was the order of the day.

Nor could one be sure where else ambition and
conspiracy might be fermenting.

Patience, Arvid, Bonde told himself. *Time is in your
favor. If he's treacherous, he'll misstep or overreach—
do something wrong—and he has no outside connections to draw on.*

❧❧   ❧❧   ❧❧

Meanwhile, Paddy's signature was authoritative. When he wrote a pass for Carlos del Passo, the new 4th usher, the guards at the palace entrance recognized and respected it, and said nothing when Carlos brought a man back in with him, even though it was night.

It was Sergeant Major Glynn the newcomer needed to see, but it was in Carlos's tiny room the three sat down to confer (Carlos had talked his way into live-in status). When they'd finished their meeting, the stranger left, to take lodging with the elderly couple he'd roomed with when he'd stayed in Hasty before.

Meanwhile, some ten hundred miles southwest of Hasty, Eskonsami Tahmm returned his communicator to his belt and walked down corridors and stairs to the infirmary. There he consulted the chief healer on the state of Master Lemmi Tsinnajinni's recovery.

❦❧   ❦❧   ❦❧

Afraid of encountering Dkota stragglers, Elvi Youngblood had left the Zandria-Cloud Highway. She'd expected the country she entered to be much like that she'd been passing through, but without the hamlets and villages having been burned. And a few miles south they *hadn't* been burned, merely abandoned.

Then her horse had gone lame, and soon even an easy trot was too much for it. It simply walked, limping ever slower, and slashing it with her quirt changed nothing. By then she was in a wild tract of forest, lakes and alder swamps, with no idea how far it extended.

Finally the animal stopped utterly, and whipping didn't move it, so she climbed down, weeping in frustration. She didn't even have a knife with which to cut it and drink its blood, and she'd eaten the last of her food the day before. Now she understood what pitiful and despondent meant.

As best she could, she shook it off and began to walk, telling herself she'd soon come to an inhabited place, over the next hill, or on the other side of the forest. She walked and walked, till she wondered if the forest had another side, a remarkable thought for Elvi, whose imagination rarely stretched in such directions.

She walked for three increasingly slow and painful hours, her feet becoming badly blistered. If she'd had a knife, she might have cut her boots to something like Roman buskins, but as it was . . . And when she tried to pull them off, she couldn't. Her feet had swollen. Feeling utterly defeated, she slumped to the ground, beset by mosquitoes, deerflies and bullflies.

So she got up and went on. She had no bedroll, having planned to plead hospitality from farm families, nor any means of starting a smudge fire to sleep by. She was hungry, with nothing to eat, and incredibly footsore, and the insects showed no mercy. She even prayed! Prayed finally that wolves would come along and put her out of her misery, but God sent not so much as a coyote.

Finally, mosquitoes or not, when it got too dark to walk, she collapsed by the road and slept.

Waking to high daylight. Stiff, sore, she got wincing to her feet, hungry beyond belief. Having no real alternative, she walked again, each step agony—until an hour later she came to a clearing. A furlong ahead was another road. Tears of relief began to flow, and she hobbled faster. Halfway to the junction, she saw a man on horseback crossing it, and cried out to him: "Help! Help!"

He stopped, turned his horse. "What's the matter?" he called.

Her weeping was no longer silent. She speeded to a half run, hobbling, crying hard, and he hurried to meet her. "All right!" he soothed, "all right! Here!" Leaning, he gripped her collar and waistband, and half lifting, half dragging, got her up in front of his saddle.

"You're all right," he said. "Everything's going to be all right."

Princess Elvi had been pointed out to him in Zandria, and disheveled and forlorn though she was now, he recognized her.

The horseman's name was Armand Schubert, an ambitious youth of twenty-five, and successful cattle broker also dealing in sheep and swine. He too had left Zandria, because when word arrived of Ellbogen being burned, it seemed to him the Dkota would burn Zandria too, stockade and all.

Unlike Elvi, he'd ridden directly south, out of the zone of abandonment, and only then eastward into refugee country. To him the invasion was an opportunity, for he couldn't imagine the Dkota conquering the kingdom. The warriors would get enough of fighting and bleeding, and ride home with their take of honors and women. Meanwhile Hasty would fill with refugees. Meat would be needed there, and he would profit from it.

So he'd left bands of refugee cattle in his wake, committed to him, to be driven eastward by drovers selected by the cattle's owners. He rode on to Hasty, to arrange their sale.

And now perhaps for something more.

After an hour of walking the overloaded horse, they reached an inn in a little place named Fes, where they stopped to eat. Because her feet were so sore, Elvi asked to be lifted down and carried. Taking her in his arms stimulated Armand, but he reminded himself who she was, and what she could mean to him, good and ill. Besides, in his young life, women had never been lacking.

At Fes he tried and failed to remove her boots for her. He would, he promised her, get them off when they stopped at the end of the day.

∝⋈∝   ∝⋈∝   ∝⋈∝

It's amazing what place names were scattered over the world by the Shuffling. Names you'd expect the ex-inhabitants would gratefully forget: Buchenwald, Treblinka, Magadan . . . Yet here they were, those names, on the other side of the world, carried along in spite of their histories. Histories one might expect their children not to know—those born in this distant place—but those who'd so inexplicably found themselves in new surroundings? Who'd brought the names with them? Who'd known all too well the places that had worn those names before? In fact they *had* forgotten; those histories were among the memories that had disappeared.

But the names remained. No one knew why, and not even the shuffled had wondered. For them it was an undefined part of something vaguely sensed as missing, that after a time dissipated without residue.

Thus a pleasant village in southern Cloud bore the name Vorkuta, and the mother tongue of the local people was Russian. Though after a generation or so, Merkan was generally known, flavored with a Russian accent, and used mostly with outsiders.

Vorkuta had an inn, not large, but the food wasn't at all bad. If you were fastidious, and paid a modest fee, the innkeeper's girl would give you a boiled mattress filled with fresh straw, and of course there was a wash house and *banya* for cleaning your body.

With his rescue of Princess Elvi, the ambitions of Armand Schubert had expanded. And his designs—fresh, new, and incomplete—were on her father, who surely would want to reward him.

Four hours after leaving Fes, they reached Vorkuta and its inn. Again he carried her inside, and this time asked for lamp oil, pouring some into one of her boots. By the time they'd finished a mug of ale, the oil had worked its way down to her toes, and pulling the boot off removed only a little skin. So they repeated the process with the other boot. It worked as well, and so had the two mugs of ale she'd drunk. She asked if they could stay there that night. More than her feet were sore, she said. Also she wanted a bath.

Her rescuer was agreeable. "Two rooms," he told the innkeeper. Then her right hand gripped his sleeve. "No," she said. "One room. Please! I'm afraid to be alone. Too many bad things have happened."

Armand rearranged his considerations. "Make that one room then, with fresh straw and a boiled mattress cover."

"A feather bed," said Elvi.

"Do you have sphagnum beds?" Armand asked.

"Of course, sir."

"Free of vermin and sticks?"

"If they're not, you're not charged."

"A sphagnum bed then." He turned to her. "They're different; you'll like it."

It turned out there was only one bath, too, and one *banya*, so they borrowed robes, and sent their clothes to be scrubbed. Twenty minutes after they'd returned to their room, her abused bare feet were waving above Armand's bobbing buttocks, and when at last the two young people slept, it was soundly. He'd wait till tomorrow to worry.

⟨⊱⊰⟩ ⟨⊱⊰⟩ ⟨⊱⊰⟩

The principal chief of the Ulster was also the leader of the northern army. A large and powerful man, his Christian name, his common name, was Gallagher, but his ceremonial name was Kills-Buffalo-With-His-Knife—something he'd done twice as a daring youth. He'd since outgrown recklessness, maturing into a man whose actions were measured. Who could make instant decisions when need be, but ordinarily thought things through in advance.

On his march toward Cloud, he'd reached the point where forest dominated the landscape. Since then he'd repeatedly encountered barriers of fallen trees, their tops daunting. Some such barriers, and the gaps in them, led into ambushes where braves were wounded and killed. Even when they didn't, they slowed progress badly, and Gallagher's braves didn't carry food enough for such slowness.

Not wanting to continue in such a manner, he ordered a great camp made, in a north-south belt of prairie. When again the sun rose, he sent out two strong patrols, one north and one south. They were to go far enough to find the end of the barriers, at the same time burning any buildings and killing any dirt-eaters they came to. And to be back at the great camp before the second night, driving with them any spotted buffalo they found.

After about two miles, the patrol that went north sent out scouts in pairs, to explore breaks in the barriers for one that might be the true end. There were numerous gaps, but always, sooner or later, they were blocked, shunted in one direction or another. After a bit, one pair came to a burned forest in its fourth post-fire summer: a broad expanse of lodgepole pine seedlings,[4] thigh deep, with islands of aspen root suckers taller than a man and slender as a thumb, amidst the charred snags of an older generation. Not an area where the hateful barriers could be felled. The scouts followed the burn northeastward for several miles, till they came to old forest again, river forest—and another hated barrier. But no sign of defenders.

The two turned north through the burn, skirting the barrier till they came to a prairie that took them to a large river. In their experience, only the Great River, the Mizzoo, was so wide. This, they realized,

---

[4] Strictly speaking, in Old Merkan, jack pine, *Pinus banksiana*

was the Misasip. So they rode back to the great camp, and reported what they'd found.

Gallagher decided they'd found what he needed.

Meanwhile both patrols found many spotted buffalo, tended by dirt-eaters whom they mostly caught and killed. The next day they brought the animals to the great camp. The army spent two more days there, resting, eating, and smoking meat. Then, before sunup, they broke camp and started northward, guided by the scouts who'd found the safe way to the Misasip.

Chapter 37
Releasing the Dead

The stockade's defenders didn't see much more of the invaders that day. The braves were busy outside Kato Town's far fringe, preparing to send the spirits of their dead to a place of beauty.

The rituals differed between the tribes, so the three principal chiefs had counseled with their principal pastors and spirit talkers. Then the braves of the three tribes separated by about six furlongs, to prepare according to their own customs. Which included butchering enough spotted buffalo to feed all the braves the next day.

The Dkota, those who did not have watch duty, spent much of that day digging a long, knee-deep trench with Sotan shovels. Dug it wider than the height of a tall man, and filled it with funerary fuel, piling it waist high above the brim. They carried off woodpiles, emptied woodsheds; broke up furniture, doorsteps, wheelless wagon beds, shutters and doors; knocked down small outbuildings. And after leveling the fuel, carefully, respectfully—tearfully!—laid the Dkota bodies on the fuel.

With the pyre completed and the bodies laid out, the pastors prepared the ceremony. It would differ in certain respects from the usual, primarily because their women weren't there. So adolescent youths would serve not only as fire-tenders, but in female ceremonial roles, and when the time came, the women's prayers would be sung by deacons. Approximately, for the women's roles were known exactly only by the women. The pastors would coach the stand-ins as best they knew how.

Finally, as twilight faded into night, Pastor Morosov stood by the long pyre and its dead, looked up at the evening stars, and raised a prayer to God, commending to his love the spirits of the dead and the living. And reminding the dead themselves that since the enemy in this place had fought honorably, and treated Dkota bodies with respect, their lodges in this place would not be burned. It was, he said, as Jesus wanted.

Then the drummers began to drum, and the dancers of both parts to pray and dance. Pastors approached with long torches, and walked along the sides of the pyre, from opposite ends, praying as they ignited the fuel, honoring the dead, commending them to God.

The fire grew and intensified. Here and there the fuel collapsed, sparks leaping upward. The fire was so large, so intense, the fire tenders found it nearly impossible to *lay* fresh fuel on it with the usual reverence, and the disturbance sent more sparks swirling. But it seemed that God approved, for in the northern sky an aurora appeared, spring green, quickening all souls.

Firelight gleamed on sweating dancers, and for a while the smell of burning flesh was almost overpowering. But in the ritual circumstances, no one seemed afflicted by it. Fire tenders poked the almost eye-searing fire with long green poles, raising and stirring it for maximum heat, and maximum consumption of bodies.

The dancing and praying continued for hours. The fire burned down, and still the tenders poked, raised, stirred. Finally Pastor Morosov sang the closing prayer, in a voice so strong and clear, one wouldn't imagine he'd been chanting all evening.

The aurora had traded its greenness for icy white, and expanded across the entire bowl of the sky, pulsing, marching, flashing. The celebrants stared upward in awe. Truly, Mazeppa thought, we witness the face of God.

Then the dancers walked reverently to the river, submerged themselves in its cooling water, and afterward dried themselves with their hands. From there they went to their robes and slept, weapons beside them, watched over protectively by cane men. But the pastors and deacons stayed near the trench, praying each according to his own thoughts now, while youths continued to stir the embers. Finally even the aurora shrank to a soft, poorly defined arc low in the north, awaiting approaching dawn.

By midmorning the fire had burnt out, the souls of the dead having ridden the purifying heat to God's higher realm. Meanwhile it was appropriate for the living to break their fast. Using Sotan kettles, meat was cooked. The braves ate, then slept again.

The proposal not to burn the town had been Morosov's, but remembering the aurora, Mazeppa had agreed. Their dead had risen to heaven here, and the site henceforth was holy.

Chapter 38
Courtship

It was newly night. An oil lamp burned in a wrought-iron sconce above the port, but its yellow light failed to find the princess's hooded face. She raised and released the heavy knocker, once, twice, a third time. Armand would have done it for her, if she'd asked, but he'd learned, during their days together, not to get in her way if she wanted to do something herself. There were things he was expected to do, of course, like pay for soft new boots, hooded cape, a horse. But to her credit, she had not insisted on royal, or even noble quality. He couldn't have managed if she had.

She'd been an education.

Again she knocked. A panel slid aside, showing lamplight through a grate. "Who knocks at this hour?" a voice asked.

"I have a message for Lord Brookins." She spoke in a husky tenor that could have been a young man's.

"I'll need to know who you are before I . . ."

"Shut up and open the slot. The matter is urgent."

"One moment."

Below the grate, a narrower panel opened. Through it she pushed the sealed counterfeit non-message she'd prepared for her escape from the Zandria stockade.

"This says to Duke Edward Maltby. He ain't here."

"Idiot! Of course he's not. Lord Brookins needs to see it, to hand to whoever he thinks best. I went to a lot of risk and expense to get this. Tell his lordship I'll wait here for him. Go now! Hurry!"

Armand stared, awed. She could seem helpless, even give the impression she was incompetent, but at others times . . .

"Yessir," the guard answered. "It'll take a few minutes."

Both panels closed, and Elvi turned to Armand. "You can go now," she murmured. "And do not forget, I owe you a favor. Meanwhile my horse is yours, to do with as you please."

He bowed slightly. "I'll remember," he answered, and backed away toward the two horses. He hadn't expected her to give back the horse, but here she'd no doubt have her choice of better. As for the favor . . . maybe someday, but he didn't think so. Best to keep clear of her, especially given what he'd learned of the new palace politics.

He unhitched the two horses, then mounted his, and with the smaller in tow, rode off wondering if the princess could free her father as simply as she'd gotten into the palace.

It wasn't Brookins the guard went to, but the duty sergeant, who thought a moment. "Fine, corporal," he said, "return to your post; I'll handle this." Then started off with the message, not to Brookins but to Colonel Bonde. For Brookins lacked authority of his own, and ambition for that matter, while it seemed to the duty sergeant the colonel would end up on the throne. Then, for having had too much power, Paddy Glynn would follow the king to the block.

Unless perhaps General Jarvi returned to intervene.

Ignoring the door guard, he knocked on the colonel's door himself, hard enough to be heard, but not enough to sound preemptory.

"Who is it?"

"The sergeant of the guard, sir, with a message." Then more softly: "It's addressed to Duke Edward, from Duke Marcel."

A moment later the door opened, and the tall soldierly form of Arvid Bonde stood looking out at him, puzzled. "From who to whom?" he asked.

The sergeant saluted, then held out the message. "From the Duke of Zandria to the Duke of Kato, sir. The messenger is waiting at the message port. He asked Corporal Maggert to take it to Lord Brookins. Maggert brought it to me, and I thought you should see it first."

Frowning, Bonde took it. "Thank you, sergeant, and thank Maggert for me. You did well, both of you." He raised a restraining hand. "But stay a moment."

"Yessir. Thank you, sir."

Bonde broke the seal and unfolded the "message." The paper was blank. Stepping back into the room, he held it to a lamp and peered carefully at both sides, in case some special ink had been used. The only writing on it, though, was the two names.

He frowned. A joke? Or was the "messenger" an assassin, trying to coax him to his death? Or . . . could the sergeant be a conspirator? He'd swear the man wasn't nervous. "Just a moment," Bonde said.

If this was a conspiracy and the guard was in on it, his situation was deadly, but he'd known from the start the game was dangerous. Going into the bedroom, he took from his closet a leather vest with a light breastplate, put it on, and over it a tunic, belted and bloused. He considered a sword as well, but settled for a dagger, threading the sheath onto the belt. The entryway was narrow for swordplay, probably the reason the guards there wore short swords.

He returned to the living room, tugging on the tunic. "One never knows," he said to the sergeant. Genially.

"No, sir." As the sergeant said it, he wondered if "yessir" fitted better. But the colonel seemed comfortable with "no sir."

They walked to the message port, Bonde feeling very alert, very alive. He'd trust the guards, and treat the messenger as the main threat. "Nagy, when we get there, have Maggert open the port. I'll welcome this messenger as an honest man, unless he shows me otherwise, but have your shortsword ready, just in case."

The moment Elvi stepped into the gate house, Bonde's eyes saw through her disguise, despite the cowl, and spoke before she could. "Ah, Charles," he said, "I thought it might be you. You've grown since I saw you last, and I suppose your voice is changing. Brookins is indisposed, so your message was brought to me. It raises questions I need answered." He gestured. "Meanwhile I'll have your dagger please. No reflection on you, but things have been . . . uncertain in the palace, and it's best to observe policy. I'm sure you understand. I'll return it to you before you leave."

He watched her unbuckle her belt and remove the dagger, sheath and all. A bit clumsily; she wore a man's gloves to hide her small hands. He wondered if the idea was hers.

He dismissed Nagy, and the two of them walked alone to his apartment, not talking till they got there and he'd closed the door.

"So, Elvi," he said genially, "let me look at you."

She threw back her cowl; she was actually smiling. Good sign. He picked up the blank paper from the table where he'd left it. "What, pray tell, is this?"

She explained it honestly, then described her ride to Hasty somewhat less honestly. Armand Schubert wasn't mentioned, but the route was basically accurate. "I first heard of father's imprisonment from the West Crossing ferryman," she finished. "Who was responsible for that?"

"Ah. I hadn't planned to bring it up so soon. When he heard about the invasion, he refused to believe it, and became violently deranged. Raging about executions."

Elvi nodded. "I thought it might be something like that. I was afraid the savages would arrive here before I could. What's being done to defend the kingdom?"

Her words, her attitude, were a greater relief than he could have imagined. "As soon as I took over," he said, "I sent a battery of light cannon, the battery your Uncle Jaako left us with, to the Knees of the Misasip, along with the 1st Rifle Company. In case the invaders get past Cloud. Since then, the other battery and the 2nd Rifle Company arrived from your Uncle Jaako. I sent that battery, too. Jaako is covering the Sota River approach, and I kept the 2nd Rifles here to defend the town and palace. Actually I'm optimistic." He paused, looking more sober now. "Your father is still deranged, suspecting everyone, yourself included. He believes you left to betray him, and—talks the most terrible filth."

She seemed untouched by that, something else he wouldn't have expected. "Well," she said after a moment, "I suppose his heart was too pure to stand Mazeppa's betrayal."

He wondered if she was serious. "Clonarty was the major source of your father's problems. We all know that." Actually, Bonde knew better; Eldred had been a molli before Clonarty had come to Sota. Still, Clonarty had no doubt made him worse. "The archbishop is also in the dungeon," Bonde added, "but in a different room."

"Room" sounded better than "cell."

"Good. And you, apparently, are in charge here now. What is your status?"

"By virtue of my military rank and Jaako's absence, I'm acting as regent—acting for the army, with the support of the palace guard, until the invaders are driven out."

Nobody had actually described it that way before, but it amounted to the truth.

"And who do you suppose that new ruler will be?"

"Yourself, now that you're here. Your father intended that Mary rule in her time, being the eldest, but she's in a nunnery now, some—five hundred? six hundred?—miles away. The council will try to impose its will, of course, and Jaako may conform to avoid violence. As for me—I'll support your candidacy with whatever force is mine."

His last words took him by surprise; but they seemed politic. He coveted the throne himself, but had no constituency, or much standing with the family. But . . . if he were to marry Elvi . . . Clearly she'd changed. She might, though, have in mind rehabilitating her father as king. And Eldred would execute for treason anyone who'd had anything to do with his jailing or the regency.

Well. If she wanted her father rehabilitated, Elvi might have to disappear. Apparently no one else knew she was here. But if she didn't— Perhaps he could marry her, and share the throne. Would the Church label such a marriage incestuous? Maybe Clonarty could declare an exemption for a second cousin. They could make a deal: for Arvid Bonde, marriage to Elvi; for the archbishop, house arrest instead of the dungeon. Clonarty could perform the wedding in his own chapel.

There was another rapping at the door, and a voice, the door guard's. "Sir, some men are here with your bath water."

Bonde gestured at the door to the bedroom, and Elvi went, closing it behind her. "Good. Let them in," he said.

There were two of them, with two large water cans on a cart. He'd been expecting, then forgotten them. "You know what to do with it?" he asked.

"Yes, milord," the elder answered.

He watched them lug one of the twelve-gallon cans into the bathroom, and heard them pour it into the copper tub. Then they repeated the performance with the other, and left with the empty cans. Before closing the door after them, he spoke to the guard. "No one else tonight, Jao," he said, then shut it, thinking about the bath. Really, he coveted the royal suite, the Garden Suite, with bath house and sauna built in, fed from a cistern with water from the roof.

Elvi removed her cape and cowl, and he hung them up for her. "I suppose," he said, "you'd like a bath after your long ride." He hoped she'd decline. He liked his hot bedtime bath, but the offer was necessary. "Let me show you where the bath is." It occurred to him it lacked equipage a princess might think necessary. He opened the door and gestured at the steaming tub, with a small bench, bowl of soft soap, and towel hanging at hand. "There you are, my dear. Is there anything else you need?"

She smiled. "Yes. I'd like you to wash my back. If you're to be my husband, I'll expect it of you. This can be your trial performance."

Chapter 39
Armies on the Move Again

After the funeral ceremonies and a day and night of rest, Mazeppa's army rose from its robes at first dawn, broke camp, and immediately after sunrise rode out of Kato Town down to the river. But not in drag-ass defeat. It galloped off whooping, as if in victory. It was the first time since they'd entered Sota that Mazeppa's braves had all been together on the march. Heretofore they'd been a gaggle of war parties, suited to the type of war he envisioned and the type of fighting men he had.

Seen from the fort, two thousand braves made a long column, but soon the last of them had galloped out of sight, concealed by terrain and the riverine forest. Headed northward, for from its elbow at Kato, the Sota River ran very nearly north for many miles, the road to Hasty keeping it company near the east shore.

The military council could see no sign that the town had been or would be set afire. Yet the Dkota weren't abandoning the war, and Frazier was in no mood for

369

needless risks. He sent orders to the civil authorities and gate guards that no one was to leave the stockade without his approval or General Jarvi's. Mazeppa might hope to draw the defenders outside, and in an hour or two come storming back, hoping to succeed by ruse where force had failed.

Then he called for volunteers to follow the invaders and report on them, and from those volunteers, appointed a dozen. After giving them instructions, he sent them off under an ensign and sergeant who knew the country.

But there was one volunteer he didn't consider sending: the one-time Dkota, Gavan Feeny. Until finding him among the volunteers, Frazier hadn't realized the young man was in the fort. Gavan, it turned out, had joined the Kato Town militia, and taken part in the defense. Withholding him from this scouting mission was not a matter of distrust. As Frazier explained to the youth, he had better uses for his knowledge, then and in the future.

Mostly the Sota River Road ran through riverine forest that spilled over onto adjacent uplands. For the first four miles, Mazeppa found the road promising: no abatises. But that changed. The road wasn't blocked, but on each side it was flanked by felled trees. Mazeppa stopped. As far up the road as he could see, there was no sign of defenders, but Sotan bowmen were quite able to lay quietly concealed. Of course, they sometimes left such barriers without a single ambusher; it was hard to be sure.

Some distance in advance, the Dkota scouts rode listening, scanning. Even the birds sounded normal. Stopping, they signed to one another, then two rode back and reported. Again the army moved. Mazeppa, who could be marvelously patient, responded to an impulse, and nudged his mount into a canter.

In fact, Katoan ambushers *were* there, and after

letting the scouts and the lead parties pass well into the trap, began to loose arrows at the column. One struck Mazeppa's horse behind the shoulder; it fell like a stone. Which may have saved the chief's life, for at virtually the same instant another hit his quiver when it might otherwise have struck him. He hit the ground rolling and came up on his feet, arrows spilling, then dove for the cover of the fallen tops to avoid being trampled. Other riders too were down.

Mazeppa didn't call a retreat; didn't have a chance. His braves turned back on their own, shouting, warning those behind. Several slowed or stopped to load the fallen onto their mounts. Others, not disabled, saved themselves, for these were men who, in the face of a stampede, might grasp the mane of a lead horse running full out, swing aboard bareback, and control it at once.

It was a one-sided gantlet run at full speed. More horses went down. Others were hit but ran on. Some not hit had riders shot from their backs. But a half minute later the Dkota were out of it. No one knew for sure how many men they'd lost, nor were they about to go back and see.

It could have been worse, Mazeppa realized. This ambush had not been heavily manned.

They continued their retreat at a trot till they came to a place where earlier, open land had been glimpsed on higher ground. Mazeppa stopped, and sent scouts to examine it. They reported a sizeable clearing, with an abandoned cabin and outbuildings. Mazeppa decided, signalled, and leading his column, urged his new mount up the sharp slope, to regroup in the clearing. On its far edge was a gap in the enclosing forest. Gesturing, Mazeppa called to his chief scout: "Leonid, see what's on the other side of that gap."

The scout signed acknowledgement, and trotted his

horse in that direction. *Now*, Mazeppa thought, *I will have my chiefs learn who, of their braves, did not emerge from the ambush.*

But that was not his prime concern. It was time to consider the morale of his braves again. Two nights earlier, they'd sent the spirits of many of their brothers to God, and this morning they'd fled headlong out of an ambush, attacked by—how many dirt-eaters? Forty? Fifty?

They left the clearing with its buildings burning behind them. Mazeppa's scouts led cross-country eastward and northward, picking their way through an irregular mosaic of forest and prairie, keeping largely to open ground and meeting no resistance. Of the woods they passed through, none had tangles of felled trees. Twice, early on, Mazeppa glimpsed the road, where it climbed out of the riverine forest to pass through prairie. That was where hills pinched out the floodplain, but inevitably the road returned to the floodplain again. He was not tempted to return to it. Enough to parallel it. In fact he tended eastward. The terrain seemed more open there. After a bit, he decided: to ride boldly east, and strike northward later. Perhaps he'd find dirt-eater settlements whose people hadn't fled; it would be good for morale.

Even riding over grassland was brightening their eyes.

From 20,000 feet, Tahmm tracked the Dkota on the screen, concerned at their unforeseen change of course. The Austin militias were moving northward up the Hasty-Austin Road, presumably led by Donald Maltby, and there seemed a real chance they'd run into the much larger invader force. The ill-coordinated militias were growing from locale to locale, picking up locals, and should grow notably at Fairbow, as it had at Tonna. But even so, if they met the Dkota in

open combat, it would prove disastrous. Militias were
trained as squads and platoons, a few as companies,
but as a battalion-sized force . . . ? Yet their involvement was needed. The trick would be to create a situation suited to them, though what that might be . . .

He triggered his radio.

Messengers had galloped in from Frazier's scouts,
reporting the successful ambush, and that the Dkota
had left the road. Frazier in turn had sent riders
pounding north up the road to let other ambushers
know.

Freddy was in his tiny command post when his com
buzzed softly. "This is Freddy."

It was a conference call, Tahmm reporting the
Dkotan commitment eastward, the progress of
Donald's militias riding north, and the potential for
their meeting. "Freddy, what can you do about it?"
he finished.

Freddy closed his eyes to better image the map in
his mind. "Luis, are you getting this?" he asked.

"Right. I need to sort out the possibilities with
Keith, but here's what I have in mind. . . ."

Good, Tahmm thought when Luis had finished.
*This crew is as good as you can hope for, but
Luis . . . came through at Eisenbach.*

❦❦   ❦❦   ❦❦

A hundred and twenty miles north, Gallagher, Goyuk
and their braves followed their guides through the
three-year-old burn. Reaching riverine forest, they
came to the barrier of fallen trees, and turning north
again, to the stretch of prairie that took them to the
Misasip.

They paused by the river.

Gallagher felt good about his decision. His scouts
were the same men who'd scouted the route in the
month of grass growing, all the way to Hasty. Men

who remember details. At the great camp, they'd said there was still a considerable distance to go, mostly through forest, before they'd reach the Misasip. To go that way, it had seemed to him, his army would spend days seeking its way around barriers, and fighting at a serious disadvantage.

It was not a way of war his people knew, and he'd wondered if his braves, many of them, might decide to go home. Many would not have come, except for what Sky Chief had said: that the dirt-eaters planned to kill all the buffalo. And a person had the right to decide that Sky Chief lied.

But today, on this new path, not a single arrow had been shot at them, and here they were at the Misasip. He wondered if the dirt-eaters even knew.

While their horses rested and grazed, the braves sat eating dried meat and pemmican. After a while, Gallagher and Goyuk sent couriers to their subchiefs, telling them the time had come to swim their horses across the river. When all had heard, he shouted a command, which was repeated by the cane men and the chiefs of war parties. Then he shook his spear overhead, strong arm pumping, and urged his horse down the river bank, a river more handsome than the Mizzoo, much less muddy. At the bank it was too deep to wade; the animal simply plunged in.

At once the cold current carried him downstream, his horse swimming powerfully, angling toward the other side, its progress as much downstream as across the current. With Gallagher's weight on its back, only its head and neck remained clear of the water. It was quickly laboring, eyes rolling. Sliding from his saddle, Gallagher gripped his horse's tail, letting it tow him. Now its back emerged; it would make better progress. An arrow struck the empty saddle, and Gallagher looked toward the shore. Here along the river there was not the tangled barrier he'd learned to dread, but dirt-eaters stood by their horses, drawing longbows, shooting arrows.

He spoke to his horse, encouraging it. "Be strong, my friend. With God's help we'll be safe."

Mostly it was the horses the dirt-eaters shot at; they were better targets. Gallagher never considered veering shoreward to fight. He knew the long knives the dirt-eaters carried. Even if his horse wasn't killed by a close-range shot, they could strike it with the blade as it struggled up the bank, and himself as he followed.

Clearly they'd known he was coming. He saw braves free-swimming now, and horses with arrows stuck in necks and backs. Other horses, dead or dying, floated with heads submerged. For the first time he peered at the far shore, the east shore. There too now, dirt-eaters on horseback jogged southward, keeping pace.

It seemed to him his army might have a long way to go in the water, maybe too far for horses to swim. Looking back, he called an order: move to mid-stream, then ride the current till they saw a place on the east bank where they could safely land.

He heard his order passed on, and forged forward to his horse's head, to guide it.

Time and the riverbanks slid by. It seemed they'd never be free of the bowmen on the shores. The cold water sucked body heat from horses and men. Some horses gave out and drowned, leaving their riders to catch one of the remounts that followed. On both banks, dirt-eater horsemen kept pace, but now, with the braves in mid-stream, the enemy saved his arrows.

At length the swimming braves saw the town of Cloud ahead on their right. From there, men rowed out in boats, wielding bows and sabers. But shooting longbows required standing, which made balance tricky, and boats were overturned by braves who'd approached underwater. The other boats drew off a ways; their people expended their arrows, then left.

Ironically it was a barrier of fallen trees that blocked their east-shore pursuers, and a prairie to the south of it saved the army. Deep-chilled, staggering, braves and horses struggled ashore. Most of the braves were too numb and dull-witted from hypothermia to pull themselves into the saddle. They scattered on foot to the fringe of the woods, where they gathered dry sticks for fires. Their sleeping robes were wet and cold, and the men spread them, rubbing most of the water out. Then left them in the afternoon sunlight, along with their saddles and other gear, to dry as much as they would.

For a time the war parties did not muster. The braves simply worked wherever they were, and Gallagher, Goyuk and their subchiefs didn't know how many men they had left. But before evening the war parties had gathered, and their chiefs counted their braves. The horse herd was gathered and guards posted.

The breeze and sun were warm. Men and horses dozed.

When they roused, they were famished. The men rummaged their saddlebags and ate. The horses grazed. In total, sixty-four braves were missing— killed or drowned. Gallagher did not doubt he'd have lost more, probably many more, if he'd fought fifteen or twenty miles of one-sided skirmishes along the road to Cloud. As it was, he still had a large and dangerous army, and they'd crossed the river. Not bad, he thought, not at all.

Night came. The men slept cold, their robes only half dried. When at last dawn arrived they rose stiffly, wrestled to warm themselves, chewed jerky with strong jaws, then mounted and rode off southward on the road to Hasty. From time to time, when they came to clearings or prairie, they stopped to spread their robes in the sun while the horses grazed. Morale recovered further as the miles passed without abatises.

Felled trees, yes, in bunches here and there, worrying and slowing them—and perhaps buying time for the dirt-eaters. A few times, Sotan sharpshooters took advantage of those tangles to shoot three or four braves before racing away, back through uncut forest. But all in all, it seemed to the Ulsters and Yellow Bears that the hard times were behind them.

⬥⬥⬥ ⬥⬥⬥ ⬥⬥⬥

That evening the Higuchians held another conference: Carlos and Paddy in the palace, Luis in his rented room, Peng in Cloud, Freddy somewhere north of Kato Town, and Tahmm and Lemmi in Tahmm's scout.

Tahmm initiated the call, and spoke first. "I can see Mazeppa's army now, and Donald's militias, so I'm in the best position to orient all of us. Freddy, where are you?"

"With Jarvi and Frazier bivouacked by the river road about thirty miles north of Kato. No tents, just sleeping under the sky and trees—so we can get on the way again early.

"We'd have made better time, but the road was blocked in places, part of the abatis system. We sent riders out ahead to get it cleared, and fortunately there were militia close by. They furnished the ax power, we did the pulling and lifting.

"The road's clear now, all the way to where we'll leave it, on what the locals call the Dindigul Trail, just south of Little Bend. It's a fairly straight shot to the Dindigul stockade.

"And that's it for me."

"Fine," Tahmm said. "Peng, tell them what you told me earlier."

Peng told about the northern army bypassing Cloud. "They took modest losses," he went on. "The locals estimate two or three hundred, so perhaps one hundred. They may reach Noka late tomorrow. The abatises there are neither extensive nor intricate; with good scouting, they can be bypassed. The Dkota experience west of Cloud has made bypassing attractive to them.

"It's not clear whether they'll try to take the Noka Stockade; it's said to be strong and well-manned. They'll probably burn the town though, which should occupy them for a few hours; it's a good-sized town.

"Carlos may want to leave Hasty in the morning, for the Knees, to provide liaison with the forces in ambush there. And that's all I have for now."

"Thanks, Peng," Tahmm said. "Lemmi's with me, and able to ride if need be. Luis asked for him earlier today, so Korri made an illicit thousand-mile sonic boom, delivering him to Kato. I took the transfer in Bishop Joseph's pasture. I'll let him off by the spring in the corner of the brother farm pasture."

He paused. "Luis, it's your turn. Take over."

"Right. Korri, if you're listening, thanks for bringing Lemmi. He and I need to be at Dindigul too. When it comes to reading Mazeppa—maybe talking with him—Lemmi knows him a *lot* better than any of the rest of us do.

"Carlos, have you got anything to say?"

"Yeah. If you're leaving for Dindigul, I better stay here instead of going to the Knees. Because something's going on here in the palace that feels important."

"Any idea what?"

"Nope, but something." He paused. "I think Paddy's got something to say. Paddy?"

"Yes sor. Oi'm worried about Luis and Lemmi and Freddy all being at Dindigul. If it falls, we'll lose them and General Jarvi's battalion too. So oi'd like to have the 2nd Rifle Company sent there, but oi'm not sure oi can get Colonel Bonde to send it. Do oi have permission to kill him if oi need to?"

"Send them if you can, Paddy. I should have thought of that myself. Work on Bonde this evening; Carlos can let me know how it goes. But don't kill him except in extreme emergency. We need the stability he provides."

Tahmm didn't comment. His proper role was support: aerial observation, and as necessary, errand boy and sounding board. Dindigul was vital to the whole operation. If it fell, the situation would be impossible to salvage. But Luis was right about Bonde's importance at Hasty, alive.

Luis continued. "At risk of belaboring the obvious, this is a good time to remember our goals. And that if we can, we need to come out of this with Mazeppa and Eldred alive. And Clonarty. And with noncombatant casualties as low as possible. We've done pretty well so far, but we need to avoid any more massacres like those at Ellbogen and Grove Falls.

"And Carlos, you're right. Stay at the palace. Something is going on there; I feel it too."

Riding west to the abandoned brother farm to pick up Lemmi, Luis thought about Dindigul. The country there was thinly peopled; rangeland, with too little wood suited for fence rails. Dindigul itself, though the seat of a barony, was scarcely even a village, and in the Royal Domains, at that. He wondered how strong the stockade was.

The answer to that could be the key to how this war played out, and to whether he and Lemmi survived to engineer a peace. If they didn't, Carlos and Peng would have a helluva job picking up the pieces.

Chapter 40
Thunder at the Slashing

Gallagher, Chief of the Ulster and junior co-chief of the Dkota, depended strongly on a young scout named Ngo, also called "Knows-What-He-Sees." At the time of birds returning, Ngo had been the first Gallagher had asked to explore the route to Hasty.

In a culture where literacy is rare, children see and hear differently, especially in a hunting-gathering culture. Sights and sounds register more strongly, are recalled more easily and clearly. In some this is especially strong, and it is they who, if they choose, become scouts.

Thus on the march, when Gallagher wanted to know what lay ahead, and how far, it was Ngo he asked. There'd been no abatises before, but by now Ngo had some sense of where to expect them. Those above and below Noka were strong, but not well laid out. Thus Gallagher's army had lost only half a day and a few lives in working around them.

Where they rode now, the bank above the floodplain was quite high. Ngo, in the lead, came to an abatis along the left side of the road, though there

was no indication it was manned: no unnatural sound
or movement, no smell of cook fires or tobacco smoke.
To the right, downhill through the trees, the floodplain road could be seen, and the mighty river.

He mistrusted the situation, and after signaling a
halt, rode back to Gallagher, who came to see for
himself. He too was ill at ease, but saw no good
alternative to proceeding. Reluctantly he led his army
slanting down the slope to the floodplain road. If it
led into trouble, they'd at least have the option of
taking to the river.

His foreboding eased greatly when the abatis ended
with a few trees chopped into, then abandoned. As
if some dirt-eater chief had changed his mind, and
called off the axmen.

Lieutenant Giao of the Teng-Xian Associated
Militias heard a distant raven call; two croaks followed
by three. He answered with a single throaty note,
followed seconds later by a single croak. Others than
the tribesmen know the sounds of nature.

His men knew what to do: lay still behind the abatis
being passed. Let the Dkota in, but not back out.

When he came to another abatis on the floodplain,
half a mile farther on, Gallagher's misgivings returned,
sharpened. *There is always the river,* he reminded
himself. Meanwhile he rode on, at a walk now, his
braves following, alert. Again Ngo rode back to him.
Ahead, he reported, the abatis ended. Beyond it,
instead of strips of trees having been felled, the whole
woods had been slashed down!

Warily they rode on, then entered the slashing.
Eerie; they'd seen nothing like it before. Why such
destruction? Here the river narrowed the floodplain
on their side of the river, crowding the road close to
the steep slope that backed it. And from some of the
fallen trees, many branches had been lopped. Why?

Gallagher could see no sense in it, and neither could Ngo.

For another half mile or more, nothing happened. Then thunderous booms erupted from partway up the slope, punching gaps in the column. Gallagher fell dead from his saddle, a grapeshot through his skull. For a long shocked moment, near paralysis prevailed. Then another volley of grape burst the silence beyond recovery. There were screams, howls, cries. The killed and wounded numbered a few dozen, but shock and terror were general, and the Ulster-Yellow Bear army dissolved. Some braves turned back the way they'd come; some rode their horses into the river; some, their horses felled, took whatever cover they could find. Meanwhile the cannon continued, firing now at will. And among the felled trees, groups of archers rose, long drilled for speed of fire as well as accuracy.

Of the braves toward the rear of the column, those not struck down were soon out of the great slashing, but behind the abatis, another rank of dirt-eaters rose, longbows dealing death. Some of the fleeing whipped their horses to run the gantlet. Others took to the river.

Many more tribesmen were struck down by archery than by artillery, though the shock was far less.

By this time fully half the northern invaders were in the water, dismounted, clinging to their horses' tails, or to the saddle, the current carrying them downstream. Where a phalanx of militia bowmen came to the shore to send arrows at swimming horses, floating men.

Those who could, pressed their mounts to swim farther out into the current, trying for safety in distance. These were the designated prey of the 1st Royal Rifles. And here Stephen Nez had shown further foresight: he'd left trees along the bank, against whose trunks the riflemen steadied their long barrels. Now a hundred yards distance gave little safety, the balls killing horses and men. And these riflemen, having mastered the drill of rapid reloading, fired three aimed shots per minute.

Downstream, the rifle fire continued, and in the water, the effort soon became to reach the far shore, where only mounted bowmen sent death. From there, those who survived could find their way home.

That, of course, was the smaller, northern army. Two or three days' ride southwest was another, much larger, with less formidable defenses awaiting it.

Chapter 41
Convergence on Dindigul

(Luis)

Lemmi was doing pretty well, but he didn't have his strength back yet. "Take it as easy as you can," rehab had told him. Tahmm could have airlifted us to somewhere near Dindigul by night. We could have holed up in a woods by the Dindigul Trail and waited for Jarvi's army. But an airlift as simple transportation was one thing. As part of a tactical operation, it would have broken External's intercessionary regulations, and ESS regs are more stringent than Bureau regs.

Besides, Paddy had somehow gotten Mary Youngblood's gelding for Lemmi, a beautiful animal, famous for its smooth-as-milk trotting gait. So Lemmi and I bedded down in a brother house hay shed, with the mosquitoes. Our muses would wake us.

At first dawn we were on a small ferry at North Landing, with me helping the night man scull across the river. Two hours later we were eating breakfast at the Last Stop Inn, at Big Ditch Junction, where the Causeway Road meets the Austin-Hasty Road.

The innkeeper fried our bacon, eggs, and mush

himself, and after he'd served us, sat down with us. "You fellas belong to some religious order?" he asked. Our clerical collars didn't seem to belong with our uniforms.

"Yep," I said. In Sota I'd generally made a point of keeping my affiliation to myself, but the situation had changed, and my brevity had been rude, so I elaborated. "Higuchian," I went on. "We're headed south."

"South." He said the word as if pondering it. No one was going south these days. "River Road?"

"Austin Road."

He shook his head. "Everything's going to hell this summer. His Majesty in the dungeon, the Dkota in the marches . . . I've had folks through here who'd left the marches—abandoned their homes just in time. Then it was folks from Kato! Kato, for God's sake! They say the militia's got all sorts of barriers and ambushes set along the River Road, and of course the army's been sent down there, so I guess that's hopeful, but . . ."

He shrugged.

I knew what he meant by "but": but what if the Dkota bypassed the abatises? And that's what they'd done. According to his aura, this peaceful innkeeper harbored a warrior's muse. After enough lifetimes, warriors don't much care for fighting, but retain the muse, which is part of them.

"The last few days," he went on, "no one's come through from the north until you two, and not many from the south. I've had to lay off my cook and serving folk." He changed direction. "Them eggs done to suit you, brothers? Is that the word? Brothers? I'm not used to Higuchians."

"Usually brothers is the word," I told him, "but we're masters. We've been sent to help stop the Dkota."

That stopped him for a moment. "Can you do

that?" he asked carefully. "Stop the Dkota? I hear there's thousands of them. And more thousands up north, coming by way of Cloud."

"We'll know in a few days," I said. "General Jarvi's down south with four companies of kingsmen, and a company of king's rifles should be coming through here today sometime, to help."

He looked more concerned than reassured. Four companies of royal ordinaries and one of rifles doesn't sound like much, compared to "thousands of Dkota." He got to his feet. "You fellas want a beer? On the house?"

"Not for me," I said. "You have sassafras?"

He nodded, and looked at Lemmi. "I'll have sassafras too," Lemmi said. "With honey."

The man brought it, then went back to his kitchen without sitting down again. We finished our breakfast and left. Interesting that our host hadn't railed against the Dkota. He was only one man, of course, and might be atypical, but come to think of it, I hadn't heard people in Hasty rail against them either.

Which was encouraging. That could help win the peace—if we won the war.

⊰⊱⊰⊱ ⊰⊱⊰⊱ ⊰⊱⊰⊱

It was high noon, and the 2nd Rifles rode at a brisk trot—through their own dust, for they were headed south, and the wind was from due north. The riflemen had been picked for their personal reputations as armsmen, and culled for their marksmanship. Their rifles were the best in weapons, and they considered themselves a military elite. They expected to fight in a battle that day, and be pivotal in winning it, a good attitude to have, riding to battle.

The company commander, Captain Hsi Chung Fong, was a distant cousin of Jarvi's by marriage, well-trained and mentally quick. He had scouts out ahead, though he didn't expect to meet the enemy this morning. The general, Fong had been told, was to reach a place called Dindigul today, to take defensive positions at its stockade. Fong was to join him there, or maybe vice versa. The Dkota weren't expected to arrive till later.

Fong certainly hoped they didn't. He wouldn't want to meet a couple thousand Dkota in the open with his 120-man company.

He topped a rise, and a quarter mile on the other side saw two men on horseback. His scouts had undoubtedly questioned them. Meanwhile his dust had preceded him, and the two had drawn their horses well aside, to avoid the worst of it. One waved his hat, perhaps to flag him down, or maybe just glad to see soldiers coming. At closer range, they seemed to wear uniforms of some sort, so raising an arm, Fong halted his column, and the two trotted over to meet him.

"Who are you?" he asked, "and where are you going?"

"I am Master Luis, of the Order of Saint Higuchi, and this is Master Lemmi. We're headed for Dindigul to assist in its defense."

Fong had heard of the Order of course, and of His Majesty's hostility toward it, but Eldred's attitude seemed irrelevant now. Jaako's was more important, and he'd told stories, years earlier, of the Anti-Pope's War, including the Order's fighting and leadership qualities.

"Just the two of you?" Fong asked.

"There is a third already there."

That hardly changes matters, Fong thought. "You're welcome to ride with me if you'd like," he said.

The man grinned. "Thank you, but Master Lemmi has recent injuries, so we must travel more slowly than you. We'll see you again at the stockade."

❖❖❖   ❖❖❖   ❖❖❖

When Luis had sent Donald Maltby off to Austin, the idea had been that after ousting Alfred Wiesendorf

as duke, the young man would ride north to Tonna
with the Austin armsmen and militias, there to gather
whatever additional militias and armsmen he could,
then ride west to Kato. Or if Kato had fallen, ride
north through Fairbow to Hasty, to help defend the
kingdom in any way he could.

During the week past, a stream of refugees had
arrived at Austin, telling of "an uncountable host" of
Dkota invaders in the marches. The villagers of Grove
Falls had mostly taken refuge not in its stockade, but
in flight to southward. It had been mostly the old and
otherwise immobile who'd sheltered inside the stockade with the duke's armsmen and militia. When the
Dkota arrived, they'd torched the town, and with fire
arrows ignited roofs inside the stockade. And because
most of its buildings had been built backed up against
it, the fires had breached the walls. What had happened to the defenders and the others there could
only be imagined.

Wiesendorf had been badly shaken by the stories,
and visited by his conscience, had prayed at length
with his Carlian confessor, for guidance. So when
Donald handed him a letter of authority from General Jarvi, the duke nearly wept with relief. He'd
convinced himself it was God's answer to those
prayers.

Wiesendorf had handed the letter to his new commander at arms. New because when word had arrived
of the events at Grove Falls, the old commander,
Captain Bevins, had dissolved in anxiety, and deserted.
Sergeant Major Banda had taken command, and a
grateful Alfred Wiesendorf had made it official,
skipping the rank of ensign and promoting him to lieutenant.

Banda had already contacted his connections within
the local ex-militia. He'd expected to hear from Master
Luis, and wanted to be ready. Now he told Wiesendorf
to stay where he was. He, his armsmen and militia,

were leaving with the younger Maltby to help drive out the Dkota. Saying nothing about the odds.

Glad to be told what to do, the duke accepted this. And prayer having worked so well the last time, he returned to it as soon as his visitors left.

While gathering the locals, Banda sent men out to alert militias from villages to the north, with instructions to meet him along the Austin-Hasty Highway. He sent the instructions in the name of Donald Maltby as commander. The name of Banda was potent among the militias in Austin, but outside the duchy he was nearly unknown. The Maltby name, on the other hand, was well-known throughout Sota, especially in the south, and carried a reputation for strength and fairness. And with Eldred's rule discredited, many would like the idea of a Maltby in command.

But stopping the Dkota was the main reason for the militia response. All they'd needed was a plausible leader. At Tonna, and again at Fairbow, Banda's long platoon—five squads—of uniformed and well-drilled dukesmen, helped inspire confidence. By Sotan standards they were a strong force, armed, ready, and matter-of-fact. It was they who converted and attached the Tonna and Fairbow baronial armsmen, and their conversion helped convince the militias, where the numbers were.

Meanwhile, at Tonna, Donald and Banda heard two new stories: one that the Dkota had taken Kato, burned it to the ground, and murdered everyone except young women and girls. The other, more recent story had it that the Kato stockade had been fought for, and the Dkota having failed to take it, had stormed off north on the River Road, toward Hasty.

So instead of turning west, Donald continued northward, hoping to get ahead of the Dkota before they reached the Misasip. Perhaps he could stop them on the Causeway Road, where marshes made crosscountry travel difficult or impossible.

Some of the Fairbow recruits were hung over, but Banda formed them up with a combination of humor, charisma, and a tongue that "could take the bark off an oak," as Donald would tell it. Then, when they were ready to ride out of town, Banda's loud voice asked Donald's leave to address the troops.

"You're welcome to, Lieutenant Banda," Maltby answered, just as loudly. As if they'd rehearsed it.

Banda turned to the mounted ranks and bellowed. "All right men, AT EASE!"

Conversations cut off. They could *feel* Banda's total, jut-jawed intention. "We're about to ride north," he boomed, "and in the next few days we'll meet the Dkota. They've never fought a force like this one, so they've got a surprise coming."

He paused, then tilted his head back and bellowed again, more loudly than before. "Battaliuuun! TENSHUT!" The order was passed down the column: "Company! Tenshut!" "Platooon! Tenshut!" Then "Road step! . . . Forwaaaard . . . MARCH!"

To Donald Maltby, the first hour and a half out of Fairbow had seemed perfect for riding—the countryside lovely and the sun warm, with a cooling breeze out of the north. Cool enough and strong enough, the flies were less active than usual. *A good day,* he thought, *to help last night's drunks recover.*

The countryside was mildly hilly and predominantly prairie, with occasional oak groves, and mixed woods on some moist sites. From time to time they'd pass two or three sets of farmsteads, typically along a creek, with small fields of corn, beans, squash, potatoes . . . Being far from the Sota River, Donald also saw loose herds of cattle and an occasional band of sheep, tended by figures on horseback.

They'd topped another rise, then ridden down its wooded north face to a brook at the bottom. There Donald called a halt, for his troops to drink, fill their water bags, and water their horses. Then one of his advance scouts came galloping south toward him. Donald nudged his horse forward to meet the man.

The scout pulled up in a puff of dust. "Sir!" he said excitedly, and waved an arm northward, "there's a very large body of horsemen ahead, sir. Horsemen or cattle, we couldn't be sure, but there's got to be hundreds and hundreds of them. The dust cloud's at least a mile long. From off west, but they're on the road ahead of us now."

Banda looked at Maltby. "What'd they want to come over here for?"

It seemed to Donald he knew. "Frazier had crews out for weeks," he said, "felling abatises along the river. They must have worked too well, and Mazeppa decided to go around."

Banda nodded. "That's it, sure's hell. So what's our orders?"

"As long as the wind doesn't shift, any time they look back, it's their own dust they'll see, not ours. And they have no reason to expect us. So after we give the horses a break, we'll follow, staying well back. And when they camp tonight, we'll run over them, kill as many as we can, and keep going north."

Banda laughed, turning heads. Some of his Austin platoon was near enough to hear, and he spoke loudly, making sure they did. "Sounds good to me, Captain. I've cheated the angel of death three four times already. Might's well do it again."

His reckless irreverence struck a chord among his men, to whom he was already an icon. And as the column moved on again, it was repeated back through the ranks, loudly and raucously, with laughter. Donald Maltby felt a sudden fellowship with these roughneck militias, and if not confidence, certainly hope.

❖❖❖ ❖❖❖ ❖❖❖

The village of Dindigul, seat of Dindigul Barony, was located on a broad, open, near-flat expanse in the southern half of the Royal Domains. There the Dindigul Trail met the Hasty-Austin Road, forty miles east of the Sota River. Its stockade stood by the road a half mile south of the junction. Since last rebuilt, the stockade poles had rotted somewhat in the ground, but it wasn't close to falling down yet. And as the baron put it in his Hindi-flavored Merkan, "The poles are piss elm. They will not burn."

And now it was strongly defended, not just by the Baron's fourteen armsmen and four platoons of ex-militia. There was Frazier's platoon of Katoan armsmen—and four companies of kingsmen, mounted infantry under Jaako Jarvi, whose long fealty to Eldred was history. Jarvi, who spoke with the authority of the king, had taken command, telling the baron and his captain what to do. The locals were grateful to him.

The baron had set up an alarm the day before. Some two miles south, atop a rise with a long view, a pyre had been built, primed with grease and dry hay. And there had posted a lookout with a spyglass and phosphor matches, watching southward for a telltale dust cloud, or any other sign that might catch his eye.

Two companies of Jarvi's infantry were manning the parapet and blockhouses; the stockade measured only eighty yards on a side. The rest of his and Frazier's men were outside, lying on the grass, napping or thinking or talking. Their horses, saddled and waiting, grazed along a picket string.

At Jarvi's order, the local garrison was busy with ladders, buckets, and the stockade's two well sweeps (the water table was at ten feet), wetting down the thatched roofs. When they'd finished, the rest of the armsmen would crowd inside with their horses.

Jarvi and Frazier had already discussed what there

was to discuss. Now they stood on the south walkway, next to a blockhouse, speaking only occasionally. Jarvi had always preferred that someone else be at the top. For fifteen years the someone else had been Eldred; the king had told him what he wanted done, and Jarvi had taken care of it. Sometimes not happily, but always ably.

At Kato he'd deferred to Frazier as knowing the area, the situation, and the enemy better than he did. And he'd come to trust Frazier's patriotism as well as his ability. So although he outranked him, he'd suggested again that Frazier be the field commander. "I'm getting old, Keith," he'd confessed. "My mind's not as nimble as it was."

Now, while Jarvi's eyes sought southward, his mind was turning over and examining things that could go wrong. (Not worrying made him feel guilty.) The one misgiving he had about Frazier was the captain's confidence in his Higuchian aide, Master Freddy. Freddy insisted the 2nd Rifles were coming—down *this* road!—and would arrive before the Dkota. But there was no way the Higuchian could know that; he had to be guessing.

Besides, the subject of the 2nd Rifles was uncomfortable for Jarvi. It was he who'd sent them back to Hasty earlier, in what he now considered an ill-decided act of caution. And their showing up here would get him off the hook too easily.

Actually, because Frazier knew now the nature of Freddy's religious talisman, he considered him his unofficial intelligence section. What he didn't know about was the eye in the sky.

Two yards to Frazier's left, Freddy leaned in another archery notch, gazing southward, reevaluating. With the 2nd Rifles, it seemed likely they could hold off the Dkota. Certainly between the rifles, archery and cold steel, they could cause a lot of Dkota casualties, especially if the Dkota persisted. But if Mazeppa's warriors were repulsed a time or two, he might bypass this stockade; it would be the smart thing to do. And from there he could lead his warriors on north unimpeded. Even if five hundred tribesmen were killed or disabled, which was highly unlikely, that would leave something like fifteen hundred. Enough to burn Hasty and ravage the countryside: destroy hamlets and villages, decimate the population, carry off women and girls . . . with tragic consequences for generations.

So they needed to do more than damage Mazeppa's army. More even than frustrate its attack on Hasty. They needed to cause its quick collapse and departure. Here. It would have to be here. And Jarvi's army wasn't enough. As for Maltby's militias—defending abatises or a stockade, they might be nearly as good as armsmen. But in the field, maneuvering, mixing it up with the tribesmen? They might have the courage, even the self-possession, but not the coordination.

Tahmm had reported Maltby's force at some six hundred, trailing four miles behind Mazeppa's. If the breeze held from the north, the Dkota main force seemed unlikely to see Maltby's dust—unless the Dkota took a break. Actually they might not take alarm if they did notice, because according to Tahmm, Mazeppa had two large foraging parties out, one off east about a mile, the other off west, each driving a large number of cattle, and lagging somewhat. Militia dust might be read as a split-off group of foragers.

What did young Maltby have in mind? What *could* he have in mind? A night charge into Mazeppa's camp, aimed at allowing Frazier and Jarvi to storm out and do heavy damage? Were the militias up to that? It was a lot to hope for.

And even if they were up to it, a lot depended on how well Frazier ran his part of the fighting, and how well the two forces interacted. All without communication or consultation.

At least the Rifles would arrive in time.

∐∑− ∐∑− ∐∑−

Mazeppa rode his favorite horse, trotting it mildly. The country was dry again, and the seven thousand hooves of his main force thoroughly pulverized the road's dried mud, raising a great dust cloud. Even near the front, he chewed grit.

They were moving more slowly than they had before attacking Kato Town. But if they were to encircle Hasty and starve out its people, they needed to gather and take with them many spotted buffalo. The problem had been to control his foragers. Only his charisma, the dedicated support of his cane men, and the firmness of Strong Wolf prevented them from hunting the woodlands for hidden women. They would, he'd told them repeatedly, have time for that later.

Mazeppa's two scouts, well out in front, were more than a mile short of the pyre when they saw its first rising smoke. One urged his horse into a gallop then, racing forward to see what was there; the other turned and raced back to Mazeppa. But the pyre had been well laid, and before the scout arrived, Mazeppa had seen the smoke for himself. So could anyone else, for miles.

Chapter 42
Battle of Dindigul

(Luis)

When Lemmi and I rode into Dindigul, it was a ghost town, with neither sight nor sound of humans. Even the drying racks were empty, without so much as a pair of underdrawers waving in the northerly breeze. We saw a few chickens running around, scratching, or pecking gravel, and a couple of dogs sized us up furtively around the corners of houses, as if they knew something bad was coming. From its south side we could see the stockade some three furlongs ahead. In between, the army's horses stood tethered on picket lines, wearing nosebags. A lot of Jarvi's and Frazier's troops were lying around in the grass napping or talking or thinking, their cap brims shading their eyes. Two mounted kingsmen trotted out to meet us. The one in charge, a corporal, recognized our uniforms, and saluted.

"Sirs," he said, "I must ask you to turn over your animals to Armsman Goulais here. He'll put them on the commanders' string, near the gate, so they'll be easily found. There's not room inside the fort yet."

I wondered what *"yet"* meant.

Lemmi and I walked the last hundred yards. The place didn't look very reassuring. It wasn't more than maybe eighty yards on a side, and part of what room there was inside would be occupied by buildings. The barony was part of the Royal Domains, where defense had been neglected for a decade, by royal decree. The walls were about twelve feet high, with three-foot archery notches, and near the ground, the poles had fungus growing out of them.

Ah well, I thought, *if mollies hadn't arisen on their own* (or had they? I'd never wondered), *the Church would have had to create them* (or had it? I'd never looked at that, either). In a universe evolving as an outgrowth of choices and their results, something like the mollies are a necessary part of the mix, if we're going to avoid another Armageddon, and have peace for an extended period of time.

If you really think about the teachings of Saint Higuchi, that's where they take you: we need the mollies.

Inside the stockade, I could see why they hadn't brought in the horses, or Jarvi's and Frazier's men. They'd have been in the way of a very important project: wetting down the roofs. There were more buildings inside than I'd expected, built of sawn lumber hauled from somewhere with a lot more forest. Except for the blockhouses, almost all the roofs were *thatched*—nice flammable thatch—and most buildings were built against the stockade walls. Set the roofs on fire and you had the makings of another Grove Falls massacre.

Someone, Keith or Jarvi or a local, had sent kids up on the roofs. Other civilians had formed bucket lines from the wells to the ladders, and the kids were wetting down the thatch to protect against fire arrows. It was taking a lot of water, and though there were three wells, with sweeps, there was more waiting than wetting. I hoped they'd started yesterday.

I scanned the south walkway and found Frazier and Jarvi standing near the blockhouse at the southwest corner. Lemmi had spotted them too. "Where do you suppose Freddy is?" he asked.

"Maybe in one of the buildings, where he can use his com."

Each walkway had a set of steep stairs near both ends. In between, here and there, ordinary ladders had been lashed in place. Lemmi went up one of them ahead of me, without any difficulty but slower than usual. I followed. Frazier and Jarvi stood at adjacent bowmen's notches looking southward.

"See anything?" I called as we approached them.

Our presence didn't startle them; Captain Fong had told them to expect us. Jarvi frowned as he turned to me. "You Higuchians are strange people," he said. "Freddy told us you'd be along, and I didn't believe him. Then Fong arrived—Freddy predicted that, too— and said he'd met you on the road."

He turned to Lemmi then, and offered a square hand. "You must be Master Lemmi. I've heard about you. I'm Jaako Jarvi, Eldred's general." He turned back to me. "Is it true you two just came from Hasty?"

"That's right. From Hasty, where Arvid Bonde is regent."

He looked as if I'd sandbagged him. Obviously Fong hadn't mentioned it. "Regent?" he said. "Has Eldred given up the throne?"

His concern seemed personal. I reminded myself they were cousins through the queen, and maybe friends.

"The word is, he went insane during an audience, and began ordering executions on the spot. I mean literally—executions right there, right then, in the audience chamber. Mazeppa's treachery may have had something to do with it. He still wouldn't admit the Dkota had invaded."

From Jarvi's expression and aura, he suspected a

palace coup. I kept talking. "So the sergeant major of the guard took command and asked Lord Brookins to suggest someone to rule as regent. Someone needed to be in charge—someone both competent and kin to Eldred. Someone the army would support. Brookins said Colonel Bonde was the best available."

Mentioning Brookins had put a different light on it. Jarvi trusted him.

"*Colonel* Bonde?" he said.

"He promoted himself."

Jarvi grunted. He was adjusting. Bonde probably *was* the best available, and his self promotion not unreasonable. "If Eldred's incapable of ruling," Jarvi said slowly, "the throne should go to Mary on her eighteenth birthday, only weeks from now. Unless she declines it. Does she know about all this?"

"Not yet, as far as I know."

"What does Elvi think of it?"

"Elvi ran away a day or two, maybe three, before you left Hasty." From his expression, Jarvi hadn't known that either. I went on. "With a young man named Halldor Halvorsen, it turned out. They followed Kaarlo Horn's platoon, and caught up with it at Zandria. But their behavior was so erratic, they were taken under protective custody.

"Later Mazeppa's northern army bypassed the Zandria stockade and rode on to Cloud, then bypassed it, too. Only to be badly shot up by a combination of archery, riflery, and artillery in a big ambush at the Knees of the Misasip. Lost their chiefs and scattered, headed for Many Geese I hope."

The victory at the Knees was the only part of it Jarvi knew about; Fong had told him. "That was Bonde's work, I suppose," he said.

I shook my head. "No, it was a Higuchian. He set it up, then recruited a small army of axmen to fell and help man abatises, and to clear fields of fire for the artillery. A Higuchian Brother talked Bonde into sending the artillery and the 2nd Rifles. And the one who set it up talked Nonchebe and a whole lot of Soggoan militia into manning the ambush. We're very proud of Stephen. He's only a novice."

Jarvi's expression had turned sour. "It seems Higuchian plottings are deeply rooted in all this."

"There are no Higuchian 'plottings' in it. Our actions have been largely impromptu, or began that way. Norlins heard rumors of the Dkota intentions last winter, through ironmongers that trade among them for furs and buffalo hides. So Lemmi and I were sent north last spring: me to Sota, to undertake an effective defense, and Lemmi to Dkota to gather information, and act as the situation required. The belief was, we had another year, not just a few weeks."

Lemmi spoke then. "Mazeppa was no more interested in changing his mind than Eldred was. But he might if we beat him badly enough here."

"What's our strategy here, general?" I asked.

"It's Keith's strategy. He's had a lot more experience with the D'kota, so I've handed him the reins. And what he's come up with is . . . One"—he counted on his fingers—"we will not let Mazeppa know in advance the strength of our forces here. Let him think this place is easy. Two, we'll parley with him, if he's willing: waste his time, exasperate him, till he wants to punish us; make him unwilling to bypass us. Three, bloody his nose when he attacks, weakening him while angering him further, making it a matter of pride to destroy us here. Four, we won't use our rifles until the time is ripe." He grimaced. "Five, keep him engaged till there's evidence that young Maltby's at hand. Freddy insists he's on his way with a large force. Six, if the Dkota get discouraged here, start to bypass us and continue on to Hasty, we'll send a force out the sally port to attack them and get their interest back. And overall, see that the Dkota feel thoroughly defeated when it's over."

"That makes sense to me, general. Why so glum?"

Irritation flashed and passed. "It's the best we're likely to come up with, but I see little prospect of success. At Kato I suggested we ride out and disperse them, but Keith said they'd destroy us if we tried it. And when I saw them demonstrate, I decided he was right."

The general shook his head, and his voice turned soft. "I do not fear dying, young man. I'm old, almost sixty. Life owes me nothing." He wasn't looking at me when he said it though, nor at Keith. "But I'm not here to die or make gestures," he added, "nor to let this country and these people down."

He shook his large, close-cropped balding head, and his voice became a monotone. "When Eldred traveled to Kato to meet with Mazeppa, he took me with him, and one day on the road I told him I didn't trust the man. That upset Eldred so, I never mentioned it again. Yet I had more influence on him than anyone except that miserable confessor of his, god damn his soul to hell. Eldred was what he was before he'd ever heard of Michael Clonarty, but if I'd persisted, even after the treaty was signed . . ."

He shook his head, his strong jaw working, controlling his emotions, his guilt and grief.

I gripped his shoulder. "General," I said, "you read your king rightly: his mind was beyond changing. And we'll never know—not in this world—why he held to this particular stance." I paused, then went on, making it casual now. "Meanwhile I don't know any better than you do how this fight and this war will turn out. But my brethren and I will do all we can to save Sota, and we're very good at what we do."

Jarvi stared at me for what seemed like a long minute, then shook his head again. "I wish we knew Mazeppa better," he said drily.

"That's where Lemmi comes in," I told him. "For several weeks he lived among the Dkota as a spy, initiated into the tribe and adopted as Mazeppa's son."

The general didn't have a chance to answer, beyond an astonished look, because a young man called: "Captain Frazier! The pyre's been lit!"

On the walkway, everyone within hearing turned to peer southward. It took a few seconds to make it out, then there it was: a slender serpent of smoke rose from the top of a distant ridge. Within half a minute, there was no mistaking it.

"Well," Jarvi said, "we'll soon learn how well we've planned." Then he sent one of his couriers with orders to bring the troops and horses inside.

Frazier turned to the courier beside him, a man who carried the captain's oral orders to others, reciting them verbatim. "Hernando," the captain said, "did you hear what the general just told the Higuchians?"

"Yes captain."

"Tell me! Show me you know! Quickly!"

After fumbling a moment, the man repeated it, not as precisely as if he'd gotten it as instructions to himself, but all the meaning was there, and nothing more.

"Good man!" Frazier said. "Now, do exactly as I tell you. Take your horse and ride eastward." He gestured. "Eastward to avoid the Dkota. Then circle southward, keeping to cover as much as possible, and return to the road well *behind* the Dkota. And take no longer than you must."

The youth nodded, looking stricken.

"When you're well behind the Dkota, hide there. Before long, a large force of armsmen and militia will come up the road from the south. Lord Donald is probably in command of it. But whoever its commander is, tell him what the general said; what you repeated to me. It could mean the difference in how this fight turns out. Do you understand?"

Again Hernando nodded. "Yes, captain."

Frazier clapped the man's shoulder. "Good! Be gone now."

Hernando saluted, then turned and jumped from the walkway, keeping his feet when he landed, and sprinted from the fort to get his horse.

Jarvi looked at Frazier. "Keith," he said, "you're as good with your men as any commander I've known."

"Thank you, Jaako," Keith replied, then turned to the young man who'd spotted the signal smoke. "Gavan, did you hear what the general told the Higuchians? What I had Hernando repeat to me?"

"Yes, captain."

"Can you repeat it?"

The young man recited it.

"Good! I want you to do the same as I told Hernando. *Except*—except I want you to start westward instead of east."

Gavan nodded, serious but not tense. His aura told me he felt sure of himself, and glad for the challenge. Then he too leaped from the walkway, landing in a peculiar sort of half-somersault, half side-roll that brought him up and running. Despite wearing a quiver of arrows on his back, and carrying a longbow! I have no idea how he did it. He didn't even spill arrows!

This time Jarvi looked worriedly at Keith. "How can you know he won't—" he hesitated "—betray us to Mazeppa?"

"I know him," Keith answered.

I did too now. Gavan. Keith had told me about him when we'd first met. And there'd been no hint of duplicity in Gavan's eyes or aura.

⁓⁓⁓⁓ ⁓⁓⁓⁓ ⁓⁓⁓⁓

The great invader dust plume settled well before it reached Maltby's column, or nearly enough settled that the eye no longer saw it. But Jean Papineau could smell it. As a boy, he'd herded cattle in the marches, and naturally alert, perceptive, curious, the herdsman's life had sharpened his senses. As an adolescent, he'd trained with the local militia. Had he been Dkota, he might have ended up a scout: a seeker of game for the hunts, a seeker of horse herds for plundering, a spy lurking unseen or unnoticed near the villages of other tribes.

But he'd wanted to experience more of the world, and through an uncle had gotten a job as post rider, carrying express mail from Austin to Hasty. Small and wiry, and a superb horseman, he'd routinely ridden the more than one-hundred-mile distance in a single day. Deep snow, lung-burning cold or extreme heat might slow him somewhat—he would not abuse a horse—but only blizzards could stop him. He had a day's layover, and a wife, at each end.

Then Eldred had installed—or ordered Jarvi to install—a puppet duke at Austin, and someone else had been given the post job. Jean had become a herdsman again, out of Tonna, with connections to the officially disbanded militia there.

Now he rode beside Donald Maltby, serving as his guide, for he knew every mile of the road as well as any human did. As they topped a low rise, his sharp eyes noticed something out of the ordinarily, just visible above the Dkota dust ahead. A tiny, distant smudge low in the sky, soon dispersed by the fair breeze.

"Smoke, your lordship," he said.

Donald peered where Jean pointed. "Smoke?"

"There. You would see it, if it were not for the dust. Or if the breeze were less."

"The Dindigul stockade?"

"No sir. The stockade is piss elm. You could not *make* it burn. The people of Dindigul are proud of it. They built it that way on purpose."

"Huh!" Donald wondered why, if that was true, all stockades weren't made of piss elm. "How far is it to Dindigul?"

"Six mile, six and a half." Papineau sniffed the air. "We are drawing up on the Dkota. I suspect they have stopped."

If we're six miles from Dindigul, Donald thought, *the Dkota are—what? Three miles at most.* Mazeppa's scouts might already have spotted the fort. Or— "The smoke's probably a signal fire lit by some sentinel from Dindigul, and Mazeppa's investigating."

It was Banda who answered. "I think that's it, sir. A signal pyre."

Donald sized up what he could see ahead. From the rise where they sat their horses, the road led down into a shallow depression most of a mile wide, and unevenly, rather thinly wooded. He turned to Jean. "What's past that next rise?"

"Mostly prairie, sir, and half a mile beyond, some woods along a slope that faces northeast. Beyond that woods, half or three-quarter mile, is the stockade. The village is a furlong farther."

Donald called his unit messengers to him. "It's time to pull up on them," he said. "But not on the road. And at a walk. If the Dkota have stopped, their dust is settling, and we don't want them to see ours. Windom, ride ahead and tell the scouts to wait until I send word again. I don't want them seen. You others, tell your commanders to spread out and ride to the far side of the woods. They're to stop there, keeping to cover. When you've delivered your messages, come back to me.

"Go now!"

Mazeppa had stopped long enough for his scouts to report back. Then, followed by his army, he advanced till he could see the stockade, his hunter eyes picking out heads in the archery notches. Halting his horse again, he signalled. Within half a minute his whole army had stopped, except for his foraging parties, trailing out on the flanks.

Face grim, eyes cold and steady, he nudged his horse again, this time to a walk, accompanied by his close men and his messengers. This was the first stockade he'd seen since Kato, much smaller, and no doubt less well defended. And he had brought with him what he had not had at Kato: from farms along the way, he'd collected hay carts, wheels intact. His braves had even loaded some of them with hay. It would be good for them to capture this place and its women, and burn all its structures to the ground.

He started forward again. Pastor Morosov moved closer to him, and spoke. "Will you send someone forward to request a parley?"

Annoyance flashed. The pastor, Mazeppa realized, hoped to avoid a massacre. "Maybe," he answered, "but first we will surround them, and demonstrate. Let them see what they are up against." He fixed Morosov with severe eyes. "Do not forget, we must break this people utterly. That means no mercy to their fighting men, and perhaps to none of them at all."

He called two messengers to him. He would send them to meet the foragers, with his orders: to continue northward till they drew even with the army, then camp and wait with their herds. He would let them know later when to continue.

They'd miss out on the fighting, and the capture of women, but they'd no doubt captured women of their own.

❖❖❖   ❖❖❖   ❖❖❖

(Luis)

After sending out Hernando and Gavan, Frazier dispatched two scouts to the next rise southward, while the armsmen and horses crowded into the stockade. The Dkota would shoot arrows into the stockade, and crowded as it was, they'd hit people and horses. It was unavoidable.

I asked about Freddy. He was on top of the

blockhouse, Keith told me, in an observation post five feet square, with two-foot parapets of thick planks, where a man could lie or crouch watching. From there he could talk with Tahmm, too, more easily than with us, actually. If he wanted to talk to me, he'd either have to buzz my com, or call loudly enough that anyone nearby could hear, or climb down through the trapdoor into the upper level of the blockhouse, then down to the walkway level, where there was a landing, and a door.

I looked up and called. "Hey, Freddy!"

"That's my name. Glad you're here. Got your amulet with you?"

"Sure do."

"Rub it for good luck."

Outside the stockade, both scouts reached the top of the next rise south, and briefly stopped, tiny in the distance. Then one wheeled and raced back. The other lingered almost till the first reached the stockade, then he too returned. No one pursued him; apparently the Dkota weren't that near yet.

Jarvi called down to Fong. "Captain, have your riflemen wait in the blockhouses, on the ground floor, ready to climb when ordered. They're to load their rifles, but none—*none* of them!—is to cock his weapon till ordered. If anyone does, I'll behead him personally! It's *essential* the Dkota don't know about them." He paused, scanning till his eyes found Baron Pannu, dark and barrel-chested, beside one of the wells. Then went down to consult with him.

When the Dkota arrived, the archery notches were fully manned, locals alternating with one of Frazier's or Jarvi's men. Jarvi's A Company waited by their horses beside the south gate, ready to sally out if need be, or climb the ladders and help defend the south wall.

B Company waited, bows in hand, manning the upper and lower rooms of the blockhouses, at twenty by thirty-inch archery slots. They'd pour arrows into any Dkota who reached the stockade walls, where the men on the walkways couldn't shoot at them. I stood at a notch, watching the Dkota line up maybe two hundred yards away—most of a furlong—where they sat two and three deep, staring toward us. My spyglass showed their faces daubed with black and red; stony faces, some of them, others eager. I didn't see any looking worried. That was something we needed to change.

The flow continued, the spillover riding around to the east, west, and finally north, surrounding us. Part of the spillover included carts, some filled with hay. Keith had foreseen that, had intended to use his own fire arrows to set them ablaze at a distance. But when Pannu had assured him the stockade wouldn't burn, Jarvi suggested letting the Dkota find out the hard way: the braves would push and pull the carts into position, and we'd shoot hell out of them while they did it. Frazier agreed. Jarvi felt pretty good about his idea.

❦❦ ❦❦ ❦❦

Jules Apodaca, known to his adoptive people as Makes-Things, was born in a village of mixed ethnicities some miles north of Kato. His father was a blacksmith, dray-service operator, and general artisan. From early childhood, Jules had helped his father, but whenever he could get away, he'd sneak off to the woods and fields. There, with his child's bow and arrows, he'd hunt and shoot animals as small as frogs and mice, moved up to marmots, then graduated to a youth's bow, and to coons, coyotes, deer, even a wolf. Increasingly he'd brought home welcome meat, but even so, the conflict between his desires and his father's demands sometimes earned him beatings.

Until, confiding in no one (remarkable at thirteen years), he'd left home on a stolen horse and ridden west to live with the Dkota. There he'd been adopted into the tipi of a hunter, and become a notable hunter himself. Like most of Mazeppa's braves, he had not chosen the way of the warrior, but like most Dkota men, he had the basic skills, and served now as a fighting man, willing if not enthusiastic.

He had a strong artisan muse, and as a boy working with his father, had learned much. Large and muscular, and willing to fight despite his good nature, he had numerous admirers and friends among his Dkota peers. And always he'd gone his own way, an acceptable trait among the Dkota.

When Mazeppa's army reached Dindigul, Jules's adoptive band, the Badgers, moved into a position north of the stockade. But Jules, instead of situating himself in the circle to await orders, sneaked into the village.

He knew how to read, and on one of the buildings saw a bilingual sign announcing LIVERY STABLE AND DRAY SERVICE. HORSES SHOD. And in the weeds out back found the dismantled remains of a wagon, its tongue broken and with two wheels missing. But the rear carriage, with its two wheels, was intact.

At the sight, a vision came to him. And in the stable were tools, rope, harness . . . everything he needed, including of all things a grapple. Meanwhile, grazing the field behind the stable were two draft horses, not animals that would ordinarily attract a buffalo tribesman, except perhaps for meat, but . . . And of course there was an oat bin in the stable. Filling its scoop with oats, he approached one of the draft horses and coaxed it inside, where he tied, then harnessed it

That done, he trotted off to get some friends. What he needed now was a heavy roof-beam, thick for strength, and long, for added weight and momentum.

❖❖❖   ❖❖❖   ❖❖❖

(Luis)

We were as ready as we could get, the stockade our

shelter and our trap. And a trap for the Dkota, with us as bait. Meanwhile Dkota scavenged the village for wood, setting aside doors as shields. Some of the wood they threw atop the hay carts.

After a while, braves began running their horses in a long loop inside the circle, yelling, yipping, displaying their horsemanship, hanging off the offside, showing us only a moccasined foot and part of a leg, then popping back up. I was impressed. They slanted in as close as fifty or sixty yards, sending arrows at us when they popped up. From the walkways, longbows were twanging. The Dkota made poor targets, but they were losing horses, so after a minute they stopped. I wondered if perhaps, in tribal conflicts, it was taboo to deliberately shoot horses. On our side of the fort only one rider was still down, thrown when his horse fell, and hit twice himself before he could be helped away. One of his rescuers had also been hit, and one of his, but all in all, it hadn't cost Mazeppa much or accomplished much

Meanwhile the Dkota were building a circle of small fires outside effective archery range. And hay carts were being drawn up. But Mazeppa sent something else first. Horsemen were poised with bows. Now they rode in lines past the fires, and leaning, lit and nocked long arrows, fire arrows. Abruptly they darted toward us, not so close as the earlier riders, and launched flaming arrows over the walls. Now we'd learn how well-watered the roof thatch was. For at least a minute the fire arrows flew, and from the bailey we heard screams, shouts, sounds of stricken animals.

I allowed myself a backward glance. Boys with rakes and pitchforks were busy on roofs, digging out burning arrows and throwing them down. So far as possible, people had taken shelter inside buildings or close to their walls, but the arrows came from all four sides.

More than fire arrows flew toward us. Other warriors sent arrows toward our archery notches. Good

targets. Men fell wounded or dead to the walkways.
And now came the hay carts, with firewood, broken-up
furniture, window shutters piled on top, pulled and
pushed by braves, while others trotted alongside
carrying doors to shield them.

It cost them men despite the shield bearers, but
as necessary, others dashed out to take over. Every
cart left casualties in its tracks, but one after another
reached the stockade, to be jammed sideways against
the walls. Then their remaining pullers, pushers, shield
bearers, raced to safety or fell to arrows. And when
a cart was in place, other warriors ran out to throw
more wood on it, each act earning honor.

The Dkota had learned at Kato that blockhouses
were major sources of casualties, so here, every blockhouse was targeted by a hay cart. One by one the carts
were set afire, and burned fiercely. Smoke arose,
obscuring targets, and the Dkota archery stopped, the
circle of warriors drawing back, waiting for the stockade to burn down. Then they'd have us. On the
walkways, the intense heat made many of the archery
notches untenable, but the hay didn't last long, and
when the fires had consumed it, the heat became less
intense. In the bailey, a few roofs had been ignited
beyond saving, and burned out of control. One by one,
more quickly than you might think, the burning roofs
collapsed, sending flame and sparks swirling upward.
Boys and men crouched on every fire-free roof, to cast
off falling embers.

The stockade itself did not take fire. Its timbers
were scorched, even superficially charred, but refused
to burn on their own. When the fuel on the carts
burned up, that was it; no more fire. Meanwhile we
had every notch manned again. Some two hundred
yards distant, the Dkota still sat their horses, but they
no longer trilled. They'd suffered numerous casualties, and their principal strategy had been defeated.

Our attention now was mainly on Mazeppa and the

cluster of men who surrounded him: Lemmi referred to them as his "close men." Most were distinguishable by the number of eagle feathers in their headbands, or occasionally in the band of a wide-brimmed straw hat. Mazeppa's headband carried the most; to accommodate them required loose ends that hung down his back to his waist. Most of the men, though, had only a few, often one or two. Lemmi said the number indicated honors, but he knew only in a general way how they were earned.

I'd kept half an eye out for some sign of Donald Maltby and his militia, but had seen nothing. I kept expecting Freddy to call something down to us, but so far he hadn't, so I stepped inside the blockhouse landing and commed him. He was still up there, but hadn't heard anything new from Tahmm.

After a few minutes, a Dkota left the circle, riding toward the stockade with a hand raised, as if wanting to parley. My spyglass told me the object he held was a tobacco pipe. Frazier gave an order to Jarvi's trumpeter, who blew the command to hold fire. I hoped the militias knew what it meant.

"That's not Mazeppa," Frazier said. "He's not tall enough. But I've seen him before. At the treaty conference."   "It's Pastor Morosov," Lemmi told us. "Among the Dkota, he amounts to a bishop."

"Do you want to talk with him?" Frazier asked. "I have no idea what to say."

"Let me," I said. "Let's keep Lemmi a secret for now."

By that time the rider had pulled up about a hundred yards away, waiting. Frazier nodded. "Go ahead."

I climbed into an archery notch and waved my arms overhead. "You're not Mazeppa!" I shouted. "We will speak with Mazeppa."

Morosov backed his horse a few steps, then it

pirouetted, and carried him back to the cluster of men around his chief. I wondered how many bishops of the Church could ride horseback like that. After a minute of conferring, a different rider trotted out.

"That's Mazeppa," Lemmi said.

"Shall we shoot him?" Jarvi asked. "Fong's men could finish him off here and now, and I doubt his people would stay, with him gone."

"We want him alive," I said. "For the peace treaty. A *real* peace treaty."

Mazeppa too stopped about a hundred yards out. In his right hand, resting on his forearm, was a pipe. Lemmi held his own spyglass to his eye. "That's not his ceremonial pipe," he told me, "but it'll do for discussion."

Jarvi started to ask what I was going to say to the chief, but my muse took over, interrupting him. There wasn't much debris below me, so I handed my spyglass to Lemmi, stepped into the notch again, flexed my knees and jumped. Landing in a Higuchian fighting roll—in this case for show—that brought me back onto my feet. Gavan Feeny would approve, and so would the Dkota. Then, my eyes on Mazeppa, I walked halfway to where he sat his horse, then stopped, arms folded across my chest. Mazeppa nudged his horse forward, cutting the distance to a dozen yards. I cut that to five. I could see his aura, even in the sunshine, and realized why Lemmi described him as charismatic.

"I am Master Luis," I told him, "of the Order of Saint Higuchi. I have come to hear what Chief Mazeppa of the Dkota and Ulster has to say to the peaceful people he has attacked."

His horse, like himself, was tall, and he remained in the saddle, taking advantage of the elevation. His voice was cold, deadly. "If the people inside come out and lay down their weapons," he said, "I will let them ride away unmolested. But they must take nothing away with them except the clothes on their bodies.

My warriors can have whatever goods they find here. You are not to destroy or remove any of it."

"There are women and children inside. Will they also ride away unmolested?"

"I have said it. All may walk away unmolested."

His aura suggested he'd keep his word, but there was an ambivalence. "What about food?" I asked. "And horses?"

"They must take no food; they can survive a few days without eating. As for horses—you have killed many of ours. We will take yours in payment."

He was no more interested in a deal than I was. He'd come out here to satisfy Morosov and perhaps other chiefs, and get us out of the fort. Then he'd have us searched, and find something to use as an excuse for butchery.

So far our voices had been no louder than necessary, for two men standing five yards apart. Now I raised mine, not quite shouting, but loud enough to be heard on the walkway. "Mazeppa Tall Man," I said, "known in your youth as He-Who-Must-Win, your ambition and arrogance have led you on a false path. Now *I* have an offer for *you*. You have found us dirt-eaters better fighters than you'd expected. You were driven away from Kato, and even at this unimportant place we have stopped you. What do you suppose will happen when you reach Hasty, if you live to reach it? Hasty, where our main army is waiting for you.

"You sent another army from the north, to Zandria and Cloud. Up the river from Hasty, it was met in open battle, and destroyed. Its survivors have scattered, bleeding and broken, many without horses, to find their way back to buffalo country by threes and fours, running by night and hiding by day.

"Why should we put our lives in your hands here? You made a great mistake, invading our country. We are many, and brave, and dangerous—and among us are wizards. Now the Dkota find themselves like the dog who attacks the porcupine. If he backs away soon enough, he may live a long life. Otherwise he ends up with his mouth and nose full of quills, perhaps with his eyes put out. Then there is nothing for him but regret and death, no matter how great his pride had been."

Mazeppa's sun-browned face had darkened; now his aura flared with anger. He'd have ridden me down, or tried, but he was within ready killing range of the stockade, and his ambition gripped him. He wasn't ready to die yet. Meanwhile I wasn't done. I raised my hand, indicating more to be said, and he did not turn to leave. I lowered my voice again.

"It is not too late for Mazeppa to turn back to Many Geese, there perhaps to take his revenge on Sky Chief, who tricked him, played with him, at the cost of many Dkota lives."

Mentioning Sky Chief and the Dkota dead had bitten deeply. Mazeppa's flushed face paled, his hand frozen halfway to his hatchet. Wheeling his horse, he rode stiff-backed toward his warriors. I turned too, and stalked to the sally port. It opened, and they let me back in. Its narrow gate had hardly closed when I heard arrows thud into it.

Almost at once, a single war whoop rose from the south, echoed a moment later by hundreds more from every point of the compass, and from the walkway, a trumpet. Seconds later hooves rumbled, and almost as quickly a new storm of arrows passed overhead, at first from the south, then from every direction.

Shouts and screams rang through the fort again, of people and animals hit. Others roared anger or bloodlust. I climbed the nearest ladder onto the walkway. In front of me, a local militiaman fell backward from his notch, his hands moving to his walnut-colored face where an arrow shaft stuck out of one cheek, the feathers showing from the other. I paused long enough to draw my knife and cut the shaft behind the head, then jerked out the now-headless shaft by the feathers. Crimson flowed from cheeks and mouth, and choking, the man rolled onto hand and knees vomiting swallowed blood.

Crouching, I moved to join Lemmi and the others. Some of our bowmen cowered behind merlons, in shock at the arrow storm. Others used the merlons as shelter in which to draw their bows, then pivot into their notch to send an arrow at the enemy; a drilled action. I stepped over a body with an arrow in its throat, and slipped in its blood, nearly falling. Just ahead of me, Jarvi stood squarely in a notch, not sheltering at all. From somewhere, probably a dead man, he'd gotten a bow and quiver, and was drawing and shooting as rapidly as possible, a living example of aimed, rapid-fire archery. For an instant I thought to pull him back; I'd want him at Hasty to help straighten things out. But my muse stopped me. The general was working out an issue of his own.

As before, Keith was doing his shoot and take cover drill. Beside him, now under his orders, crouched Jarvi's wide-eyed trumpeter. White-knuckled, the boy waited, gripping his instrument. I spoke to Keith, and he turned. "Are you all right?" he asked.

I was bloody from the man shot through the face. "Yeah," I said, "I'm fine."

Lemmi grinned at me from the next notch. "Nice work," he called. "You really kicked the hornets' nest." Then, with his head, he gestured upward toward where Freddy was lying, or had lain, on the blockhouse roof. "Maltby's militias are drawing up a mile or so south."

So Tahmm had buzzed him. I knew Donald's warrior muse was a strong one; the question was how well he listened to it. In his position, a wrong move could be disastrous, for him and for Sota.

The archery exchange continued for several minutes, and I wondered how many packhorses of arrows Mazeppa had brought with him. Then, abruptly, the

Dkota arrows stopped. Jarvi's trumpeter blew the order to draw sabers. Even as I drew mine, the Dkota charged. Within seconds their lariats were snaking upward, settling over merlons, and the fight became bloody chop and thrust.

During the archery exchange, enough armsmen and militiamen had fallen that numerous notches were undefended. Agile braves were on the walkways, hatchets in hand, and the din of shouting, shrieking, crying out, was deafening. A section of the decaying east walkway collapsed, dumping struggling men onto a roof just below, from which they slid or rolled or jumped into the bailey. Meanwhile the archery from the blockhouses was furious and deadly, sweeping the ground outside the walls, finding horses and men. The fighting on the walkways was intense, most of the combatants heedless now of danger.

Briefly it seemed the Dkota might prevail, but not enough made it over the walls. The assault had struck and piled up, and after brief savage minutes, those who hadn't found their chance at a merlon, rode or ran back to the circle. While those who'd made it over, died. Then a ragged cheer broke out on the walkways, growing into a full-throated cry of victory that was taken up by the folk in the bailey.

It seemed to me the Dkota would not charge again. Leaning through my notch, I scanned the ground outside and was impressed by the carnage. Our folks began to throw out the Dkota bodies lying on the walkways.

Jarvi and Keith too had looked over the killing ground. Now they were scanning the walkways, getting an idea of our own losses. We'd lost a lot fewer than Mazeppa had, but percentage-wise? Now Captain Fong stepped out onto the walkway, his face and voice stiff with upset. "General," he reminded his uncle, "you did not call on my riflemen."

"I'm aware of that, Captain," Jarvi answered. Point-edly; the young commander was imposing on their familial relationship. "I'll let you know when the time is right." He said the last dismissively. Fong, know-ing he'd overstepped, saluted sharply and reentered the blockhouse. Jarvi turned to me unhappily. "What about that?" he asked. "How do we know when the time is right?"

They'd been waiting, a squad in the lower level of the blockhouses, having to keep out of the archers' way. "It's time to order them upstairs now," I said, "so they'll be in position when Maltby's militia is ready. Meanwhile they need to be reminded not to fire till ordered."

He frowned, digesting that. "When Maltby's mili-tia is ready. Why didn't you say so earlier?"

I liked and respected the old man. He'd been more agreeable than I'd had any right to expect, and more importantly, I depended on his good will. "Earlier I wasn't sure enough," I answered mildly. "Higuchians, especially masters, live and act in the moment. We plan so far as we reasonably can, so far as circumstances permit, but we *act* according to the situation, and trust our judgement."

He wasn't ready to give up being irritated yet. "As a negotiator," he said, "you almost got us all killed. I can't imagine an enemy more aroused than the Dkota were."

"Credit Mazeppa for that, general. Mazeppa and the Dkota's warrior tradition. As for negotiating? It's not time yet. I was *goading* him. We have the advantage here. The fort is ours, and it allows us to kill more of them than they do of us. I was operating on points two and three of *your* strategy: exasperate the enemy, make him unwilling to bypass us. And *weaken* him; we cer-tainly did that."

Keith was taking in all of this, his eyes intrigued. Jarvi snuffed his resentment and nodded, impressing me again. "So," he said, "what next?"

"That depends on what Maltby does. And Mazeppa, of course. I'll call for your riflemen when it seems to me they'll make the difference between the war ending here, or the Dkota rampaging through the rest of Sota."

The general frowned, but his voice was not hostile. "When it seems . . ." he echoed, stressing "seems."

"That's the best we can do," I told him.

He settled for that. Then Freddy buzzed me from the roof, and I put my amulet to my ear, keeping it on low. "Someone just rode out of that strip of woods behind the Dkota. Two of them, shirtless, and too far away to recognize faces. I think they're ours; I think they're wearing boots, but the grass is up to their horses' bellies. One of them may be Maltby. It's hard to be sure."

"Lemmi," I said, "get on your horse and be ready to meet Mazeppa. Maybe we can entice him to pick up his casualties; that'll stall him for a bit." Freddy would hear via his com, and understand.

Lemmi nodded and headed for a ladder. I didn't suggest anything more. He'd know what to say. After he left the walkway, I stripped off my shirt, tied the sleeves to a borrowed bow and waved it overhead.

❧❦ ❧❦ ❧❦

While other braves launched arrows at the stockade and its occupants, Jules Apodaca and several friends had assaulted an elderly, forty-foot-long hay barn next door to Dindigul's livery stable. With axes found in the woodshed, two of them attacked its strong corner posts, while Jules himself coaxed up and harnessed the other draft horse. Then, with the corner posts seriously compromised, he cast the grapple over a tie beam, and with the horses, pulled the structure down.

Their labor had just begun. Working rapidly with smith's hammers and crowbars, they freed the ridge-pole of rafters and roofing, then looped strong ropes around one end and pulled it out of the hay and debris. All against a background of yelling and screaming—and cheering—half a mile away.

With horses, ropes, pry poles, strong backs, a heavy smith's bench, and trial and error, they lifted and lashed the roof beam securely onto the available wagon carriage, balanced so the center of gravity was slightly to the rear of the axle. Four men could easily raise the trailing end, push with it, and use it to steer.

❖❖❖   ❖❖❖   ❖❖❖

Donald Maltby had left his militia in thin young forest, in the hands of Lieutenant Banda, taking with him Frazier's two messengers, Gavan and Hernando, and two of his own. He was riding shirtless, a form of long-distance disguise. He'd promised Banda to return within an hour. Neither man had a timepiece, but as a ducal guardsman, Banda was experienced with clocks, and had a fair sense of how long an hour was.

The five of them had crossed a stretch of prairie grass deeper than their stirrups, then reached a slender band of woods where the downslope leveled out. From the fringe of the woods they'd watched from the saddle, the young trees obscuring their outlines. Most of a mile ahead he could see the south side of the Dkota ring, and the blockhouses.

And rising above the stockade, smoke! It made his stomach knot. A moment later they heard what might have been a cheer. "That doesn't sound like Dkota," Gavan said. Donald hoped the other youth was right. Though his stomach was knotted, his hands were steady. He took his spyglass from its case, certain his plan couldn't possibly work, and at the same time determined to *make* it work. A look through the glass told him he was too far away to distinguish faces in the archery notches.

He spoke to his couriers, "Gavan and I are going to where I can see more. You others stay here, but

watch me. If I turn my horse and look back, and raise
my arm overhead, Hernando will ride to Lieutenant
Banda and tell him to bring the troops up to where
we are now. That's *if* I turn and raise my arm overhead. But if I *don't* turn—if I don't turn, and I *wave*
my arm overhead"—he demonstrated—"that means
I'm signaling the people in the fort, so they'll know
we're here." He tested Hernando's recall, and received
the message back verbatim, including emphases.

Then Donald and Gavan rode into the open at an
easy trot, eyes on the Dkota in the near distance.
Three furlongs ahead stood a solitary burr oak, its
trunk thick and rugged, its crown broad. When they
reached it, they stopped in its shade, and Donald
realized that his tension, his edginess, had passed,
replaced by calm. It seemed to him he was inside
himself looking out, and at the same time outside
looking at himself. An electric chill ran over him.

He raised his spyglass again. On the stockade wall,
a man stood up in one of the archery notches. After
a moment he either jumped or fell, perhaps hit by
an arrow. Donald couldn't see him hit the ground; the
Dkota were in the way.

Staying where he was, he scanned, watching, waiting for some indication of what was going on. Time
passed; tension returned. Then someone waved what
looked like a shirt, tied to a staff by its sleeves. A
surrender?

He needed to get closer. From where he was, he
could miss the critical point, the time to strike. The
thought triggered a pang of anxiety, but he brushed
it away. After telling Gavan to stay where he was, to
relay any signals, he rode forward another furlong, and
paused to scan again. This time he saw an irregular-
ity in a blockhouse roof: the upper part of a head.

And Donald knew! The man was looking through
a spyglass! At him! At once he waved his left arm
overhead, widely. The face disappeared, was replaced

a moment later by something round and gray, held motionless. A hat, broad brimmed with an oval crown—a Higuchian hat! It disappeared, replaced again by the forehead and spyglass.

A grin split Donald's face. Once more he waved his arm.

Then he examined the backs of the Dkota ahead. There was no sign that any had noticed anything remarkable. Something else held their attention, he decided. Something compelling.

Turning in his saddle, he signalled Gavan.

When Mazeppa saw the shirt-flag waving, he decided. The dirt-eaters in this place had shown less respect to the dead than those at Kato had, but perhaps they had Dkota wounded inside they were willing to give back. And he was willing to trade—one dirt-eater woman or child could be let go for each of his own wounded returned.

He told his close men what he had in mind, then rode into the no-man's land between his circle and the fort. This time no one leaped from the wall. Instead a narrow gate opened, and a man rode out, tall, lean, and dark. For a moment he didn't recognize him. When he did, he stopped, not in rejection but in consternation, staring.

Lemmi didn't stop till he was only ten feet away. "Hello, my father."

"You!" The word was little more than breathed. Mazeppa rallied. "Truly, Helverti Chief has played me false."

"Helverti Chief is done for," Lemmi said. "He has powerful enemies among his own people, the Sky People. I told you, before: there are players in this you know nothing about. *Players who seek no one's destruction*, who prefer to be no one's enemy. Players who have much influence with the Sotans, and follow the teachings of the Christ."

Lemmi's words registered, but Mazeppa did not heed them, his mind held by mystery: Helverti Chief had stolen him, then healed him and given him to the dirt-eaters. For what purpose, this? What purpose any of it?

"I do not hate my father-of-choice," Lemmi went on, "he who took me into his tipi. I was sent to you to undo, if I could, the evil done by Helverti Chief, that master deceiver, a servant of Skunk Bear. And to prevent this war that now threatens the Dkota with destruction."

He paused, examining Mazeppa's aura. "Perhaps you are remembering the voice that whispered to you on your vision quest. Such whispers can come from others than Jesus. Skunk Bear also whispers into the minds of men, as is well known."

This comment truly shook Mazeppa. Had he ever told that story to anyone besides Pastor Ipatiev? In particular, had he told his son-of-choice? Surely not. He'd confided his mission, yes; his life goal, yes. But anything more? *Perhaps Elder Ipatiev, before he died, told Morosov, and Morosov had . . .*

Reading Mazeppa's inattention, Lemmi backed his horse a few steps, as if about to leave, the movement recapturing the chief's focus. "Jorval treats people as he'd treat a mullein leaf," Lemmi said. "He wipes his anus with it and throws it away. If you take your braves back to Many Geese now, he will know, and gnash his teeth, tear his hair, for you will have wrecked his larger plan. But if you stay here, using up your people in his service, he will shake with mirth. And for the rest of his life tell the story of his victim Mazeppa, and the destruction of the Dkota."

The words froze Mazeppa. Briefly, the young Dinneh examined him, then turned his horse and trotted back to the sally port. When he reached the walkway, it was Frazier who asked what success he'd had.

"He's not able to back down," Lemmi answered. "He's obsessed with his dream now: to rule the Misasip, and save the buffalo peoples from a threat that doesn't exist.

"But he's no longer the man he was when he left Many Geese. Not even the man he was a few hours ago. He's losing his grip."

When Mazeppa returned to his close men, he almost didn't see them. Things Lemmi Dark Skin had said, and before that the one called Luis, had seriously confused him. He could no longer see clearly the world around him.

A familiar voice snapped him out of it, one of his close men, Utkur War Spear of the Badger Band. A young man was with Utkur, nearly as tall as Mazeppa, and strongly built. Like Utkur, he wore the Badger totem painted on his breast. He'd been sweating heavily, the sweat full of dirt.

"Mazeppa," Utkur said, "this young man has brought you a new weapon, one to break down the gates of the fort."

This wakened Mazeppa. His eyes sharpened. "Tell me about this weapon," he said.

⊰⊱⊰⊱ ⊰⊱⊰⊱ ⊰⊱⊰⊱

(Luis)

Despite what Lemmi had said about Mazeppa losing his grip, there was no sign now of withdrawal or indecision. The tribesmen were waiting for something—some signal, some order—and none of us had a notion of what it might be. But every one of us was concerned, because for whatever reason, when Mazeppa returned to his close men, everything around them seemed to pause. Followed by a sense of intention and expectancy, of something brewing, and I wondered if it was connected to what Freddy had forwarded to Tahmm awhile earlier: that in the village, a building had been pulled down by men with horses.

After a little, Freddy commed from his post on the roof. "Donald's moved closer," he said, then followed that with a broken series of observations. "The man with him is Gavan, I think . . . He's looking us over with a spyglass . . . I think he saw me! Yes! He just waved! That took guts."

"Does he know you saw him?" I murmured.

He didn't answer right away. Then, "I'm sure of it," he said. "I held my hat just above the parapet, and he waved again, this time standing in his stirrups . . . Now he's moving back toward the woods. I think he signalled someone there, too."

That was reading a lot into a little, but knowing Freddy, I'd bet on it. "Any indication the Dkota know he's there?" My impression was, they didn't miss much that went on around them.

"No sign of it."

"Any sign of what he has in mind?"

"None," he said, then, "let's talk about that later."

I stepped back out on the walkway to a puzzled glance from Keith. Meanwhile our riflemen were in the blockhouses now, in the upper level at the firing ports. Jarvi, through Fong, had ordered them to target men with the most feathers, and to sort out the targets in advance with the others in their blockhouse. They were to target individual chiefs, or failing that, their horses.

The principal exception to that rule was Mazeppa, who was NOT to be shot. His horse, yes, but we wanted its rider alive, in our hands. He was easy to recognize, by his height and his headdress. The best marksman in the 2nd Rifles had been assigned to him. A second exception was Morosov, easily recognized by the slender, short-armed, six-foot crucifix he carried. The third we assumed was the chief of the Wolves. His headdress rivaled Mazeppa's, and his spirit chief carried a staff with a wolf's head on it. He sat his horse only a few yards from Mazeppa, listening but not saying much. From time to time he sent what seemed to be messages to the braves on the east, or maybe the north side of the circle.

Now something unexpected began. Mazeppa, the Wolf Chief, and their close men left their command area, riding to the southwest corner of the box they had us in, then north out of my sight.

Where's he going? I wondered. Freddy commented as if he'd heard me: "Mazeppa's either making a circuit, or . . ." He paused. "Something's going on in the village." His next pause was longer, ending with "Mazeppa's stopped opposite the northside gate. It appears he's going to stay there."

Jarvi was staring at me, so on an impulse I kissed my "amulet." Then I told the others what Freddy had told me, without saying how I knew. Keith knew, and of course Lemmi. Jarvi accepted it, sending orders to the southwest and northwest blockhouses, moving riflemen to keep them with their known targets, rather than orienting on new. We moved to the north walkway too, to keep Mazeppa in front of us. We didn't have a notion of what was going on.

Soon the commanders on the other walkways sent word that the warriors facing them were acting as if readying to attack again. Then Freddy, who'd remained on the southwest blockhouse, had an update: Donald's militias were moving out of the forest. He could see them now.

Meanwhile something was coming out of the village, too, and I realized why the Dkota had pulled down a building: for its ridgepole. They'd made a battering ram out of it. "They're going to try knocking down the north gate," I said, pointing. A slope led down from the village. Nothing much—a drop of a couple feet per hundred horizontal; enough to help build momentum on the dry, hard-packed road. I wondered who among the Dkota knew about singletrees and eveners, or recognized the potential in a roof beam and a pair of wheels. The men bringing it stopped about two hundred yards off. Two of them unhitched the horses; others led them away.

Two hundred yards. According to Jarvi, that was a long rifle shot for a human target, even with the uniform batches of gunpowder he boasted of. Accuracy was the problem, he said. The balls, if they hit their targets, would do their job well, even beyond two hundred yards.

Mazeppa and his chiefs had gathered around, examining it. Mazeppa had dismounted, to study the wheel and axle assembly, kneeling, bending, moving around. "Stand still," I muttered, "stand still." Twenty warriors had lined up along the ram, ten on each side, a shield bearer by each of them. Then Mazeppa and the others who'd dismounted went to their horses and mounted again. Distantly I heard him shout, an order to be passed around the circle. It was time.

"Fire," I told Jarvi. "Fire!" he told his trumpeter. The youth blew a brief phrase, even as the ram crew raised the trailing end and pushed, setting the ram in motion. It took little time to pick up speed, no longer than it took the riflemen to lay their sights on their targets. Already arrows were being launched from the Dkota circle, to be answered by bowmen on the walkways. Then a ragged salvo of gunshots boomed from the blockhouses, and from the middle section of the north wall. I saw chiefs fall from their horses, saw horses shot down under chiefs. Saw the ram picking up speed as if it had life of its own, its crew running alongside as if there'd been no thunderous salvo. Saw arrows stuck in shields, and in several fallen men. Saw Mazeppa reel in his saddle—struck by an arrow! Heard another boom, too soon to be a reload, and his horse collapsed under him, falling to one side on its rider, raising dust.

Saw Jarvi fall to the walkway; he'd been standing at a notch again, fast-firing. I liked and admired the old soldier, and needed him in Hasty, so I shouted for an aid-man, then dropped to my knees to see what I could do for him. He'd been gut-shot, and the arrow hadn't gone all the way through. Drawing my belt knife, I cut the feathered end off and pushed hard, forcing the pointed, sharp-edged head out of his back, then pulled it the rest of the way by the head.

Heard and felt the ram strike. There were war cries at the gate, and roars of Sotan anger. The impact had broken the heavy bar and partly dislodged one gate, making a gap wide enough that Dkota warriors fought their way through with spears and hatchets.

Rifle fire hadn't ended with that first salvo. Behind each rifleman at a firing notch was another. When one had fired, he stepped back to reload, and another stepped up to replace him. Thus a second, less selective salvo followed quickly. After that the marksmen fired at will, favoring warriors with multiple feathers.

On the walkways we had worries of our own, for the whole first rank of braves had charged the walls. Again lariats snaked upward, and again we were busy hacking. Where the east walkway had collapsed earlier, its defenders stood in the bailey, their bows sending arrows point blank at the warriors clambering through unmanned notches. By then, of course, the Dkota arrow flights had stopped, and the war cries and bellows of rage had been largely replaced by grunts of effort, cries of pain.

Then war cries swelled again—an exuberant unified roar from outside the south wall. I knew at once whose shouts they were. Donald Maltby's force had arrived.

Part Five

AFTERSHOCKS

Chapter 43
Closure at Dindigul

Seen from outside, the stockade was chaos. The Dkota were in mid-attack, braves climbing the walls, fighting and dying on the walkways, milling and dying at their base, striving in mortal combat inside the north gates, or crowding and clamoring to get in, all individual effort and focus now, uncoordinated, bloody, man to man. They had a toe-hold inside, and leaderless or not, they showed no sign of quitting.

Perhaps half of Mazeppa's men still waited in the circle, actually more box than circle, and now only seventy or eighty yards from the stockade. They'd moved inward during the attack for more effective archery, fragmenting as chiefs fell to rifle slugs, and as impatience sent braves yipping and yelling toward the wall to prove themselves.

The booming of rifles had less psychological effect on the Dkota than Frazier, Jarvi, and the Higuchians had hoped. The braves had connected the opening salvo with the decimation of their chiefs, but they hadn't panicked. Their focus was too strong, and it was on the scene in front of them—the stockade, the fighting, and the breaking and destruction of the obstinate dirt-eaters.

Then Donald's force charged, trotting at first, speeding to a gallop for the last hundred yards. The first rank was of armsmen, well-drilled and with no space between the riders, a solid, slightly angled chevron of fighting men, their knees meshed with the knees of the men on each side of them. At least that was the drill. Their execution was less than drill-perfect, but effective, firming their solidarity and nerves, locking their chevron into a solid, on-rushing wall.

As ordered, they charged without shouting or cheering. The approach of twenty-five hundred hooves at a fast trot might have warned the braves, but an attack from behind hadn't occurred to them, and there was that intensity of focus. Some in the rear, less rapt and eager, did become aware when the galloping began, and turning, reacted mostly with a moment of shocked paralysis, followed by a yelling attempt to scatter. But it was too late.

The impact of the charge was audible, a crash of horses, and the agreed-upon release of exultant shouts. Screaming horses, screaming braves fell, were over-ridden, and initially, in that solid chevron, most of the sabers found nothing to strike. The horses were the weapons, sweeping the circle away, trampling fallen bodies.

At forty-yard intervals behind the chevron came two much longer and less solid ranks, the militias, whose sabers were busier. They finished any overrun braves who somehow arose after the shock wave had struck, and their wings rolled up the flanks of the Tlahta facing the east and west walls.

The chevron's compactness and regularity, and much of its momentum was broken by the impact, but it continued forward, scattering and decimating the braves milling at the south wall. Then, careening

round the corners of the stockade, it flanked the
attackers there, who only then realized what was
happening. Some fled, some fought, but most who
fought, fought singly.

Despite their pre-attack briefing, the natural tendency for the victors was to pursue fugitives, but
Maltby's trumpeter trumpeted an order, and most
continued as squads and platoons to clear the attackers around the stockade. On the south side, the Dkota
were mostly down—wounded or dead—and most of
the wounds were grievous, from sabers and trampling.
On the other sides, many escaped, but others threw
down their weapons, and raised their arms in surrender.
Then, briefly, the main job of officers and noncoms was
to prevent the killing of surrendering braves.

❦ ❦ ❦

(Luis)

Many of the warriors who ran away fled homeward,
either due west, or backtracking southward, then west.
Still others gathered in impromptu bands in the vicinity
of Dindigul, and sent spokesmen to negotiate surrender. Apparently none of them seriously considered
continuing the war, though some who rode on to Many
Geese committed depredations along the way.

All three tribes had lost their major chiefs. Both
Mazeppa and Strong Wolf had been disabled, Strong
Wolf when a slug intended for his horse had shattered
his femur, costing him a lot of blood, and leaving him
crippled. Mazeppa, from the crash with his horse, had
ribs broken and a lung punctured, plus severe concussion, pelvic damage, and more. The arrow wound
was minor.

We didn't know the details then, of course. All we
knew was, the great chief was unconscious, and
seemed at death's door, and that's what Lemmi and
I radioed Tahmm. Who knew, of course, that we
considered Mazeppa a key to future peace.

"Is he important enough for me to order a medical intervention?"

We told him yes; he'd have been disappointed if we hadn't. It was he who'd taught us that the mission came before careers and convenience, and that the spirit of the law was more important than some senior ESS bureaucrat's interpretation.

So that night Freddy and I lugged the unconscious—and heavy!—Mazeppa half a mile by stretcher, to rendezvous with a courier fitted as an ambulance. It would deliver him to the infirmary at the Sangre de Cristo headquarters. Along with Lemmi to be his guardian, and afterward his anchor point, so to speak. There, before ever regaining consciousness, he received emergency and reconstructive surgery, then was stashed in an isolated room for a week, undergoing deep regeneration. All under a medication that would leave his memories of the infirmary vague and dreamlike. He wouldn't know what to make of them.

They repaired the critical damage, but not all the—call it peripheral damage. They were stretching regulations as it was, and being partially crippled would give Mazeppa a different view of life.

Jaako Jarvi didn't get surgical intervention, but we were pretty sure he'd pull through with Higuchian therapy, and the medicines the courier delivered. What wasn't clear was how well he'd do afterward.

Freddy acted as his nurse and therapist, which would help a lot. Freddy had to stay at Dindigul anyway, along with most of Jarvi's armsmen and many of Donald's men, to deal with our 714 prisoners, many of them wounded. The stockade became a prison. Keith's men, along with some of Donald's, set off to hunt down and run off—or finish off—any tribesmen who might hang around to make trouble.

Strong Wolf was in custody at the stockade, and Mazeppa would be returned there. When Lemmi and

Mazeppa got back, I'd come back too. Then Lemmi and I would engineer peace terms, and send the prisoners back to Many Geese. Or not, depending on how things developed. Fortunately we had the cattle the Dkota had captured, to feed them.

Meanwhile, with the invasion broken, I had to get back to Hasty. Carlos hadn't responded when I'd initiated my report after the battle. He had, I'd learn later, been handling 4th usher duties in the palace, and both hands had been full, but meanwhile I was worried. And at any rate Sota needed to be stabilized, and left with someone ethical in charge. From what Jarvi had told me—and they were kinsmen—Bonde wasn't the man. But neither was Jarvi, for now, not with his wound.

I'd leave at dawn, I decided, leaving Donald in charge at Dindigul, with Freddy as advisor. Tomorrow they'd set prisoners to work preparing for the cremation ceremonies. Some would dig the trenches, others would cut and drag up firewood, and still others would lay out the dead and wash their faces. Bossed by Pastor Morosov, and two Wolf "guides of the spirit."

To properly send off the souls of the dead would help heal the living, and the sins of the pre-Armageddon past.

Dawn had begun infiltrating night, and I was eating an army breakfast, when Carlos called, and I learned how dangerous the situation had become at Hasty. I ended up getting away two hours late—and *not* alone. Jarvi, sick and hurting though he was, signed a quickly written document placing Captain Fong and his 2nd Rifles under my command. The old warrior was too groggy from painkiller to ask how I knew what I knew, and he'd come to trust me. I hoped never to betray that trust.

Chapter 44
A Fisherman Interrupted

In this universe, much of Terra was wilderness. Tahmm had flown some hundred and fifty miles since he'd last seen a village or field, or what passed for roads. Nor a solitary hut, though he might have missed a few hidden under trees. He'd seen thousands of square miles of pine, spruce and fir forest, with here and there groves and stands of leafy trees. And open bogs. And lakes by the hundreds, probably the thousands, not including ponds and beaver flowages.

Close up, one could find animals small and large, including insects in countless zillions, most notably mosquitoes. But surveys from near space had found almost no sign of humans. In the early post-glacial history of the pre-Armageddon version, there'd been scattered bands of hunting-fishing-gathering cultures there, but apparently not in this new version.

At last his scanner registered what he'd come to find, and the scout adjusted course. Soon he spotted a shuttle resting on an AG cushion, barely above a shelf of nearly black rock extending into a lake. Smooth-looking stone, polished by a long-gone glacier, and the combined action of wind and lake ice in countless springtimes.

A hundred yards from it floated a small watercraft, anchored, for the lake was ruffled by a breeze. In the boat sat another Fohannu, playing a fish; a pike weighing sixteen pounds, though Tahmm didn't know that. The lure itself had been a live ten-inch sucker. Now the pike broke the surface, thrashing, lashing its head, trying to dislodge the hook from its hard, needle-toothed mouth.

Fishing had a certain following on r'Fohann, but Tahmm hadn't thought of it as something a chaos cultist would care for. He'd approached the boat unnoticed from behind, sledding diagonally down across gravitic vectors; had very nearly stopped and was reaching for the loud-hailer switch, when another male Fohannu stepped from the shuttle onto the black rock, waving his arms, shouting to the fisherman. Who turned his head. There, twenty feet above the water and twenty-five feet behind him, was an armed scout.

The glance was fleeting, then he turned back to the pike, which had sounded. Tahmm watched the fisher play it, plunging his rod tip into the water when the fish darted under the boat. The breeze had died for the moment, and the surface was smooth. Through water dark but clear, Tahmm could see the pike fighting the tension of line and rod. Then it wrapped the line around the anchor rope. Picking up his landing net, the Helverti reached elbow deep into the cold water, netted the fish, then took out his sheath knife, cut the line, and boated the pike. He rapped it on the head with a billy, killing it, then reached in and took it from the net, holding it up for Tahmm's approval. From twenty feet now; Tahmm had inched in a bit.

Now the fisherman saw who sat beside the pilot. "I've been expecting you," Jorval called.

Even from fifteen feet (for Tahmm continued to

edge in), the fisherman's aura exposed the lie. "My name is Eskonsami Tahmm," Tahmm said, "and yours is Charconvera Jorval. And this of course is—" He gestured.

"I *see* who it is." Jorval grimaced as if something smelled and tasted bad. "So you turned on me, Ench."

Old resentments, ugly and bitter, flared in the youth. Tahmm could *feel* them in Ench's energy field. Though Jorval's question had been rhetorical and directed at his nephew, it was the COB operations chief who replied. "He told me nothing, Jorval, not a word. I asked questions, fed him sorting terms, and showed him maps, all the while reading his energy field."

"Then why bring him here?"

"So you could see I have him. He saw his best friend killed in *your* war, the war you instigated for nothing more than your own degenerate pleasure. He was wounded himself in the attack on the fortress at Kato. Fortunately he was rescued by one of the indigenes; one of ours, not yours. Mazeppa lost the battle there, and a few days later lost again, badly, at a rural stockade. A little place named Dindigul. His northern army had already been crushed and dispersed in a battle by the Misasip, northwest of Hasty.

"At Dindigul, the indigenes captured Mazeppa himself, badly wounded. That magnificent human specimen, crippled. How does that seem to you?"

He didn't wait for a reply; simply continued. "As a matter of fact, the Dkota and their allies never won a battle. A few skirmishes, but never a battle."

Jorval brushed absently at mosquitoes. "Why should I be interested in any of this?"

"Because I'm going to send you to Dzixoss. We've been interested in your project, and as soon as we had Ench in custody—as an active, extraterrestrial combatant in the fighting—we had legal grounds for a whole new level of counter-actions. So of course we sent a corvette to Charon—the ice ball where Captain Vazzo had *Satan's Delight* parked. From him we learned enough to debrief his shipsmind, and . . ."

Jorval's free hand waved full-time at the mosquitoes now, their stings distracting. "You couldn't have!" he said. "It would have—"

"It didn't, and from it . . ." Tahmm's left hand gestured a Fohannid equivalent of a shrug. "Well, here I am and here you are, and over there must be Lorness and Harmu and the others. You started with certain strategic advantages, but now, to use a Terran anachronism—I hold the trumps."

"Not all of them. Lorness has a beam gun trained on you . . ."

Tahmm raised a hand, clucking. "Jorval, surely you know better. Why has your insect repellent field quit on you? One of the advantages I had from the beginning is the power to lock your beam generators, small as well as large."

The courier was barely eight feet from the boat now, and half rising, Jorval threw himself headfirst into the lake. Calmly Tahmm watched him swim downward out of sight. After twenty seconds, bubbles surfaced, and Tahmm saw the cultist rise into sight again. The white, tightly-furred head broke the surface gasping, sucking air. Briefly Jorval clung to the boat, then tried to pull himself over the side. His solid weight almost overturned it, so he worked his way along the gunwale to the transom, where he pulled himself over the stern, to lie gasping on the bottom.

"You look like the pike," Tahmm said.

"Ah, shut up!" Jorval looked truly defeated, despite his ill-tempered words.

Tahmm changed tack. "No need for embarrassment. Drowning by willfully staying under water is not easy to do," he said, wondering if it was true. He turned to the compartment behind him. "Cyth, take Charconvera Jorval into custody."

❧❧❦   ❧❧❦   ❧❧❦

A hum became audible as the AG generator changed modes, and Jorval might have turned his head to look out the window, but his seat restraint field held him too firmly. Thus he didn't see the COB personnel carrier as it settled beside the shuttle to pick up the others. Peripheral vision, however, let him see Cyth, the non-homid agent who'd manhandled him into the courier, and sat now in a customized seat at his side. The creature had produced a syringe from one of the pockets in its harness. A sedative? Jorval wondered. He felt the syringe held to his neck. It chuffed.

Relaxation spread through him, and he thought a thank you to the agent. Then nothing more, all the way to the Sangre de Cristo Mountains.

Chapter 45
Intrigue and Violence

Arvid Bonde laid aside his fork. *You need to rein yourself in at table,* he thought, *or you'll get fat like Eldred. Though Eldred's no doubt getting thinner now.*

Bonde had long been vain about his physique, and at thirty-five years considered himself in his prime. From early youth he'd practiced regularly with weapons and at military horsemanship, but as regent he'd been too busy. These past few days, his only exercise had been in bed, with Elvi the eager, the insatiable. Well, not quite insatiable. She no longer required another go when she woke up.

This morning he was to inspect the 1st Rifles, newly back from the Knees. He'd wear his blue sash, he decided, in honor of the victory there.

Elvi came into the room wearing a light robe. The morning air was cool. "Good morning, nymph," he said.

"Good morning, mighty stallion," she answered. "I've been thinking."

"Ah? What about?"

"I want to be king."

"King?"

"Yes, I know: women who rule are called queens. But I want to be *king*, and I want you to help me, as my prince consort."

"Hmh! I believe I could do that. But Sota already has a king. Will he approve?"

"My father is insane. You told me so yourself. He'd be better off—happier—with the angels."

Bonde's brief frown was serious. *With the angels? She's inviting me to do him in!* "Shall we hold off till the war is over? Your father's death would cause turmoil in the palace, and Mazeppa is on his way north with an army much larger than ours. Let's give your uncle Jaako and his armsmen time to deal with the Dkota. Then we'll make you king."

Bonde took another sip of sassafras, then restirred it. He liked lots of honey in his tea, and it tended to settle out. Putting Elvi on the throne, especially with himself as consort, would be easier if Jaako's army took heavy casualties. Especially if Jaako was one of them.

"How long will it be before they beat the Dkota?" Elvi asked.

"The 2nd Rifles should join Jaako tomorrow, at a place named Dindigul. That's where he plans to break the invasion. His battalion of ordinaries should get there later today."

"Then the battle should be won by the day after, and Uncle Jaako may be back on Friday. We need to take care of father before that; give the palace and town time to get used to it." She nodded, as if coming to a decision. "Father will die tonight, of apoplexy, and tomorrow we'll move into the royal apartments, with a real bath, and sauna."

Bonde looked startled. "Don't worry," Elvi said. "I'll announce daddy's death to the staff as soon as we discover it, and send the royal heralds to announce it through town in the morning." She smiled, then bent, her robe parting at the top, and kissed Bonde on the lips. He felt his loins stir. "I'll design a prince consort's crown for you," she added. "You'll look so handsome! And Uncle Jaako is too old to command the army. That will be your other job. I'll retire him to his estate. He's always spent as much time there as he could. His lake is beautiful, and fishing is his favorite pastime now. He told daddy he got tired too easily to care for hunting anymore."

For a moment Bonde was stunned, as if he'd been run over by a team and wagon, but he shook it off. If Eldred was to die, why not today? The more awkward matter was explaining Elvi's presence in the palace. What had she been doing there? And why hadn't people known?

As for prince consort? A foot in the door, a further chance to prove himself. And with Elvi, things would be more than interesting. She'd have no trouble at all making decisions.

He excused himself, saying he needed to send a page to Captain Manty, delaying the inspection till midafternoon. Then he'd see to Eldred's apoplexy. As he walked to his office, another thought struck him: he still hadn't done anything about Mary. She might be in a nunnery, but that didn't mean she'd stay there. She'd hardly be more than a postulant yet. And if she returned, Elvi would want her dealt with, he did not doubt. What explanation could he come up with for that?

For now he'd hope Mary would remain a religious. It seemed likely, but . . . He wondered if she was half as good in bed as Elvi. She'd always seemed so virginal. But he'd never imagined Elvi interested in coupling, either. At least from a little distance she'd seemed boyish, even after she'd grown breasts.

Mary would be saner by a mile and a half, but a bird in the hand was worth two on the roof. And in bed—the elder twin might prove frigid as an ice statue.

Don't worry, he told himself. *She knew she was Eldred's chosen when she went off to Sanlooee, and went anyway.*

Captain Eli Carnes, Bonde's adjutant, stopped at the distance prescribed when entering the royal presence, but instead of bowing, he saluted. "You sent for me, Colonel."

Rumor had it that Captain Uuka arranged disappearances. Carnes would know whether or not it was true. "Send me Uuka," he said, watching Carnes's eyes. "Privately. Do you understand?"

Carnes nodded. "Yes, your lordship, I quite understand."

The regent's gaze was hard. "And say nothing of this to anyone."

"Of course, your lordship."

Bonde watched him leave. Interesting, that switch from "colonel" to "your lordship," and directly after asking for Uuka.

Carnes strode down the corridor feeling grateful that Bonde was turning to Uuka for whatever this business was. He didn't want to know any more about it.

Carnes had been Eldred's adjutant, too, and when His Majesty wanted someone to disappear, he'd send Carnes to Uuka, his intelligence chief. Uuka would then turn to Corporal Djati; that was the belief among the old hands, and he had reason to credit it. Carnes wanted nothing to do with Djati. The man was a troll. Worse. Over the years he'd risen twice to sergeant, and been broken to private each time, for acts of insane rage. Men had quit the service because they were afraid of offending him. Djati would have been discharged, or worse, but Eldred had come up with another solution.

Carnes recalled a royal dinner party for in-laws. He and His Majesty had been in their cups, and stepped out on a balcony for fresh air. The king had just pardoned Djati for a senseless, brutal beating, and transferred him to dungeon master. Carnes had asked why.

"Compassion," Eldred had replied blandly, then frowned, tasting the word. "Compassion. If I discharge him, send him out into the population, he'll commit much worse outrages than he has in the service. End up hung or beheaded. But as dungeon master he'll provide a benefit. There are things a king needs done that cannot be dealt with by laws."

The dungeon at Hasty Castle was bigger than it appeared. Except for its small office and guard quarters, it existed below ground, along damp unventilated corridors lit sparsely by stinking oil lamps. What little light reached its inmates penetrated, like the lamp fumes, through twelve by six-inch openings in the doors—openings that could be shut from outside. Prisoners breathed a miasma of lamp fumes and their own body wastes.

The stone walls, stone floors, short maze-like corridors and heavy oaken doors effectively muffled sound. The dungeon seldom had more than a handful of inmates, rarely more than one on a corridor, and never more than one in a cell. Just now, because of recent arrests for sedition, it held more than a dozen, distributed to prevent prisoners from calling back and forth.

It was Corporal Djati's personal domain, and just now he strutted through its corridors followed by two henchmen, men who laughed at the right times. Toadies to whom no order was too outrageous to carry out. Even aping Djati's swagger, they slunk.

All three were of middle height, and strong, Djati the largest, squat and powerful. More important were their similarities of limitations and attitudes. They were able to function only in a simple, narrow context, which the dungeon provided. The world at large was too dangerous to cope with. And each recognized only one human being: himself. Everyone else was simply part of the environment: deadly, threatening, and beyond understanding. Also, their cruelty provided more than pleasure. It provided security—irrational and precarious, but a sort of security: the power of fear, of vengeance.

It was to the most remote cell they marched. There Djati handed the lamp to one of his men, and used the key himself. They went in. Eldred did not cower in a corner like the archbishop. For fifteen years he'd been king, and the abuses visited on him here had not made him forget that, even squealing with pain. For Djati had no sense of loyalty, none at all. And the order not to torture Eldred, he'd interpreted to mean acts that maimed; that visibly damaged the body. If the results were not conspicuous, it wasn't torture.

At any rate, this morning he had another purpose: He'd been given a small flask of wine, mixed with unnamed powder, and told to see that Eldred drank it. That was the extent of the order. But Djati knew the drill; that night there'd be another order.

The lamp flame glittered in his black eyes. "I have a drink for you, Your Majesty," he said. "Wine from your own cabinet."

Eldred said nothing, simply clamped his mouth shut.

"Come now, Your Majesty, don't be difficult."

One of the toadies snickered. Djati turned and scowled, and the snicker cut off. "Hold his arms," he ordered.

The man who held the lamp put it on the floor in the far corner; then the toadies grabbed Eldred's arms. He resisted furiously, but after a struggle they levered them behind him, twisting so he cried out. With fierce fingers, Djati gripped Eldred's nose painfully, so he'd have to open his mouth to breathe. With his other hand, he held the flask ready.

Eldred foiled him, breathing between slitted lips, and when the flask was brought to them, he shook his head from side to side. With a sudden oath, Djati let go the royal nose, drew the dagger at his belt, and gashing lips, pried Eldred's teeth apart. Blood flowed from lips, gums, tongue. Eldred roared, lashing his head, worsening the damage but avoiding the flask.

A growl swelled from Djati's throat. "Jong," he said, "take both arms and don't let them go. Owens, grab his hair and hold his head still." He helped them, till panting and cursing they got it done. "Now, Your Majesty," he said chuckling, "it's time to drink." With the pommel of his dagger, he smashed already ruined lips, and broke clenched teeth. "Pull his head back." It was done. Now the defiance was gone; Eldred's eyes were wide with fear. Djati pushed the mouth of the flask into the bloody opening and poured. Poured till the flask was empty, some of the contents inside the king, some out, some on Djati. The king gagged, first on blood and wine, then on his own thin vomit. The gagging repeated, once, twice, as he struggled, then weakened. After a minute or two he was either dead or moribund.

They left him lying in his own blood and puke. They'd return with a bucket of water and a broom, strip him, and clean the worst of the filth off the body before bundling him up.

Carnes caught Bonde just about to go to the quadrangle. The 1st Rifles were waiting. "Your lordship!" he said, in little more than a whisper, "this is urgent!"

Bonde felt fear grip his gut. "Out with it then." He spoke as softly as his adjutant.

"That goddamned Djati. He . . . took care of His Majesty. With poison. But the king refused to drink willingly, so he smashed his mouth to pour it in. His lips are all gashed and split, and his front teeth are broken out. We dare not show him to the public, or even the embalmers."

Oh shit! That stupid bastard! "How did it happen?"

"Djati says his orders were to see that the king drank the wine. So he did 'what was necessary.' Apparently before, the bodies were disposed of secretly, not shown to anyone. They'd tie a bag over the head, wrap the body in canvas, and at midnight, Uuka would send someone with a horse cart to haul it away. Bury it somewhere. Djati thought this would be done the same way."

Bonde's gut shriveled to a heavy knot. He took a deep breath and exhaled. "All right. I'll think of something. Right now, though, I've got to inspect troops. Stay here. Right here. I'll be back in half an hour."

Carnes saluted. "Yes your lordship!"

As Bonde walked to the quadrangle, thoughts crowded his mind. Pretend a plot to rescue the king. The royal corpse could be spirited from the dungeon that night just as Djati expected, by men in disguise— or better, have some living man pretend to be him. Have him smuggled out by "rescuers" on horseback. Other men would follow, and they'd pretend to fight. And the pretended king . . . No, that would never work. Too many people involved; too many tongues to wag; too many things to go wrong.

By the time Bonde met with the 1st Rifles, he'd decided: The king would simply disappear, as other men before him. Late at night. But not buried. Hauled to the dump, with firewood buried by hay; fires were always burning there. Burn the body. Ash it. Break the bones up too fine to identify as human. Or maybe lime them—Uuka would know—and bury them amidst the other refuse. The resulting suspicions would require delaying the royal succession, but he'd work things out.

That evening Corporal Albin Blom came to Paddy Glynn. He'd been given an order by Captain Uuka, he said, bypassing the sergeant major. At eleven that night he was to sign out a team and cart from the stable, along with a short load of hay and a short rick of firewood, then pick up the kitchen trash. (Kitchen trash? The intelligence chief?) Then drive to the dungeon guard house, where Corporal Djati would load another bundle of trash. He, Blom, was to haul it all to the dump. "And I'm afraid what the bundle might be," Blom finished.

Or *who* it might be, Paddy thought. Luis very much wanted the king alive; he had a role for him in the peace. And regicide, if that's what this was, would set a terrible precedent. Quietly Paddy gathered four men he trusted for their honesty, toughness, and competence. Then, armed, they went to the dungeon guardhouse together, and found the three guards with a pitcher of beer, playing cards. Saber in one big fist, Paddy ordered Djati to take them to the king. "You two," he ordered the others, "come along."

Then Paddy and his four men followed Djati and his two down to the bottom level. At the foot of the stairs, three oil lamps burned on a ledge. "Jong, take a lamp," Djati ordered. Jong did, and they started for the dead king's cell.

Djati didn't really plan, he simply intended: Go to the king's cell, send Jong in ahead, gesture Glynn and his men to follow, then slam the door behind them. Lock it and close the shutter. Then get something that when burned, would give off poisonous smoke. Uuka would know; he'd get it for him. Come back, open the shutter, dump the something inside, throw in burning lamp oil . . .

Djati's pulse raced with anticipation. When they reached the cell, he took the key from his belt, unlocked the door and pulled it open. "Go ahead Jong," he said, and the man stepped inside.

Paddy, however, didn't follow the script. "You next, Djati," he ordered.

Djati had lived by the premise that if anything went wrong, act at once. His right hand flashed to his dagger—and almost as quickly the heel of Paddy's hand slammed forward, taking Djati between the eyes and catapulting him unconscious into the cell, the dagger clattering on the stone floor. Owens fought wildly but very briefly. Slugged, and slammed against a wall, he too lay quickly unconscious. Jong, on the other hand, froze—surrendered without a fight. He'd been the one with the best weapon, the open oil lamp.

Paddy tried the key on the next cell. It opened; apparently one key served all. They dragged the two unconscious jailers into it and locked them inside. Then, finally, Paddy entered Eldred's cell with the lamp. What he saw sickened him. *What have I done!* he thought.

Briefly he questioned Jong, who proved anxious to please. He laid the blame on Djati, of course, which was where it mainly belonged.

When Paddy knocked at Brookins' door, Sir Lawrence was working by lamplight, entering debits against inventories. In the past, his servant would have handled the interruption, but Terence was one of those who'd fled the town, whether inspired more by the internal discord or Mazeppa's armies, Brookins didn't know. "Who is it?" he called.

"Sergeant Glynn, sor." The answer was barely loud enough for Brookins to hear. The old nobleman got up hesitantly, then decided, and moved quickly; Glynn was a man to trust. He opened the door, and after a final glance up and down the hall, Glynn entered.

"Sor," he said, "you're a man well-known and respected. And its necessary that oi take action now. Against Colonel Bonde. But oi don't want bloody skirmishes in the corridors again."

He spoke in a near whisper. "Eldred is dead in the dungeon, murdered by Corporal Djati. They brutalized him; he looks terrible. Oi've witnesses to the act, Djati's men. One of them's told me everything. And Corporal Blom's been ordered by Captain Uuka to transport a body secretly, which probably means Colonel Bonde's behind it. Uuka can tell us, and maybe Carnes."

Brookins nodded. He knew palace lore, the true and the untrue.

"If you can get Captain Ylvessalo and maybe Captain Horn to back me," Paddy went on, "oi'll take some men and arrest the colonel. Oi think we can do it without violence."

Brookins wondered what Jarvi would think of that. Probably he'd approve; at any rate it seemed necessary. "Very well, sergeant," he said, "let's talk with Ylvessalo."

It was then Paddy remembered the archbishop: it was like a punch in the gut! Clonarty was in the dungeon too! He'd ordered him there himself, then forgotten him! Well, first things first.

Paddy and two guardsmen found Bonde literally with his pants down, in his office toilet with no weapon at hand. The sergeant major dealt courteously with him, waiting outside the door while the indignant regent tidied himself. When Paddy told him what he'd seen and learned, Bonde caved in, and the sergeant major led him to the dungeon.

With Bonde locked up, Paddy asked to see the archbishop. "Sergeant," the new dungeon keeper said quietly, "I don't think you'll like what you find. When I came on duty, the first thing I did was look in on my lodgers. The archbishop was terrified; he pleaded, begged. I tried to settle him down, but it took several minutes before he stopped his clamor. Then he curled up in a corner and wept. He wouldn't look at us, or say another word. I believe he's lost his mind."

God forgive me, Paddy prayed silently.

"Later I had Armsmen Morgan and Contreras provide all the prisoners with a lamp, water and broom, to clean their cells. When that was done, each was given more water and a bowl of soap to clean himself. And a clean shift to wear. But the archbishop cleaned neither cell nor self. He just huddled there, weeping."

Paddy gusted a sigh. "Let's see him," he said.

When they got there, the cell door was ajar. "I left it like that," Corporal Grosman said. "I thought when he noticed—if he noticed—it might help."

Paddy dismissed the jailer, and with broom and water, scrubbed the cell himself, quickly and thoroughly, all the while talking calmly to Clonarty. The activity stilled the weeping, but the cowering persisted, though it seemed to Paddy the man peeked past a sheltering arm. By the time the scrubbing was finished, Grosman was back with basin, soap, and the rest. There was no dry place for the towel and shift, so Paddy had the corporal hold them, then took the rest to the archbishop, who shrank away from him.

"Yer reverence," he said, "Corporal Djati's locked away. He'll never trouble you again. Here now, oi've water and soap for ye. And Corporal Grosman has a towel and clean shift for when yer done washing. After that we'll have someone bring your own clothes to ye, and take you home."

Slowly, cautiously, Clonarty straightened a bit. "First leave my room," he whispered. "I'll not disrobe before you."

"Of course, yer reverence."

Perhaps the poor man was coming around.

⊰⊱ ⊰⊱ ⊰⊱

(Luis)

I'd been cagey when I told Fong why he and his rifle

company were going with me, saying only that the king was dead, and there was trouble at Hasty. Carlos had brought me up to date soon after we left Dindigul, so on our first break I gave Fong a fuller picture. He assumed, of course, that I'd received a messenger at Dindigul—how else could I have heard?—and he wasn't happy about that. He thought I hadn't trusted him to know till we were away from the stockade, away from the rest of Jarvi's troops.

But I nonetheless had Jarvi's letter of authority.

Then I announced the king's death to the troops: They knew of course that he'd been locked in the dungeon; they'd heard that before they'd left Hasty, and had pretty much approved. Now I told them that on Colonel Bonde's orders, the king had been murdered. Beaten, stabbed in the face, then poisoned. When it was learned that the execution order came from Bonde, the palace guard had arrested him for regicide, and locked him in the dungeon. Captain Uuka had also been jailed. He'd been the go-between, who'd delivered the order to Corporal Djati, who'd done the actual killing.

Till then, Fong's men weren't sure I was telling the truth, but mentioning Djati changed that. I could feel it: they despised and hated the man. On the other hand, telling them Lord Brookins was acting as regent had little effect. These weren't palace guard. Few or none of them, other than Fong himself, had heard of Brookins.

Bonde they knew well. He was a genial officer, big, good-looking and soldierly, with a reputation as a horseman, swordsman, and supposedly cocksman. And they assumed he'd had the king done in because of Eldred's refusal to defend his country and people. The brutality had been Djati's.

What I told them next was even more troublesome: the palace guard held the palace, and the key to Bonde's cell. But the 1st Rifles held the town, and weren't letting anyone or anything into the palace now, including food. Until, they said, Bonde was reseated as regent. Our job, I told them, was to break the siege: talk Captain Manty into letting Sotan law determine who would rule, and letting Bonde and Uuka stand trial.

Meanwhile, I went on, Lord Brookins had sent a message to Princess Mary, in Sanlooee, asking her to come home as quickly as she could. It was widely believed her father had intended her as his successor. Actually I was being selectively honest there. Brookins *had* sent a messenger, but Carlos had already radioed the brother house near Sanlooee. They were to notify the hospital convent at once.

Tahmm hadn't volunteered to fly her up though; that would be a *major* breach of policy. Besides, the odds were she'd be on her way home no later than the next day. Though she wouldn't reach Hasty for maybe three weeks; it was upstream all the way.

The break cost us an hour on the road, but it was necessary. And afterward I didn't push as hard as I might have.

It was early evening when we made camp just outside Big Ditch Junction. The mosquitoes were fairly bad there, despite the dry summer, because of all the marshland to the east, but there was nothing I could do about that. The troops pitched their squad tents, and afterward made smudge fires on the side facing what breeze there was, while I went to the Last Stop Inn to see if the innkeeper would sell me two kegs of beer. He was glad to, he'd had zero travelers stop there since Lemmi and me.

His brewer shipped his beer in twelve-gallon oak kegs, so I got twenty-four gallons. It came to a bit less than two pints per man, not much for armsmen, and they were bound to suspect my motives: I was trying to get on the good side of them. But the brew was good, and free, and they'd appreciate it, and meanwhile no one would be sick or hung over from two pints of beer.

I borrowed a trestle table to set the kegs on, and each man had a pint mug in his camp gear. Fong and I had charge of the spigots, and when the men had lined up by platoons, I told them each man would get one full mug the first time, and part of a mug the second. Then Fong and I started serving.

Actually I'd had their good will before we left Dindigul; I just wanted to repair it. When Lemmi and I had first met them on the Austin Road, the word had passed through the ranks that we were Higuchians. Which interested them right off, because of the Higuchian reputation. Then at Dindigul we'd fought together, which made me good with them—unless and until I proved otherwise. Some had seen me jump off the stockade to confront Mazeppa, and been impressed, and those who hadn't seen it would have heard about it, with no loss in the telling.

And not least of all, they felt good about themselves. They'd done major damage to the invader, and having mostly been in the blockhouses, rifleman casualties had totaled only four wounded, none severely. They were in a mood to be generous.

While they drank, Fong got with the 1st sergeant to set up watches, not for security, but to keep the smudge fires alive so the men would sleep better. Some of the men drank their firsts pretty quickly, and were back early for seconds. So after a bit, I passed the word that everyone who wanted seconds—which was all of them—should line up by squads. If their mug wasn't empty, we'd give them their seconds on top.

We did a pretty good job of judging. When the last man had been served, what remained went to the senior sergeants for thirds. Then the 1st sergeant detailed men to return the table and empty kegs to the inn.

Fong and I strolled after them through a pleasant summer night. I ordered a bucket of beer for the two of us, and we went to a table at one end of the otherwise empty tap room. The innkeeper brought the bucket, and we ladled our mugs full with the dipper provided.

I knew Fong had to be curious, so I waited for him to start the conversation. It didn't take long; maybe two swigs.

"You're not a king's man," he said. "Where did the money come from for the kegs?"

"From Norlins. The Holy Father."

"And your authority to spend it like this?"

"Same place. Norlins knew last winter what Mazeppa had in mind. We just didn't expect it so soon. And of course Norlins knew that Eldred was a molli. So Master Lemmi and I were detailed to come up here and see if we could prevent the war. If we couldn't prevent it, we were to see that Sota won, which it has. Norlins also knew the war would end up with Eldred deposed, and there'd be the matter of succession to deal with. There might even be civil war, and who knew what kind of government. Except for defense, Eldred was a pretty good king."

Fong nodded. "So," he said, "meanwhile we drink the pope's beer." He finished his mug and ladled another. I was a little slower. "Who do you want for king?" he asked me.

"Mary's the one with the best claim. But she'd have to want the job, and there'd have to be enough support for her among the dukes. If she doesn't want it, or they're not willing for her to have it, Elvi's next in line, but the dukes wouldn't go for Elvi. So if not Mary, then someone else. And that's where the main danger lies; of civil war. Jarvi would suit me, but I doubt he'd take it. He might agree to be regent though, while something else is arranged. Or—"

I let it hang there, and we both drank. After a

minute I added: "Bonde seems to want the regency, at least, and he has support within the army. And we don't know all the circumstances of Eldred's murder. But it would set a terrible precedent to crown the man who'd ordered the king's death, if in fact Bonde's the guilty party."

Now I was getting to my main reason for buying this extra beer; we'd be up pissing half the night. "I don't really know Bonde," I said. "What kind of person is he?"

Bonde and Fong were kinsman; I'd had that from Jarvi—members of that loosely defined class lumped as cousins of the queen. Fong took another swig. "I was never close to Arvid," he told me, "so what I can give you is mostly hearsay. Family lore. I've always been a line officer, and Arvid's always been staff. He ended up in charge of all the training. He's a helluva good horseman, letter perfect in cavalry skills, and the men have always liked him."

I'd been keeping an eye on Fong's aura. "Who doesn't like him?" I asked.

That took him by surprise. "His parents, actually. His mother didn't care much for children, so she farmed out the mothering to nannies. And if Arvid didn't like a nanny—say one of them crossed him— he'd go crying to Lovisa. That's his mother. And she'd fire the nanny. At least that's the family lore. Apparently he was pretty spoiled."

"What about his father?"

"Einar didn't like him at all."

That came with another interesting aural reaction. "Why not?" I asked.

The captain emptied his mug; he was wishing this conversation hadn't begun. The beer was getting low, so I poured him a refill from the bucket. "I've got some difficult decisions to make," I went on, "and I need all the information I can get. Especially about Arvid Bonde."

He nodded glumly and took another swig. "It's been rumored in the family that Einar didn't think he was the father, though I never heard anyone else suggested. Anyway, when Arvid was a baby, Einar never bounced him on his knee, never blew on his little belly, never ate his little face the way fathers do, that makes them squeal and laugh.

"Then, when Arvid was seventeen, he got one of the maids pregnant. That's not so rare, but this one was only twelve years old, and supposed to be slow-witted. Einar thrashed him for that, really cuffed him around. A big strong man. Then Lovisa raised holy hell with Einar. His beating on Arvid upset her a lot worse than Arvid's getting the child pregnant.

"So Einar told Lovisa fine, he's yours; I wash my hands of him. And supposedly he never spoke to Arvid again, not even at table. Wouldn't surprise me a bit. Einar was a hardhead."

After that, neither of us said anything more till we'd finished the beer.

The next day, at the West Crossing ferry dock, we found a sign giving new service hours—nothing before noon unless you hired a man with a rowboat. The surge of refugees from the Marches and Kato was days past, and normal travel was dead. To swim the horses across, we'd have to unload the packhorses and wait for someone to ferry the gear. So taking a squad of riflemen, I went to find the owner-skipper of the largest ferry barge. By that time of morning the village was well awake, and in thirty minutes I had the skipper and eight oarsmen at the dock. All of them unhappy, because by law they couldn't charge us. Nor did telling them we'd just whipped the Dkota at Dindigul brighten them as much as I'd expected. To them, I suppose, it seemed like an anti-climax, after Gallagher's army had been broken at the Knees.

What did brighten them was my paying nine pieces

of Norlins silver—one for each oarsman and one for the ferryman. Not as much as the ferryman would ordinarily make, but very good money for the oarsmen. Also we did our own rowing, south to north, then they'd recross the river empty, to pick up another load. In three hours the whole company was across, men and horses.

There weren't many people on the road to Hasty, either, but to those we met, we announced the victory at Dindigul. And now the villages at both landings knew. Before long, all of Sota would. Good news, if interesting enough, travels as fast as bad.

We got to Hasty in the middle of the day, to find the town gates closed, but the guards opened them for us without being asked. They were allied to the 1st Rifles, and thought we were too. We told them about the victory at Dindigul, but they didn't seem greatly relieved. Their minds were on the local troubles. I'd expected we'd be hailed as saviors of the kingdom; it would help in straightening things out. But it wasn't happening.

The streets were quiet. A lot of people had left when the Dkota took the warpath, and few had come back despite the victory at the Knees. Those who remained were worried about a fight between Manty's 1st Rifle Company, backing Bonde, and Ylvessalo's garrison company and Horn's platoon supporting the palace guard.

For years Eldred had been an affable ruler who'd provided decent government. And when the Dkota invaded—he'd virtually invited them—people had been less angry than disillusioned. That's how popular he'd been. It was claimed he'd gone mad, that a palace coup had locked him in the dungeon, murdered him, set up a kinsman of his wife as regent. And who knew what would happen next?

I wished Jarvi was with us. He was prominent, respected, and a good man. But as they say back in Mizzoo, wishing won't buy you a twist of forty-rod.

⋘⋙ ⋘⋙ ⋘⋙

Halldor Halvorsen, the produce boy, had continued to deliver vegetables. He needed income till it was safe to go home again. Meanwhile he'd found a girl who liked him, a farmer's daughter at the co-op market, who sold what the farmers sent to town. On this particular day, while delivering to the palace, the gates there were shut and barred, closing him inside. The palace, said the guards, was officially under siege.

The only thing Halldor could think of to do was push his empty cart back to the unloading dock and ask advice. From the new 4th usher, Carlos, who seemed like a good guy. Maybe he could help.

"You're in luck," Carlos told him. "We're short-handed in housekeeping." Then he took him to the housekeeper, and she'd sent him to livery. There a small, baldheaded man had given him a quick but knowledgeable look, pulled a wooden hanger from a long rod, and from it took an ash-gray work shirt and breeches. They fitted nicely. "Your own shoes all right," he said. "Now go back to Mrs. Hah."

Housekeeping. To Halldor that smacked of dusting, mopping, washing windows—things hired girls did. Mrs. Hah showed him a diagram of the second floor, and pointed to a small suite. "Go this apartment," she said. "Door unlocked. Roll all rugs, take in corridor. Then come back here. I tell what next."

He found the suite. There was a wardrobe in the living room, and he peered inside. Empty. He rolled up the small rugs, moved the furniture, all of it heavy, onto bared places, then rolled up the large central rug and dragged it out.

Besides the hall door, the living room had two others. He opened one of them and found a bathroom, with a vanity against a wall, a commode with a lid, and a copper bathtub. The floor had two small rugs, one of them covering a trapdoor. Curious, he raised it, peered in, and found a crawl space. Closing it, he took the rugs to the hall, and put them atop the others.

Then he went to the third room, a bedroom. It had a door that opened into a walk-in closet with uniforms. Large uniforms. And more—a shaft of morning sunlight showed him two extraneous legs. Not just uniform legs, but legs in uniform. His first impulse was to close the door and pretend he hadn't noticed, but somehow the words "Oops, excuse me" came out.

"Who are you?" said the legs.

"I'm in housekeeping," said Halldor. "I'm taking the rugs out to be cleaned."

"Halldor? Is that you?"

"Elvi?"

She came out from behind the uniforms. "Oh my god, it *is* you!" she said. "Halldor! How did you . . . ?"

Briefly they exchanged stories. *Very* briefly. He needed to get back to Mrs. Hah before she sent someone looking for him.

"A state of siege?" she said. Someone outside wanted in, she realized, to free Arvid. "Look, I haven't eaten since yesterday. And I know a way out of here, out of the palace grounds, without being seen. But it needs to be after dark. Come back this evening. *Bring food!* Then we'll leave together." She patted his butt. "Well, maybe not right away."

His loins stirred. "Suppose someone else comes?"

"I'll hide in the closet again. Now go."

He left wondering at her bravery. And she planned to be *king*! What a woman! He'd forgotten all about his bitterness at Zandria. She'd as good as said they'd couple that evening before they escaped. Probably afterward, too, it seemed to him.

(Luis)

With Fong's 2nd Rifles behind me, and Jarvi's letter of authorization, I had no problem getting a meeting with Captain Manty. Fong went with me; he took the letter seriously, and didn't trust Manty. Now that was interesting. Maybe he thought Manty might arrest me, or worse. It turned out Manty was older than Fong by about ten years, and me by closer to twenty, and resented not being senior in grade and authority.

But at the same time he was in a difficult situation. He couldn't storm the palace successfully, and it takes time for sieges to work. Even if the palace wasn't well prepared for one. I didn't tell Manty about Jarvi's wound, and neither did Fong, so for all Manty knew, the old general would arrive in a few days, with his battalion and his own ideas about how to fix things here. Which would hardly include Bonde as regent.

As far as that was concerned, with Freddy giving Jarvi healing sessions, he might still be able to ride in ten days or even less. And with the Dkota beaten, the dukes would be taking sharp interest in the succession.

I didn't point out any of that. Manty knew it, and his aura marked him as a stubborn sonuvabitch. Pressured, he'd likeliest dig in his heals and resist. So I tried sweet reason.

"There's more than just the palace guard inside," I told him. "But I'm sure you know that. There's Ylvessalo's company, and Horn's platoon."

"They don't worry me," Manty said. He lied.

"So what I'd like to do," I went on, "if you'll go along with it, is meet with Brookins and Horn, and make a deal. So you folks don't end up killing each other. They keep the palace, but they move Colonel Bonde out of the dungeon into house arrest. He'll be as comfortable as before, but held on charges of not keeping His Majesty safe while in his custody."

Manty beetled his brows impressively. "I wouldn't trust any of them," he said. "They're in this for the influence and promotion."

"The general won't be," I pointed out. "He'll be here in a week or so, maybe sooner, and no one will hoodwink him."

That did get to Manty. His aura suggested someone whose first response to a situation is emotional, leading to action. Intellect tends to enter in after the fact, to evaluate, rationalize, excuse what he'd done. But hopefully he was taking a fresh look at his own motives now.

"Who'd judge the charges against Bonde?" he asked.

Good. He was thinking. "If Ylvessalo and Horn and Brookins have any sense at all," I said, "they'll leave it to the general. And it might be well to have it all buttoned up before Princess Mary gets here. Brookins has sent for her. It'll take a while, but she'll get here, and I don't know what she'll think when she learns how her father died."

As I said it, it occurred to me I didn't know either. But I was optimistic, especially if Kabibi had any influence on her. Manty, on the other hand, was shaken. He'd forgotten about the princess, and knew how he'd feel if the murdered man had been his father. "Tell you what," I said. "Which of your officers would you trust to go in and see to the colonel's comfort? I'll make that a condition when I talk to Ylvessalo and the others."

Manty felt actual pain, making up his mind. Finally he nodded curtly. "If Jaako trusts you, I suppose I should. And you've spoken fairly enough, I must say."

I could feel Fong's resentment. Manty hadn't included Fong's trust as a factor. Which relieved me somewhat. I hadn't supposed Fong would knuckle under to the older officer, but now I felt sure he wouldn't. And he was the more intelligent of the two.

By the time I started for the palace gate, he'd be planning the disposition of his company, just in case Manty thought about catching him flat-footed.

The palace gate guards examined me through a grill-work that wouldn't pass arrows. They were in no mood to let anyone in, I felt that without seeing their auras or even their faces. This project was really bringing that out in me.

And I was a stranger, an unknown quantity. The eyes that peered out at me either didn't recognize my uniform, or didn't like it. So I slipped a wild card out of my sleeve. "I want to talk to Paddy," I said. "Tell him Luis is here."

Carlos had told me Paddy wasn't the boss any longer. He'd gotten rid of that responsibility as soon as he could. Brookins was the man who made decisions now, and Ylvessalo was in charge of carrying them out. But Paddy was the man that Brookins and Ylvessalo trusted to know what was going on, and to get things done; in other words continue as sergeant major of the Guard. And Paddy was one of them. His men more than trusted him. The Guard would talk about Paddy Glynn for a long long time.

"Just a minute," the guard said. "I'll send someone."

Paddy himself let me in, clapping my shoulder. "Oh sor, am oi glad to see you! What can oi do for ye?"

I showed him Jarvi's letter. He conned it, then I told him briefly why I was there. "Good! Good!" he said. "Ol'll take ye to Lord Brookins. Oh, this is like the sun coming up!"

We left the gate guards awed.

A dozen minutes later I was talking with his lordship and the two captains, Paddy behind me. I didn't have to explain my thinking; they saw the situation basically as I did. We held the cards. All we needed to do, at least for now, was avoid a fight with Bonde's advocates until the general arrived, or Mary if the general didn't recover as quickly as I expected. With every day that passed, Manty'd be worrying, having second thoughts. Which could lead to backing out of the contest—or to some act of desperation.

Now there was a thought. I could imagine a man or men, in uniform on fast horses, rushing south to "see how the general was doing," then killing him, perhaps with poison.

So I asked who might be in this with Manty. Was he acting alone, or as someone's front man, or what?

Both Brookins and Ylvessalo thought Manty was acting on his own, but would have notified Bonde's Uncle Fritjof, who'd headed the Bonde clan since old Einar had died. Manty was the youngest of three surviving brothers, which made him Arvid's Uncle. Apparently Arvid Bonde was the family black sheep, personable and admired, but not always approved of.

Paddy's muse was strong, and he'd recognized almost at once what he faced: an everlasting kettle of aristocratic ambitions and opportunism, that in good times was on the back burner with the lid on, but in times like this could boil over. A situation best dealt with by someone who knew it. So he'd turned to Brookins, who beneath his courteous gentility, knew the game and could play it if he had to.

Brookins and Ylvessalo agreed almost at once to the terms I'd gotten Manty's approval on. Mainly what we talked about were the risks of Bonde's people agreeing, then trying to stab us in the back. Uuka was also in the dungeon, and we agreed that no one from outside would be allowed to contact him.

Finally his lordship sat down to pen a formal legal agreement.

I excused myself to use the toilet, for the usual purposes plus a conference call to Freddy, Tahmm, and Peng. And Carlos, the smartest 4th usher the royal palace would ever have. I warned Freddy of possible risks to Jarvi, and that Mary might be at risk of interception and violence on the river. Maybe Fedor could provide an escort from Moleen north, some brothers in a fast boat, with several well-muscled novices to help with the rowing. I also told Tahmm what I thought of Paddy's work at the palace. "He's been the key to everything good that's happened here," I said. "And that's not to slight Carlos."

I had no doubt at all that Paddy was headed for the Academy when this was over. He'd turn out to be one of the best men the Order ever had, I did not doubt.

For just a moment I thought of Jamila. She'd had even greater potential, till she was murdered. The thought took me so unexpectedly, I almost wept. I'd thought I'd had all the grief drained off that at the Academy.

I couriered the proposal for Brookins myself. He'd signed it as "regent acting for the Crown Princess Mary." Manty's mouth twisted sourly when he read that, but he signed too. It seemed to me he still had hopes of Bonde taking the throne, but I didn't read anything in him that worried me particularly. He'd already decided on his liaison with Bonde: a man who looked enough like Manty to be his younger brother. A cousin I supposed, or nephew, an Ensign Wu. My read was, they'd wait to hear from Arvid Bonde before trying to cook anything up.

After I'd shaken hands with Wu, he went with me to the palace's front gate. We'd see what happened next. Hopefully not much.

⬦—⬦   ⬦—⬦   ⬦—⬦

Mrs. Hah kept Halldor busy. She intended to clean several unoccupied suites and rooms from floor to ceiling while she had the chance. So he'd stripped them all of their rugs that day. Besides Elvi in Arvid Bonde's old lodging, only one room or suite had a personal item of any consequence at all—a leather-covered flask, holding two or three ounces of brandy, lay flat on a wardrobe shelf. The chamber maid had been too short to see it. Meanwhile the water pitcher remained half full, so from it, Halldor filled the flask before putting it back where he'd found it.

Word of the victory at Dindigul had penetrated the palace, but it didn't reach Halldor's ears. Most of his day was spent hauling rugs to the rug frame out back, and after hanging them up, beating them with a rug beater till his arm was ready to fall off. Mrs. Hah sent a girl to approve his work, and she flunked the first rug she checked. A peasant girl! Humiliating! But he was learning to take setbacks and adapt, so he walloped them all again, thoroughly, and all of them passed her next inspection.

Filching food wasn't as simple as Elvi had assumed. Nothing was, Halldor suspected. Ordering was her job; doing was someone else's. He'd learned that weeks before, but the coupling had made it worthwhile; and it would again, he told himself. He had no access to the staff kitchen, only the staff dining room, where there was no privacy. Meals were served at set times, everyone eating together, ordinarily. But at supper he managed to tuck bread inside his shirt, next to his skin: two slices stuck together with butter, then two more.

After supper he reported back to the housekeeper. "You do good!" she said. "All done till tomorrow. Rest!"

He bobbed an almost-bow, thanked her and left. He'd feared she might discern the bread inside his shirt, but apparently not. One comes to appreciate small victories, he told himself.

He was indeed learning.

−−− −−− −−−

Growing up in the palace had given Elvi some sense of the demands and limits on domestic servants, and she showed no sign of impatience when at last Halldor arrived back—with bread and butter, and water with a distinct flavor of apple brandy. She'd bolted the door behind him and kissed him hungrily before asking what he'd brought to eat. She still had water in the laquered pitcher by the wash basin; it was food she was ravenous for. They sat together on the bed while she ate the bread and butter. When she'd finished, they undressed, fondling as they went. Then she rolled him onto his back and mounted. "For I will be king," she murmured, and began to ride.

When they were done, they drank the brandied water. "Your gift of brandy," she called it, and giggled. He'd never heard her giggle before, and felt like the luckiest young man in the world. It showed in his eyes, and sobering, she touched his face with gentle fingers. *Arvid would never look at me like that,* she thought. "I'm very fond of you, Halldor," she said. "If anything ever happens, I want you to remember that."

His heart melted in his chest.

It was getting dark. She'd lit a lamp earlier—there were phosphorous matches on each lamp shelf—and now, she said, it was time to escape the palace. Then she showed Halldor the closet. Colonel Bonde's clothes were gone. Some men had come and taken them.

"But where . . . how did you . . . ?

"Hide?" She giggled again, "Under the bed. They were guardsmen," she went on. "I could tell by their boots." Sobering she added, "We really have to leave now. I have to save Arvid, and I cannot do it as a prisoner." She looked penetratingly at Halldor. "He is my champion, you understand. Without him I cannot become king."

He nodded, also soberly. Then she led him into the bathroom and raised the trapdoor. "You first," she

said. "I'll pass the lamp after you're down. We must
be very careful with it."

The opening was small and the space cramped, but
he sat down on the edge, then wiggled and slid, and
found it adequate. When he was in, he turned over
in order to crawl, feet first of necessity. The place
smelled of human waste. The toilet pail. Elvi handed
down the lamp, which he set carefully to one side,
then she followed, also feet first, the only direction
possible. "A few feet farther and you can stand up,"
she said. "You'll be in a passage then."

The passage served the toilets of all the rooms and
apartments on that side of the corridor. A clever
arrangement, he told himself. A servant could come
with clean five-gallon buckets, replace the fouled ones
in their frames beneath the commode, and lug the
wastes away. Then the contractor would empty them
into his odorous wagon, and some unfortunate would
clean the empty buckets. It occurred to Halldor he'd
been lucky in his job assignment.

The passage was lit by twilight through louvered
slots, and by the oil lamp they'd brought. At its end,
stairs led down to a ground floor landing, and a longer
flight to a cellar smelling of damp stone, where the
lamp gave the only light. There they followed a corridor a short distance, to where Elvi opened a side
door into a short, narrow, low-roofed tunnel that
seemed to dead end. They entered in a crouch. The
air smelled and felt as if the tunnel hadn't been
opened since the door was hung: dank, heavy, and in
spite of its mortared stone walls, smelling of moist soil
and tree roots. Halldor's eyes were large and round
as he followed Elvi. Even rats, he thought, would not
come here.

The dead end was illusion. The tunnel right-angled,
then left-angled, then dropped two steps and proceeded straight. Here Halldor could walk upright,
barely, stumbling twice on tree roots. It took them

sixty or seventy yards, he guessed, then widened a bit and stopped. This dead end was no illusion.

To Halldor it felt like a tomb. "Now what?" he asked.

Crouching, she set the lamp down by the wall, and turned to him. "Now you lift the flagstone overhead, and we climb out. Into a tiny park by the river, outside the palace. Outside the city wall. Daddy showed mother and Mary and me, when we were little. Eight or nine, I think. It was a way we could escape if we were ever in danger."

Halldor looked worriedly at the stones overhead.

"The center one, the round one," she told him.

"It looks heavy."

Her voice sounded strange to him, so matter of fact in such a creepy place. "That's what mama said: 'it looks heavy.' But it's not. Daddy raised it easily, and then he had mama raise it too. It was night, and daddy lifted us out into the little park above the river."

She gestured, stepping behind him. "Go ahead. Lift it."

He raised his hands and pressed. *Heavy.* Her mother must have been a *strong* woman. Bending his knees, he pressed upward again with all his strength, grunting. Felt it raise, inches, a foot. "There!" he said. "It's off."

Searing pain struck the back of his neck, and he collapsed to the stone floor, almost knocking Elvi down. She hadn't expected it to be so sudden. Crouching again, she wiped her stiletto on Halldor's breeches, then slipped it into its sheath.

"That didn't hurt, did it," she said, a statement, not a question, her voice unnaturally calm. "I didn't want it to hurt. I like you too much. I like you better than Arvid, quite a lot, even if he is a better lover. But Arvid can make me king, you see. I was born to be king. I practiced and practiced. But Mary'd tricked me; she came out first. She wasn't supposed to. We'd agreed."

Only now did she look upward. No twilight entered from outside. It was as if the stone had fallen exactly into place again. Cold settled over her. Quickly she set herself, reached up, placed her hands on the flagstone and pushed.

It didn't budge. Not an inch. Not a hairsbreadth.

Resetting her feet, bending her knees once more, she tried again, sounds of effort straining from her throat. Nothing.

"Heavier than you thought, isn't it?"

Fear flowed through her like ice, her short hairs rigid, exquisite fear at the limit of bearing. Slowly, holding her breath, she turned and looked down. Halldor lay as if his strings had been cut. Then a greater cold wrapped her, like two arms. "Who?" she whispered.

"Who else?" Halldor's voice was soft. "There are only the two of us here, and we have all the time in the world."

Shrieking, Elvi flailed, staggered away—felt a hand on her foot, like iron, and fell senseless to the stone floor.

Chapter 46
Sorting It Out

Sergeant Major Paddy Glynn had just made the rounds of the walls enclosing the palace complex. Now he sat alone in his small office, eating lunch: rye bread with cheese, a bowl of barley porridge, a big mug of sassafras, and a side dish of prunes. The siege was still in effect, kind of, because until the 1st Rifles left its positions outside, Paddy was letting no one in or out without a pass, and there were almost no passes.

Colonel Bonde was back in a guest suite, Ensign Wu with him, but Bonde was upset with it. He wanted the same suite he'd had before. Brookins had explained that the old one was being cleaned and painted—the rugs had even been hauled out for cleaning. If the colonel wished, he could visit it. And at any rate it would be ready for him the next day.

At that, Bonde had settled into a black mood that perplexed even Wu. He wouldn't say what was wrong, only that Brookins was toying with him. Luis was still the go-between for Brookins and Manty, and Manty wouldn't remove his troops until Bonde's complaints had been satisfied. Luis said he'd certainly try, if Bonde would say what was wrong. He'd even bring him to the gatehouse and let Manty try to get it out of him.

That wasn't good enough, Manty had answered, but at the same time he'd calmed down.

Manty had also been making a big point of his greater time in grade, and that Fong needed to obey his orders. Fong had replied he was following the *general's* orders—which put him under Luis's command. Then, with Luis's agreement, Fong had moved his 2nd Rifles to the military reservation four miles north of the city, out of Manty's ready reach. Manty was welcome to come after them, of course, but he'd have to bring his company, and chase the 2nd Rifles all the way to the wilderness. Which meant abandoning the siege.

A ridiculous mess. Paddy felt an urge to slap the snot out of Bonde, but that would accomplish nothing except exercising his own exasperation, and cause God knew what further problems.

His clerk came to Paddy's door. "Sergeant Major, sir, Mrs. Hah, the housekeeper, wants to talk to you. She says there's something suspicious about Colonel Bonde's old quarters."

A rush ran over Paddy from scalp to knees. "Let her in, Issa. Oi'm interested."

Half a minute later the tiny housekeeper stood before his desk. "Mr. Sergeant Major!" she said. "This morning girl come to me. Had been in Colonel Bonde's old suite. Someone did coupling on bed. Stain on sheet. Also, whiskey bottle on table. In toilet, trapdoor raised, one lamp gone." She paused meaningfully, holding Paddy's gaze. "Also, one person not come work today. Must be somewhere in palace. He work that suite yesterday."

A trapdoor raised. And someone missing. Paddy got to his feet. "Thank you, Mrs. Hah. Just a minute." He went to his door and gave instructions to his clerk. Ten minutes later, the formidable sergeant major, with two armsmen, were tagging behind the birdlike housekeeper, across the quadrangle to the royal residence, headed for the suite she wanted him to see. On the way, they picked up the chief of building maintenance, a raw-boned, strong-looking older man who would know the buildings, service facilities included, at least as thoroughly as anyone.

Together they looked at the evidence Mrs. Hah had reported. It was obvious from the disturbed dust in the crawl space that someone had exited via the trapdoor. It seemed to Paddy the trapdoor was too small for him, certainly given the cramped space it led into. He turned to Mr. Gonsalves, the maintenance chief. "You say there's a service passage back there. How else can we get into it?"

"There are several ways. I can show you. But when we get there, then what? The honey man walks it every day, up and down, carrying buckets. It wouldn't be possible to track someone."

"Show me," Paddy said.

So Gonsalves took them down corridors and stairways to a long service dock; the far end was where the honey wagon parked. Stacks of nested five-gallon copper pails stood nearby waiting, cleaned and shiny, lids stacked beside them. Gonsalves opened a door and they went inside, into a landing at the end of a passage. Stairs led up and down.

"From the second-floor passage there is no other exit than the stairs," Gonsalves said. Then paused in afterthought. "Except—someone could enter any rooms or suites where the crawl-space trapdoors were unbolted. But if they came downstairs, it would bring them here. Then they could leave the building. If they went up, they would come to a dead end."

"And if, from here, they went down *those* stairs?" Paddy asked gesturing.

"They lead to the cellar. There is nothing there but storerooms."

Paddy stood frowning, feeling his muse nudging. On a ledge stood a row of oil lamps, like covered gravy boats with ears for carrying. One was lit. He used it to light another, then led off down the stairway to the cellar level, the others following. At the bottom there was only one way to go. He took it, eyes prowling, twice opening sidedoors into storerooms, where he expected and found nothing of interest. Farther on he opened a door into—not a room but a cramped, dead-end passage, perhaps five yards long and five feet high. Wide enough for Paddy's big shoulders, but little more. It might have seemed an abandoned beginning of something, had it not been walled, floored and ceiled with stone and mortar.

"What's this for?" he asked.

For a long moment, Gonsalves didn't answer. Paddy was about to prod him, when the man spoke. "It's . . ." He gave the sergeant major a deeply troubled look. "I cannot say," he whispered. "I am sworn. I myself dug it, hauled out the dirt and laid the stonework, all by night. It took a long time. I expected to be killed for what I knew, but instead His Majesty gave me my position, God bless him." He crossed himself, then gestured forward. "Go. See for yourself."

Paddy peered, scowling, then in an awkward crouch entered. The dank air smelled like a newly dug ditch. Or grave. *This is it,* he told himself, though what *it* was . . .

The dead end was an apparency. Actually the tunnel turned right, then left. Beyond the second turn, the floor lowered two steps, but the overhead continued level; now Paddy could walk upright, barely. He'd gone fifty yards farther before he made out something ahead on the floor. When they got there they found two bodies, the first a young woman in an armsman's uniform.

Gingerly he turned her head. One of the princesses.

Elvi. She seemed to have started back out, but a tree root had caught her foot, and tripped her. Probably, he thought, she'd struck her head. She wasn't stiff: She might still be alive.

Behind her, nearly at the tunnel's end, was a man with the rigor of recent death. He lay on his back, his face with a hint of surprise. There was no sign of what had killed him, nor visible blood.

Mrs. Hah bent beside Paddy. "That Harald Andersen," she said. "Boy who beat rugs."

Paddy turned him over, and on the back of his neck saw blood. Saw the wound. Whoever had stabbed him knew what they were doing. Had struck from behind, upward into skull and brain.

Then he peered at the stones overhead. The round one. "An escape hatch?" he asked.

Gonsalves nodded. The center stone was about twenty inches in diameter. Paddy reached up and pushed. It did not raise easily, or readily move aside. Something was on top of it. He let it back down. "What's up there?" he asked. "Something's sitting on the stone."

"There shouldn't be."

"Do you know where it is?"

"Yes, sir."

"Yer going to carry the princess to the infirmary. Oi'll carry the dead man. Then oi want you to go look at this exit from outside. By yerself, saying nothing. See what the trouble is."

Paddy shouldered the corpse, while Gonsalvez lifted the princess in his arms. Wondering if she might still be alive.

⋘⋙ ⋘⋙ ⋘⋙

(Luis)

They took both Elvi and the corpse to the infirmary, and sent for me. The palace physician confirmed her identity, and when I got there, I confirmed the corpse's identity: Halldor Halvorsen, Elvi's sweetheart, the lordling son of a baron.

Elvi was breathing, and had a pulse. A slow pulse. The physician, her cousin Koivun, could find no evidence of injury beyond a bruised chin. When I saw her, she lay on a cot, covered by a blanket. Her clothes were folded on a table, her boots beneath it. Her belt bore a sheath, and I drew the stiletto from it, a slim sharp wicked-looking thing. Expensive. There was no gleam to it though; it needed cleaning. Blood had congealed at the juncture of blade and cross-guard. I touched the blade. It was slightly sticky. The murder weapon, I did not doubt, and presumably Elvi was the murderess.

But why? A lover's quarrel? Did it matter? I had more important things to deal with, but my muse was telling me to have Elvi questioned.

"Paddy," I said, "have someone bring Carlos to me."

"Oi'll get him myself," he said, and was on his way.

I could have gotten her conscious; the procedure was simple enough. But when she woke up, she'd recognize me, remember me from the Zandria Road, and wouldn't cooperate if her life depended on it.

When Carlos arrived, I took him out of the room— a hysteric in a coma might register our conversation— and asked him to waken and question her. Find out how she'd come to be in the palace, and what she'd been doing there. I paused. What was I leaving out? "Oh, and Carlos, address her as 'Your Majesty.'"

He cocked an eyebrow at that, then grinned and nodded.

I hoisted the corpse and carried it off. There wasn't a priest on the premises, so I lugged it to a service gate, where the guards let me out, then walked down the street with the remains of Halldor Halvorsen over my shoulder, to the offices of the archdiocese. A junior priest met me, and scurried off round-eyed to fetch Father Akimoto. Akimoto recognized my uniform—

it did not please him—but he accepted jurisdiction of the dead man. He would, he said, have a corpse washer deal with it.

I nodded gravely. "While I'm here, father," I said, "tell me how Archbishop Clonarty is doing. Sergeant Major Glynn feels terrible about what happened to His Reverence."

Akimoto had his own emotion about that: anger. He was Carlian, and I Higuchian.

"His reverence is recovering," he said, enunciating stonily.

It seemed to me aural healing would be useful, but the good father would not be friendly toward Higuchian procedures. So I simply told him more about what had happened. "Sergeant Major Glynn had already jailed the jailor. But by then the archbishop was in a state alternating between apathy and terror; he could do nothing at all for himself. He'd become unable even to use his waste bucket. The sergeant major himself scrubbed the cell, hoping the activity would bring the archbishop out of his terror. And when it did, to a degree, it was Glynn who brought soap and clean water and cloths, and coaxed the archbishop to bathe himself. Which after a bit, with privacy, he did. It was then the sergeant major sent for you. He's a good man, Glynn is, a man truly of God."

This hadn't seemed to accomplish much, but I went on. "When His Majesty went insane and began ordering executions, the whole government came unhinged. There was fighting in the corridors. Men were wounded. Two died. It was the sergeant major who got it stopped, and took over the palace until Colonel Bonde agreed to be regent."

I paused. "The kingdom was already at war, you understand. The Dkota had arrived. Presumably that contributed to His Majesty's madness; he couldn't accept a world in which his peace treaty could be so cynically used to destroy the kingdom."

Akimoto's face and voice remained cold, hostile. "The archbishop should never have been locked up!" He bit the words out; a zealot all the way. I wondered if he'd really heard anything I'd said. "Indeed he shouldn't," I replied, adding silently *house arrest, yes, but not the dungeon.* "Sergeant Glynn's intention," I went on, "was to get the archbishop out of harm's way until the immediate danger had ended. Then, amidst the turmoil and confusion, he was forgotten. There's nothing more I can say, except that we regret what happened. I've already notified Norlins. I suggest you do the same."

Akimoto's aura seemed unchanged.

"My Order has effective healing procedures," I added. "If you wish, I will arrange to have His Reverence treated."

"We will continue to look after him ourselves."

"Of course," I said, and left. I'd expected nothing better, but I'd done what I could. And it might, at some level, set small roots.

Later Grosman told me some things I hadn't known. Akimoto had arrived with the archbishop's hairbrush, sandles, and white robe. Clonarty, in a voice quavering but imperious, ordered the priest to stay out; he wasn't done washing yet. He washed for a half hour longer, requiring more buckets of water, stopping only when Grosman told him he must either leave or stay overnight. Then Akimoto dried and dressed his archbishop, and led him out, Clonarty with his cowl raised, his face hidden.

When I heard that, I understood better Akimoto's bitterness.

When I got back to the palace, Gonsalves was waiting to tell me what he'd learned: a small stone shrine to Saint Carl had been placed, no doubt inadvertently, on the passage's round flagstone lid.

❦❦ ❦❦ ❦❦

From there I visited the infirmary, to talk with
Carlos about Elvi. Before deposing her under oath,
he'd interviewed her on cube without her knowing.
She'd wondered where she'd been, and what had
happened to her, and what he told her was true, but
not the whole truth. She'd fallen, he said, and struck
her head. Then he'd asked how she'd come to be in
Hasty—that the last the palace had heard, she'd been
in protective custody at Zandria.

She told him she'd returned to assume the throne,
and that Colonel Bonde had agreed to be prince
consort.

"When did he agree to that?" Carlos had asked.

"Three or four days ago."

Carlos raised an eyebrow. "You have him, you
know."

I told him to inform everyone in our com circle,
then left.

As things worked out, it was four hours before I
was ready to visit Arvid Bonde. First I talked to Djati
and Uuka in their cells, with Lord Brookins and
Captain Ylvessalo as witnesses. Then I then went to
get Manty.

Manty wasn't interested. He didn't trust me at all,
not even when I told him I had a new proposal for
the colonel, one I felt sure he'd accept. Especially he
didn't trust me when I refused to tell him what the
proposal was. What broke his resistance was my utter
certainty, and my avowal that I asked it only so he
could witness that the proposal had been made, in
case somehow the colonel rejected it, or Brookins had
second thoughts. Then I sealed it by covering his butt
for him; I sent a messenger to Fong, ordering him
to ride in and stay as a hostage with Manty's second
in command.

❦❦ ❦❦ ❦❦

When we walked into Bonde's sitting room, he had two friendly faces to look at: Wu's and Manty's. I had Brookins and Ylvessalo with me. Opening with a slight bow, I addressed Bonde as "your lordship." "I have a proposal for you," I said, "one I think you'll find hard to refuse. But first—we've found what you left in your previous guest suite."

His expression had been sternly imperious. Now he sneered. "I doubt it," he said.

"She tells us she intends to rule as king—not queen, but king—and has promised to make you her consort."

That shook him; especially the word *"king."* No one but Elvi could have told us that. He didn't much change expression, but he paled, and his aura shrank. Manty looked thunderstruck; he had not missed the Colonel's loss of color. Wu stared literally open-mouthed.

Still, Bonde's reply hardly lagged at all. "True," he said. "With Mary in a nunnery, Elvi is next in the succession."

"When did she propose this to you?"

Though he stared distrustingly, he failed to see the trap. "Three or four days ago. I don't remember exactly."

"Then her father was still alive."

For a moment his self-possession broke. "He . . . uh . . . she . . . was predicating a future when His Majesty would have been tried, and forced to abdicate."

"Ah. Apparently you're unaware that Captain Uuka is under arrest. He and I have talked, just today." My smile finished him. "And of course Captain Carnes. You asked Carnes to tell Uuka you wanted Eldred disposed of. Uuka in turn told Djati, and provided the poisoned wine."

Bonde was in shock now, near collapse. Manty glared at him.

"Now for my proposal. If you confess to ordering

the murder of Eldred Youngblood—King of Sota, your uncle by marriage—I will recommend a trial before a special court. A court consisting of relatives no more than twice removed from the king or his deceased wife. They will also be your relatives. I believe you'll find more mercy there than in an Assembly of Dukes. In either case, if a court sentences you to death for the crime of regicide, the Princess Mary shall have the power to spare your life."

Arvid Bonde stood utterly defeated.

"I believe she is a young lady of considerable compassion," I added. "And if it comes to that, I will recommend her mercy. You have these witnesses to my word."

Chapter 47
Closure

(Luis)

It took awhile to wrap everything up—trials, ceremonies, appointments . . . Then I more or less collapsed, burned out. It wasn't so much the war as the events at Hasty. I'd manipulated, withheld, told half-truths—and sometimes flat-out lied—in the hopeful cause of saving and bettering lives. The dishonesty takes its toll.

As cadets, our instructors, our reading, our meditations had prepared us for such things. Basically, society and civilization are the products of human beings. Particularly human beings with energy and ambition, who too often are also greedy and more or less ruthless. And to help humankind survive and evolve, in a free-choice universe, someone has to deal with the more dangerous of them. So said Saint Higuchi.

And that's what the Order is trying to do, as honestly as we can, as dishonestly as we must. Coercion, in the long run, is a crutch that fails. Survival and evolution require an increasing degree of freedom, which of course is dangerous stuff. It's a privilege to serve, but it can be hard on the soul. So I was ready for a few weeks at the Academy, enjoying R&R—rest and retrospection—and hiking in the Sangre de Cristo, indulging my nature-boy muse.

In Sota, over the next few months, numerous loose ends were tied up.

Lord Brookins formally accepted the regency until Mary Youngblood could relieve him. He promptly seated a court to try those involved in the death of her father, so that the trial might be over before she arrived. Two courts, actually. One for *Djati*, *Owens*, *Jong* and *Uuka*, the other for *Bonde*. All were found guilty of regicide, and sentenced to death by hanging, but their executions were postponed until the young queen should be ready to act on my requests for clemency. *Carnes* was found guilty of contributing to regicide, and received a suspended sentence dependent on satisfactory completion of suitable penance.

Shortly after her return from Sanlooee, *Mary Youngblood* was crowned queen of Sota. She did, in fact, grant clemency to all five murderers. Their sentences were reduced to life in the dungeon.

The young queen announced that an Althean convent would be established near Hasty, to train women in the healing arts.

Duke Edward Maltby's improved health enabled him to take over completely the management of his duchy again.

Donald Maltby returned to the brother school, not to become a brother—he and Mary Youngblood soon had other plans—but because he wanted the knowledge and skills he could gain there.

Stephen Nez also returned to the brother school. Tahmm has an eye on him as a likely future cadet. His performance as a novice had been unprecedented.

Kabibi Christian agreed to continue her duties as Mary Youngblood's secretary and companion on a temporary basis. Tahmm has plans for her at the Academy, not as a cadet, but a scholar, and later an instructor. The COB intends gradually to staff the Academy and the Terran COB operation entirely with us indigenes, and I'm sure we'll handle it suitably. But I'm glad we don't have to yet. I can't imagine not having Tahmm here.

Princess Elvi disappeared on the second night following her discovery in the tunnel. No one knows what happened to her.

Although he hadn't known it, *Paddy Glynn* had been earmarked for the Academy before leaving Moleen. All he'd lacked was a major field mission as a brother. This one had been about as major as they come. He's now at the Academy as a cadet.

When *Lemmi Tsinnajinni* and *Mazeppa Tall Man* arrived back at Dindigul from Mazeppa's healing, the chief's fighting days were over. But Mazeppa is basically healthy, and can walk and ride. Lemmi is riding with him to Many Geese, to begin the healing of the Dkota war wounds, through *Mazeppa* and *Pastor Morosov*. Leaving loose ends like those is akin to evil.

He'll also guide both men to a recognition of the effects of fasting and ambition on visions.

Jorval and his people are on their way to Dzixoss, in stasis, aboard the *Satan's Delight*, commanded by a fleet officer, its crew supervised by Commonwealth marines. According to Tahmm, Jorval's trial will almost certainly sentence him to rehabilitation, followed by an amends project that will occupy most of his remaining life. However, he'll have the option to choose life imprisonment at hard labor, instead.

⊰⊱ ⊰⊱ ⊰⊱

Ench pleaded not to be sent to Dzixoss on the same ship as his uncle, even though they'd both be in stasis. So Tahmm exercised his executive authority to assign Ench as orderly to the marine officer barracks at the Sangre de Cristo HQ. He'll be sent to Dzixoss on the biennial personnel rotation flight. Meanwhile he spends much of his off-duty time reading Commonwealth history, and exploring his "subconscious" with an Academy supervisor of mental-spiritual training.

I never got to know him, but I wish him well.

Jaako Jarvi agreed to continue as general of the Royal Sotan Force-at-Arms, and break in his successor. He chose Sulo Ylvessalo for the job, and promoted him to major.

Gavan Feeny had preferred life as a buffalo hunter over life on the farm, but wasn't comfortable with the prospect of returning to the Dkota. So I sold him on trying something way different than either. He's a novice now, training under Carlos and Peng. I have no doubt he'll fit in well there.

DAVID WEBER

The Honor Harrington series: *(cont.)*

Field of Dishonor

Honor goes home to Manticore—and fights for her life on a battlefield she never trained for, in a private war that offers just two choices: death—or a "victory" that can end only in dishonor and the loss of all she loves. . . .

Flag in Exile

Hounded into retirement and disgrace by political enemies, Honor Harrington has retreated to planet Grayson, where powerful men plot to reverse the changes she has brought to their world. And for their plans to succeed, Honor Harrington must die!

Honor Among Enemies

Offered a chance to end her exile and again command a ship, Honor Harrington must use a crew drawn from the dregs of the service to stop pirates who are plundering commerce. Her enemies have chosen the mission carefully, thinking that either she will stop the raiders or they will kill her . . . and either way, her enemies will win. . . .

In Enemy Hands

After being ambushed, Honor finds herself aboard an enemy cruiser, bound for her scheduled execution. But one lesson Honor has never learned is how to give up!

Echoes of Honor

"Brilliant! Brilliant! Brilliant!"—*Anne McCaffrey*

continued ☞

DAVID WEBER

The Honor Harrington series: *(cont.)*

Ashes of Victory

Honor has escaped from the prison planet called Hell and returned to the Manticoran Alliance, to the heart of a furnace of new weapons, new strategies, new tactics, spies, diplomacy, and assassination.

War of Honor

No one wanted another war. Neither the Republic of Haven, nor Manticore—and certainly not Honor Harrington. Unfortunately, what they wanted didn't matter.

AND DON'T MISS—

—the Honor Harrington <u>anthologies</u>, with stories from David Weber, John Ringo, Eric Flint, Jane Lindskold, and more!

HONOR HARRINGTON BOOKS by DAVID WEBER

On Basilisk Station	(HC) 57793-X /$18.00	☐
	(PB) 72163-1 / $7.99	☐
The Honor of the Queen	72172-0 / $7.99	☐
The Short Victorious War	87596-5 / $6.99	☐
	7434-3551-6 /$14.00	☐
Field of Dishonor	87624-4 / $6.99	☐

continued ☛

DAVID DRAKE RULES!

Hammer's Slammers:

The Tank Lords	87794-1 ◆ $6.99	☐
Caught in the Crossfire	87882-4 ◆ $6.99	☐
The Butcher's Bill	57773-5 ◆ $6.99	☐
The Sharp End	87632-5 ◆ $7.99	☐
Cross the Stars	57821-9 ◆ $6.99	☐
Paying the Piper (HC)	7434-3547-8 ◆$24.00	☐

RCN series:

With the Lightnings	57818-9 ◆ $6.99	☐
Lt. Leary, Commanding (HC)	57875-8 ◆$24.00	☐
Lt. Leary, Commanding (PB)	31992-2 ◆ $7.99	☐

The Belisarius series with Eric Flint:

An Oblique Approach	87865-4 ◆ $6.99	☐
In the Heart of Darkness	87885-9 ◆ $6.99	☐
Destiny's Shield	57872-3 ◆ $6.99	☐
Fortune's Stroke (HC)	57871-5 ◆$24.00	☐
The Tide of Victory (HC)	31996-5 ◆ $22.00	☐
The Tide of Victory (PB)	7434-3565-6 ◆ $7.99	☐

The General series with S.M. Stirling:

The Forge	72037-6 ◆ $5.99	☐
The Chosen	87724-0 ◆ $6.99	☐
The Reformer	57860-X ◆ $6.99	☐
The Tyrant	0-7434-7150-4 ◆ $7.99	☐

Independent Novels and Collections:

The Dragon Lord (fantasy)	87890-5 ◆ $6.99	☐
Birds of Prey	57790-5 ◆ $6.99	☐